Available
from Mi

BLAZE 2-IN-1
A Body to Die For
by Kimberly Raye
&
Flashpoint
by Jill Shalvis

His Christmas Fantasy
by Jennifer LaBrecque

Restless
by Tori Carrington

A BODY TO DIE FOR

He'd fantasised about kissing her so many times over the years.

But nothing, not even the most decadent dream, prepared him for the real thing.

Her lips were soft and full beneath his plundering mouth and an electrical current ran from his lips, straight to his growing erection. He pushed his tongue deep, stroking and delving. He was through denying himself. He meant to sample every inch of her, savour her essence on his lips, make her writhe and moan until she knew without a doubt that he was her equal – a seductive, mesmerising vampire with pure sex on his mind.

FLASHPOINT

Oh, boy. She recognised the heat in his gaze and felt a matching heat in her belly.

And her nipples.

And between her legs.

A kiss. She wanted just one kiss. Was that so bad?

"Because I think we've started something very interesting here. Something we should finish. What do you think?"

"I…uh…"

"I'm all ears," he murmured and shifted just a little closer. So close that she had to tip her head up to see into his eyes, giving her an up-front and personal view of the scar that slashed his right eyebrow in half. Her gaze dropped from that scarred brow to his mouth.

Way too dangerous.

First published in Great Britain 2009
Harlequin Mills & Boon Limited,
Eton House, 18-24 Paradise Road, Richmond, Surrey TW9 1SR

A Body to Die For © Kimberly Raye Groff 2008
Flashpoint © Jill Shalvis 2008

ISBN: 978 0 263 87499 0

14-1209

Harlequin Mills & Boon policy is to use papers that are natural, renewable and recyclable products and made from wood grown in sustainable forests. The logging and manufacturing processes conform to the legal environmental regulations of the country of origin.

Printed and bound in Spain
by Litografia Rosés S.A., Barcelona

A BODY TO DIE FOR
BY
KIMBERLY RAYE

FLASHPOINT
BY
JILL SHALVIS

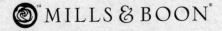
MILLS & BOON

A BODY TO DIE FOR

BY
KIMBERLY RAYE

Bestselling author **Kimberly Raye** started her first novel in high school and has been writing ever since. To date, she's published more than forty-five novels, two of them prestigious RITA® Award nominees. She's also been nominated by *Romantic Times BOOKreviews* for several Reviewers' Choice awards, as well as a career achievement award. Currently she is writing a romantic vampire mystery series for Ballantine Books that was recently optioned by ABC for a television series. She also writes steamy contemporary reads for Blaze®. Kim lives deep in the heart of the Texas Hill Country with her very own cowboy, Curt, and their young children. She's an avid reader who loves Diet Dr Pepper, chocolate, Toby Keith, chocolate, alpha males (*especially* vampires) and chocolate. Kim also loves to hear from readers. You can visit her online at www.kimberlyraye.com.

For all of you hopeless romantics out there…
We rock!

1

HE SMELLED LIKE SEX.

Rich. Potent. Mesmerizing. Like a creamy dark truffle mousse with a drizzle of imported white chocolate, a dollop of whipped raspberry cream and a sprinkle of cinnamon-crusted pecans.

The crazy thought struck as she stood in the middle of The Iron Horseshoe—a rough and rowdy bar just off the interstate—and stared at the man who sat at a nearby table.

Crazy because Viviana Darland didn't normally think in terms of food.

She didn't do chocolate or whipped cream or pecans. She didn't do anything edible, period. She was a vampire who thrived on sex and blood, and so her thoughts rarely read like a transcript of the latest Rachael Ray episode.

But sheer desperation—coupled with the past two days spent holed up at the Skull Creek Inn, watching the Food Network and trying to work up her courage to approach Mr. Luscious and Edible—was new to her and so it only made sense that she would act out of character.

After all, her days were numbered.

A wild, rebellious southern rock song poured from the speakers and vibrated the air around her. Her heart beat faster, keeping tempo with the steady ba-bom ba-bom ba-bom of the drums. A neon Harley Davidson sign glowed above the bar and various motorcycle memorabilia— from studded leather chaps to an *Easy Rider* poster— decorated the walls.

Several truck drivers, their big rigs parked out back, sucked down a round of beers at a nearby table. A group of leather-clad bikers clustered around a dartboard in the far corner. A handful of men sporting long hair, beards and Golden Chopper Motorcycle Club jackets chugged Coronas at the massive bar that spanned the length of one wall.

The loud clack of pool balls echoed above the music. Cigarette smoke thickened the air. The sharp smell of Jack Daniels hovered around her.

It was a far cry from the latest "it" bar down in West Hollywood. She swallowed against a sudden lump in her throat.

So?

You're a vampire. You adapt to any place, any time, any situation. Stop making excuses, walk over and just tell him what you want.

The command echoed in her head and urged her forward. Unfortunately, her body didn't obey any more now than when she'd first spotted him a few days ago.

The memory rolled through her as she turned left and headed for the bar. She angled herself between two big bruisers and ordered a house beer.

She'd been on her way into the desperately small Texas town when she'd seen the hunky guy parked outside the city limits on the side of the highway. Wishful thinking, or so she'd thought.

But Garret Sawyer had been more than a figment of her imagination.

He'd been flesh and blood and oh, so real.

As real as the day she'd first met him. Touched him. Kissed him. Loved him.

Talk about opportunity. Forget tracking him down and arranging a chance meeting. She could dispense with formality and cut right to the chase.

At least that's what she'd told herself when she'd climbed out of her car and approached him.

But then she'd glimpsed the surprise in his gaze, the anger, the hurt and her resolve had crumbled. She'd barely managed a "Long time no see" before she'd hightailed it back to her car.

She hadn't seen him since.

But she'd asked around.

With Skull Creek being the quintessential small town, she'd gotten an earful from everyone—from the clerk at the Piggly Wiggly, to the fry guy at the Dairy Freeze.

She'd learned that Garret was the skill and expertise behind Skull Creek Choppers, the town's one and only custom motorcycle shop. He'd opened his doors a few months ago and bought a small ranch just outside the city limits. He had two business partners—Jake McCann handled the design and Dillon Cash monitored the software and computer system.

Garret bought coffee at the local diner every evening and subscribed to the *Skull Creek Gazette*. He also sponsored a local little league team, donated to the senior's center and served on the board of the Skull Creek Chamber of Commerce.

Exactly what she would have expected from a thirty-something businessman trying to establish himself in a new location.

Exactly what she wouldn't have expected from a two hundred-year-old vampire who'd always avoided hanging around too long in any one place.

"It's on me," the bruiser to the right said when she slid a five across the bar to pay for her drink.

Her head snapped up, and she found herself staring into a pair of interested brown eyes.

The man had long, black, greasy hair and a thick beard. He reeked of beer and cigarettes and sexual frustration. He missed his wife. But not because she'd been a fine upstanding woman who'd taken her vows seriously. No, she'd been the opposite. A slut who'd slept around on him every time he'd pulled out of town.

What he missed was having a warm body to turn to in the dead of night. He'd never been much of a player, and so he hadn't actually dated much before he'd met his missus. He wasn't even the type of man who offered to buy a woman a drink.

Until tonight.

Viv read the truth in his eyes and felt his desperation. And suddenly it didn't matter that he wasn't the most attractive man she'd ever met. All that mattered was the sexual energy bubbling inside of him.

The desire.

The need.

Her own hunger stirred, reminding her just how long it had been since she'd fed. Her chest tightened, and her stomach hollowed out. Her hands trembled, and it took all of her strength not to reach out and take the man up on his blatant offer.

But this wasn't about getting a quick fix and fulfilling some stranger's fantasies.

This was about fulfilling her own.

"Thanks, but no thanks." But you might try with the blonde over there in the corner, she added silently. I think she likes you.

He fixated on Viv for a few long moments before the message seemed to penetrate. Finally, his eyes sparked, and hope fired to life inside of him. He turned toward the woman who sat nearby, nursing a margarita and eyeballing him.

Viv took her beer and shifted her attention back to the real reason she'd come to the Iron Horseshoe in the first place.

He sat facing her, his back to the wall, his feet propped on the table in front of him. He wore faded jeans that outlined his trim waist and muscular thighs. A frayed black T-shirt, the words Easy Rider emblazoned in neon blue and silver script, hugged his broad chest and sinewy biceps. Black gloves, the fingers cut out, accented his large hands. A tiny silver skull dangled from one ear. The only thing about him that didn't scream bad-ass biker was the black Stetson sitting on the table near his beer and the black cowboy boots that covered his feet.

She eyed the scuffed toes of the boots before dragging her gaze back up, over his long legs, the hard, lean lines of his torso, the tanned column of his throat.

Her attention stalled on the faint throb of his pulse, and her mouth went dry. Despite the crying guitar and pounding drums, she could hear the steady pump of his heart. The sound called to her, inviting her closer, while fear held her stiff.

Her fingers flexed on the ice-cold bottle of beer. Her gaze stalled on his face, and she licked her suddenly dry lips.

He had short, cropped brown hair and the rugged features of a man who'd spent more than one day in the saddle. A day's growth of stubble darkened his jaw and outlined his sensuous lips. Pale blue eyes collided with hers.

There was no flicker of surprise, no glimmer of pain. Just pure, unadulterated lust.

As if he'd been waiting for her, wanting her, as much as she'd been wanting him.

A fierce longing knifed through her, and for the first time in a very long time—one hundred and eighty years to be exact—she felt her legs tremble.

The reaction fortified her courage. It also erased any lingering doubts about her decision to leave L.A. and her freelance career as a tabloid photographer, for a small Texas town and an assignment with a regional travel magazine.

She'd ditched it all for sex.

For him.

Because Garret Sawyer had been the first man to give her a mind-blowing orgasm.

The only man.

And Viviana Darland wanted one more before her past finally caught up with her, and she bit the dust for good.

HE HAD TO BE DREAMING.

Another full-blown, heart-stopping, aching hard-on fantasy.

Because no way—no friggin' way—was she really here.

Right here.

Right now.

She eased off the bar stool and stepped toward him, and reality sank in.

Shit.

That's what his head said. But his damned traitorous body wasn't nearly as pissed.

His muscles tightened. His spine stiffened. Heat swept through him, firebombing his dick until it throbbed to full awareness. His eyes drank in the sight of her, roving from her head to her red-tipped toes and back up again just as she reached his table.

She looked different now. So damned different.

Instead of being pulled back, her long black hair

hung in soft waves around her face, accenting her bright blue eyes and full pink lips. A fitted navy blue jacket molded to her lush breasts and tiny waist. A matching skirt outlined her curvaceous hips. High-heeled sandals made her legs seem that much longer than the full skirts and petticoats she'd worn way back when.

Different, yet she still had the same glimmer in her eyes. The same confidence in her stance.

His nostrils flared, and he drank in the same warm scent of apples and cinnamon that he remembered so well.

"Is this seat taken?" Her soft, familiar voice slid into his ears and jump-started his heart. Before he could reply, she pulled out the chair opposite him and folded herself into it.

The music blared a fast ZZ Top song that kept time with his racing pulse. "What are you doing here?" he finally asked after a long, loud moment.

She held up a bottle of Lonestar and gave him the faintest smile. "Thought I'd sample some of the local brew."

"Not here at the Horseshoe." His gaze narrowed, colliding with hers. "Here. This town."

She shrugged. "I'm on assignment."

That's what she said. But her eyes. Those bluer-than-blue eyes said something much different. He didn't miss the flash of desperation. Or the glimmer of need.

"We haven't had any alien abductions or Elvis sightings in a while," he said, sarcastically.

"I'm not working for *The Gossip Guru* anymore," she said, referring to the national tabloid that sat next to the cash register at every grocery store and gas station in town. "I'm freelancing now. I'm doing a travel article on small towns." Her gaze collided with his. "Sexy small towns."

Her words stirred a rush of memories he'd buried a long, long time ago. Memories of the two of them having wild and crazy—

Garret hit the brakes and made a U-turn before he wasted another second going down the wrong road.

He'd traveled that path once before, and he'd crashed and burned in a major way. Sure, he couldn't help a wet dream every now and then. But that was pure fantasy. An escape from the monotony of living year after year after year.

He sure as hell wasn't stupid enough to go for the real thing.

Not ever again.

He leaned back in his chair and folded his arms. "It's dusty here. And hot. And it smells like cow shit when the wind blows due south. We're smack dab in the middle of ranch country. There's nothing sexy about it."

"Not to you because you live here. But if you were stuck in New York or Chicago or Detroit, it would be a different story. There are quite a few people who would love to escape the daily grind of civilization and get back to nature. In a small town, you can do that. There's no traffic congestion. No pollution fogging the air. No concrete jungle. Just lots of birds and trees and rolling countryside." She smiled. "Come on, you have to admit the view around here is pretty incredible."

Damn straight.

She paused to lick her lips, and he couldn't help but follow the motion with his gaze.

His stomach did a one-eighty, and the words were out before he could stop himself. "I suppose it's nice enough. But sexy?"

"It can be. If you're with that special someone. There are couples all over the world eager to find an old, quaint small town with friendly people and lots of local color for a romantic getaway."

"You've just described every town from here to the Rio Grande. That still doesn't answer my question— why this particular town?" My town? His gaze collided with hers and he found himself wishing he could read her thoughts the way he could read those of humans.

But she was a vampire.

She always had been.

A knife twisted in his gut, and he stiffened. "Why Skull Creek?" he pressed.

She didn't say anything for a long moment. Instead, she licked her lips again. Once. Twice. If he hadn't known better, he would have sworn she was trying to work up her courage.

But he knew better.

Viv had never come up short on courage. She was a bloodsucker who took what she wanted. And discarded what she didn't want.

He knew that firsthand.

"Why not Skull Creek?" she countered. "Besides, it's not the only town I'm featuring. Just one of five I'm visiting for this particular article." The music closed in on them for several long seconds as Bob Seger launched into "Night Moves."

"A travel piece, huh?" he finally said. "Sounds tame compared to the stuff you're used to."

She shrugged and took a swig of her beer. "I was due for a change of pace."

"And here I thought you'd come all this way to see me."

"Actually…" Her voice faded as she seemed to search for her next words. "I did." Her gaze locked with his, and he saw it again—the flash of desperation, along with a glimmer of fear. "I…" She swallowed. "That, is, I know you recently opened a motorcycle shop in town, and I thought maybe I could take a few pictures for my article. You know, to showcase all that Skull Creek has to offer. I've taken shots of Mr. McClury's jasmine fields and the gazebo in the town square. I know a motorcycle shop doesn't seem all that sexy, but it's the implication. Two lovebirds riding off into the sunset." When he didn't say anything, she added, "It's just a few pictures. You won't have to do anything. Just be there to let me in and out and answer a few questions."

"What's in it for me?"

"Free promotion. In exchange for the photos, the magazine will mention your contact information and even give you a free half page ad." She smiled and he had the sudden urge to get the hell out of there while the getting was good.

The last thing he needed was to let Viviana back into his life, even for a measly travel article. He'd had a hard enough time putting the past behind him.

Better to keep his distance and his sanity.

At the same time, he couldn't stifle the voice that told him there was something up besides his traitorous cock.

She wanted more from him than a few pictures, and he couldn't shake the sudden urge to find out exactly how much.

No way did he want to spend any time with her because he still had feelings for her. Anything he'd once felt had died a long time ago, right along with his humanity. The only thing left now was the lust that lived and breathed inside of him. And that, he felt for every woman.

A lust he'd been denying since he'd moved to Skull Creek. He was tired of the endless one-night stands. Even more, he was tired of being a vampire.

He wanted out.

He wanted his humanity back.

"I'm busy with a project right now—a custom chopper we've designed for some bigwig up in Dallas. You'll have to stay out of the way."

She nodded. "No problem. You won't even know I'm there."

He sucked down the last of his drink. "Tomorrow night then. Seven o'clock."

Excitement lit her expression as she got to her feet. "It's a date."

If only.

He squelched the thought, sipped his beer and watched the push/pull of her denim skirt as she turned to walk away.

Watch being the key word. A word that implied distance and perspective and hands off.

But looking...

Well, there wasn't a damned thing wrong with that.

2

EVERY INCH of Viv's body screamed with awareness as she left Garret staring after her and headed for the nearest exit.

Her hands trembled. Her stomach tingled. Her nipples quivered. Heat flamed her cheeks, and she felt a buzzing awareness from her hair follicles to the balls of her feet. The chemistry between them was even stronger than she'd remembered.

Which explained why she'd chickened out with her real proposition.

She wanted a lot of things from Garret Sawyer—his hands on her skin, his lips eating at hers and his body full and thick inside of her—but a picture wasn't one of them.

Unless said picture included all of the above.

But still shots of his motorcycle shop?

Forget desperate. One hundred and eighty years without an orgasm had finally taken its toll. She'd crossed the line from desperate to completely deranged.

"Hey there, sweet thing."

Her gaze snapped up just as a man stepped in front

of her and blocked her escape route. It was one of the bikers who'd been playing darts when she'd first entered the bar.

He slid his arm around her shoulder and leaned into her. "Why don't you and I have a seat and get to know each other better?"

That's what he said, but she knew the truth. He didn't want to get to know her. Not her mind, that is. As for having a seat… The only seat he had in mind involved her straddling his lap and doing her best rodeo queen imitation.

"No, thanks."

"Aw, don't be like that." His thick fingers stroked her arm. "I just want to be friends."

"I doubt that." Garret's deep voice drifted over her shoulder and prickled the hair on the back of her neck.

The man turned and his eyes went wide. "Where'd you come from?"

"Do you really want to know?"

The man blinked and shook his head. "Weren't you just sitting clear across the room?"

"I've got fast reflexes." When the man didn't look convinced, Garret added, "Shouldn't you be at home with Liza?"

Shock fueled the man's expression and his gaze narrowed. "What do you know about my wife?"

"I know she left your sorry ass because you've got a hair trigger when it comes to sex. I also know that the two of you are still married even though she's staying at her mother's." Garret's expression was as hard as granite. "You shouldn't be here hitting on women. You should be begging Liza's forgiveness."

The man looked confused for a long moment before an idea seemed to strike. "You're one of them superheroes, ain't ya?"

"Not even close," Garret replied.

"What about a psychic? My Aunt Bertie was a psychic. She had forty cats and swore she could talk to every one of them. Always knew when one was getting sick."

"I'm not psychic either. I'm pissed. So get your hands off the lady. Now."

"Like hell—" he started, but his voice faded when Garret's gaze collided with his.

"Go home," Garret told the man.

And beg your wife to take you back. Viv added the silent thought when the man's gaze finally shifted to hers. He nodded and released her arm.

"Thanks," she told Garret when the man finally walked away. "But you didn't have to do that. I can take care of myself."

"I know." His gaze drilled into hers, and for a split second time pulled her back, and the wall between them seemed to crumble.

Concern sparkled in his eyes, along with a fierce protective light that stalled her heart.

"About those pictures," she heard herself say. "I…" *I was lying. I don't want to take your picture. I want you. Wild and naked and inside of me.* She opened her mouth, but despite the moment of déjà vu, she couldn't seem to force the words past her lips. "I—I can't wait to get started," she heard herself say. "See you tomorrow." And then she turned and pushed through the Exit door.

The sweltering Texas night sucked her up, and the door rocked shut behind her. Gravel crunched as she headed for the silver Jag parked at the far end of a row of motorcycles. Her ears tuned for any sound that would indicate that Garret followed.

Nothing.

A wave of disappointment crashed through her, followed by a surge of relief.

Relief? What the hell was wrong with her?

She should have hauled him outside with her, shoved him up against the nearest wall, kissed him full on the mouth and made her intentions crystal clear.

That's what she would have done with anybody else. What she'd always done to keep up her strength and feed the hunger that churned deep inside her.

But while she'd soaked up plenty of sexual energy from her partner's orgasms, she'd never closed her eyes and lost herself in the feel of her own body convulsing and splintering into a thousand little pieces.

Not since her last night with Garret.

She'd been a vampire back then and he'd been just another mortal, but the encounter had rocked her unlike any other. They'd had phenomenal sex and she'd been hooked.

And so had he.

The crazy fool had actually proposed to her.

She touched her bare ring finger. She could still feel the metal sliding over her knuckle. In her mind's eye, she saw the ornate gold band and the bloodred princess-cut ruby. It had been small. Very small but pretty. His grandmother's, he'd told her.

She'd smiled indulgently and played along for a while. The way she always did when it came to men.

She was a vampire. Charismatic. Mesmerizing. She could be dressed in baggy sweats, having the worst hair day on the planet, and men would still find her ir-resistible. It hadn't been a bit surprising that Garret had fallen so hard for her so fast.

No, what had really startled her was what she'd felt for him.

She'd actually liked him.

He'd been a patriot of Texas. Strong. Noble. Coura-geous. And from the moment he'd walked into the small saloon where she'd been working, aka feeding, she'd been attracted.

So she'd done the unthinkable—she'd slept with him not once but several times. Even more than the sex, they'd actually spent time together.

They'd gone on moonlit walks, held hands beneath the stars and confided their dreams to each other.

Wild, far-out dreams of love and marriage and kids and a real home.

She'd been a newly turned vampire back then, des-perate to ignore the truth of what she'd become. Likewise, he'd been a man eager to escape the death and destruction that lived and breathed all around him.

And so she'd pretended, and he'd pretended.

She'd seen the love swimming in his eyes, and she'd let herself believe it was real.

But it hadn't been.

Not then and certainly not now.

He was no longer a weak human mesmerized by her vampiric charm, and she was no longer denying her true nature.

They were both vampires, fully rooted in the present. When they had sex again, there would be no soft words between them, no foolhardy talk of happily ever after. No false promises.

Just lust.

Raw.

Primitive.

Savage.

If they came together.

The doubt pushed its way into her head as she climbed behind the wheel of her car and keyed the ignition.

There could be no if.

Sex had to be a sure thing, and the lame excuse she'd given him tonight would work in her favor. Pictures meant more than one. Which meant they wouldn't be spending five minutes together sharing small talk. It would take hours, maybe even days, for her to set up her equipment—the cameras, the lighting, the background—and get just the right shots. She had no doubt that the more time they spent with one another, the more explosive the chemistry would be.

Because he wanted her as fiercely as she wanted him.

Even though she could no longer stare into his eyes and see his every thought—vamps couldn't read other vamps the way they did humans—she'd seen the tell-tale spark in his gaze when she'd sat down at his table. She'd felt the rush of jealousy when he'd come to her rescue.

Something was bound to happen between them.

Eventually.

Before Cruz and Molly caught up with her again?

The question struck, and her survival instincts kicked into gear. She swept a glance around her, drinking in the half-full parking lot. Her gaze sliced through the darkness, pushing back the shadows, searching. Her ears perked, and her nostrils flared, but she smelled nothing except stale beer and cigarettes and her grip eased on the steering wheel.

She was safe. She knew it. She felt it.

For now.

Over the past year, it had taken at least a week or two for the other vampires to track her down once she'd given them the slip.

With the exception of their last encounter, that is.

When they'd left her for dead.

She'd been sensationalizing the latest in a string of serial murders in state courtesy of the Butcher.

The Butcher had eluded police over twenty-nine murders, and he was still on the loose. While true crime wasn't usually something picked up by a tabloid, the Butcher was the exception because he was rumored to be a Hollywood celebrity gone bad. At least that's what he'd told the world when he'd left a bloody message on the wall of his first victim's apartment. Every tabloid was now hot on the trail to discovery his identity first. Viv had been covering his handiwork from the beginning, from his first kill down in West Hollywood, to an elderly couple in Portland, to the recent handful of bodies found in an abandoned cabin outside of Tacoma.

She'd been scoping out the actual crime scene when she'd been discovered by local law enforcement, specifically a hard-ass sheriff by the name of Matt Keller. Keller had been about to grill her with questions—who did she work for, how did she hear about the murders, why was she there—when he'd been called back to the police station. He'd threatened to throw her ass in jail for trespassing and then he'd escorted her off the property. His parting words? "Stay the hell away from here."

She should have listened to him.

Instead, she'd gone back. She'd been snapping pictures when she'd been attacked by the two vampires who'd been hot on her trail for over three years. They'd staked her out on the front porch of the cabin and left her to fry.

But Molly's aim had been off. The knife had punctured her at an angle, a scant half-inch to the right. Rather than hitting her heart, they'd stabbed the inner right lobe of her lung. While not life-threatening, she'd still been hurt badly. She'd bled all over the porch, her blood mingling with that of the Butcher's other victims. She would have burned to a crisp at the first sign of dawn if she hadn't managed to drag herself through the front door. Inside, she'd hidden in one of the closets.

It was there, as she'd cowered beneath a mound of stale clothes, her St. Benedict medal clutched tightly in her hand, that she'd felt vulnerable for the first time in her life. Hurt. Nervous. Scared.

Cruz and Molly wanted their humanity back and they would stop at nothing in their quest to destroy the vampire who'd taken it from them.

She could still see their faces, the first time she'd met them all those years ago. Eighty-seven to be exact. She'd been in some hole-in-the-wall border town looking for her next meal when she'd happened upon a white slavery ring holed up in a house on the outskirts of town.

Molly had been chained in the cellar and Cruz had been one of her abductors. He'd fallen in love with her and tried to help her escape, and so he'd ended up chained next to her.

After a violent encounter with the one guard on duty (the rest of the slave traders had been upstairs passed out from a case of tequila), Viv had freed a cellar full of prisoners made up of primarily women and children.

Most of the prisoners had taken off up the rickety steps, desperate to get away before their abductors sobered up.

Except for Cruz and Molly.

They'd seen the truth about Viv, and they'd wanted a different means of escape.

The voices echoed in her head, so strong and clear, as if it had been just yesterday that she'd descended into that hell-hole prison.

"YOU CAN'T JUST leave us." Cruz held Molly's hand in one of his and a buck knife he'd taken off the guard in his other.

The man's body slumped in a nearby corner. He was out cold. For now.

"They'll track us down," Cruz went on. "They will." He nodded frantically. His eyes glittered with the horrific memories of being beaten and locked up and humiliated. He'd watched the woman he loved being raped. Over and over. And he'd been powerless to stop it.

He still was.

The truth burned inside of him, feeding the desperation and fear coiling his body tight.

"You have to help us," he added, his gaze as pleading as his words.

"Leave now," Viv told him. She couldn't do what he asked. She wouldn't doom anyone else to the darkness. Never again.

"You'll have a good head start," Viv continued. "Take Molly and go. I'll stall them for you."

"Kill them?"

But she couldn't do that either. While she'd made her fair share of vampires, she'd never actually caused anyone's death. No, she'd saved them from it.

Or so she'd always thought.

"I can't do that." She shook her head. "But I'll slow them down. That's all I can do."

"It won't be enough," came Molly's small, hollow voice. She shook her head, her eyes wide and vacant, as if the men had stolen her spirit right along with her innocence. "They'll find us."

"They won't," Viv reassured them. "But you have to go." She motioned toward the rickety steps leading to the dark, cold night. "Now."

"You don't know them." Cruz shook his head, a strange look in his eyes. He let go of Molly's hand and lifted the knife. "They'll catch us and make us pay. And I won't be able to stop them. I can't. Not like this."

The blade flashed and before Viv could blink, he sliced through his left wrist clear to the bone. Blood gushed, spurting out onto the floor at an alarming rate.

"Please," he mouthed, and then he sank to his knees as his life slipped away.

VIV BLINKED AGAINST the sudden burning in her eyes at the vivid memory. She hadn't been able to stand by and watch him die. Not after the suffering he'd already endured. And so she'd turned him.

And he'd turned Molly.

And then the two newly made vampires had doled out revenge.

But what they'd first seen as their salvation, they'd come to realize was more a curse.

One they now meant to break.

They'd finally figured out that if they killed her, they

could free themselves from the chains of darkness that bound them, silence the hunger that ruled their existence and become human again.

It had been eight days since Viviana had crawled into that closet and faced her mortality. She had no doubt that Cruz and Molly knew that they'd failed by now.

They would come for her again. To do the job right this time. And she would let them.

Because along with fear, she'd felt something else, as well, while she'd been holed up in that closet. As her body had healed, her mind had relived the past. She'd spent three days hiding, healing and thinking about her life, about all those people she'd tried to save from death.

She'd finally admitted the truth to herself—despite her intentions, she hadn't really saved anyone. No, she'd doomed them to a fate worse than death.

The darkness.

The hunger.

No more.

She figured she only had a few days before Molly and Cruz caught up with her again. When they did, she had no intention of fighting them. Rather, she would face her mistakes this time, and set things right. She would give them back their humanity.

But before she submitted to her own death, she wanted to feel truly alive one more time.

One last time.

She retrieved the medallion she'd left hanging from

the rearview mirror, slid the gold chain over her head and tucked the warm metal deep in her cleavage. Gunning the engine, she put the car in gear and headed back to the motel.

3

SHE WAS PERFECT.

Garret watched the redhead make her way across the sawdust floor. His nostrils flared. The faint scent of strawberry shampoo drifted through the fog of beer and cigarette smoke. Her breaths came quick, her lips parting ever so slightly. Her small breasts bounced with each draw of oxygen.

It had been an hour since Viv had left the bar.

An hour spent thinking and wondering and fantasizing.

He drop-kicked the last thought as soon as it waltzed into his head and focused on the hunger gnawing at his gut. His stomach clenched, and his muscles bunched. Heat clawed low and deep. His throat tightened.

His gaze narrowed, and he fixated on the woman again. He noticed everything about her—from the way her eyes glittered with excitement and fear to the slight sway of her walk, as if she hadn't pulled out the high heels in a really long time.

And then he noticed that no one else seemed to notice her.

The other men didn't stare or drool or eat her up with their eyes the way they'd done Viv.

Because there was nothing supernatural about this woman.

She was real.

Ordinary.

And so the men kept drinking and shooting the shit while the woman slid onto a bar stool and crossed her legs.

As if she felt his attention, she turned. Her green gaze collided with his, and the truth echoed in his head.

This was the last place she wanted to be, but she was sick and tired of sitting home alone, mourning over a recent break-up with her long-term boyfriend. She needed to ease her sexual frustration, get over him once and for all and get on with her life.

She needed rebound sex.

And Garret needed the energy bubbling inside of her, especially now that Viv was back in his life. If he meant to keep his head on straight and his dick in his pants, he needed every ounce of strength when he faced her tomorrow night.

He needed to suppress the hunger.

Satisfy it.

He pushed to his feet despite the promise he'd made to himself to give up the endless string of one-night stands that came with being a vampire. The constant need for blood and sex. The blood he couldn't deny himself. He'd been bagging it, courtesy of a contact he'd made at the Austin Blood Bank. But the sex... He wasn't going to sleep his way through Skull Creek the way he'd done every other town. He was tired of moving from place to place. Running. Existing. He wanted to live again.

He wanted his humanity back.

He could have it, too. It was just a matter of finding and destroying the vampire who'd turned him.

A nearly impossible task or so he'd thought. Until Dillon Cash—the computer genius behind Skull Creek Choppers—had come through with a solid lead.

It had started with a cheesy blog Dillon had started a few months ago to locate Garret's sire. Surprisingly enough, the blog had gained popularity. People had started to comment.

While the majority of visitors were vampire wannabes, there were a few legitimate posts. Enough for Dillon to come up with a lead on the vampire who fit the description in Garret's memory.

He didn't remember much. Just a dark, looming shadow, a sweet, succulent scent, and a gold medallion.

He'd sketched the medallion, and Dillon had blogged about it and now they had a name.

One that might lead him absolutely nowhere.

At the same time, there was a chance—however slim—that Garret might find himself that much closer to the Ancient One.

He'd hired a private investigator to track down the name. Dalton MacGregor, the decorated Green Beret and ex-cop who'd taken the case, had promised to have an address by the end of this week. Reason enough for

Garret to ignore the hunger churning inside of him and head for the door instead of the woman.

Five steps, and he reached her. Desire sparked in her gaze, and she licked her lips. A wave of self-consciousness swept through her, and she stiffened. She damned herself for not wearing the pink tank top instead of the white. White always made her look so flat-chested.

He dropped his gaze and let it linger on her cotton-clad breasts for a brief moment.

Nice. He sent the silent message and shifted his attention to her face in time to see her smile.

"What are you drinking?" he asked.

"Corona." She licked her lips again, and her heartbeat kicked up a notch.

The fast rhythm of it echoed in his head, and his gut tightened. He could see the faint pulse of blue at the base of her neck, and a knife twisted inside of him. He signaled the bartender to bring her a beer and ordered a shot of Jack Daniels for himself.

A few seconds later, the bartender deposited a frosty beer mug in front of the redhead and a shot glass in front of Garret. The man poured two fingers of fiery liquid before setting the whiskey bottle aside and rushing toward the opposite end of the bar to fill another request.

"Thanks," she said as she took a tentative sip from her mug. "So, um, do you come here often?"

"Every now and then."

"That's nice." She nodded and took another sip. "I've never been here myself, but I've always wanted to give it a try." She glanced around. "It's a little noisier than I expected. Not really ideal for getting to know someone." She shifted her gaze back to his, suddenly eager to cut right to the chase now that she'd worked up her courage. "Maybe we could, um, go someplace quiet. That is, if you want." She took another sip.

Her red lipstick left an imprint on the frosted mug. The sight stirred a rush of memories, and just like that he was back in the Texas Star saloon with his regiment.

A drink.

That's all he'd wanted at first, but then he'd seen Viv Darland standing near the bar, and suddenly alcohol hadn't been enough.

He'd wanted her warm skin beneath his hands, her legs wrapped around his waist, her mouth soft and open beneath his own. He'd followed her upstairs, and he hadn't come down for days. He'd ended up staying so long he'd almost been declared AWOL by his commanding officer.

Not that he'd cared.

Everything else—his family, his passion, his duty—had ceased to exist when he'd stared into Viv's blue eyes. He'd been hooked. Infatuated. Mesmerized.

Because she was a vampire.

He hadn't known then.

Sure, he'd seen the signs.

Her usually blue eyes had seemed purple at times, green at other times. She'd been stronger than most women, uncorking her own whiskey bottles and dealing with drunken brawlers all by herself. And, of course, her aversion to sunlight. But she'd been a saloon whore, plying her trade all night and sleeping all day, and so he hadn't thought much about it.

He'd fallen hard and fast, and he hadn't been able to pick himself back up. Hell, he hadn't wanted to.

She'd been the first thing he'd thought of when he'd opened his eyes every morning and the last thing when he'd closed them at night.

He'd even imagined her there at the end, leaning over him as he'd sprawled facedown on the ground, his blood seeping out into the dirt. Her scent had filled his head. Her soft, silky hair had brushed his temple. And just like that, he'd been distracted from the pain and suffering of the knife wounds.

A hallucination, of course.

He'd been miles away from the saloon when he'd been attacked by a group of Mexican bandits, robbed and left for dead.

An easy target for the vampire who'd come along to finish the job.

He could still remember the presence looming over his wounded body, the strong hand gripping his hair and yanking his head back, the razor-sharp fangs piercing his throat.

One minute he'd been hanging onto his life by a thread and the next, the line had snapped. Death had taken him, only to spit him back out when the vampire had rolled him over and drip-dropped his own blood into Garret's mouth.

Garret hadn't even caught a glimpse of his sire.

He'd been too weak to see more than a shadow looming over him.

Seconds later, he'd been alone, sprawled on the ground without a clue as to what had just happened. Until daybreak arrived and the first rays of sunlight topped the horizon.

The past pushed and pulled, snatching him from the here and now and luring him back to the morning of his turning.

He fought against the pain gripping him and forced his eyes open. He felt cold. So cold. His teeth chattered, and his body shook. He stared through blurry eyes. Orange topped the trees, promising warmth and a rush of relief went through him. Now he would warm up.

In…just…a…few…seconds…

A shaft of light fell across his face, and pain sliced clear to his bones. A hiss worked its way up his throat as he jerked his head to the side. The heat slashed across his shoulders, and he scrambled away. He staggered to his feet. Pain beat at his temples as the light cracked at his body like a red hot whip.

He stumbled for the trees, but they weren't enough to shield him completely. His skin burned and sizzled and he moved deeper into the forest. Light filtered down through the branches, stabbing him at every step. The pungent scent of charred flesh clogged his nostrils and choked him. Smoke burned his eyes, blurring his vision as he glanced around, frantic for a place to hide.

Another shaft of light broke through the trees, and he dodged to the left. His foot came up against a rock and he pitched forward, landing facedown on the ground. Clawing at the ground, he pushed until he managed to lift his head. A black hole loomed in front of him.

He dug his fingers into the dirt and pulled himself forward, over sharp rocks and prickly cactus until he managed to crawl inside. He went deeper, deeper, until the light disappeared and he found himself sheltered in the dark, cool interior.

Heaven.

That's what Garret had thought. The deep, narrow cave had been his shelter. His salvation.

But over the next several hours as the hunger had taken full control, the small space had turned into his own personal hell, a place where he'd fought a losing battle for his soul.

It was a battle that had lasted several days, as Garret remained hidden away in the cave, resisting the blood-lust and trying to come to terms with what he'd become.

Meanwhile, Viv had been back at the saloon, seducing any and every cowboy who'd walked in. Talking them into drinks. Luring them back to her room. Spreading her legs and opening her arms.

Deceiving them the way she'd deceived him.

The realization had come when he'd finally given in to the hunger and left the cave. He'd gone back to town in search of food. But before he'd sank his fangs into anyone, he'd gone to the saloon first. He'd meant to explain things to her, to beg for her help and her under-standing.

But she'd already understood because she was every bit the vampire he'd become.

Even so, he'd thought that she still felt something for him. Something that went beyond the bloodlust and the need for sex.

Love.

He'd been wrong.

"I can't be with you like this. Not now. Not ever again."

He could still hear her voice as she'd turned her back and walked away from him.

She'd left him because he'd become a vampire who could see through her lies. A vampire who could no longer give her the sustenance she needed—the sexual energy—because he needed it for himself.

And so she'd abandoned him to find someone else to feed the beast that lived and breathed inside of her.

As for love... She hadn't loved him, and he hadn't really loved her. He'd been mesmerized by her, seduced by her vamp magic like any other weak human.

But he wasn't susceptible to her now.

Even if he did have an aching hard-on.

"What do you say?" The soft voice pushed into his thoughts and pulled him back to the present. To the smoke-filled bar and the horny woman sitting next to him. "Would you, um, like to come back to my place?"

Yes.

The answer was there on the tip of his tongue despite his self-made vow. He needed her. To ease the pain inside his body, feed the hunger and fill him with a burst of energy.

He felt so tired at that moment.

So damned hungry.

His gaze hooked on the lipstick imprint on her glass again, and his chest tightened. "I'm afraid I'm a little busy right now." He slid several bills onto the counter and reached for the bottle of Jack Daniels. "But you have a nice night, sugar." He turned and left her staring longingly after him.

Because even more than Garret Sawyer needed to feed, suddenly he needed to forget.

The dark hair.

The true blue eyes.

The luscious body and fragrant skin.

The damned voice that echoed over and over in his head "I can't be with you like this."

And so he sank down at the nearest table, touched the open bottle to his lips and did what he hadn't done since Viv Darland had walked out on him all those years ago.

He started to drink.

And he didn't stop.

4

"HOW'S THIS?"

"Move a little to the right," Viv told the short, balding, forty-six-year-old man who stood behind the counter of Skull Creek's one and only motel.

It was two hours since she'd left the Iron Horseshoe, and she was desperate for a distraction. Something to pass the time and get her mind off Garret and the anticipation bubbling inside of her.

Enter Eldin Atkins.

He was the owner of the Skull Creek Inn and, more importantly, the oldest bachelor in town. He'd inherited both the motel and his grandmother, Winona, when his parents had retired to a small fishing port on the Gulf Coast. Eldin made all the reservations and looked after Winona while she puttered around, straightening rooms and poking her nose in everyone's business.

Or so Viv had heard from the waitress over at the diner.

Since Winona did most of her nosing around during the day when Viv had her door barricaded and her shades drawn, she'd yet to run into the old woman.

Eldin was a different story altogether.

The minute Viv had mentioned that she was a photo journalist, he'd gone above and beyond the call of duty to make her stay as memorable as possible.

He'd brought fresh towels every morning and had even upgraded her room for free. She now occupied the one and only deluxe suite with a full-size bathroom and a kitchenette.

Not that she needed the latter, but Eldin didn't know that. He was just out to attract as much attention as possible because he'd already tried every on-line dating service in the free world, and he still hadn't had any luck with the opposite sex.

He was hoping like hell that some poor, lonely female read the travel article, saw his picture and realized that, despite his thinning hair, introverted personality and live-in grandmother, he was a halfway decent catch.

He didn't wear women's underwear (not since Double Dog Dare Ya night back in the tenth grade) and he didn't suck his teeth and—and this was the biggee— he had his own business.

Sort of.

Technically, his parents still owned the place, but once they kicked the bucket, the Inn would be Eldin's free and clear.

Well, his and Winona's, but his grammy was already older than dirt, so how much longer could she actually last?

Bottom line, he wasn't such a bad guy. The article

would be a prime opportunity to show the single women of the southwest (and a few east coast states where the travel mag had been picked up) all that he had to offer.

Tonight he wore an orange Hawaiian-print shirt, beige walking shorts and a pair of tan boat shoes with tube socks. He had a king-sized Snickers bar in his left shirt pocket and a Slim Jim in the right.

"You're going to put my e-mail address in the article, right?" he asked. "Just in case somebody is of a mind to reach me? For a room, that is."

Or, more importantly, a date.

"E-mail and snail mail," Viv promised. "Say cheese."

"Wait a second." Eldin slicked his eyebrows down, threw his shoulders back and puffed out his chest. One hand paused on the wall of room keys and the other gave a little salute. "Okay, I'm ready."

"So, Eldin," Viv said as she checked the shutter on her camera, "do you always stand that way when you're checking someone in?"

He seemed to think before letting out a deep breath. "'Course not." He switched angles and struck the same pose. "I usually stand like this on account of it's my good side," he said, his words tight as he tried to suck in his sizeable beer belly. "Go on," he gasped. "Shoot."

Viv snapped a few pictures before pausing to check the shots on her digital screen.

"Where do you want me next?" Eldin asked after gasping for several deep breaths. "Over by the fireplace? I could build a fire. I know how."

"That's good to know. And I would take you up on it in a heartbeat…" Viv checked her flash. "…if it wasn't ninety plus degrees outside."

"Forget the fire. I'll just hold a few chunks of wood. Maybe I should take my shirt off to look like I've been out chopping all day—"

"No," she cut in, desperate to ignore the sudden image of Eldin shirtless. "These are supposed to be action shots. A day in the life of stuff." She stared deep into his eyes to press her point home. "That means natural."

He looked confused for a split-second before he seemed to relax. "Let me just straighten the magazines here like I do every night on account of my granny and her dad-burned group are always messing things up. Why, it takes days to get this lobby back to normal after one of her danged meetings."

"Shame on you for talking about an old lady," said a crackling voice as an ancient-looking woman walked from the back room.

She wore a purple flower-print dress, white orthopedic shoes and knee-high panty hose. She had a shock of white hair curled into tight sausages that covered her head like a football helmet. Bifocals hung from a chain around her neck and sat low on her nose.

"If I was a few years younger," she continued as she deposited a cardboard box on the counter and wagged a finger at Eldin, "I'd take a skillet to your hind end. Just pay him no nevermind," she turned to Viv. "He hates my meetings because he has to give up the TV and bide his time until we're finished."

"You took three hours last time," Eldin whined. "I missed *Grey's Anatomy* and *So You Think You Can Dance*."

"You watch too much TV. You ought to be doing other things with your time."

"Like what?"

"The front walkway needs power washing."

"But that'll take hours."

"That's the idea."

"But I been standing all day. My feet hurt."

"That's 'cause you're putting on too much weight." She snatched the Snickers bar out of his pocket. "Steer clear of the snack machine, and you won't have such a big gut puttin' so much pressure on your tootsies. Why, I been standing over eighty years, and my feet don't hurt a bit."

"But that's my dessert." Eldin eyed the candy bar in her hand. "Dessert is one of the four basic food groups."

"Is not."

"Is too. There's fruit, potatoes, steak and dessert. A man needs all of 'em if he wants to keep up his stamina."

The old woman seemed to soften as she eyed him. "I s'pose you'll need your energy to handle that power washer." She handed the candy bar back to him. "Take it and skedaddle." She waved a hand and motioned him out. "My students will be here in less than fifteen minutes. I'm Winona Atkins," she added, turning to Viv. "Are you the one who called yesterday about joining my group?"

"I'm afraid not. I'm a guest. Room 12."

"You're the one from California? The one with the flashy sports car?"

"Guilty."

She seemed to think. "Had me a little Pinto once. It wasn't much too look at, but my husband—rest his soul—souped up the engine for me. It was the fastest ride in town. Faster than that old Mustang Merle Shanks used to hot rod around in, I'll tell you that much." She opened the edges of the cardboard box. One shriveled hand dove into the box, and she pulled out an enormous purple vibrator—

Oh, no, she didn't.

Viv blinked, but sure enough it was purple, it was a vibrator and it was enormous. A neon blue version followed. Then an orange. A yellow. Pink. Aqua.

"What exactly does your group do?" Viv asked as she watched the old woman unpack the box as nonchalantly as if she were setting out crochet needles instead of sex toys.

"A little of this. A little of that." Winona shrugged. "Tonight we're learning how to give a blowjob without biting. We're also going to talk about how to respond when your partner approaches you about a blow job, or vice versa. You'd be surprised how many gals just ain't that good when it comes to tellin' their men what they want."

Tell me about it.

"So it's like a self help class to overcome shyness?"

"It's a class to pull the stick out of your ass."

Viv couldn't help but smile. While the old woman had plenty of snow on the roof, she was all fire and spunk inside.

"I teach women how to loosen up and relax," Winona continued, "so's that they can enrich their relationships with their fellas. It's all about using what you got to spice things up and keep your man screaming for more. I'm a carnal coach. Coach Winona." She pulled a penis-shaped name tag out of her pocket and pinned it to the front of her dress.

"We also have refreshments," she added. "Mary Lou's bringing her famous pigs-in-a-blanket and Jennie Sue's making a coffee cake. I'm even baking a few batches of pleasure bites to get everyone feeling frisky. They're small, round little tastes of heaven made primarily of the one thing no sexually repressed woman can resist."

Viv arched an eyebrow. "Chocolate?"

"Alcohol." Winona adjusted her glasses. "See, I've got a lot of introverts in my class, like poor, timid Ellen Jenkins—she's the local librarian. That woman won't even send her hamburger back when they load it with ketchup instead of mustard. She sure as shootin' can't work up the nerve to tell Oren—that's her husband—that he's just not satisfying her in the sack. So instead of calling him out, she joined my class. She figured if she got better at doin' it, then she could make up for what he lacked. I had my doubts about that. Oren wasn't the best-looking catfish in the pond, and so the girls never paid him no nevermind growing up. He's definitely a plate short of a place setting when it comes to physical relations. But Ellen paid her registration in full, and I wasn't one to argue with cold hard cash.

Anyhow, sober she could barely sit through a lecture without blushing. A few pleasure bites, and she all but fought me for the pole when I did my strip-your-way-into-his-heart seminar."

"They sound very effective."

"And pretty darned tasty. You really ought to sit in tonight and try a few for yourself. You might even pick up some pointers on how to be more sexy." She wiggled her eyebrows. "I'm going to reveal my ten Do-Me-Baby Commandments after we finish blow jobs. It's a special list I put together over the past few months based on my own experience as a vibrant, sexually active woman." When Viv looked doubtful, she added, "Back in the day, that is. I'm not nearly as sexually active as I should be right now on account of I'm still pining for my late husband."

That and she was still waiting on Morty Donovan to haul his carcass out of his rocking chair and ask her for a date. Morty was in charge of Bingo over at the senior center. He also had the whitest dentures in town because his grandson was a cosmetic dentist, and Morty got free bleaching with every visit.

"If you can manage to learn all ten of them," Winona said, "there ain't a man alive who'll be able to resist you."

While Viv had no trouble consuming liquids, anything solid (even if it was one hundred and eighty proof) was completely off-limits. Even more, the last thing she needed was a how-to list to beef up her sex appeal. She'd been oozing vampire mojo for over two centuries. She already knew that no man could resist her.

But Garret Sawyer wasn't a man.

He was a vampire.

Larger than life. Tall, dark and totally immune to her supernatural charms because he had plenty of his own.

Forget being a persuasive, seductive female vampire. From here on out, it was all about being a persuasive, seductive female, period.

A scary thought for a woman who'd been turned before she'd even lost her virginity. A woman who'd been so desperate for survival that she'd never learned how to rely on good, old-fashioned feminine wiles.

No flirting or teasing. No licking her lips and batting her eyelashes. No being overly affectionate one minute and hard-to-get the next.

She'd never played games with men.

She'd never had to.

"The first class is free. What do you say?" Winona asked, arching one silver eyebrow. "You want to join us?"

Viv grabbed a rubber penis and glanced around. "Just tell me where to sit."

5

THE HALLWAY BENEATH the house was pitch-black, but it didn't matter. Garret's gaze sliced through the darkness and fixated on the door knob. Yes, he could see it, all right. He just couldn't get his fingers around it because it kept moving.

A little to the left…

A little to the right…

There.

Wood creaked, and the door slammed inward.

A single lamp burned on the nightstand and pushed back the shadows. The walls of the massive room seemed to vibrate. The plasma TV mounted on the opposite wall swam in front of him.

He meant to pick his leg up and take a step inside, but damned if his body would cooperate. He slid forward. The rug caught the tip of his boot, and he tripped. His shoulder hit the edge of a thick maple dresser. His head slammed into the mirror. Glass shattered and pain cracked open his skull. He doubled over. His stomach churned and his throat burned and—

Shit.

He shouldn't have drank so friggin' much.

No matter how desperate he was to forget.

Images of Viv pushed into his head, and he could see her looming above him. Her long, silky black hair falling down around her shoulders. Her deep blue eyes glittering with pleasure. Moonlight bathed her pale breasts, her nipples red and ripe and so damned tempting. She braced her hands against his chest as she straddled him. Her head fell back, and her eyes closed. She started to move, her body lifting and sliding as her heat slithered down over his cock, and she rode him hard and deep and—

Shit. Shit. Shit.

Garret forced his eyes open and stared through a watery haze. A few blinks, and his vivid memories faded into the polished wood paneling. He gripped the edge of the dresser and hauled himself to his feet. Three steps, and his knee caught the nightstand. Wood crashed. Shafts of light bounced off the walls as the lamp toppled over and rolled across the hardwood floor.

The noise knifed at his throbbing temples. He fell to his knees, floundering for the king-sized bed. Finally his hands made contact with the down comforter, and relief rushed through him. He needed to lie down for a little while.

Sleep.

When he woke up he would realize that it was all just a dream. Viv wasn't really here in town, and he didn't still want her so badly he could hardly stand it.

He sprawled on the bed and closed his eyes, determined to shut out the thundering in his head, the pain in his body and her.

Especially her.

But he hadn't drank nearly enough for that, and so the damnable vision followed him into the blackness. Teasing and taunting and reminding him of just how good they'd been together.

How good they could be again if Garret let his guard down.

But he wouldn't.

He'd been burned once before, and he wasn't jumping into the fire again.

No matter how much he suddenly wanted to.

HE FELT LIKE horse shit.

A big, thick pile of the stuff that had been baked a day or two in the hot, sweltering Texas sun.

Garret pushed to a sitting position, his muscles screaming with the effort. He blinked against the fluorescent bulb hanging overhead and willed his eyes to focus.

They watered instead, and he blinked. Once. Twice. He raked a hand over his face and glanced at his watch. It was just a little after six in the evening. The sun wouldn't set for at least another hour, which explained his exhaustion.

And his pounding head? He had to give the empty whiskey bottle next to him all the credit for that one.

He fell back to the mattress and closed his eyes.

A hangover.

He had a friggin' hangover.

Not that the concept was foreign to vampires. Just the opposite, in fact. A vampire had heightened senses, which meant that everything—taste, touch, smell, sight, sound—was magnified a thousand times over. If the average human could tie one on with a few beers, a vampire could get rip-roaring drunk on a helluva lot less. He could also pass out quicker from the effects and hurt even more the morning after.

Or, in his case, the night after.

He'd learned that the hard way the night Viv had left him. He'd been so drunk that he'd wandered out into the woods and passed out. The first rays of sunlight were just creeping over the horizon when he'd finally come to, and he'd suffered some serious burns before he'd managed to get his ass up and out of there.

He hadn't exceeded his two drink limit since.

He pushed his eyelids open again and swept a gaze around the shambles that had once been his bedroom. His dresser lay on its side, clothes spilled out onto the hardwood floor. His nightstand was upended. A lamp lay several feet away near a big screen TV. The bedroom door sat wide open, the rug bunched where he'd stumbled in last night.

He glanced up at the open beams of the ceiling. He'd left the rafters exposed when he'd bought the ranch house and converted the basement into a "safe" space—the perfect place for a vampire to sleep while the rest of the world went about their daily business. He'd wanted the rooms to seem larger and less cramped.

He hated being cooped up. Smothered. Cursed.

He stared at the door situated directly across the hall. The basement consisted of two rooms separated by a main hallway that led upstairs to the kitchen.

Newly made vampire, Dillon Cash, had been living in the opposite room while Garret had helped him learn the ropes of being undead. Meanwhile, Meg Sweeney, Dillon's best friend and now his girlfriend, had been helping him learn the ins and outs of great sex.

The great sex had quickly morphed into a bona fide relationship. Dillon and Meg were now living together at her place, and Garret was once again on his own in the sprawling ranch house with its state-of-the-art security system.

Garret's spread sat on over one hundred and twenty acres. The two-story rock house, as well as the barn and bunk station, had surveillance cameras around the entire perimeter.

But while the cameras could warn him of intruders, they couldn't do anything when it came to sunlight, and so he made sure to stay below ground until the sun set.

He smiled. Most of the old myths people believed about vampires didn't hold true. They didn't turn into bats or sleep in coffins. They weren't the least bit bothered by crucifixes or holy water. But sunlight… Talk about frying to a crisp.

A thought struck, and panic bolted through him.

He threw his legs over the side of the bed and pushed to his feet. The floor tilted for a long second before finally settling down. He picked his way through the bedroom and out into the hallway. He stumbled up the basement steps and sure enough, the door at the top stood wide open.

Because he'd been too shit-faced to remember to close it.

A shaft of light spilled down into the corridor and brought him to an abrupt halt.

He stared at the sliver of fading daylight and couldn't help but remember the long days in the saddle when he'd been just a man.

Before he'd gone off to fight for Texas independence, he'd helped on his family's horse farm. He'd set a horse for hours on end back then, rounding up wild broncs and breaking them. He could still see the stretch of empty plain in front of him, feel the sun beating down on the top of his head, the warmth surrounding him.

Before he could stop himself, he reached out. His fingertips brushed the light and pain wrenched through him. A sharp hiss vibrated his vocal chords.

The smell of burned flesh filled his nostrils as he stared down at his seared fingertips. A wave of regret washed through him.

Regret for the warmth he'd lost.

The life.

The love.

He forced the last notion aside. He hadn't loved Viv. He hadn't, and so there was no use regretting what he'd never had. As for his life… He missed it, all right. He missed the sun and his mama's homemade cornbread and freedom.

He retraced his steps back down into the basement and spent the next half hour cleaning up the mess he'd made. By the time he'd finished and taken a shower, dusk had settled around the house.

Only shadows crowded the staircase as he made his way upstairs and into the kitchen.

Unlike the rest of the ancient ranch house with its stone fireplace and authentic hardwood floors, the kitchen had been completely redone. Black granite countertops ran along the perimeter. There were new appliances and hand-carved oak cabinets. It was a chef's dream and a constant reminder of the man he'd once been.

The man he wanted to be again.

Grasping the stainless-steel handle of the refrigerator, he hauled open the door and retrieved a plastic bag of blood from one of the shelves. He nuked the bag to warm it up and cut the coldness, and then poured himself a glass. The first drop hit his tongue and sent a shiver through him. Warmth slid down his throat and spiraled in his gut, but it didn't ease the clenching inside of him.

If anything, it made it worse.

While the bagged stuff provided sustenance, it didn't give him the same satisfaction as sinking his fangs into a sweet, warm neck. Feeling the pulse against his tongue. Tasting the life that pumped through someone else's veins.

It was pure ecstasy, and at the same time, the worst kind of pain because it only made him want more.

That's why he refrained from biting as much as possible. Because it increased the craving as much as it satisfied it.

His hands trembled as he poured another glass and pulled out his cell.

"You sound like shit," Jake McCann said when Garret asked if he was at the shop yet.

Jake was his best friend and business partner. He was also a vampire, thanks to Garret.

It had been the anniversary of Garret's turning and he'd instinctively returned to the place of his death to relive those last few moments when his humanity had slipped away and the hunger—the damnable hunger—had seized control. Like any other vampire experiencing the turning, he'd been out of control. Jake had crossed his path, and Garret had attacked him. And then he'd tried to right his wrong by giving Jake back the life that had been stolen from him.

Or rather, a new life.

One born and bred in darkness.

He'd doomed Jake to the same fate, just as Jake had doomed Dillon. Jake hadn't been the one to attack the young man. No, Garret had done that during the most recent anniversary of his turning. In yet another thirsty craze, he'd attacked Dillon and inadvertently left him on Death's doorstep. Luckily, Jake had been on hand to turn Dillon before he completely bled out.

"What the hell happened to you?" Jake asked.

"Two bottles of Jack."

"Only two?"

"I lost count after two." Before Jake could push for more information, Garret rushed on, "Did you finish the design on the Harwell bike?" Ethan Harwell was CEO of a multi-million dollar oil company who'd commissioned a specialty chopper that incorporated his company's theme and logo.

"I'm putting the final specs on the oil well shaped spokes tonight. Late tonight. It's Saturday night."

"And?"

"Saturday night is date night. I promised Nikki I would take her out." Nikki was Jake's girlfriend and the best hairdresser in town. She was also human, and Jake meant for her to stay that way. He refused to turn her. Not while there was still hope of reclaiming his own humanity.

Hope that hinged on Garret.

Since he had sired Jake and Jake had sired Dillon, finding and destroying the vamp who'd sired Garret would start a domino effect that would free all three of them.

"We're meeting Meg and Dillon over in Karnes County for the rodeo. After the bull riding, we'll head back to the shop and catch up."

"Since when do you like bull riding?"

"Since forever." Jake had been a real cowboy back in the day. He could ride and rope almost as well as Garret. "Why don't you come with us?" Jake added.

"I've got a meeting with someone about some free PR for the shop."

"You work too much, bro."

"Yeah, well, somebody has to while the rest of you are goofing off."

"It's called having fun. You should try it sometime."

"Trust me. I have plenty of fun."

"You mean plenty of one-night stands."

"Same thing." At least, it had been. A long, long time ago when he'd first turned.

But after one hundred and eighty years and too many women to count, he didn't enjoy it nearly as much as he used to. He wanted more than sex. He wanted an actual relationship. He wanted someone to love. Someone to love him.

"He needs a real date," came Nikki's voice in the background.

"I don't need a date."

"I don't know, buddy." Since settling down with Nikki, Jake had done a complete one-eighty when it came to women and relationships. Ditto for Dillon since he'd landed Meg. While Garret knew that a real relationship could exist between a vampire and a woman, he knew his buddies were the exception rather than the rule. Dillon and Jake had gotten lucky, and Garret had never been long on luck.

"A date might lighten you up," Jake continued. "Take the edge off. You sound really tense."

"I'm fine."

"Nikki's got this friend—"

"Later." Garret hit the Off button. He was over one hundred and eighty years old, for Christ's sake. He didn't date.

Dating implied liking and liking implied a relationship, and a relationship implied a mutual give and take between two individuals. Other than fantastic sex, Garret had nothing to offer a woman.

Not until he managed to find and destroy the vampire who'd made him.

He chugged the rest of his blood, grabbed his Stetson and headed outside to the barn.

For so long he'd run from the past, from the man he'd been. He'd dressed differently—all bad-ass biker with his leather and bandanas and chains. He'd avoided small towns and clung to the cities, desperate to trade the rolling pastureland for miles and miles of concrete. He'd even refused to sit a horse.

But seeing Jake so determined to break the curse, to have a real future with his human girlfriend, Nikki Braxton, had reminded Garret of the man he'd been.

A man who'd loved horses and lived in the saddle, one who'd enjoyed the fresh air and freedom. A man who'd fought hard for what he believed in—his family and his land and his right to have both.

Until he'd been turned.

Even then, he'd held tight to the man he'd been. He'd wanted to save himself. He'd fought the damnable hunger for so long, and he'd kept fighting. But eventually, he'd gotten tired. Exhausted. Giving in had been easier.

No more.

He was through running. Forgetting.

He still hadn't climbed back into the saddle yet, but that was just a matter of time. He'd recently purchased several horses, and taming them would take a while.

One in particular—Delilah. She was the toughest of the bunch and the most stubborn.

So was Garret.

He wouldn't give up on her any more than he would give up on finding the vampire who'd turned him.

He held tight to the thought and spent a half hour pitching hay and pouring oats.

When he finished, he checked the gates, grabbed his chopper keys and headed into town to find out what Viviana Darland really wanted from him.

6

IT WAS TOO SMALL, too cramped, too quiet.

Viv wanted to move, to open the door and crawl out of the stifling closet. The sun had already set, and there was safety in the darkness. Right?

She touched the sticky wetness soaking her chest. The blood wasn't coming as fast as when Molly had first staked her, but it was still flowing, saturating her shirt and oozing onto the scarred wooden floor of the abandoned cabin.

She tried for a breath of air and a white-hot pain cut through her. Molly had been aiming for her heart, but she'd missed. Barely.

Still, the puncture hurt like a sonofabitch, and she was still bleeding heavily.

With every beat of her heart, more blood gushed from the open wound and made her wonder if—despite the fact that they'd missed her heart—she might die anyway.

Maybe this was it.

Her last few moments in existence.

The past flashed through her mind as she lay there,

like images advertising the birth of America on the History channel. The names echoed in her head.

Names she would never forget.

She saw Jimmy, the dying confederate soldier she'd gathered in her arms when she'd found him sprawled on the battlefield. She heard the anguish in his voice as he begged her to save him. She felt the tightening in her chest as she tried to resist.

But he kept begging, and her own heart kept hurting, until she gave in. She leaned over, sank her fangs into his neck and tasted the sweet heat. Pure ecstasy rolled through her body, along with a rush of dizzying energy, followed by a wave of regret.

Because as much as she wanted to save him, she knew the hunger he'd soon experience would be far worse than death.

She knew, but she turned him anyway because she couldn't help herself. She couldn't watch him die. She couldn't watch anyone die.

Never again.

Fast forward to an Apache raid. Or what was left of one.

She saw herself wandering through the demolished camp. The voices of the dying echoed in her ears. One man in particular called out to her. Travis. He was a farmer whose wife and three children had just been abducted. He was their only hope. He had to follow them. Save them.

But first he had to stop bleeding.

"Please," he begged and she couldn't resist. Not the desperation in his voice or the sweet scent curling in the air, luring her closer to his slaughtered body.

Her nostrils flared, her hunger roared, and she dipped her head. She lapped at the blood pulsing from one particular wound and awareness ripped through her. Her senses came alive, and it was as if an amplifier switched on in her head.

The whisper of the wind became a roar as it whipped through the trees. Crickets buzzed so loudly that she wanted to cover her ears. Horse hoofs thundered, and she flinched. Women pleaded and begged. Children whimpered and sniffled.

"Daddy!"

The desperate cry filled her head. A girl. Travis's youngest.

The hungry red haze that clouded her vision faded until his broken and battered face came into sharp focus. She saw the faint laugh lines around his eyes, the tiny scar that ran along his cheekbone, the deep pores of his skin. Recognition sparked as he stared up at her, and his lips moved.

"Do it," he rasped. "Help me. You have to."

She didn't. She shouldn't. She knew that.

At the same time, she couldn't stand the blood on her hands. The death on her conscience.

Not just Travis's death, but that of his wife and three daughters.

The horse hoofs kept pounding the ground, fading ever so slightly with each passing second. The little girl's voice faded, too. The crying. The pleading. The praying.

Anxiety rushed through Viv and she bared her fangs. Sinking them deep into her own wrist, she drew blood and held it to Travis's lips, and then she gave him back the precious life that was fast spilling out all over the dusty ground.

Her past kept replaying and she saw the others. Mary. James. Walter. Francis. Ruby. Ben. Molly and Cruz. Caroline. Mitchell. Richard. Loretta.

She could see their faces, hear their anguished voices, feel their pain and suffering.

She meant to say no to each and every one of them. To satisfy her own hunger and walk away. That's all that should have mattered. Feeding the beast inside of her.

At the same time, she couldn't resist the tears, the fear, the desperation. And so she tried to help, to cheat death out of yet another precious life.

But while she robbed death of victory, she didn't really save anyone. Rather, she doomed them to the hunger.

She'd doomed Garret.

Her stomach convulsed and her chest hurt and the blood kept coming, flooding the floor of the small closet. The ripe, sticky scent mingled with the smell of mothballs burned her nostrils. She held her hand to the wound and prayed for sleep. For peace.

She needed to heal. To forget.

Instead, she remembered.

Garret sprawled on the ground.

Broken.

Bleeding.

Dying.

"No!" She touched her lips to his and felt the weakness of his breath, the coldness of his skin.

One sharp slice to her neck, and her lifeblood spilled out, running in tiny rivulets down her skin, falling onto his pale lips, giving him new life all the while his old slipped away.

Slowly the color returned to his face, and his heartbeat grew strong and sure against the palm of her hand. She started to move, to leave him to heal before he opened his eyes and realized what had happened. She drew her hand away, but strong fingers clamped around hers and jerked her back down. A growl vibrated up his throat and his fangs flashed. He opened his eyes and instead of a warm chocolate, they burned a fierce, vivid violet. Her own heart catapulted with excitement, and lust rushed through her.

He turned her, pinning her to the ground.

She arched against him as he ripped her clothes away, until she felt his bare skin against her own. His hands swept up and down, touching her everywhere as he drew one nipple into his mouth and suckled her so hard that she moaned long and deep and… Ahhhhhh.

Strong, purposeful fingers found the wet heat between her legs and plunged inside. She gasped, wiggling her hips and drawing him another inch deeper… There. And there. And there.

Sensation coiled, and she felt herself winding tighter. Her hands roved over him, and she felt the bunch of his muscles as his excitement multiplied.

Her own hunger stirred, eager for a taste of the climax building inside of him. She threw her head back and arched her body, ready to feel his fangs sinking deep, and his hard erection pumping between her legs.

Sex and blood.

It was an intoxicating duo. One she'd never enjoyed with any man. Not at the same time.

But Garret was different.

Because she loved him.

Because he loved her.

Her body throbbed, and her hands trailed up and down his back, begging and pleading with him to touch her faster, harder, deeper—

The thought shattered as pain sliced through her from her collarbone, clear to her belly button. Her eyes went wide and she saw him poised above her, his hands wrapped around the sharp stake that protruded from her chest.

Blood spurted and steamed, the sound sizzling in her ears.

She opened her mouth, but her throat closed in on itself, and only a gurgle bubbled past her lips. Her gaze collided with his, and she saw the anger that burned a hot, vicious red in his eyes.

He knew the truth now, and he hated her for it.

"You did this to me," he growled. "You."

VIVIANA BOLTED UPRIGHT, her heart pounding.

She touched her chest, feeling only the soft cotton of her T-shirt and the warm metal of her St. Benedict medal.

No stake. No blood.

A dream.

That's all it had been.

Just a wild, horrific nightmare.

She and Garret hadn't made love that night, and he certainly hadn't tried to kill her.

He'd been too busy hurting. Dying.

She forced aside the memory of his body riddled with stab wounds and glanced toward the window. Shadows pushed past the edge of the blinds, a tell-tale sign that the sun had already set.

She eased from the bed and headed for the bathroom. She didn't bother to turn on the overhead bulb. She didn't need to. She could see every detail of the ancient powder-blue tile, the old-fashioned sink, the small medicine cabinet. She stared at her reflection in the mirror and noted the frantic rise and fall of her chest.

She was so freaked out she was actually breathing.

Closing her eyes, she counted to ten. Until the breaths stopped coming and her hands stopped trembling.

While the dream was a far cry from reality—she hadn't so much as kissed him that night—she had found him broken and bleeding, and she'd done her best to ease his pain.

She closed her eyes against a rush of tears and swallowed against the sudden tightening in her throat. She hadn't meant to hurt him.

But she had no doubt he would see things much differently.

That's why she'd left him so long ago. She'd been afraid to see the hatred in his eyes should he discover the truth.

She was still afraid.

He won't find out.

Even if he did, it wouldn't matter.

Cruz and Molly would catch her, and she wouldn't fight them. The curse would end and Garret would have his humanity back.

When they caught up with her.

She left the bathroom to double check the lock on the front door. As her hand closed over the doorknob, a strange niggling awareness worked its way up and down her spine. It was the same sensation she'd had up in Washington. When she'd been sensationalizing the Butcher's latest handiwork and Sheriff Keller had escorted her from the crime scene.

She could still feel his strong fingertips on her arm, hear the leaves crunching beneath his boots as they'd walked down the mountain, smell the sharp scent of pine trees and fresh blood and something else…

Someone.

They were getting closer. She knew it. She felt it. But while the feeling was there, it wasn't nearly as strong as it had been in Washington.

She double-checked the lock and headed back to the bathroom. Drawing back the shower curtain, she turned the shower on full force and stepped beneath the icy spray.

Dunking her head under the sluice of water, she closed her eyes and fought to control the frantic beating of her heart. Eventually, the tears faded. The fear started to seep away and spiral down the drain along with the ice-cold water.

By the time she stepped from the shower and reached for a fluffy towel, she'd managed to tamp down on her regret and gather her control.

Think tonight.

Think seduction.

Think Winona's ten Do-Me-Baby commandments.

Or, at least most of them.

While she fully intended to bat her eyes and lick her lips as often as possible, she wasn't so sure she was going to slap Garret's ass or tickle his balls (numbers seven and eight on the list). At least not until they were already naked and in bed.

That was the goal.

To turn him on to the point that he toppled her onto the nearest horizontal surface and initiated the sex so she didn't have to.

She'd spent an eternity being the aggressor, mesmerizing men and bending them to her will, acting rather than reacting.

No more.

Yes, she would be suggestive, seductive, inviting. But she wouldn't make the first move. She was leaving that up to Garret.

She had to.

That's why he'd been the first and only man to give her an orgasm. He'd been the aggressor. He'd been the one to take the initiative and approach her first—before she'd "vamped" him. He'd swept her off her feet and ravished her, and all because of his own passionate nature. Because he'd really and truly wanted her of his own free will. Unlike the others, who'd been puppets manipulated by her vamp charm.

She wanted Garret to want her again. She wanted to taste his excitement, his fervor, his passion once more because she knew it would feed her own and give her one last climax.

The thing was, she hadn't been trying to attract him back then. It had just happened. One look and bam, he'd been over the top for her. Out of control.

But now… She would have to use everything in her mortal female power (as untried as it was) to tempt him past the point of no return.

With that thought in mind, she stashed her St. Benedict medal in her suitcase and pulled out her clothes.

She didn't have a tank top and Daisy Duke shorts (commandment number two), so she opted for the closest thing she could find—a red silk shell and a fitted black skirt. She bypassed the undies (commandment number one), added a spritz of perfume to the inside of each thigh and her belly button (number four) and donned her outfit.

She finished with a pair of stilettos and grabbed her camera bag. She had the rest of her supplies—backdrops, lighting, extra cameras, several stands—already packed in her car. Taking one final look at the list of notes she'd taken during Winona's class, she mentally checked off the first five commandments (the rest would have to wait until she came face-to-face with Garret) and fought down a wave of nerves.

By the time the evening ended, he would be begging her for sex.

Or so she desperately hoped.

7

GARRET WASN'T begging Viv for sex.

He wasn't begging her for anything—because he wasn't there.

Disappointment rushed through her, along with a burst of anxiety as she walked into the spacious machine shop that housed Skull Creek Choppers.

It was just after sunset. Shadows crowded outside the glass windows that lined the front wall facing Main Street. Fluorescent lights blazed overhead, illuminating the stainless steel work tables covered with tools. Some she recognized—screwdrivers and wrenches and pliers—but most were totally foreign to her. An assortment of saw blades covered one twelve foot surface. An industrial strength welding unit overflowed a nearby corner. A grinder and several sprayers edged the sidelines while three large work tables dominated the center of the room. On top of one sat the shiny silver skeleton of a motorcycle. On another sat a large chunk of metal that vaguely resembled a gas tank. The third table held several long strips of metal that had been cut to resemble lightning bolts. They sat next to something that looked like a large welder. It had clamps and a curved wheel.

While Viv was no expert, she would have been willing to bet the machine had something to do with shaping and molding the fenders.

Her ears perked. She tuned in to the whir of the air conditioner, the tick-tock of a nearby clock, the hum of the massive computer system that sat in a small adjacent office just to the right. Another wall of windows separated the space from the actual shop.

There was nothing else. No deep, familiar rumble of his voice or the pounding of his heart or the pulse of his blood.

Her nose twitched, and she caught a sharp whiff of oil and engine fluid. The musky mingling of rubber and exhaust. The sterile scent of industrial strength soap and disinfectant.

The place was empty, all right. Despite the lights that blazed and the door that had been left unlocked.

Then again, this was a small town with zero crime.

She knew the type, which was why she'd made it her business to stick to the big cities. For the anonymity. The throng of people. The safety.

Garret was asking for trouble settling in such a rinky-dink place.

That, or he was just tired of running. Maybe he wanted to settle down and have the normalcy she'd robbed him of so long ago.

Guilt niggled at her the way it always did when she thought of the past, but she pushed it aside this time.

She was through living with the regret. She was doing something about it now. She was giving back.

But first…

She cast another glance around and blew out an exasperated breath. She busied herself snapping a few pictures, desperate to calm her trembling hands and rein in the sexual frustration that whipped through her.

He would be back soon, and she would get on with the matter at hand—seducing him past the point of no return.

She was armed and ready. She'd dabbed a few drops of Winona's Strawberry Seduction behind each ear. She'd gone over her notes another ten times before climbing out of the car. She was in full-blown seduction mode, her body quivering in anticipation, and he was MIA.

For now.

He would be back soon. He'd agreed to the date, and he'd always kept his word. He'd probably gone out for supplies or coffee or a quick bite.

The last thought stirred a rush of jealousy that made her stiffen.

She shifted her attention to the bike, eager to ignore the sudden image that popped into her head. Garret leaning over some woman, holding her, sinking his fangs deep—

She shook away the vision and reached out to trace the silver metallic skull and cross bones etched into the chopper's rear fender. A flaming silver skull blazed on the gas tank. The seat was rounded and curved with skulls embossed on the leather. The rims were made up of a center skull with four metal-shaped "bones" for spokes. Every detail, from the skull-shaped headlight to the red cross-bone brake lights played into the theme. It was the coolest and most unusual bike she'd ever seen.

Even more, it was sexy.

It was Garret.

A tiny thrill ripped through her. Sure, it was just a pile of metal—a motorcycle, not a man—but the man had been the one to put it together.

He'd smoothed and molded the steel. He'd attached the pieces. He'd touched and shaped and put his heart and soul into the machine to the point that she couldn't see it and not think about him.

It looked like him—sleek and masculine and dangerous. It felt like him—hard and cool and stirring. It even smelled like him—a heady mixture of rich leather and fresh air and pure adrenaline that made her heart beat that much faster.

Before she could stop herself, she set her camera on a nearby table and hiked her skirt up. Leather met her bare bottom as she straddled the seat and awareness crackled through her. Goosebumps danced up and down her skin and her nipples pebbled.

She wiggled for a better position and sensation speared her. She gasped and caught her lip against a sharp, sweet zap of lust.

No, no, no!

The chant echoed through her head because this was

not what she wanted. She'd had a zillion orgasms before, but none with a man.

Just him.

Only him.

At the same time, it felt so good, and she was so wound up. A little rocking back and forth, some wiggling side to side, and she could relieve some of the tension winding her so tight. No way would she make it through the first five minutes without doing something totally crazy. Like jump his bones the moment he walked in the door.

A disastrous move, she knew.

While he still wanted her—she'd seen it in his eyes—he didn't want to want her. To feel the attraction. The lust.

He was still hurt. Angry. Furious.

No way would he let his guard down, stop resisting what he felt for her and simply act on it.

Not yet.

She had to get him to relax, which meant she needed to bide her time and seduce him slowly.

Right.

She was too wound up. Too close to pinning him against the nearest wall and ravishing his hot, hunky body. She needed to take the edge off.

Right here.

Right now.

She leaned forward to grasp the handlebars. Her bottom slid a scant inch across the cool seat. Leather rasped her clit and desire knifed through her. She shivered. Her vision blurred. Her ears rang. Pleasure gripped her for a long, delicious moment and she caught her bottom lip.

And then she adjusted her grip, braced her thighs and started to ride.

SHE WANTED SEX.

The realization echoed in Garret's head as he stood in the office of Skull Creek Choppers and stared through the glass wall that overlooked the machine shop.

A realization that had nothing to do with the fact that he was a highly sensitive, mind-reading vampire and everything to do with the fact that he was a full-blooded male.

His heart jumped, pounding harder and faster. His muscles went tight, his spine stiff. His gut clenched and his cock throbbed as his gaze roved over the woman perched atop his latest custom chopper.

It was a project he was doing for a high profile rock star. The lead singer for some insanely popular band. Jake hadn't wanted to do the bike because they were already so busy and the guy wanted it ASAP, but Garret hadn't been able to pass up a PR op. The exposure alone would be worth the added stress of getting the bike done on time.

Even so, Garret had tacked on a hefty fee for a quick turn-around. They would make three times their usual amount on this one project. With Jake swamped, Garret had done both the design and the build. He'd put on the final touches—a silver skull gas cap and a cross-bones kick stand—just yesterday.

The finished product had been, hands-down, the most beautiful sight he'd ever seen.

Until now.

He watched as Viv arched her body. Her head fell back. Her long, dark hair spilled down her shoulders. Her eyes were closed, her neck arched. Her full, pink lips parted on a gasp as she slid her bare ass across his leather seat…

Beautiful.

The notion stuck as he watched her move. Her breasts quivered. Her nipples pressed provocatively against the thin material of her blouse. She slid along the seat again and her hands tightened on the handlebars, her knuckles going white. A pink flush crept up her neck, over the frantic throb of her pulse and higher into her face. She worked the skirt up an inch higher so she could spread her legs wider and make better contact.

His mouth went dry, and his heart shifted into overdrive. A sliver of excitement worked its way through him, followed by a rush of whoa, buddy.

She wanted sex, all right.

What vampire didn't?

It was the nature of the beast.

The consequence of the curse.

And it was the only explanation for his nearly irresistible urge to stride into the room, haul her off the bike, shove her up against the nearest wall and plunge deep, deep inside her hot, tight body.

Where he'd been a slave to her hunger before, he was now a slave to his own.

He sure as hell didn't want her because he actually felt something for her.

Or rather, because he thought he felt something.

He'd thought a lot of things way back when. He'd thought that maybe they would get married. Settle down. Raise horses and a family. That they would spend Christmases decorating a tree and hanging up stockings. That he would work the farm while she kept house, and at night they would fall into bed together.

But nothing had been real.

Not her.

Not his feelings for her.

Not his damnable dreams.

It had all been an illusion spawned by her vamp powers because she wanted sex from him. Energy. Strength.

He knew, because he'd created the same illusion for the women he'd fed off of over the years. He'd mesmerized them with his charm. Swept them off their feet with his hot, wet kisses. Spoiled them for any other man with his sexual expertise. And then he'd taken from them.

He'd done to other women exactly what she'd done to him. With one exception. He hadn't talked of dreams and the future and a real, bona fide relationship. He'd wanted one thing and one thing only—a one-night stand—and he'd made his needs crystal clear. He hadn't toyed with anyone's emotions.

It had all been about sex.

The hunger roared to life, as demanding as ever. His groin tightened and his body trembled and he barely managed to resist the need screaming inside of him. His fingers balled and his muscles bunched as he turned and walked back outside.

He had to get a grip.

Resist.

The shadows welcomed him as he moved silently around the side of the building toward the back parking lot. A few feet shy, he stopped and leaned against the cold steel.

The amp in his head switched on, bombarding him with sounds. The chirp of crickets. The squeal of tires as someone burned rubber down the street. The tick-tick of a parking meter a block away.

Her soft moans pushed through the blare of noise, and he knew she was close to coming. So damned close...

He drew several deep breaths, hoping to cool the fire that raged inside of him.

Fat chance.

He closed his eyes, counted to ten, and did his best to concentrate on the sound of his own voice rather than her whisper-soft oohs and ahhs.

He hit ten and kept on going.

It wasn't until he murmured one hundred that he finally managed to soothe his frantic heartbeat and regain his composure.

When he could think of something other than the

sexy woman riding his newest creation just a few feet away, he headed back around to the front of the shop.

At one time, the place had been a service station. The ancient pumps were still there, still working, along with the original Davey's Fill-r-Up ball that rotated atop an iron pole. He had a thing for vintage, and so he'd left the old Coke machine, along with a Fanta sign and one advertising Mmm-Mmm Good Moonpies. The only thing to clue anyone in that the place had been turned into a state-of-the-art chopper shop was the neon blue Home of Skull Creek Choppers that hummed in the front window and the hi-tech security pad that sat next to the entrance.

Punching in the code (the door locked automatically every time it shut), he walked inside and went out of his way to make as much noise as possible.

He slammed the door a little harder than usual and hit the edge of the filing cabinet. The metal rattled and shook, the sound bouncing off the office walls. He paused to shuffle papers and move a few things around near the computer.

He didn't have to look through the windows to see if she'd heard him. He heard her loud and clear.

Her surprised whimper, followed by the faint gasp of leather and the grumble of steel as she scrambled off the seat. The soft click as her shoes hit the concrete. The swish-swish of fabric as she shoved the skirt down to a modest level.

Disappointment rushed through him, feeding the insane urge to waltz in and rip the damned thing off of her. He wanted her naked and ready and—

Whoa. The word thundered through his head, yanking him from his ridiculous thoughts and reminding him that he couldn't. He wouldn't.

Not Viv.

Not ever again.

Bracing himself, he hauled open the door that separated them and walked into the shop.

8

FINALLY.

That was the first thought on Viv's mind when she heard the door open and close. Despite the fact that she'd almost been caught having a pretty fantastic orgasm.

Sex was a necessity. Like oxygen to the average human. She didn't usually feel guilty over it. Or mortified. Or embarrassed.

Not until she soothed her skirt down one final time, hooked a now damp tendril of hair behind one ear and turned toward Garret.

He wore a soft cotton T-shirt that molded to his broad shoulders and solid chest. Worn denim cupped his crotch and hugged his muscular legs. He wore the black Stetson she remembered from the bar. The hat brim tipped low, casting a shadow over the upper half of his face.

Her gaze collided with his and there was just something about the gleam in his pale blue eyes that said Gotcha.

Heat flooded her cheeks and awareness sizzled up and down her spine. "I, um, was just seeing how she handles," she blurted, suddenly desperate for a plausible excuse.

He tossed his keys on a nearby work table. His boots thudded on the stained concrete floor as he stepped toward her. "What's the verdict?"

"Nice." And how. "That is—" she licked her lips, "—the handlebars felt good. Solid."

He seemed almost angry at her answer. His gaze narrowed, and his jaw went tense. But then she licked her lips, and his attention snagged on the sweeping motion of her tongue. Just like that, his defenses seemed to lapse, and his body relaxed just a fraction. Strong, sensuous lips crooked in a faint smile. "So you had a pretty good grip, then?"

"Very."

The animosity between them slipped away, and the air charged with a sudden awareness that made her spine tingle. He was flirting with her. Teasing. Tempting.

Because he'd seen her.

His eyes sparkled like ice reflecting rays of sunlight and her tummy tingled. "How about the seat? How did that feel?"

Fan-friggin'-tastic.

That's what she wanted to say, but she caught her bottom lip just in case she was overreacting and he wasn't being nearly as forward as she hoped.

"Comfortable." Viv nodded. "Not too hard. Not too soft. Just—" she swallowed against her suddenly dry throat "—right."

"That's good to know." He raked a gaze over her,

from her head to her toes and back up again. His attention lingered on several key places.

Her nipples throbbed, and she felt the sudden wetness between her legs. Her heart pounded with excitement.

"You know," his voice slid into her ears and rumbled across her nerve endings, "if you really want to get a feel for her, you need to crank her up." He hooked a leg over and straddled the seat. Large, strong hands rested on the gas tank. "You don't want a bike that vibrates too much." His gaze caught and held hers. "You need a nice, steady hum so you can get into a groove when you're on the road."

He was flirting with her, all right.

His words stirred a very vivid picture of the two of them zooming along, finding their groove. Moonlight spilled down around them. Her hands gripped the handlebars while his hands stroked the wet flesh between her legs.

Despite her orgasm, she felt herself winding right back up. His scent filled her head, and the raw timbre of his voice tickled her ears. His tall, sexy body filled up her line of vision.

She shook her head, desperate to remember her objective.

Slow. Easy.

"I, um, wouldn't know. I've never actually ridden a motorcycle."

Liar. That's what his gaze seemed to say, but he didn't voice the sentiment out loud. Instead, he shrugged.

"That's a shame. You're really missing out. There's nothing like climbing on the back of one of these babies and cutting loose."

Amen.

She could still feel the handlebars in her grasp, the gas tank between her legs, the cool, delicious leather rasping her—

"—try it at least once if you're going to write about it."

His voice shattered the memory and snatched her back to the present. "Excuse me?"

"I said you'll have to take at least one ride." His gaze sparked. "A real ride," he added, "if you really want to get it right for your article." Suspicion worked its way into his expression. "That's why you're here, right? To get info for your article?"

"Of course." Not that he believed her. She could see the doubt in his guarded expression and the way his body stiffened. The muscles in his arms rippled and tensed. "Why else?" She went for the wide-eyed, innocent look that had rated number nine on Winona's list.

It was a look that appealed to a man's baser instincts. It said poor little old me needs big strong you, and it was guaranteed to make a man forget everything—the football game, the yard work, the cute little honey washing her car next door.

He stared at her, as if he could see the answer if he looked long and hard enough. He couldn't. Thankfully. And so he finally shrugged. "It just seems a little too coincidental that you showed up here. Now. Don't you think?"

"Not really. Stranger things happen all the time." Before he could say anything else, she rushed on, "You're right. I definitely need to take a real ride if I want to write about the activity with any enthusiasm. But since I'm out of my element I'd really like to get some background info first." What was she saying? If the man wanted to give her a ride, then all the better. But a ride and a ride were two different things, and if they got that close, she could forget slow and easy. She would take the lead and be the aggressor and that would surely kill her chances at an orgasm.

Better to slow down for now. A little small talk and his guard would ease. He would go back to flirting with her, and the situation would escalate from there. "I'd really like to snap a few pictures right now."

"If I didn't know better, I'd say you were scared. But then you're a vampire, and vampires aren't scared of anything." He meant the comment as a dig. A reminder of how she'd deceived him so long ago.

But she didn't need any reminders. She lived with the guilt every day. She shrugged. "I wouldn't say that. I'm a big sissy when it comes to sunlight. And wooden stakes. And reality TV."

The sudden tension between them seemed to melt and his mouth hinted at a grin. "Whatever happened to sitcom re-runs?"

"You obviously don't have cable. They've got a channel for that. They've got a channel for everything now. Thankfully. Otherwise, how else would we keep up with the times?"

"*Car and Driver.*"

"Excuse me?"

"That's how I keep up with the times. I read a lot of *Car and Driver.* And *Hot Rod.* And *Motorcycle Mania.*"

"Maybe I'm dense, but I don't see how that keeps you up on popular culture."

"Then you haven't read an issue. See, the actual machines keep me up on technological changes. And the car girls…" His smile was slow and wicked and fueled with enough innuendo to make her heart stop. "They keep me updated on popular culture."

"How so?"

"Take Daisy, for instance. She was the centerfold in the last issue of *C & D,* along with the latest eco-friendly Porsche that just rolled off the assembly line. She was wearing a recycled string bikini and sipping a fruit smoothie. One glance at her and I knew green was in."

"One glance at the *TV Guide,* and you'd know that. There are at least a dozen recycling shows on and QVC has an entire hour dedicated to environmentally friendly cosmetics. And neither contributes to the exploitation of women," she added.

"If I didn't know better, I'd say you were jealous." His grin widened. "But then vampires don't get jealous any more than they get scared."

It wasn't a dig this time. Just a simple fact that reminded her that no matter how much she wanted

Garret, she didn't like him. Not genuine, 'til-death-do-us-part like. Maybe a long, long time ago. But even then it hadn't been the real thing. There'd been too many lies between them for the emotion to have been genuine.

She dismissed the strange jealousy niggling at her and said, "I can see how *Car & Driver* would have its benefit for someone in your line of work."

"I don't get a chance to watch much TV, so it's the magazines or nothing else. I stay pretty busy with my choppers."

She eyed the motorcycle skeleton sitting atop the center table. "New project?"

He nodded. "Just one of a dozen on the schedule for this week."

"Sounds like business is good."

"Very. We've got this new software that saves us not only money, but time—"

"Wait." She motioned to him before reaching for her purse. She retrieved a small, hand-held tape recorder from her bag and tried to ignore the hunger yawning inside. Punching the record button, she set the device off to the side. "In case I miss something."

While the article was just a cover to get her here with him, she was still responsible for turning something in to the travel mag who'd fronted her the money for her trip south.

She motioned to him. "Go on."

"We can design, build and finalize a bike in a third the time it used to take."

"We?"

"Jake McCann, Dillon Cash and yours truly. Jake does the design, I do the actual fabrication and Dillon handles overall operations. We don't just handcraft made-to-order custom bikes," he went on, "we're also doing several spec choppers. They're selling like crazy, and so we're getting busier by the minute. This is one of a dozen we're doing for a bike shop in Austin." He hit a button on a nearby computer screen and a 3-D image appeared. "This is what it will look like on completion." Another few buttons and the layers of the bike started to peel away. "This is where we are right now."

"Seems pretty high-tech."

"It is. At the same time, it's still good old-fashioned hard work that makes each bike come to life. We shape everything by hand. The computer software just gives us accurate specs and a list of supplies so that we don't make any costly mistakes along the way." He eyed the recorder. "You sure you want to hear this stuff? I can't imagine you'll include it in a travel article."

"Maybe not, but it gives me an overall handle on the business, which will help with the writing." Hey, it sounded good. Besides, she liked hearing him talk. That had attracted her to him almost as much as the sex. He'd never been one of those men to roll over and fall asleep. He'd pulled her closer into the crook of his arm, rested his head atop hers and talked. About any and everything. About nothing.

She missed his voice almost as much as she missed the toe-curling orgasms.

Almost.

"I need as much information as possible when I write," she went on. "Even information I might not end up using. So how long have you been working with Dillon and Jake?"

The easy rapport they'd lapsed into seemed to melt away, and the tension pushed back in. He grew wary, as if he didn't like her bringing up his coworkers.

He didn't. She could see the hesitation in his gaze, the tensing of his muscles as he fortified his guard.

She didn't think he would answer her, but finally he murmured, "Dillon just came on board about six months ago. He's a local."

"A vampire?"

"Now."

She wanted to ask what that meant, but the dangerous gleam in his gaze warned her off. "What about Jake?"

"We've been friends since the eighteen hundreds."

Which meant he was a vampire, as well.

She wondered if Garret had turned him or if they'd merely banded together as a means of survival. She opened her mouth to ask, but she didn't get the chance.

"I've really got a lot of work to do." His expression closed. "The others will be in later if you have any questions for them. There are several choppers in the holding room." He pointed to a nearby door. "That's where we keep the finished bikes that are waiting to be shipped out. Feel free to set up in there and take as many pictures as you need."

Before she could protest, he pulled on a welding mask, fired up his unit and went to work on the strips of metal sitting on the opposite table.

So much for small talk.

9

VIV SPENT THE NEXT half hour snapping pictures of the various choppers in the holding room. She made sure to leave the door open so she could get in the occasional sultry smile if Garret should happen to glance her way.

He didn't.

No hungry glances. No I-want-you-but-I-don't-want-to-want-you smiles. No I'm-a-sex-starved-vampire-and-I-can't-control-myself stares.

Nada.

"It's not working," she told Winona a few minutes later when she retreated into the ladies room and pulled out her cell phone.

"Who is this?" asked a groggy voice.

"Viv. Viv Darland. The reporter staying at the motel. I sat in on your class tonight." Winona mumbled a groggy "Oh, yeah," and Viv rushed on, "I'm sorry to call so late, but I didn't know what else to do. You said you were available for dating emergencies."

Bedsprings groaned in the background, followed by a faint click as a light switched on. "Are you on a date?" Winona went from groggy to excited in a nanosecond.

"No. I mean, yes. I mean, I'm here and he's here and we're alone, so I guess that qualifies."

"I'm in bed with my cat, Pumpkin, but that doesn't make him my significant other. Scoot, Pumpkin," the woman ordered. "Can't you see I'm working?" Sheets rustled, and a frantic meow echoed in the distance. "Does this man even know you like him?" Winona's attention shifted back to Viv.

She thought of Garret's knowing expression when he'd first walked in on her. The glimmer in his eyes. The sexy murmur of his voice. "Maybe. I'm not really sure."

"Does he like you?"

"I'm not sure about that either. I followed the commandments, but they don't seem to be working. He's ignoring me."

"Maybe he's just trying to come off like he's ignoring you."

"You really think so?"

"That depends. What's he doing right now?"

"Welding."

"All right, so he's ignoring you. But that doesn't mean the commandments aren't working," Winona rushed on as if sensing Viv's disappointment. "It just means you haven't been using them long enough. Just hang in there, and stick to what I taught you. He'll come around eventually."

"The eventually is what I'm afraid of. I don't exactly have a lot of time."

"I know. Eldin told me that as soon as you're finished

with your article, you're moving on. The life of a reporter ain't really conducive to a relationship, is it?"

"No, ma'am." Which was exactly why Viv had chosen it. It kept her moving. Running.

Not anymore.

She swallowed back the sudden lump in her throat. "I would really appreciate any advice you could give me to speed things along."

"Let's see…" Winona seemed to think. "You might try dropping a few knick-knacks. That always worked with my dear, departed husband."

"Knick-knacks?"

"You know, anything. Everything. The point is to give him an eyeful when you go to pick up whatever it is you dropped. Either it's an eyeful of cleavage or your ba-donk-a-donk. Why, I was bent over cleaning dust bunnies out from under the fridge when my oldest daughter was conceived. Can't get a better success rate than that."

"Thanks."

"Thank you. I charge extra for on-call. I'll drop a bill by your motel room first thing tomorrow morning." A loud click punctuated the statement.

Viv dropped her cell back into her purse, splashed some cold water onto her face and summoned her courage. She walked back into the large room where she'd set up her equipment and slid a glance toward the open doorway that led to the fabrication shop.

Garret wore heat-resistant gloves that went clear to his elbows. A welding mask hid his face as he torched the edge of a metal strip before hammering it down.

Torch. Hammer. Torch. Hammer.

She fought down a wave of self-consciousness and reached for a roll of film. After plucking the package from her equipment bag, she half-turned. Her fingers went limp, and the roll hit the concrete with a soft thud.

"Oh, no. Clumsy me," she said, her voice a few decibals louder than normal. She gathered her determination, bent at the waist and did a slow motion retrieval that would have perpetuated the Adkins gene pool for the next fifty years.

Just as her fingers closed around the film, she stalled for a few seconds to give Garret an eyeful.

He didn't spare her a glance.

Instead, he bent over the metal, his attention fully focused on his task.

Torch. Hammer. Torch. Hammer.

Her gaze snagged on one bicep and the familiar slave band tattoo that peeked beneath the edge. The sight reminded her of her own markings, and guilt spiraled through her followed by a wave of self-doubt.

Maybe he was really and truly no longer attracted to her. Despite the hunger that lived and breathed inside of him.

Because of it.

Because he could satisfy his need with any woman. Every woman. He didn't need her. Not emotionally or physically. He never had. He'd just been mesmerized.

Her chest tightened at the thought.

Not that it mattered.

All that really mattered was that she needed him.

While he could get what he craved from any female, she could only get what she so desperately wanted—a bona fide orgasm—from one male.

Him.

If she really wanted to orgasm with an actual partner, she couldn't let herself get discouraged.

She wiggled just a little to emphasize her breasts before she straightened and put the film back into her bag. Her hand brushed the lens cap sitting on the table, and it tumbled over the edge.

"Whoops," she said again. Louder this time. "I swear I'm all thumbs tonight."

If at first you don't succeed. . .

IF SHE DROPPED ONE more thing—anything—he was going to stake himself with the nearest sharp object.

That is, if he didn't burst into a ball of flames first.

He hit the Off switch on the welder, and the blue flame died. But it did nothing to ease the fire that burned inside of him.

He was too worked up.

Too turned on.

Too damned intent on retaining his control and keeping the hunger contained.

Lust pushed and pulled inside of him. His nerves buzzed. Electricity sizzled across his skin, and he grew hotter by the second.

He tugged off his T-shirt, but the rush of air against his bare skin did little to help. He reached for a plain sheet of metal. The cool material heated instantly beneath the hot pads of his fingertips. The air seemed to shimmer with the heat radiating from his body.

As if confirming his worst fear, the temperature-sensitive fans near the computer table kicked on with a click and whoosh. They revved, cranking up to full blast to cool down the rapidly warming equipment.

He heard the glub, glub, glub of bubbles. The sharp scent of boiling gasoline spiraled from the half-full gallon-sized container sitting near the doorway.

And all because of her.

Because he wanted her, and he couldn't—wouldn't act on it.

Don't look.

That's what he told himself.

But damned if his eyes would cooperate.

When she leaned over just the way she was doing right now, her backside to him, he couldn't not look.

He caught a glimpse of the dewy pink flesh between her legs. The tender insides of her thighs. The tiny beauty mark that dotted her left ass cheek.

His groin throbbed, and his gut clenched. He felt the sharp graze of his fangs against his tongue. The heat sizzling his fingertips—

Damn it.

His gaze dropped to the smoke spiraling from his grip on the piece of metal. He dropped the material and stared through the shimmering air at his seared black skin.

"Just call me klutz." Her voice slid into his ears and snagged his attention.

He glanced up in time to see the bright blue of her eyes and the fullness of her lips just before she bent forward—facing him this time—to retrieve her lens cap. Her blouse ballooned, and her breasts quivered. He glimpsed one ripe nipple as she shifted and reached.

Every muscle in his body went tight. He balled his fingers against a wave of white-hot need that drenched him. His vision blurred, and his ears started to ring.

Through a haze he saw her straighten. She tugged at the collar of her blouse, as if she felt the heat as much as he did. Her gaze collided with his. Desire brightened her eyes, along with a glimmer of desperation that reached across the distance separating them and sucker-punched him right in the gut.

She made a big show of dropping another roll of film, and Garret reached his limit.

He was halfway across the room, his fangs extended, his heart pounding, his hunger raging, when the gas can exploded.

10

THE NEXT FEW MOMENTS seemed to go in slow motion as the fire blazed from the container's spout, shot up the wall and ate up the door frame.

Viv's expression went from startled to scared as she inched backwards, away from the bright orange waves that now separated them.

The fire alarm sounded, and the overhead sprinklers kicked on.

The cold water hit him, and everything seemed to speed up then. He grabbed a nearby fire extinguisher and rushed forward. White foam spewed, drenching the flames until the last lick of orange fizzled. In a matter of seconds, the wall went from a fiery blaze to a smoldering black mess.

Garret chucked the extinguisher and crossed the threshold. He reached for Viv. "Are you okay?"

She nodded, but he wasn't convinced. Fear brightened her eyes, and his chest tightened. He swept his gaze from her head to her toes and back up again. She was soaked from the sprinklers and still a little freaked out from the sudden fire, but otherwise she looked okay.

His gaze collided with hers, and the strange glimmer seemed to fade into the blue depths. Her eyes glittered, the color shifting, morphing, into a brilliant blaze of purple.

And suddenly she looked more hungry than afraid.

Time seemed to stand still for the next few moments as they stood there staring at each other. The sprinkler rained down on them, cooling off the temperature in the room. But it didn't begin to touch the heat that churned inside of him.

His body tightened and his vision blurred, and he knew his eyes gleamed just as hot, as bright, as wild as hers.

The air sizzled, and steam rose. The water chugged and splattered for several more seconds until the automatic shut-off finally kicked in.

"What just happened?" Her voice, soft and breathless, barely pushed past the frantic beat of his heart.

He licked his lips and gathered his control. "The, um, air conditioner has been acting up." Like hell. But it was the best he could come up with and a damned sight better than the truth—that he wanted to kiss her.

He wouldn't.

No matter how much he suddenly wanted to.

"I guess it finally blew," he added.

His hearing perked and through the sound of dripping water he could hear the steady drone of the central cooling unit.

Judging from the "yeah, right" look on her face, so could she.

"Temporarily," he rushed on. "It must be one of those things that comes and goes. You know, one minute the problem is here, the next it clears itself up."

"Probably." That's what she said, but he could see the doubt in her gaze. He could also see a hell of a lot more thanks to the sprinklers.

Her clothes were soaked. Her silky red shirt plastered to her breasts and outlined her hard, ripe nipples. Water ran in tiny rivulets down her face, her smooth, curved neck, to disappear in the deep V between her luscious breasts. She was soaked, her skin slick and gleaming, and he couldn't help but wonder if she was just as wet between her legs.

He could easily find out. All he had to do was reach out. Hitch up her skirt. Trail his palms over her soft, smooth ass. Plunge his hand between her silky thighs. Dip his fingers into the hot, sweltering folds. Stroke her swollen, throbbing clit.

As if she read the decadent thoughts wreaking havoc on his control, her nostrils flared and her chest hitched. Urgency gleamed in her gaze, and he knew she wanted him to touch her and find out.

If only. But she didn't want him. He could have been any man. He was nothing but a meal ticket to her.

Nothing.

That's what he told himself, but he didn't quite believe it. Not with the two of them standing so close, the air so steamy and hot as they gazed at each other, into each other. While he couldn't read her the way he did a human, he could see the uncertainty in the way she caught her bottom lip and gripped her hands together.

The sight chipped away at his control because Viv Darland didn't feel such things. She was a vampire, for Christ's sake.

Commanding. Determined. Self-assured.

She looked anything but at the moment, and it tied his damned self-control into knots.

That, and he couldn't forget the fear in her eyes. The real, raw fear caused by the fire.

"You should really get that fixed," she told him, as if eager to ease the tension that crackled around them. "The air conditioner, I mean. I would imagine it gets pretty hot in here what with all the equipment."

"Yep, it's definitely an equipment problem."

Her gaze slid past him to the welding unit, the sheet cutter, the shaper. "What with all the stuff in here, the place could go up in flames if you're not careful." She glanced at the ceiling. "But then I guess that's what the sprinklers are for."

"Yes." His gaze dropped to her nipples pressing provocatively against the drenched fabric before shifting back to her face, and suddenly he couldn't help himself.

He reached out.

His fingertip circled one hard tip outlined beneath the wet fabric of her shirt. She hissed and went perfectly still.

"There's nothing like a good sprinkler system to calm things down," he murmured. A few more strokes, and she clamped down on her bottom lip. "Or liven things up."

"I…" She seemed to be fighting hard for her own control. As hard as he'd fought just a few moments ago. But the battle was futile. The pull between them was too fierce. Too compelling. And suddenly it was all he could think of.

His gaze collided with hers. "You look good wet," he murmured, and then he pulled her into his arms.

GARRET SAWYER had lived and breathed in Viv's memory for so long. The feel of his hard, hot body pressed against hers, his arms locked tight, his lips eating at hers. But the memories were nothing compared to the real thing.

Electricity skimmed her skin and heat firebombed the pit of her stomach as he drew her close.

Closer.

His hands spanned her waist, slid over her ass and cupped the round fullness. He pulled her flush against him and lifted her. Her legs came around him, and he hoisted her, sliding her up the hard ridge of his erection until he was eye-level with her chest. His tongue flicked out, and she barely caught the moan that worked its way up her throat.

Heat licked the tip of her nipple, and a burst of pleasure zapped her brain. She bowed toward him.

He touched her with his tongue again and licked her longer, more leisurely, savoring the ripeness of her. She gasped and clung to him.

His lips closed over her nipple. The wet material of her shirt provided little protection against the searing inferno of his mouth. Heat surrounded her areola as he drew on her, sucking long and hard.

She threaded her fingers through his hair, tilted her head back and gave herself up to sensation.

The pressure of his mouth increased. His tongue stroked. His lips suckled. Each pull on her nipple sent an echoing tug between her legs. She clutched at his bare shoulders, desperate to relieve the pressure building inside of her.

It was coming. She could feel it.

His hands held her steady, scorching her as he nestled her crotch against the ripped hardness of his abdomen.

Then he moved her, a frantic brush of her sex up and down the muscled ridges, and the pressure neared maximum intensity. She was so close.

Too close.

As wonderful as it was, it wasn't what she wanted.

She wanted him inside of her when she went over the edge. She needed it.

Stop!

The command echoed through her head, and her fingers tightened in his hair. But instead of pushing him away, she couldn't help herself. She pulled him closer and rubbed herself against him and…there. And there. And, oh, yes, there.

She felt the waistband of his jeans rasp her slit, the metal of his button a cold shock against her ultra-sensitive clitoris, and a lightning bolt went through her. Her nerves tingled, and the sharp edge of her fangs pressed against her tongue.

Desperation rushed through her, and she lifted herself for another slide and shimmy. He stopped her cold, his arms tightening in a grip that rendered her immobile.

Her eyes popped open to see a fierce look on his face. His grip tightened for a split-second before it loosened and her feet hit the floor.

The next few moments passed in a dizzying blur. One minute they were pressed against each other, and the next she was standing alone as Garret threw open a small storage unit on the opposite side of the room.

A heartbeat later, he was back. He tossed a Skull Creek Choppers T-shirt around her shoulders. Large hands tugged her wet skirt down around her hips just as the outer doorway opened and two couples filed into the adjoining office.

They were laughing and talking and then bam, four pairs of eyes stared through the wall of windows and fixated on her. Everyone went silent.

Viv gathered the extra large tee around her and tried to control her frantic heartbeat.

But Garret was still too close, his hard body just to her right. In her peripheral vision she could see him wipe his drenched face with a second T-shirt before scrubbing at his hair. Her skin still burned where his fingers had rubbed her thighs as he'd tugged the skirt down to a respectable level.

The hunger raged, urging her to turn and reach for him. To beg for his touch all over her body and finish what they'd started regardless of the audience.

But it was too late.

While he stood only inches away physically, emotionally he'd already traveled a few hundred miles.

Gone was the desire that had brightened his eyes. Ice blue chips glittered back at her when she chanced a glance at him. Regret glimmered in the translucent depths and her chest tightened.

She blinked against the sudden burning in her own eyes. "I—I really should be going."

"Yeah."

"I'll finish up tomorrow night after everything dries out." She snatched up her soaked camera bag. "I'll need to pick up some new lighting equipment. Is it all right if I leave all the wet stuff here for now?"

Without waiting for a reply, she sailed past him and pushed through the nearest side door marked Exit. She didn't slow down until she reached the opposite side of the small parking lot where her car was parked.

She stalled for a few seconds and drank in a heavy draft of air.

As if that would help.

She climbed behind the wheel, keyed the ignition and revved the engine.

The roar did little to drown out the sound of his heartbeat that echoed in her ears and followed her as she turned out onto Main Street. Along with the voice that whispered in her ear.

"It's not happening between us."

She knew then that while she'd won the battle tonight, she wasn't even close to winning the war. He had no intention of having sex with her no matter how much he wanted her.

Or how much she wanted him.

"Never, ever again."

His deep voice followed, whispering in her ear, stirring her insecurity and her doubt.

She shouldn't have come here.

She wouldn't have if she could just forget.

The feel of his arms, his hands, his lips…

Her body tingled, and heat spiraled through her. No, she couldn't forget. And while he might regret what had just happened, the point was, it had happened.

Which meant that it could happen again.

Garret would lose control, they would go all the way, and she would get one more chance to experience the earth-shattering orgasm that had eluded her since she'd walked away from him all those years ago.

That's all she wanted from him, she reminded herself. She certainly didn't want him to need her. To like her.

This was all about sex.

Breath-stealing, toe-curling, bone-melting sex.

At least that's what she told herself as she headed back to the motel.

11

"YOU'VE BEEN HOLDING OUT on us." Jake stared at the Exit door where Viv had just disappeared.

Garret shook his head. "It's not like that, man."

"Isn't it?" Jake arched an eyebrow and gave Garret a knowing look. Not because he'd actually witnessed the wet and wild bump and grind.

He hadn't.

Garret had felt his fellow vampires long before they'd keyed in the security code and opened the outer doorway.

No, Jake knew because of Garret.

Because he was staring at him right now, and he could see the brightness that lingered in his gaze. The tension in his body. The hunger that radiated from him, along with a shimmer of heat. He wasn't anywhere close to starting another fire thanks to the douse of water and the arrival of his friends, but he was still worked up.

"Who is she?" Jake asked.

"A freelance reporter." When Jake didn't look the least bit satisfied, Garret shrugged. "Just somebody I used to know. A long, long time ago."

"Vampire?" The question came from Nikki. Her lips hinted at a grin and curiosity danced in her excited expression. Garret nodded and she added, "No wonder you're not interested in a fix-up. Donna Sue's got a pretty big dose of sex appeal and can give the hotties in this town a run for their money, but she doesn't have anything close to vamp charisma."

"So you like this woman?" It was Meg's turn.

"No." Like didn't begin to touch what he felt for Viv Darland.

Disappointment? Definitely.

Resentment? Ditto.

Fear? A little.

Lust? A shitload.

But that was it.

Nothing else. Nothing powerful.

He ignored the small voice that insisted otherwise and shifted his attention to Dillon.

The younger vampire stared at the Exit door before his gaze slid back to Garret. You are so busted gleamed loud and clear. The younger vamp opened his mouth for confirmation, but Garret spoke first.

"Don't ask."

Dillon shrugged. "Hey, your sex life is your own business."

"They didn't have sex." Meg nudged him. Excitement lit her face and her eyes swiveled to Nikki. "Did they?"

Nikki looked at Jake. "Honey?"

"Garret?" Jake arched an eyebrow.

"I'm out of here." Garret turned and reached for his keys.

"We'll take that as a yes," Nikki's amused voice followed him to the doorway.

"A big fat yes," Meg added.

If only.

Garret shook off a pang of disappointment. He wasn't having sex with Viv Darland. He wasn't.

His head knew that, but his damned body didn't seem to be getting the message.

His groin throbbed, and his muscles ached. Hunger twisted at his insides, fighting and clawing for sustenance.

He tamped down on the urge to find the nearest woman and end the torment eating away at him. He could, but that would mean breaking his vow, and he wasn't about to do that.

He'd held out this long, and he wasn't caving now. No sex. Not with Viv. Not with any woman.

Not until he'd reclaimed his humanity.

In the meantime, Garret did what he'd been doing for the past few months when the need grew too great. He headed home to chug a few bags of blood and climb into an ice-cold shower.

"DO YOU ALWAYS wear a suit and tie when you deliver extra towels?" Viv asked when she arrived at the motel to find Eldin waiting on her doorstep.

He wore a pin-striped navy suit, a red dress shirt, red tennis shoes and a wide smile. "It's part of our first-class treatment here at the Skull Creek Inn." He handed her a fluffy stack of folded white cotton and stepped back while she slid her key card into the slot and unlocked the door. "That, and I like to be ready for any late night dating opportunities." The door opened, and he followed her inside. "You can quote me on that."

"Will do." Viv set the towels on a nearby table and moved to close the door.

Eldin didn't budge. Instead, he stood rooted just inside the doorway, an expectant look on his face.

Realization dawned and she shrugged. "I can't take any pictures tonight. I lost most of my film in a freak fire over at the chopper shop." Okay, so that wasn't the complete truth. While she had, indeed, lost the rolls she'd had with her, she kept an extra stash in the trunk of her car, along with two back-up digital cameras. But the last thing she wanted was to spend the next fifteen minutes taking pics of Eldin. She was too worked up— too hot—and she needed a cold shower in the worst way. "The inside sprinklers came on and ruined every-thing." She indicated her damp clothes.

As if noticing them for the first time, he nodded. "You're all wet."

"And so is my film. I'll have to pick more up at the pharmacy tomorrow."

"Just write down what you need, and I'll fetch it for you first thing in the morning."

"I couldn't put you to so much trouble."

"No trouble at all. Just part of our VIP Ultra-Deluxe vacation package which also includes free muffins, a

Buy-One-Get-One-Free entrée coupon for Little Pigs Barbecue just a spit and holler down the road and an unlimited supply of Tums. You'll need it after eating the ribs." He pulled a folded sheet of paper from his pocket. "This outlines all the different packages we offer, and it also includes the itinerary for the vacation I'm taking this summer."

Viv scanned the page. "You're taking a couples cruise? I thought you were single?"

"At the moment, but I'm hoping your article can hook me up before I sail. I prefer a blonde, but at this point I'm willing to look at most anyone who might be interested. You can quote me on that, too."

"Um, yeah." Viv grabbed the door. "I'd really like to get out of these wet clothes."

Eldin still didn't budge. "How you doin' on ice? You need another bucketful before bedtime?"

"I'm good." She stepped forward, urging him back a few inches.

"Complimentary soap?"

"I'm still working on the six extra bars you left yesterday." She took another step, but he stalled in the threshold and she added, "They really work up a good lather."

"They should for what I'm paying Marvin over at the pharmacy. He says I ought to order the stuff in gross if I want a discount."

"Sounds like a plan."

"Shower cap? I'd be happy to fetch you another."

"The one I have is still working like a champ." She

stared deep into his eyes and sent a silent message. Go. He backed up, and she moved to close the door. The minute their gazes disconnected, however, his hand shot through the crack to grip the doorjamb.

"If you need anything else, you know who to call. Me. Eldin. That's E-L-D-I-N. Some folks spell it with two Es, but my parents wanted something unique."

"I'll make a note of that."

The hand loosened from the doorjamb only to tighten again. "Oh, I almost forgot. You had a couple of phone calls."

Viv opened the door a few inches. "Who?"

"One was a Cindy Marsfield with Southern Travel. She said her assistant lost your cell number. Since we're not set up for voicemail here, she asked if I could relay a message. She said they moved up your deadline. It's two weeks from today."

Viv nodded. She'd planned on turning it in to Cindy sooner anyway because she knew the odds were that Cruz and Molly would find her before then, and she didn't want any loose ends left hanging. Cindy had given her the job that had led her back to Garret. She owed the woman.

Article? Check.

Orgasm? Check, check.

At least that had been the plan.

"Never, ever again."

Garret's deep voice echoed in her ears, and she focused her attention on Eldin. Anything to ignore the doubt that gripped her.

"What about the other calls?"

"There was just one." He shrugged. "Don't know who it was. The man didn't leave a message. He just asked if I had a Viviana Darland registered here and what room she was in." He must have noticed the sudden stiffening of Viv's body, because he rushed on, "But don't worry. I didn't give you up. If there's one thing we pride ourselves on here at the Skull Creek, it's protecting the privacy of each and every celebrity guest. Why, we had Norm Shannon here last year, and not so much as one groupie wiggled past yours truly."

"Norm Shannon?"

"He hosts a local AM radio show. He does cow impersonations," he added, as if that explained it all. "The FFA kids over at the high school just love him. He was in town to speak at their annual banquet, and he was really worried that he wouldn't be able to get a decent night's rest on account of his ratings recently tripled— he started doing chickens in addition to the cows. But I sat in the parking lot with my BB gun and made sure none of them youngsters got within twenty feet of him. I didn't have to shoot anybody, mind you. The darned thing wasn't even loaded. It was more of a bluff than anything else, but it worked like a charm. So don't you worry a bit. If anyone tries to bother you while you're here, I'll deal with them. I know you famous writer types like to keep a low profile."

Writing articles for a sleazy tabloid hardly qualified her for celebrity status, but she appreciated Eldin's protective instincts all the same.

Not that a BB gun would be of any use against Cruz and Molly. They wanted their humanity back, and they wouldn't stop until Viv was dead for good this time.

Time.

The word lingered in her mind as she closed and locked the door behind Eldin and tried to shake the tingling awareness that gripped every inch of her.

The same awareness she'd felt walking down that mountain, away from the site of the Butcher's latest bloodbath, with Sheriff Matt Keller.

She'd known then that Cruz and Molly were close.

Just as she knew now.

The truth closed in on her, and she trembled.

While they were just calling around right now, checking facts, it wouldn't be long before they got enough confirmation to draw them here in person. It would be just a matter of days—if that long—before they finally showed up for a repeat of the Washington ambush.

She turned on the cold water and peeled off her shirt. Anxiety gripped her body, along with frustration.

Her gut clenched, and hunger gnawed at her. Her hands trembled, and her nipples throbbed.

She ignored the doubt that nibbled away at her determination and focused on analyzing the evening and what had driven Garret over the edge.

He'd managed to resist her while they were in different rooms, but when the fire started he'd come to her rescue. Face-to-face, with the heat burning between them, he'd been unable to hold back.

Close.

That was the key. All she had to do was stick to him like glue, and they would be doing the nasty in no time.

She clung to the hope, shimmied off her skirt and stepped beneath the icy spray.

_12_

DISTANCE.

That was the key to resisting Viv and keeping his fire insurance coverage from going through the friggin' roof.

Garret tossed another hay bale from the bed of the 4 x 4 Chevy pick-up. It landed in a pile near the three others he'd already unloaded. He jumped down off the tailgate. One hand dove into his back pocket and retrieved a pair of wire cutters.

He snipped the tie on each bale before climbing back into the cab. He gunned the engine and headed for the adjacent pasture to drop off the last bale for the handful of broncing bucks he'd purchased last week.

He'd yet to turn them out with the rest of his herd. He wouldn't until they were broken.

If they were broken.

When he'd been just a man, he'd been able to tame the wildest horse. But now... Now he couldn't get within fifty feet. The horses saw his true nature, and they feared it.

He didn't blame them. He would have pissed himself

if he'd known who—what—Viviana really was when he'd first met her. And he sure as hell wouldn't have put his trust in her.

Her image popped into his head, and he saw her the way she'd looked on that first night. Her luscious body clad in white cotton bloomers, her cleavage pushing up from an ultra-tight corset, her long dark hair flowing down around her shoulders. She'd been beautiful. Mesmerizing. Irresistible.

Then and now.

Only the circumstances were different now. He didn't want her because of what she was. He wanted her because of what he was. Because he'd been mainly bagging it since he'd come to Skull Creek, and he was desperate for the real thing.

Blood and sex.

His muscles tightened, and his gut clenched as he snipped the wire on the last bale. He'd been cold turkey for so long, and he was starting to feel it. That was the reason for his temporary loss of control tonight. A loss that wouldn't have occurred if he hadn't been in a confined space with her.

He ignored the tiny voice that whispered there was nothing confining about a massive fabrication shop with three spacious bays and twenty-foot ceilings.

He needed distance. Space.

His nerves twitched, and his gaze shifted to the faint orange line outlining the distant trees.

Forget space. What he needed at the moment was to get the hell out of here before sunup. Already he could feel the heat creeping toward him and smell the sunshine hiding just behind the cluster of oak trees.

His skin tingled, and his hands clinched.

As anxious as he was, there was a small part of him that refused to hurry. He couldn't help but wonder if the sun still felt as warm, as honest as it once had so long ago.

It did. He knew it. It was a certainty that grew stronger with each day that passed since he'd moved to Skull Creek, Texas.

Moved, but not settled.

No, Garret Sawyer was still very much unsettled. Still restless. Still waiting.

For the chance to breathe again, to feel, to live.

He shifted his attention back to the cutters in his hand. A quick snip, and the wires popped. He lifted the bale and scattered it for several feet.

He could have easily paid someone to do the work for him. Or even bought one of those state-of-the-art balers that could cut and drop in a fifth the time it took him to load his truck and do the job himself.

He had the money thanks to the success of his choppers.

But it felt good to get his hands dirty.

Normal.

The thought struck and he pushed it away. He was anything but, and he had a burnt mess back at his shop to prove it.

No, he wasn't normal.

He might never be normal again. He saw the proof

in the glittering black eyes of the nearest horse. Delilah. The rich, sweet smell of hay filled the air, and her nostrils flared. She took a few steps toward him, only to draw up short several feet away.

Garret walked back to the cab and pulled a bag of apple slices from the dashboard. He pulled out a slice and held it out to her. The animal drew another step closer, her nose twitching, her hunger battling with her survival instincts.

A knowing light gleamed in her eyes as she stared at Garret.

"It's okay," he murmured, but the animal wasn't the least bit fooled.

Garret's fingers itched to cross the space between them and stroke the animal's soft fur. It had been so long since he'd felt the silky horsehair.

Too long.

He knelt and set the apple slice on the ground, and then he turned and climbed back into the truck. Behind the wheel, he pulled out his cell and thumbed through his messages.

He had three, but none of them were from Dalton McGregor. Not that he'd expected one this soon. The man had given him a respectable timetable, and Garret had done enough reference checks to know that he kept his word. By Saturday MacGregor would have the information Garret so desperately needed to reclaim his humanity.

Two days, he reminded himself. Two days, and he would be one step closer to the man he'd once been.

The notion didn't excite him half as much as the thought of seeing Viv again.

Understandable, of course. He was so damned hungry, so fucking desperate for a woman, that he couldn't think straight. It wasn't her.

It never had been.

The hunger clawed inside of him, and his fingers went stiff as he pocketed the cell phone. All he had to do was head for the interstate and the nearest bar. He could take his pick of any woman there and forget all about Viv Darland.

He shifted the pick-up into gear, gunned the engine and headed for the far gate. Once out on the main road, he idled for a split-second, indecision pushing and pulling inside of him. Finally, he hung a right onto the dirt trail that led back to the ranch house.

As much as he hurt, he wasn't acting on it. He didn't have time. The sun was already creeping over the horizon which meant he was bagging it today.

And tomorrow.

And the next day.

Because he'd made a promise to himself. One he didn't intend to break, no matter how hungry Viv made him.

The next time Garret climbed into bed with a woman, it would be because he wanted to. Not because he had to. Because he craved the feel of her body and the smell of her skin and the dizzying energy as she came apart in his arms.

An image slid into his head, and his stomach muscles

bunched. Heat spiraled through him, making him harder and hotter.

He cranked up the air conditioner, gathered his resolve and forced Viv out of his head.

He was keeping his priorities straight and his distance where she was concerned. Even more, he wasn't getting stuck under the same roof with her while she leaned this way and bent that way and worked him into a sexually frustrated frenzy.

Never, ever again.

"FORGET THE EQUIPMENT BAG," Garret said when he met Viv in the parking lot of Skull Creek Choppers on Wednesday evening. "We're traveling light."

Viv eyed the black and silver motorcycle with the skull and crossbones motif that now sat parked near the doorway. "A ride?"

"A road trip. I've got to test out this bike and make sure she performs up to spec before I send her out. The only way to do that is to take her out and open her up."

Excitement flared in her gaze for a split-second before she seemed to tamp down on it long enough to give him a calm, controlled, "Sounds good." She pulled out her camera before tossing her bag into the car, then slammed and locked the door. "So," she said, turning back to the bike and hooking the camera strap over her shoulder. "How do we do this? Do I get on first or last?"

"First."

When she started to straddle the chopper, he caught

her arm. Skin met skin and the air around them seemed to crackle. She stalled, and her gaze locked with his. For just the smallest moment, the past seemed to fade. The hurt. The betrayal.

Suddenly it was just the two of them standing beneath the stars, staring into each other's eyes the way they'd done so long ago.

When he'd been a man, and she'd been just a woman.

Or so he'd thought.

He stiffened and let his hand fall away. "Not that one." He pointed to another chopper parked a few feet away near the back door. It was a silver and pink number he'd just completed for a runway model from New York. "That one. I'm shipping it out next week, and I want to do some final tweaks. You're about the same size as the client, so you can give me a feel for how she'll handle."

"But I can't ride." For a split-second, there was more than simply dismay in her gaze. He saw a glimmer of uncertainty. Fear. And something softened inside of him.

"You can ride a horse, can't you?"

"Sure. About a hundred years ago before I grew vampire cooties."

A smile tugged at his lips. "It doesn't matter. Once you've done it, you never forget how. Just stash your camera in that compartment beneath the seat, climb on, keep your knees locked and your hands steady, and you'll be fine."

She looked hesitant, but finally she walked over, stashed her camera and straddled the bike. Her fingers tightened on the hand grips. "I hope you have good insurance."

"Why's that?"

"Because if I fall off this thing, I'm going to sue." When he started to remind her that her injuries would heal faster than he could call 911 or pull out a first aid kit, she added, "For the emotional duress I'm going to suffer when I fall on my ass in front of everyone and make a complete idiot of myself."

"We're taking the backroads, so the only one likely to see you on your ass will be me. I've busted my own more than once, so you'll be in good company."

She looked doubtful. "You've really fallen off one of these things?"

"One or two times." He shrugged. "Or forty-three."

"You're not making me feel any better." She eyed him.

"I was popping wheelies or racing or doing something equally stupid when I bit the dust. You won't have that problem because we're going to go nice and slow."

She eyed the bike again, and disappointment glimmered before diving into the deep blue depths of her eyes. "I guess I don't really have a choice, do I? If I want to ride, it's this or nothing."

"This or you can take pictures inside and wait for Jake and Dillon. I'm sure one of them would double up and give you a tour of the town when they come in."

"But not you?"

"I've got my own bike to evaluate. I need an accurate

ride," he added, suddenly eager to convince himself. "Two people throw the balance off. I need to make shock and alignment adjustments. If you climb on, my readings will be messed up." And so would his control.

Already, he could feel his body temperature rising. His hands trembled, and it was all he could do not to reach out and pull her close.

He wanted to taste her again.

To feel her.

"I'm crunched for time on this. The bike has to go out tomorrow."

She sat there for a long moment as if trying to make up her mind. Stay or go. With him or without him. "It's heavier than it looks," she finally said, turning the handlebars from side to side.

"Only because it's stationary. Once we start moving, she'll loosen up."

Indecision faded into serious intent. "I really could use some firsthand experience," she admitted. Then, eyeing the bike as if she were a bullfighter about to climb into the ring, she asked, "What do I do first?"

13

IT WAS NOTHING like riding a horse.

The cold metal against the insides of her bare knees. The hot exhaust blowing around her ankles. The soft, cushiony seat pillowing her bottom. The steady vibration between her legs.

A horse wasn't nearly this exciting.

This stirring.

This decadent.

The wind whipped at her face and lifted the neckline of her blouse. Air teased her nipples, stirring them to a full, throbbing awareness. Electricity rippled up her spine and she chanced a glance to the side to see Garret staring back at her.

Again.

As reassuring as he'd been about her ability to ride, he seemed intent on keeping a close eye on her.

A strange warmth blossomed in her chest. A crazy feeling because the last thing she wanted from him was his concern.

Her nipples pebbled, and she shifted on the seat. A bad move even though she'd worn panties tonight. They were thin enough to be non-existent, and desire spurted through her, along with a rush of anxiety.

"How much longer until we get where we're going?" she asked. Where the wind would have masked her voice to the normal human, Garret heard her loud and clear.

"It's not about getting somewhere. It's about the ride, sugar. Just relax."

Sugar.

The sentiment stuck in her head, and the warmth spread from her chest throughout the rest of her body. Need spiraled through her, dive-bombing several erogenous zones and making her that much more uncomfortable. And desperate.

She tightened her grip on the handlebars and did her damndest not to shift on the seat. No problem when they were on the main highway. But when Garret turned off onto an old dirt path, Viv knew she was in big trouble.

Sure enough, she bounced this way and slid that way and rubbed up and down and—

Easy.

Yeah, right. By the time they came to a stop by the edge of a sprawling river, she was this close to going up in flames.

She killed the engine and sat there for a few seconds trying to gather her control. Just one teensy, tiny move and she was going to—

She bit down on her bottom lip and fought back the burst of dizzying pleasure. Her vision clouded, and she clamped her eyes shut. Her ears rang. She could feel her fangs sharp against her tongue. Her hands tightened on the handlebars, and she braced herself.

Not yet. Not like—

"Are you okay?"

Garret's voice pushed past the roar in her head, and she forced her eyes open to find him staring back at her.

He sat a few feet away on the black and chrome chopper. His hands rested atop his thighs. He looked as relaxed as ever except for the tense set to his jaw. As if he knew the turmoil her body was caught in, and it took all of his strength not to climb off the motorcycle and help her out.

"I…" She swallowed against the tightness in her throat and summoned her control. "I'm just feeling a little dizzy. It was a rough ride." And not nearly satisfying enough. "I… Just let me sit here for a minute and catch my bearings."

She waited for him to remind her that she was a vampire who wasn't susceptible to motion sickness. She could leap tall buildings and levitate and walk on water, for Pete's sake. Motion sickness? Forget about it.

He didn't say a word. Instead, he gave her a thoughtful look before he finally shrugged and climbed off the bike.

He walked over to the edge of the water and hunkered down. Pulling out a shiny black PDA, he started keying in notes. He seemed oblivious to Viv, and she sent up a silent thank-you.

She spent the next few minutes telling herself every reason why she shouldn't climb off the bike, march over to him and jump his bones.

Slow, she reminded herself. Easy. She needed him to be the aggressor. That's why she'd had an orgasm in the first place. Because he'd seduced her. He'd turned the tables on her and taken control. That's what had sent her over the edge.

If she took the lead, she wouldn't be any more satisfied than she'd been with any other man. She had to wait on him.

She eyed his broad back outlined by the moonlight reflecting off the calm water. Her tummy tingled and her knees shook and desperation coiled low in her belly.

No, she wasn't going to jump him.

At the same time, she wasn't going to sit here and just wait. She had to do something.

"Shimmy, shake, shazam." Winona's crackling voice echoed through her head.

It had been the woman's last piece of advice when Viv had called her on the way to Skull Creek Choppers that evening.

"If the drop and retrieve didn't send him over the edge, you have to get more aggressive. You got to send a crystal-clear message that says you're ready for sex, and nothing does that better than stripping buck naked smack dab in front of him."

"Isn't that a little too aggressive?"

"Not if you don't say the words. See, telling a man you want to have sex with him takes all the guesswork out of it, which takes away the challenge. Every man wants what he can't have. So the key here is to let him see what it is he can't have. Sort of like dangling the carrot in front of him. Then when he makes like Bugs Bunny and tries to grab you, you back off."

"Why would I back off if he tries to grab me?"

"'Cause you're dangling, darlin'. Trust me, if you strip naked and employ my infamous Triple S, he'll make another move. And then another. My rule of thumb is three moves minimum. Then you can give in. Just remember to shimmy and shake every time you take off something."

"What about the shazam? How do I do that?"

"It's not something you do, darlin'." The old woman laughed. "That's what happens when that man finally gets ahold of you. Shazam!"

Viv gathered her courage and turned on the state-of-the-art sound system built into the chopper's dash. A frantic heavy metal song blasted from the speakers, and she punched the buttons until she found a soft, slow country song with just enough beat for what she had in mind.

She climbed off the bike. "Nice sound system," she commented. "Is it standard on all your bikes?"

"We don't have a 'standard.' We cater to each customer." He didn't spare her a glance. "Some want more power than others. Some want CD only. Some want XM. Some want it all. We give them what they want."

"It's nice." She fingered the edge of the red sequined tank top she'd bought today just minutes before the boutique had closed. Actually, they'd already turned off the sign, but she'd used her persuasive gaze to get the salesclerk to open up for one final purchase—a blue jean mini-skirt, strappy tank and a pair of killer red heels. "So, um, how did your bike handle?"

"Fine, with the exception of a few suspension problems. But they're easy to fix." He still didn't turn her way.

"So," she came up next to him on the riverbank, "where exactly are we?"

"The river."

"I know that. What river?"

"It's really deep, so the folks around here call it the Bottomless Pit."

"That sort of kills the mood."

A warm chuckle vibrated on the air. "Black Bottom River is the official name."

"Oh." She went silent for a few moments as the night's sounds closed in on her. The occasional hooting of an owl, the faint ripple of water, the click of his fingers on the PDA, the distant drone of the highway miles away. Wind rippled, sneaking beneath the edge of her skirt to tickle her thighs and the tender flesh between her legs.

She shifted. "Garret?"

"Yeah?"

"Could you look here for a second? I've got something to show you."

He didn't budge. "I really need to finish these adjustments for the suspension system in case I forget something."

She would lay money down that he never forgot a

thing, whether keyed in or not. She tamped down on her disappointment and gathered her courage.

"Boy, it's hot out here." She slid a hand under her hair and lifted it. Her back arched and her breasts pushed up and out, but he didn't spare her a glance. "Maybe I'll just cool off." She knelt near the water and splashed some onto her face, careful to let it drip down into her cleavage. "Uh-oh. I'm all wet now."

In more ways than one.

He still didn't look at her. "I've got an extra T-shirt under the seat on my bike if you need to dry off."

"Thanks, but I'm fine." She pushed to her feet and barely resisted kicking him in the side. That would get his attention.

And cause major damage. She wanted him in her bed, not the hospital. "It's a really nice night. Would you look at that moon?"

He didn't, and she re-evaluated her earlier decision. The toe of her shoe caught him in the ribs.

Hey, he was a vampire. He would heal.

"Ouch!" His head whipped around, and his ice-blue gaze stared up at her. "What the hell was that for?"

She shrugged. "Sorry." She gave him an innocent smile. "I guess I lost my balance."

He didn't look the least bit convinced, but at least he was looking at her.

Before she could reach for the strap of her tank top, however, he turned back to his PDA.

"My front drive shaft was a little shaky," he commented, as if trying to get his thoughts back on business. "I'll have to make some tweaks to it."

"This place is really great," she tried for more conversation. "Do you come here often?"

"I live here."

She glanced toward the opposite bank and the lush green grass that stretched toward a distant wall of trees. "Unless you're pitching a tent over there every night— one with Kryptonite walls—I doubt you live here."

A grin tugged at his mouth. "Kryptonite's for superheroes, sugar, not vampires, and I didn't mean here at the river. I meant here on the property." He motioned to the north. "I've got a place just beyond those trees over there."

"Oh." She remembered the name of the river and a light bulb went off in her brain. "Black Bottom as in Sam Black." The man he'd once been.

The man she'd betrayed.

"I…" she started, only to clamp down on her bottom lip. She couldn't change the past with a simple I'm sorry, no matter how heartfelt. And she certainly couldn't erase the hurt.

The only way to ease that would be to give him back the humanity that she took from him, which she fully intended to do.

Soon.

The hair on the back of her neck prickled, and once again she felt the strange awareness. They were catching up to her.

"So, um, do you come here often?" It sounded

cheesy even to her ears, but it was the only thing she could think of to say.

She needed to talk. To cut the tension that stretched so tightly between them.

"Every now and then. It's peaceful here. And wide open." He spared a glance at his surroundings. "It helps me think."

Because he couldn't think when he was cooped up and barricaded in during the day. Hiding from the sunlight. Smothering because of what he was.

"I know the feeling," she blurted before she could think better of it. "My folks had this old farmhouse, and I used to hide under the boards when I was first turned. I hated it. It was so dark. So damp. But at least it was safe."

"What about your folks?" He spared her a glance then, his gaze drilling into her for a long, piercing moment. "Did they really die in a fire? Or did you lie about that, too?"

She ignored the urge to turn, to run the way she'd been doing her entire life. But she couldn't escape her past. She knew that now. What's more, she didn't want to. Instinctively, her hand went to her throat, her fingers searching for the St. Benedict medal. Bare skin met bare skin, and she remembered that she'd left it back in her suitcase.

She stiffened and gathered her courage. "My mother did die in a fire." She hadn't deceived him about that. Not completely. "But my father…" She caught her lip for a long moment before the words trembled out. "My father is the one who turned me." She'd never actually said the words out loud to anyone. She'd never been able to.

Until now.

Suddenly, she couldn't seem to stop herself. Even more, she didn't want to.

She wanted to tell him the truth. And she did.

14

"HE WENT OUT gambling one night and didn't come home for three days." Her voice broke the calm silence. "That was typical for him, though. He was always leaving us, disappearing for days." She stared out over the water, seeing the old farmhouse instead.

Her father stood on the front porch. He wore his usual stained overalls, his shirt sleeves rolled up to reveal meaty forearms. The stench of moonshine rolled off him, along with something else.

A dark, forbidden anger that never failed to send her running into the fields to hide from him.

Her palms started to sweat, and she clutched at the medal that dangled around her neck. It matched the one that her mother wore. St. Benedict. The protector. The medal felt cold against her palm, and anxiety rolled through her. Along with fear.

Run. Hide.

She'd done just that so many times.

Often he'd found her, but sometimes—those blessed few times—he hadn't.

Run. Hide.

She hadn't had a chance to do either that night.

"I thought he was just drunk at first," she said, her lips trembling around the words. "He had that crazy look in his eyes the way he always did. But there was something else...I didn't know what it was at first. But then he opened his mouth, and I saw his fangs." She blinked against the sudden burning at the backs of her eyes.

"He attacked my mother before I could blink," she went on when she managed to find her voice. "One minute she was standing there, and the next her throat was ripped open and she was bleeding out onto the floor." He'd snatched the medal off the older woman's neck and lapped up the blood while Viv had watched. Terror pumping through her small body. Her own medal digging into her small hands. "He turned on me then. I tried to get away." A lump pushed its way into her throat, and she swallowed it back down. "I ran for the door, but he caught me. I fought him and knocked over one of the lanterns." She shook her head. "One minute my mother was just lying there, and the next her dress was on fire. I tried to help, but then he grabbed me and..." The words stumbled into one another, and she swallowed again.

The past was there, right in front of her. She could see the bright orange flames, feel the heat and the pain and the terror.

"That explains why you looked so freaked out at the fire back at the machine shop." His deep voice slid into her ears and drew her away from the carnage, back to the present.

The images faded, and she found herself staring at a lush stretch of green grass that led to a thick patch of trees.

She nodded. "By the time he was finished drinking from me, I was almost dead, and my mother had burned beyond recognition. It was too late for him to turn her. I wanted him to let me die, too, but he didn't. He wouldn't."

Because he was a cruel bastard who'd done nothing but hurt her since the day she'd been born. As a vampire, that cruelty had been magnified.

"He turned me and then he disappeared. I haven't seen him since." She faced Garret then, her gaze finally meeting his. "He didn't die like I told you, but I wished he had. He was a hateful man. He hit my mother and he…" She caught her bottom lip, fighting back the darker images—the ones she'd buried deep down inside—that threatened to swamp her. "He wasn't much better to me."

Garret's gaze brightened into a vicious red, and she knew he was pissed.

At her? Because she'd lied to him?

Or for her?

If she hadn't known better, she would have put her money on number two. But she'd hurt him too badly for him to care one way or the other.

She shrugged. "I've had a long time to come to terms with what happened to me, and I'm okay with it. But still, he should have died in that fire. In my mind, he did."

The red faded into an icy blue, and she was left to wonder if she'd only imagined his rage. "My dad eventually died of a heart attack," he told her, as if one admission deserved another. It didn't, but oddly enough, hearing his voice soothed the frantic beat of her heart and calmed the images that pushed and pulled inside of her. "My mom died of consumption. Not that I was there. I didn't trust myself to see them after I turned, so I took off."

"How did you find out what happened to them?" She shifted her attention away from her own demons, and concentrated on his.

He held up the PDA. "Technology is a beautiful thing." He grinned, easing the dark mood that had gripped them. His expression faded. "I'm really sorry about your mother."

He looked as surprised by the sincerity of his words as she was. But then the look vanished as he shifted his attention back to his PDA. "I really need to finish a few notes."

She stood there beside him for the next few moments trying to ignore the past that fluttered in and out of her head. Not the bad memories. No, those had faded along with the conversation. The memories that haunted her now featured the two of them. Outside. In the moonlight.

Talking. Sharing. Making love.

Not. Making love required being in love, which they weren't. No matter how much she'd pretended otherwise back then.

Rather, they'd had sex. Lots and lots and lots of sex.

Her body stirred, still fired up after her frenzied state

just moments ago. Hunger clawed inside of her. She felt itchy and tight. Anxious. Alive. And painfully aware of the vampire who sat so close.

Physically, that is.

Emotionally, he seemed a thousand miles away.

"I—I really ought to take some pictures of this for my article." With the information she already had from Eldin and several other businesses around town, she'd written the copy on Skull Creek, calling it the "sexiest small town in Texas." She'd e-mailed it to her editor tonight. All she needed now were a few more photos to support the text, and she would be finished.

The river and the moonlight definitely portrayed the sexy image she was trying to project to her readers. Besides, a few pictures would give her something to do while he finished with his notes. Then he would look at her long enough for her to seduce him.

She meant to walk to the pink chopper and retrieve the camera she'd stowed under the seat. She really did. But her feet seemed to have a will all their own. Instead of turning, she stepped forward, out onto the water. Her feet barely skimmed the surface—another vamp perk—as she made her way around in front of him.

He didn't glance up from his PDA.

Doubt pushed past the determination dictating her actions, and she almost turned and headed back to the riverbank. She should wait.

She would wait.

If she had the time.

But the minutes were slipping away, and Molly and

Cruz were getting closer. The phone call was evidence. Enough to prompt her to finish the article and tie up that loose end. The prickling awareness that followed her around, reminding her of Washington and the ambush, was even more proof.

It was now or never.

She backed up several feet, putting a little distance between them while she worked up her nerve. Finally, she stopped.

Her ears tuned to the music, and she closed her eyes for a long moment to block out the man hunkered down on the riverbank. The beat filled her head and thrummed through her body as she started to move.

She swayed, a subtle rotation of her hips from side to side. A vision slid into her head, and the past pulled her back. To the small barn where she'd found him saddling up to ride out and join his regiment.

One look into her eyes, and he'd forgotten all about the horse. He'd stripped them both down to nothing and pressed her down into the soft, sweet-smelling hay one last time.

He spread her legs wide and plunged deep inside. Her eyes closed as pleasure swelled and crashed over her. Her nerve endings came alive. Her heart thundered. Her ears rang. Her blood pounded.

She wasn't sure how she heard his voice, but she did. The deep timbre pushed its way past her thundering heart and sizzled along her nerve endings.

"Look at me, Viv."

The memory faded as she opened her eyes to find

Garret—a very real Garret—staring back at her, and she realized that the voice hadn't been her memory this time.

She had his full attention now.

He'd pushed to his feet, the PDA forgotten in his hand as he stared across the mirrorlike surface at her. His ice-blue eyes gleamed in the moonlit darkness. Tension held his body tight. His muscles bunched beneath his T-shirt. Taut lines carved his face, making him seem harsh, fierce, predatory.

He was every bit the vampire she'd made him.

At the same time, there was something familiar in his eyes.

Passion.

Lust.

Love.

She ditched the last thought. He'd never loved her. Not then, and certainly not now.

But want...

He definitely wanted her.

Enough to forgive the past, forget the hurt and betrayal, and take the initiative?

There was only one way to find out.

WHAT IN THE HELL was she doing?

Garret watched as she started to move to the slow, sexy song that poured from the radio. Her hips shifted from side to side in a seductive way that made his muscles bunch and his groin tighten.

She slid her hands beneath her hair and lifted the silky curtain before letting it fall back down around her shoulders. She wasn't as practiced as an actual stripper, but she was pretty damned good.

Enough that his dick throbbed and hardened and, just like that, he had a massive erection.

It's not her. It's you, buddy. It's who you are. What you are.

She arched her back, and her breasts jutted forward, her hard nipples perfectly outlined beneath her sparkly tank top. His mouth watered at the memory of the throbbing tips deep in his mouth, her skin slick and wet beneath his hands. His entire body shook with need.

Hunger sliced through him, and his groin tightened.

He tried to fight the primitive urges that gripped him, but instead found himself thinking that maybe, just maybe, having sex with her wouldn't be such a bad thing.

It wasn't like he was falling for her all over again.

He was stronger now. Immune to her vamp mojo because he had his own.

No, this wasn't about falling for her. It was about falling into bed with her. Or, in this case, smack dab onto the river bank.

A little body-slapping, and he would see that she was nothing special. That he'd simply been mesmerized all those years ago.

He wasn't mesmerized now.

He was hungry. Horny.

He needed to press himself between her legs and drive into her slick flesh over and over until she climaxed and he drank in her sweet energy.

Even more, he needed to shatter the illusion that had haunted him for the past two hundred years.

Viv Darland wasn't his one and only—she never had been—and having sex with her was a surefire way to prove she was no different from any other woman out there.

Then he could stop fantasizing. Dreaming. Remembering.

Once and for all.

15

SHE'D FINALLY GOTTEN his full, undivided attention. She just couldn't decide if that was a good thing or a bad thing.

His expression was unreadable, his eyes hard and unwavering, his mouth set in a grim line as if he fought some internal battle.

Viv trailed her tongue over her bottom lip, determined to do everything she could to tip the scales in her favor. She touched a finger to her throat. A few fluttering strokes against the steady beat of her pulse, and her own hunger stirred. Her ears prickled, sifting through the sensory overload—the buzz of crickets, the scurry of critters, the whistle of the breeze, the occasional whinny of a horse—until she heard only the thud of her own heart and the slow, intoxicating melody drifting from the speakers.

A deep voice on the radio crooned about making love all weekend, and she slid a finger to the edge of her tank top, tracing the line where flesh met soft cotton before moving to the strap. Hooking her finger beneath, she eased the material down over her shoulder. Lifting her opposite arm, she did the same with the other strap until the cotton sagged around her shoulders.

She gave her upper body a little shimmy. The tank top rode lower on her torso until the material caught on her bare, aroused nipples.

Garret swallowed, and the air grew hot and shimmery between them.

She could feel the heat rolling off his muscular body, see the frantic beat of his pulse at the base of his neck, smell the rich, musky aroma of hot, aroused male. She knew then that he wasn't half as indifferent as she'd first suspected.

A surge of feminine power went through her, and she pushed the straps of her shirt down until the material hugged her waist. Grasping the cotton, she eased it over her hips. She gave a little shake, and the top slid down her thighs, past her knees to puddle around her ankles. Leaning down, she caught the edge of the material and stepped free. Then with all the confidence of a sexy woman who'd been seducing men forever, she smiled. Just a faint crook to her lips that told him there would be more—much more—to come.

Cool night air slid over her bare arms and breasts, but it did little to ease her rising body temperature. His hot molten gaze fanned the flames, heating her body, her blood, until she felt the air sizzle around her.

She touched the undersides of her breasts, cupping the full mounds, weighing them and feeling the heat of her own fingertips against the soft flesh. All the while she imagined that it was Garret's touch that seared her.

She skimmed her palms over her nipples, and they throbbed in response. Her stomach quivered beneath her fluttering fingertips as she moved on. Down. Around her belly button. To the zipper of her skirt.

A few tugs, and the opening slid free, her zipper parted and the material sagged. She rocked her hips in time to the slow, sweet, twangy song that filled the night air, and the skirt slithered down her hips. Her legs. She toed the denim to the side with her high heel.

She wore a silky red thong that matched her high heels and made her feel just as decadent. She traced the very edge before trailing her fingertips over the satin V. Back and forth. Side to side. Desire speared her, so sharp and potent, that her vision clouded, and her nipples hardened and quivered. Her eyes closed, and her need magnified.

Anxiety rushed through her and made her entire body tremble, but she wasn't giving in to it.

Not just yet.

She gathered her control and focused on his burning gaze rather than the damnable hunger that pushed and pulled inside of her. With one fingertip, she teased the elastic at the edge of her undies before dipping a finger beneath. She touched the damp, swollen flesh between her legs, and her nerves hummed. Another lingering stroke, and she pushed deep inside her drenched flesh.

Pressure spiked through her, and she gasped.

She'd touched herself many times in this exact same way during more than one fantasy starring the hot, hunky vampire standing in front of her. But it had never felt the way it did now.

So real.

So intense.

So…pleasurable.

Another move of her fingers, and her body swayed from the sensation rippling along her nerve endings. But it wasn't enough to satisfy the restless need inside of her. Not even close.

She didn't want her own touch. She wanted his.

Sliding her finger free of her panties, she hooked the edge and slid the material down her legs. Stepping free, she faced him, her skin bathed in moonlight, her nipples hard and inviting, her body wet and ready.

He just stood there.

Watching.

Waiting.

"I came here for this," she heard herself say. Her gaze locked with his. "For you."

She wasn't sure why she told him the truth. Except that she'd already put herself out there by stripping naked, so there seemed no point in denying it anymore. That, and she wanted him to know that he wasn't just any man to her.

Not then and not now.

He didn't move for a long moment, as if letting her words sink in. Disbelief flashed in his gaze, followed by a strange glimmer that burned up any and everything else. He dropped his PDA to the riverbank and reached for the hem of his T-shirt. Pulling the soft cotton over his head, he tossed it to the side.

He was every bit as rough and rugged as she remembered.

Muscles carved his torso, from his bulging biceps and shoulders to the rippled plane of his abdomen. Dark, silky hair sprinkled his chest and narrowed to a tiny funnel of silk that disappeared beneath the button fly of his faded jeans.

Her gaze swept down to the prominent bulge beneath his zipper, and her pulse quickened.

His boots barely made a ripple as he strode across the water and ate up the distance that separated them. He stopped just inches shy.

Close, but not close enough.

"I'm not the man you remember." She wasn't sure if it was an admission or a warning.

Her doubts stirred and suddenly, she couldn't help but wonder if maybe, just maybe, she'd come to Skull Creek for nothing.

He was different now.

And there was a very real possibility that her reaction to him would be different, as well.

Maybe sex with him would be as uneventful as it had been with every other male in her past.

Maybe.

Probably.

"I'm not a man at all," he added.

She clung to a small ripple of hope and fingered her sensitive nipple. "Neither am I."

A grin tugged at his lips, followed by a fierce, hungry look as he watched her play with herself. She plucked the ripe tip, rubbed and stirred until a gasp worked its way up her throat.

"I've pictured you like this, you know." He reached out to replace her hand with his own. The rough pad of his thumb flicked her, and the tip hardened even more. Her areola tightened and puckered. A growl vibrated up his throat. "Standing in the moonlight with your eyes bright and your body trembling." His gaze flashed and his mouth opened just enough for her to see the gleaming white tips of his fangs. "In my dreams. My fantasies."

Excitement stirred deep inside of her, along with her own hunger. Her gut clenched, and her legs quivered. "I've fantasized about you, too." She wasn't sure why she told him, except he spoke so freely and suddenly she wanted to, as well.

She wanted to talk to him the way she had back then. And she wanted him to listen.

To care.

The notion struck, and she stiffened. Caring? This wasn't about caring. It was about passion. Fast, furious, blazing passion.

He thumbed her nipple again before dipping his head. His tongue flicked out, and he licked her. Once, twice.

Slowly. Meticulously.

Because he wasn't turned on enough. Not yet.

Dangling, she could almost hear Winona say.

"Geez, it's getting hot," she commented as he slid his hands under her breasts.

"Not nearly hot enough." He kneaded the soft, round globes.

Excitement flared in the pit of her stomach, and she closed her eyes for a long, nerve-wracking moment. She couldn't... She wouldn't...

She opened her eyes and stared at her feet, focusing on the quickest means of escape from the delicious sensation wreaking havoc on her control.

"I—I think maybe it's time to cool off." She willed herself to drop, plunging straight down into the water and out of his grasp.

The cool liquid closed over her head, and she relished the sudden change of temperature. She needed to calm down, to douse the inferno that raged deep inside and threatened to seize control.

She wasn't taking the lead and killing her chances for a bona fide orgasm.

She wasn't.

She stayed under for several long moments, until her heart calmed enough for her to actually think again.

Finally, she moved her arms and legs, swimming back toward the shimmering moonlight overhead. She broke the surface with a soft plunk and opened her eyes to find him nowhere in sight.

She wiped a hand over her face. Other than the two motorcycles, the bank sat empty, the trees shrouding everything else in darkness.

Surely, he wouldn't leave his motorcycle?

Then again, if he'd changed his mind...

Instead of upping the challenge, maybe her retreat had given him time to come to his senses.

To run.

The truth echoed in her head as she did a complete three-sixty in the water, her gaze searching every inch of the surrounding bank. A faint rustle thundered through her head, and her gaze snapped to the stretch of lush vegetation to her right. A rabbit darted across the ground before disappearing into the trees. A cricket buzzed, hopping from one distant branch to the other. A firefly sparked, bobbing through the trees.

She glanced down at the water, her gaze pushing into the dark depths, but she saw only the steady kick of her own legs, the flap of her arms. On the surface, her reflection stared back at her.

Her hair was plastered to her head. Water dripped from the tip of her nose. Black circles rimmed her eyes and made streaks down her cheeks—

What the hell?

She peered closer, and a sinking feeling gripped the pit of her stomach. She hadn't used waterproof mascara. She hadn't even thought about it.

But then, she hadn't had a clue she'd be going for a swim. No, she'd pictured herself having sex tonight, not playing cat and mouse in the river.

She wiped frantically at her face, but that only smeared the black even more. She'd just splashed a handful of water onto her face to try to wash some of it off when she felt the soft brush against the inside of one ankle.

She jumped, kicking her legs and flailing around. While she might be up to a game with Garret, she wasn't going one on one with a fish. Or a snake.

Not that she was vulnerable to snakes. It was just the

thought of something she couldn't see slithering around her ankles that sent goose bumps dancing up and down her arms. She definitely didn't do snakes.

Just as the notion struck, something brushed her other ankle, and she kicked out.

To hell with this.

She focused, gathering her strength and energy, and started to lift herself out of the water. But then the faint brush turned to a steel-like grip as fingers wrapped around her ankle and jerked her back down.

The water closed over her and she went completely under. Deeper and deeper. She flailed, fighting for a split-second until she felt the strong arms close around her, and she knew it wasn't a snake.

Her eyes opened and through the shimmering water, she saw Garret, his face only inches from her. His eyes blazed with a hunger so bright and intense that she felt like she'd go up in flames.

She had the sudden thought that she should definitely give Winona a great, big fat bonus for her advice, but then his lips touched hers, and she stopped thinking altogether.

Shazam!

16

HE'D FANTASIZED ABOUT kissing her so many times over the years. But nothing, not even the most decadent dream, prepared him for the real thing.

Her lips were soft and full beneath his plundering mouth and an electrical current ran from his lips, straight to his growing erection. He pushed his tongue deep, stroking and delving. He was through denying himself. He meant to sample every inch of her, savor her essence on his lips, make her writhe and moan until she knew without a doubt that he was her equal—a seductive, mesmerizing vampire with pure sex on his mind.

He pulled her flush against his body as they hung suspended in the sparkling depths of the water. He let his hands roam over her naked body and marveled at the feel. She was softer than he remembered. More voluptuous.

Impossible, he knew.

She was a vampire. The same yesterday, today, tomorrow. He knew that, yet he found himself slowing down and re-learning every inch of her anyway.

The dip at the base of her spine, the soft hollow just beneath her rib cage, the roundness of her ass, the smooth, sensitive inside of each thigh.

He drew her closer, pulling her legs around him and locking her ankles at the small of his back. Then he settled her firmly against the rock-hard length barely contained by his zipper.

She wrapped her arms around his neck and hung on as he rocked her. The coarse material of his jeans rasped against her clitoris, and he felt her tremble.

The water stirred around them, bubbling from the heat rolling off their bodies. At the rate they were going, it wouldn't be long until the entire river started to steam.

He focused his thoughts and willed them to move toward the surface and higher…until they cleared the river completely and levitated a few feet above. Water dripped off of them, sprinkling down as he moved them toward the opposite river bank and the soft patch of thick grass.

When his bare feet touched the lush growth, he kissed her again, exploring and tasting for the next few frantic moments before he loosened his grip. Easing her to the ground, he slid her down his hard length, letting her feel every inch of how badly he wanted her.

A gasp parted her lips. He caught the sound as he kissed her again, hard and insistent. His hands were everywhere, touching, branding, reminding her of the past and how much he'd changed.

That was the goal here. To prove that he wasn't the same man any more than she was the same woman.

He'd been as charged up sexually, of course, but he'd had a far different goal in mind.

Back then, he'd been concerned with both giving and receiving pleasure. But now… Now it wasn't about having his own orgasm. It was about sustaining himself, growing stronger, feeding.

It was about giving her an orgasm and soaking up the energy he so desperately needed.

Ditto for her. Or so he thought. But she made no move to turn him on and push him toward the edge. Rather, she seemed content to be on the receiving end. As if her goal had nothing to do with the beast that lived and breathed inside of her and everything to do with the woman who stood before him.

As if.

He had to give her credit. She was one hell of an actress. Then and now.

Desperate sounds worked their way past her luscious lips as he touched her. Her breasts plumped beneath his fingertips. Her nipples hardened.

He moved lower, stroking the heat between her legs, plunging, mimicking what he was going to do to her. He slipped his hands between her legs to find her warm and slick and oh, so ready.

She managed to tear her lips away. "No," she gasped the minute his fingertip pushed a delicious inch into her steamy heat. "Not like this…I…" She licked her lips, her eyes bright with desire. "I—I want you inside of me."

He wanted it, too.

He wanted to bury himself deep and forget the rest of the world and explode.

A realization that made him all the more determined to hold back.

The way he would with any woman.

That's all she was to him.

Any woman.

Every woman.

He ignored the last thought and slid a finger deep inside of her. She moaned, the sound vibrating up her throat, feeding the excitement that coiled inside of him.

"No," she said again when he plunged a second finger inside, but the word was softer, weaker.

He withdrew and pushed back in. Her muscles quivered around him, and a drop of wetness slid across his palm. Her lips trembled as he took her mouth in another kiss. Deeper than the last. Hotter. Wetter.

He pleasured her with his hand and his mouth for the next several moments until she clung to him. A soft cry bubbled from her lips. A tremor went through her, and energy rushed into him from every point of contact.

He fixated on the empowering buzz and let it feed his strength. His senses sharpened and magnified and the fog in his head seemed to clear.

But it wasn't enough, he realized when her climax subsided and the buzz faded to a distant hum. The beast stirred, restless and demanding and not the least bit satisfied, and a growl worked its way up his throat.

The deep rumbling pushed past the ringing in Viv's

ears and drew her gaze to his. She pulled away to stare up at him.

His eyes fired with a predatory light. A hiss slid past his lips and he opened his mouth. His fangs flashed, gleaming in the moonlight, and a crazy excitement welled inside of her.

Crazy because she couldn't let him actually bite her. She wouldn't. If he drank from her, or vice versa, it would forge a nearly unbreakable bond between them. They would be one.

He would know her darkest fears and her deepest secrets.

He would know the truth.

She stumbled back, but he refused to let her retreat. He matched her step for step until she came up against one of the massive trees that circled the clearing.

Gone was the passionate man who'd pleasured her for hours on end. Instead, he'd turned into a raw primitive savage.

A vampire.

The truth stirred a wave of guilt, but then he reached for her.

One hand dove into the hair at the base of her skull while the other pressed into the small of her back. He tugged her head back until her neck was fully exposed. The sharp edge of his fangs grazed the tender flesh, rasping and prickling just enough to draw one sweet drop.

She hissed, warning him away, but he wasn't about to be put off.

He followed the crimson trail with his seductive

mouth and licked his way over her clavicle, down the slope of her breast until it reached her nipple.

He sucked her into his mouth, and a burst of pleasure sliced through her from her head clear to her toes.

But while he rasped her with his fangs, he didn't sink them deep. She realized then that he didn't want the bond between them any more than she did.

Relief swept through her, followed by a surge of disappointment.

He didn't give her a chance to analyze the strange reaction. He urged her down to the soft grass and straddled her.

The faded material of his wet jeans hugged his hard thighs, showing every ripple of muscle. His bare torso gleamed with a fine sheen of water that caught flickers of moonlight.

She reached up and trailed her hands along his slick muscled flesh. His shoulders rippled and bulged beneath her palms. She splayed her fingers in the hair covering his chest, her touch tentative, restrained as she followed the whorl of silk as it narrowed and descended to his abdomen. She stopped just shy of the waistband to his jeans.

Her hunger raged, urging her on. She balled her fingers against the need. Her body stiffened. She forced her gaze away, up over his rock-hard abdomen, his broad chest, his corded neck, to his face.

His eyes burned, reflecting the pure, ravaging hunger that she felt inside.

"Please," she heard herself beg. Because she'd gone without the sweet, drenching heat for so long.

Without him.

As if he read her mind, he leaned down. His tongue flicked a ripe nipple, and she gasped. His mouth was hot and wet as he drew her in, tonguing and laving the stiff peak until she arched against him.

"Unzip me," he said when he finally drew away. He caught her hand and pressed it to his crotch.

Her fingers fluttered over the zipper, the metal hot beneath her touch. Because he was hot, his skin on fire. The air around them shimmered, and she could practically see the sparks in the translucent depths of his eyes.

"I can't…" Because if she reached out this time, she wouldn't be able to stop. She would unzip him, roll him over and straddle him, and that would be the kiss of death. He had to be the leader.

"You can," he said. "And you will." He leaned down and flicked her nipple again, teasing and torturing even longer this time until she couldn't not touch him.

The zipper hissed, and he sprang hot and eager into her hands. Her attention riveted on his heated, pulsing flesh. He was as smooth as satin and rock-hard.

She trailed her fingers over him, touching the ripe head of his desire. He jumped in her hands, and she barely resisted the urge to dip her head, to taste him.

Instead, she wrapped her arms around his neck and pulled him down for a kiss that surprised them both. It was a bold move, but not half as aggressive as what she wanted to do to him.

Her passion seemed to feed his, and soon he was back in the driver's seat. He kissed her harder, faster, deeper. He pulled away long enough to peel off the wet jeans and then he joined her on the soft grass.

He parted her legs and settled himself between them. He rasped his erection up and down her slick folds before entering her in one powerful surge.

The sudden sense of fullness deep inside sent shockwaves pulsing through her body. Her inner muscles contracted, sucking him in. Pressure erupted in her belly.

He started to move, plunging and withdrawing, over and over, and the pressure mounted. His movements picked up and he pumped harder, faster, pushing her closer to the edge just the way he had so many times in the past.

But the heat felt sweeter this time, sharper, more intense than anything in her memory.

The pinnacle was steeper this time, the crest higher. When she finally reached the top and plunged over the edge into orgasmic bliss, it was much more powerful than anything she remembered.

Sensation crashed over her and sucked her under for several long moments. Her heart pounded, and her blood rushed. Her body clenched around his and held on. Pleasure drenched her, all-consuming for the next few moments as her heart stopped and her body clenched.

She stared up at him, into him, waiting for the rush of warmth as he followed her over the edge.

But instead of pushing even deeper and letting

himself go, he pulled out a few inches until only the very tip of his erection stayed inside. His muscles bunched as he held himself back and loomed over her. His eyes grew even brighter and a growl rumbled from deep in his chest. He trembled as he drank in the sweet sexual energy of her climax.

She felt the draw where the very tip of his penis nestled inside her slick folds. The tremble of flesh against flesh turned her on as much as the actual sex. Her nipples throbbed, and her clit started to quiver again. Her body vibrated, and sensation rushed through her.

And then all of a sudden it was happening again. Pleasure crashed over her. She cried out, closing her eyes and arching against him for several long moments.

Until her body calmed enough for her to open her eyes.

She found him still poised above her, his body tense, his teeth clamped together as if he'd been waiting on her to look up before he let himself go.

Sheer longing flashed in his gaze. Or so she thought. But then he blinked, and the emotion faded into the icy blue depths of his eyes and he did the last thing she expected.

He pulled away.

"We should be getting back." His voice was gruff as he turned away from her, his erection still rock-hard. He reached for his jeans. "I've got a lot of work to do."

"I. . ." She caught her bottom lip to stop its sudden trembling as she pushed herself into a sitting position and tried to calm the shock beating at her temples. "I— I need to get back to work myself."

Silence stretched around them as he stepped into his jeans and pulled them on. A hiss vibrated up his throat as he tugged the zipper over his erection. She almost reached out for him. A few strokes of her hand, the warm heat of her mouth, and she could give him the release he so desperately needed.

Then again, maybe he didn't need her. Maybe he wasn't aching or hurting.

Maybe he was more than satisfied from her climax alone.

The possibility haunted her as he helped her to her feet. There were no lingering touches. Rather, he dropped her hand as quickly as possible. In the blink of an eye, he stood on the opposite river bank where the motorcycles sat.

By the time she joined him, he'd retrieved the spare shirt he'd mentioned earlier from beneath his seat. He tossed it to her before turning to pick up his own T-shirt that still lay where he'd left it.

Her gaze went to the water. She'd done her striptease on the river, which meant that her own clothes were several feet under by now. She debated a quick dive to see if she could find at least her undies, but Garret straddled his motorcycle and gunned the engine and she knew she didn't have time.

Not if she was going to follow him back.

She slipped the giant T-shirt over her head. The cotton dropped to mid-thigh which afforded her enough modesty to climb onto her own motorcycle.

"Let's go." He didn't wait for a reply. He gunned the

engine, shifted into gear and took off as if the Devil himself were in hot pursuit.

Viv blinked back the sudden stinging behind her eyes, gunned the engine and followed.

You did it, she reminded herself as she trailed behind.

Sex.

Orgasm.

Shazam!

Oddly enough, she didn't feel any more satisfied than when they'd first ridden out to the river.

It was the bike, of course.

She wasn't wearing undies, and the steady pulse of the engine was getting to her.

No way was she feeling so out of sorts because Garret hadn't had his own orgasm. So what if he'd held himself back, content just to drink up her energy?

He was a vampire, and that's what vampires did. Sure, he never would have done such a thing if he'd been human, but he wasn't. And what difference did it make anyway?

She hadn't come to Skull Creek to give him an orgasm. She'd come in pursuit of her own.

Which meant that what he had or hadn't felt didn't concern her. She'd accomplished her goal, end of story.

That's what she told herself. But she couldn't shake the hollowness in the pit of her stomach or the ache in her chest. Feelings that magnified when she followed him into the back parking lot of Skull Creek Choppers.

He was already climbing off his chopper when she killed the engine. "You can leave the keys in the ignition.

I'll grab them later." And then he turned and walked away from her without so much as a "See ya."

Viv watched him disappear through the back door before she climbed off the chopper and headed for her car. A lump worked its way up her throat as she climbed behind the wheel and headed back to the motel.

She swallowed and blinked frantically a few times. She wasn't going to cry. She should be happy. She was happy.

She'd done it. She'd had an honest-to-God orgasm.

And just in the nick of time, she realized when she reached her motel room.

The thought struck the moment she unlocked the door and stared into the pitch-black interior. She stalled in the doorway. Awareness crawled down her spine and her survival instincts fired to life.

Turn. Fight. Run.

No more.

She closed her eyes as the shadows closed in and a hand clamped around her throat.

It was finally time to set things right.

17

IN THE BLINK of an eye, she found herself whirled around and shoved up against the nearest wall by a hard male body. Bright green eyes stared down at her, and her memory stirred.

"Sheriff Keller?" Her gaze sliced through the darkness and drank in the familiar face of Matt Keller, the sheriff who'd threatened her with trespassing and escorted her off the mountain in Washington.

"No, it's the Easter Bunny."

It was him, all right.

He stood well over six feet with dark black hair cut short and neat. A day's growth of stubble shadowed his angular jaw. A scar zig-zagged its way from his temple down his right cheek. He wasn't the most handsome man, but he had a rough edge about him that no doubt attracted more than his share of women.

She wasn't one of them, of course. Despite the hunger that lived and breathed inside of her, she hadn't been the least bit attracted when she'd first met him.

She'd been too preoccupied with her story, too worked up over the strange prickling awareness that Cruz and Molly were catching up to her.

"You went back to the crime scene," he told her, "I know because we found a strange DNA on the front porch." His gaze hardened. "You compromised the evidence."

"I didn't mean to. I—I went back to get a few pictures and I cut myself."

"There was an awful lot of blood for a minor cut."

"I'm a heavy bleeder."

He didn't look as if he bought the explanation, but he let go of her anyway. But not before his gaze brightened to a brilliant, glowing green, and she started to wonder if there was more than rugged good looks feeding Matt Keller's success with the ladies.

Especially when she stared deep into his eyes and saw…nothing. No hang-ups. No family history. No work-related goals or plans for the future. Just a blank wall.

A vampire?

Nah. She would have sensed as much. As it was, she felt only a humming awareness, as if Molly and Cruz were close. But not too close.

Not yet.

She stared into Matt's eyes, searching for some clue that he was anything other than a human who'd managed to shield his thoughts. Some could, particularly if they knew there were vampires out there trying to crawl into their heads. She focused all of her attention, determined to crack the wall and see the truth.

As if he knew what she was up to, he turned away,

averting those glowing green eyes as he flipped on a nearby light.

"There," he said. "That's better." He closed the motel room door. "Now we can talk."

"About?"

"The Butcher. You went back to the scene of the crime. You took pictures. You gathered evidence. I want it."

"But I didn't. I meant to, but then I—" she swallowed "—cut myself and I had to leave to find a first aid kit."

He didn't buy it, but he didn't call her out, either. "Still, you've been following the case from day one. The West Hollywood murder. The Portland couple. You've taken pictures and asked questions and I figure you know a helluva lot more than you realize."

"So you came all the way to Texas to pick my brain?"

"I'm this close to cracking the case—and that's the problem. I'm too close to the killer." He shook his head. "I thought if we compared notes, it might help me figure out what I'm missing. This guy claims he's a celebrity, and you know celebrities."

Which is why she'd gotten involved in the first place. Gossip rags didn't cover grisly murders unless there was the possibility of something really sensational. Like Brad Pitt or Tom Hanks or some other A-list actor being possessed by the ghost of Ted Bundy.

It wasn't all that likely, but then neither was the three-headed alien baby born in Oregon.

"I seriously doubt my notes could help you very much."

"I'll be the judge of that once you hand them over."

"I'd be happy to, but I gave everything to my editor at the magazine." Along with her resignation. She scribbled down a phone number. "Call and ask for Louise. Tell her I gave you the number. I'm sure she can e-mail you a copy of my notes."

He nodded. "I talked to her when I started looking for you." He must have noticed her curious expression because he added, "I followed your paper trail. You used your Visa to buy the airline ticket from L.A. to San Antonio. From there, I followed you to a gas station about twenty miles up on the interstate. I made a few phone calls to the surrounding towns until I hit pay dirt here. Some clerk answered at the motel, and when I mentioned your name, he seemed nervous. Now I know why."

"You couldn't have just tracked down my cell phone number and called me up?"

He shrugged. "I didn't think about it."

Yeah, right. A phone number was more than a logical answer if all he'd wanted was to ask her a few questions. Unless he hadn't been half as anxious to talk to her as he was to find out her whereabouts.

To find her.

Unconsciously, her hand went to her throat, her fingers searching for the comforting warmth of her St. Benedict medal before she remembered that she'd stashed it in her suitcase.

"Sorry about the choke hold," he said, noticing the path of her hand. "You broke the law once, and I wasn't one hundred percent sure you wouldn't add assaulting a police officer to your rap sheet."

"I doubt I could take you."

He didn't look as if he believed the statement anymore than she did. As if he knew she wasn't the mild-mannered reporter she pretended to be.

"I seriously doubt you'll find any solid leads in my notes," she blurted, eager to ignore the strange thought. He wasn't a vampire, which meant he couldn't know the truth about her.

"I'll be the judge of that." He stashed the slip of paper with the contact information in his shirt pocket. "I'm staying just down the hall. I'll give your editor a call first thing in the morning. You'll be around tomorrow, right? In case I need clarification on anything?" She nodded, and he stared at her again, his gaze glowing, searching. "We'll talk once I figure things out," he finally said.

"I hope you find what you're looking for," she called out to his retreating back.

"I already did," he said and then he disappeared.

What was that supposed to mean?

The question haunted her as she stared at the closed door. He'd gone to a lot of trouble to find her just to get his hands on her notes.

Unless the notes were just a cover, and he wasn't half as interested in her research as he was in her.

"I already did."

His words echoed in her head, and his image flashed in her mind—his knowing expression, his odd gaze.

She'd noticed his eyes back in Washington when he'd escorted her off the mountain. But then she'd been

ambushed by Cruz and Molly. She'd forgotten all about
Keller, about the strange glow of his eyes and the fact
that no matter how hard she'd tried, she hadn't been
able to read his thoughts.

She'd forgotten about everything except surviving.

The notion stirred her suspicion.

Sheriff Matt Keller had shown up just minutes
before Molly and Cruz back in Washington. Had he led
them to her?

Was he leading them to her now?

The question stalled in her head and sent a burst of
fear through her. She threw the lock on the door and
peered past the edge of the curtains.

The shadowy walkway remained empty. In the
distance, she could see a light on in the lobby. Eldin sat
behind the registration desk, his gaze hooked on a nearby
television, his hands busy with a platter of nachos.

Relief swept through. A crazy feeling because she'd
already accepted her fate. The possibility that Sheriff
Keller might be speeding up her fate by leading Molly
and Cruz to her shouldn't have freaked her out.

It did.

Not because she was afraid to die, but because she
was afraid to die without knowing the truth about her
feelings for Garret.

The truth crystallized as she stood there in the
window, her hand gripping the drape, her body still
throbbing from their earlier encounter.

She wanted to right off the pounding of her heart and
the trembling of her hands as fear. Because there was

a very real possibility that Keller was linked to Cruz and Molly. But she knew it was more.

It was Garret.

Because she loved him?

She'd never thought so. Sure, she'd pretended that what she'd felt had been the real thing back then, but she'd never known. How could she? Her parents' relationship had been one of fear and dominance. There'd been no kind words, no soft feelings. She'd never seen love firsthand, and she'd never, ever felt it. While her mother had, indeed, cared for her, she'd been too busy worrying over her own survival to have anything left over for her daughter. And her father… He'd shown her only cruelty and hatred. Likewise, her existence had been a string of meaningless encounters, all fueled by hunger.

And so she'd written off the tingling in her stomach, the trembling in her knees and the strange warmth in her chest as pure, uncomplicated lust.

Physical rather than emotional.

She'd convinced herself that the only reason she'd reacted to him so intensely way back when was because he'd taken the lead and swept her off her feet. He'd treated her like a woman and so she'd reacted like one.

But if she gave in to the hungry beast inside of her and swept him off his feet, she wouldn't come anywhere close to having an orgasm.

Right?

Maybe.

Probably.

Still, she couldn't help but wonder as she stepped into the shower, if maybe there was more to it.

If he was more.

Maybe she reacted to him not because he was the only man who'd ever taken the lead, but because he was the only man, period.

Her one true love.

It shouldn't have mattered. Regardless, it wouldn't change her fate. If anything, it would make her all the more determined to set things right. She knew that, but she still couldn't close her eyes and push him out of her head when she finally toweled off and crawled into bed.

Instead, she tossed and turned and ended up staring at the ceiling.

She'd spent far too long—almost two centuries to be exact—wondering what it would feel like to love and be loved. While she had no illusions that Garret felt anything that strong for her——he'd been far too controlled tonight—she knew there was a real possibility that she loved him.

She climbed from the bed and reached for her clothes. While she had no clue if what she felt even came close to the real thing, she wasn't going to pass up the chance to find out.

To feel it. To really and truly feel it.

If only for a little while.

18

"THE MAN'S REAL NAME is John Darrington. It's probably an alias like the other, but there's no way to know for sure without checking further. His last known address is in Chicago," Dalton MacGregor's voice carried over the cell phone the minute Garret picked up. "I'm e-mailing it to you right now, along with my notes."

Garret paused, pitch fork in one hand, his cell phone clenched tight in the other. "You're sure it's him?"

"Based on the information that you gave me, this is the man you're looking for. He had actual contact with the blogger who gave the description of him. Based on everyone I've talked to, it's him, right down to the medallion that you described."

Garret could still feel the cold metal dangling over him, brushing his skin as the figure loomed over him.

"Do you want me to fly to Chicago and check it out myself?"

"You've done enough. I'll take it from here. Send me everything, and I'll leave first thing in the morning." Garret hung up and dialed Jake.

"We've got him," he told his friend.

"Really?" Excitement fueled the one word. "You're not shitting me, are you?"

"I'm flying out at sundown tomorrow to check it out. Twenty-four hours from now, you just might be getting ready to watch the sun rise."

"I'll go with you."

"No. You stay with Nikki and the others. This is something I need to do by myself."

Garret needed to face his past, to finally see the man's face. He wanted the bits and pieces of what he remembered to finally fit together in a clear, solid picture.

And then he wanted to shatter that picture and destroy the man who'd destroyed him.

He did.

So why didn't he feel even a fifth the excitement he'd heard in Jake's voice?

Because killing the Ancient One wouldn't solve Garret's problem.

It wouldn't make Viv love him the way he loved her.

Wait a second. Love? She couldn't love him any more than he could love her.

Hell, he didn't love her.

Tonight had proved as much. He'd held tight to his control and resisted the urge to climax.

Barely.

The realization followed him around the barn as he pitched hay for the three mares he had stabled inside. They were about to foal and he wanted them comfortable.

The horses stirred, dancing around their stalls, completely alert to his presence and fearful of it.

For now.

But come tomorrow night things would be different. He could help foal the mares, and he could start taming Delilah. He would have his life back. His humanity.

If only he wanted it half as much as he wanted Viv.

The truth pushed and pulled and haunted him for the next half hour as he tried to work off the sexual energy stringing his body tight. He couldn't, regardless of how hard he pitched or how fast he moved.

He wanted her.

In a way he'd never wanted any woman before.

Because she meant more to him than an easy lay and a way to feed the beast inside of him.

Much, much more.

He didn't want to believe it, but then she appeared in the barn doorway, and the sight of her outlined in the moonlight stopped him cold.

There was nothing provocative about her faded pink sweats and worn tennis shoes, but his gut tightened anyway. Her eyes sparked a bright, brilliant blue, and the minute his gaze locked with hers, his heart stalled in his chest.

He loved her, all right, and that made him all the more determined to resist her when she stepped forward. He'd given her his heart once before. He wasn't about to make the same mistake twice.

No, he would play it cool. Controlled.

"What are you doing here?" he asked, trying to sound indifferent.

"I thought I'd see where you live." She glanced around. "It's nice."

"It's a barn."

"Yeah, well—" she shrugged "—it's a nice barn."

The tension eased for a few moments, and he couldn't help the grin that tugged at the corner of his mouth. "I'm really busy. I've got a lot to do before I fly out tomorrow afternoon."

The news seemed to startle her. "Where are you going?"

"Chicago."

"Business?"

"It's personal."

"Oh." She looked surprised, and a little hurt, as if she suspected he might be flying off to meet someone.

Some woman.

"I've got an address," he heard himself blurt. He knew what she was thinking, and while it shouldn't have mattered, it did. "By this time tomorrow night, the Ancient One will be history." He shook his head. "I'm through living like this."

She stiffened. "Is it so bad?" she finally asked after a long, silent moment. "Being a vampire?"

"Isn't it?"

"It could be worse." She shrugged. "My actual life wasn't all that great, so I guess I don't have much to compare it to."

"You could, you know." He wasn't sure why he said the words, except that she looked so sad and lonely all of a sudden, and he couldn't resist the sudden urge to ease her pain. "You could find your father and break the curse," he reminded her.

"By killing him?" She shook her head. "I could never do that." She seemed to gather her resolve. "I wouldn't do that."

"You don't owe him, Viv. Not loyalty. Not respect. Nothing."

"But I owe myself." Her gaze locked with his. "Don't you see? I can't do to him what he did to my mother. No matter how much he deserves it. That would make me no better than he was." She seemed to gather her courage. "I'm different. I am. I don't hurt people. Not on purpose. I…" Her eyes burned with desperation, and he had the sudden thought that she wanted to tell him something.

But then she seemed to think better of it. Determination lit her expression, burning up everything else, and she reached for the hem of her T-shirt instead. "We still have some unfinished business," she said. And then she pulled the cotton up and over her head.

She wasn't wearing a bra. Her bare breasts trembled as she tossed the cotton aside and reached for the drawstring on her pants. Her fingers hesitated, and he knew then that she wasn't half as confident as she pretended to be. And damned if that knowledge didn't slither across the distance to him and keep him rooted to the spot when he should have turned and hauled ass the other way.

He didn't need another test on his already tentative control.

Oh, but he wanted one. One more touch. One more kiss. One more chance to be inside of her.

She stripped completely down and stepped toward him.

Dropping to her knees in front of him, she gripped his zipper. Metal hissed, and he sprang into her hands. She trailed her fingers over him, circling the ripe, plump head of his erection.

"I wanted so much to touch you before. Too much, that's why I didn't."

He groaned. A drop of pearly liquid beaded on the head of his penis. She leaned down and closed her lips around the smooth ridge. Her fangs grazed the tender underside, and a bolt of electricity zinged through his body. Desire rushed hot on its heels. She suckled him then, and his cock throbbed in the warm heat of her mouth.

He ground his teeth together, fighting the sensation that gripped his body. He had to hold on, to hold back.

At the same time, with her mouth drawing on him and her hands tugging at his waistband, peeling the denim down his hips, it was hard to remember his objective.

Brakes, his conscience quipped. *Put on the friggin' brakes.*

He couldn't.

He pushed himself deeper into her mouth, his hands cradling her head as she sucked on him, and then he waited to see what she would do next. A long list of possibilities rushed through his head, but none of them were half as exciting as what she was doing right now.

Because it was real.

Because she was real.

Because he loved her.

Viv's last little bit of hesitation vanished when she glanced up and saw the dark desire swimming in the depths of Garret's eyes. He was following her, relishing her touch, eager for it.

She sucked him harder for several more moments before she finally pulled away and stripped the jeans completely down his legs. Then she pulled him down to the ground, urging him backwards onto the soft cushion of the hay. She climbed over him and sank down onto his hard, hot length.

Flesh met flesh as her body closed around his and ecstasy pulsed through her.

She moved, rotating her hips, her inner muscles contracting, sucking at him as the delicious pressure built inside of her.

A groan worked its way up his throat, and she saw the startled glimpse in his gaze, as if he felt everything as intensely as she did, and feared it.

When he grasped her buttocks, she thought he meant to slow her down, but he didn't.

His voice, raw and husky, echoed in her ears. "I've missed you so much." His fingers sank into her flesh. He tightened his pelvis and thrust upward at the same time that she pushed down, and it was like pure magic.

Sensation swept her up and pushed her to the edge as she sank deliciously deep. The sensation receded when she withdrew, and then hit her again when she slid back down.

Up and down.

Over and over.

Again and again.

Until pleasure crashed over her, and the most decadent orgasm flowed through her body. Along with a rush of pure joy that had nothing to do with the way his body pulsed deep inside of her and everything to do with the way he was looking at her.

His eyes blazed with passion and desire and a possessive light that said he would never, ever let her go again.

His fingers tightened on her bottom. The muscles in his arms bulged. His body went taut and a deep, husky growl rumbled from his throat.

His eyes fired even hotter, and his fangs flashed in the moonlight.

Before she could stop herself, she threw her head back and offered her neck to him.

She had the fleeting thought that he would refuse. While she truly felt something for him, she had no illusions that his feelings went any deeper than the lust that lived and breathed inside of him. No way would he want to bond himself to her.

But then his mouth closed over her neck, and his tongue stroked her pulse point. And then…he sank his fangs into her.

She'd thought the orgasm phenomenal, but it paled in comparison to the dizzying rush that crashed over her in that next instant, gripping every inch of her body.

She rode the tide of pleasure, holding tight to his shoulders as he feasted on her and heightened the sensation.

But then he pulled away, and the feelings disappeared.

He stared up at her, disbelief blazing in his eyes. Reality crashed down around her, and she knew then that her worst fear had been realized.

He'd drank from her, bonded with her, and now he knew her head. Her heart.

He knew the truth.

"You did this to me," he growled, and the betrayal in his gaze hurt far worse than the stake she'd envisioned in her dreams. "You."

19

Garret didn't pull out a stake and punish Viv for turning him all those years ago.

No, what he did next was much more painful.

He pulled away from her.

"I couldn't just let you die," she said as he turned his back to her and reached for his clothes.

"It was you," he said again as if he couldn't quite believe it. But he did. She saw it in the stiffness of his body as he yanked on his pants, the tense set of his shoulders as he worked at the zipper on his jeans. Anger warred inside of him, battling with the hurt.

"I'm so sorry," she said, but he didn't so much as spare her a glance as he pulled on his boots and pushed to his feet.

She didn't blame him. She'd lied to him too many times for him to believe her now.

She'd lied to herself.

No more.

He knew the truth, and so did she.

She loved him. She always had, she'd just been too naive to realize it. Too scared. She'd been hurt so much

by the people that she loved and so she hadn't wanted
to love anyone.

She hadn't wanted to love him.

But she did, and so she let him walk away. Words
were little solace for the pain she'd inflicted on him. An
apology wasn't going to erase the past. There was only
one thing that could do that.

She pulled on her clothes and headed back to town
to confront Matt Keller.

If her instincts were right about him, Cruz and Molly
wouldn't be far away.

"I'M SORRY."

Her soft, desperate voice echoed in Garret's head as
he gunned the engine on his motorcycle and hit the dirt
trail that led across the North pasture.

A rut caught the front tire, and the handlebars shook
with the force of it. The custom chopper wasn't made
for this and he damn well knew it, but he couldn't stop
himself. He tightened his grip and opened the bike up
as fast as it would go. He had to outrun the voice. The
past.

The truth.

She was sorry.

He knew it as surely as he knew the sun would rise
in a few hours. The knowledge sat deep down in his
bones. His heart.

She hadn't wanted to turn him anymore than she'd
wanted to turn all the others in her past. He'd seen their
faces when he'd drank from her—faces that haunted

her dreams and refused her any peace—and he'd felt her remorse.

The bike jumped, startling him as much as the regret now swimming inside of him. Her regret.

For ruining so many lives. For betraying him.

She hadn't meant to.

Rather, she'd saved him because she hadn't been able to bear losing him. And then she'd turned her back on him because she hadn't been able to bear his hatred should he discover the truth.

Because she loved him.

Then and now.

Always.

The realization sent a burst of pure happiness through him, followed by a rush of dread. He gunned the engine faster, pushing the bike as fast and as far as it would go. Because maybe, just maybe if he burned up the engine he could escape the inevitable that beat at his temples.

Viv was the vampire. The one he and Jake and Dillon had been searching for all these months. The key to his humanity. The answer to his desperate prayers.

The Ancient One.

And she had to die.

It was the only way to free all of them. To free himself. He was tired of being a slave to the beast inside. He wanted to be normal again. To laugh. To love. To be whole.

He slammed on the brakes and skidded to a stop. The transmission screamed as he swerved the bike in a one-eighty and shifted into gear. And then he did what he should have done in the first place—he headed for town.

It was time to reclaim his humanity.

"WHERE ARE THEY?" Viv demanded when Sheriff Matt Keller hauled open the motel room door after her second knock.

"Do you know what time it is?" He wiped at his tired-looking face and glared at her.

"Cruz and Molly. You know them, right?" She pushed her way into his room and kicked the door shut. Her gaze sliced through the darkness, touching every corner as if she expected the duo of vampires to pop out at her.

Or rather, she hoped. Then it would all be over and the pain twisting at her heart would end.

"You led them to me in Washington, and you're leading them to me now," she told him. "Where are they? Just tell me, and I'll go to them. I'm tired of waiting. I want this over with."

He flipped on a nearby light. The small bulb pushed back the shadows to reveal a worn duffel bag sitting next to the bed. His badge and gun lay on the nightstand next to a half empty bottle of soda. He eyed her. "Have you been drinking?"

"I know you know where they are. Tell me."

"I don't have a friggin' clue what you're talking about, lady, but I'll make sure to add 'crazy' to the other list of offenses on your rap sheet."

"I know you didn't come here just to get my notes

on the Butcher. You're working for Cruz and Molly. What are you? A blood slave?" That would explain why she hadn't been able to read him. If he were feeding one of the vampires, they would have control over him. They could block his thoughts. They could wipe his mind clean until he was little more than a zombie.

But they couldn't make his eyes glow.

She watched as the green depths magnified, growing brighter and more intense.

"What are you?" she asked again. As much as she was hoping for the blood slave explanation, she had a gut feeling she wasn't even close.

"I should be asking you that question." He stepped closer then. "I know you're not human. I can feel it." His tall body loomed over her, backing her up a few steps.

Insane, right? She was a big, bad vampire.

But Matt Keller seemed just as dangerous. Strength rolled off him, along with a feral air that stalled her heartbeat and made her wonder if he didn't intend to save Cruz and Molly the trouble and kill her himself.

"You're like me, aren't you?" he demanded. Before she could respond, he continued, "You are. You have to be. You're too strong to be human. Too different." His gaze grew brighter, hotter and his mouth opened. She saw the teeth then. Not just a pair of fangs, but two full rows of them. A growl vibrated up his throat. A wildness lit his eyes and carved his expression. Reality dawned.

"You're a werewolf?" It had been hard enough accepting the truth of what she'd become, and she'd lived every painful moment of the change. Denial pumped through her. There had to be another explanation. "I don't believe this. There's no such thing."

His lips pulled back and he growled, a strange, inhuman sound that slid into her ears and chased away all doubt.

"Oh, my God."

"God didn't have anything to do with it." His expression relaxed, and the savage air that had gripped him seemed to ease. The muscles in his face shifted, his bones pushing and pulling until the familiar face of Sheriff Matt Keller stared back at her. "It's genetic, at least that's what my father told me. And it's rare."

"I hate to break this to you, but I don't howl at the full moon." When he gave her a sharp look, she added, "Not that your instincts were wrong. I'm not human, but I'm not a werewolf, either. I'm a vampire."

He looked at her as if she'd just confessed to giving birth to the three-headed alien in Oregon. "There's no such thing."

This from the Wolf Man? "Listen, buddy, if werewolves can exist, so can vampires."

"Werewolves don't exist. Just one. Me." He looked so alone in that next instant that she could actually understand why he'd come all the way from Washington. "I'm all that's left since my folks died. That's why I was so determined to find you. I thought maybe... Finally..." He shook his head and eyed her. "You're sure you're not a werewolf?"

"Trust me." To prove her point, she flashed him her fangs. She went on to tell him the short version of her life story—namely that she was being hunted by two vamps determined to destroy her. She finished with "That's why I barged in just now. I thought you knew them. I'm really sorry." She glanced at the rumpled sheets. "I didn't mean to wake you."

"I couldn't sleep anyway." He eyed the open window. Beyond, the moon hung huge and round, and his eyes glowed for a split-second. "It's two days until the moon is at its fullest. I'm supposed to mate then. At least, I think I am. But then, I've never actually done it because there are no female werewolves around. Which means I end up with a human female." He shook his head. "It's not the same. Not that I actually know, I just feel it. I keep thinking there ought to be more excitement to it. More oomph…" He let his voice trail off as if he'd already said too much. "I don't mean to dump all of this on you. I just don't get a chance to talk about it much. Don't sweat the barging in. I never really sleep much, especially this time of the month. I've tried pills, warm milk, the works, but nothing helps."

"Do you really howl at the moon?"

"Do you really suck blood?"

"Point made." She grinned and he grinned and despite the fact that he was a werewolf and she was a vampire, she actually felt a sort of camaraderie. Not the same connection she felt with Garret, of course. That was deeper, more profound.

But this… This was nice.

Suddenly, she could understand why Garret was so anxious to find and kill the vampire that turned him.

He wasn't just doing it for himself.

He was doing it for his friends.

At least, he wanted to. But he wouldn't get the chance because Cruz and Molly were about to beat him to it.

She knew it the moment the hair on the back of her neck stood on end. Awareness raced down her spine. Every muscle in her body went tight. The door crashed open behind her.

Viv whirled in time to see Cruz lunging for her, a stake in his hand and murder on his mind.

20

VIV DIDN'T MOVE as the vampire lunged. Instead, she closed her eyes and braced herself for the pain.

But instead of feeling the sharp stab of the stake, she felt Matt Keller's hand on her arm.

"Run," he told her as he shoved her out of the way. The stake caught him in the shoulder, and a loud howl filled the room.

His eyes glowed, and he reached for Cruz, his hands going for the vampire's throat. Before his fingers could make contact, Molly flew into the room.

"No!" Viv cried, but the female vampire had already caught Keller and jerked him backwards. Her fangs sank into his neck.

She lunged to her feet and rushed forward, but Cruz caught her by the hair.

"You're going to die this time," he spat as he yanked her around and shoved her back up against the wall.

Her head smashed into the sheetrock. Pain split open her skull, and her gut clenched. Anger rolled through her, along with the need for survival.

Live, the beast chanted. *Fight. Destroy.*

"Do it," she ground out. It was too late to save Keller, but it wasn't too late to save everyone else. "Just go ahead and do it."

He raised the stake high into the air and she closed her eyes.

"No!" Garret's voice pushed past the frantic beat of her heart. Her eyes snapped open in time to see him catch the stake mid-air.

Cruz turned on him, his gaze flashing red fury as he lunged at Garret.

Viv moved forward to help, but Molly tackled her. She hit the wall again, and chunks of plaster flew. Blood dripped from the woman's mouth and streamed down her neck as she gripped Viv by the collar and threw her against the opposite wall.

Her vision blurred from the impact, but a loud wail yanked her back to the present.

Viv scrambled to her feet just as Garret sank the stake into the crazed vampire's chest.

Cruz stumbled backwards, a surprised look on his face. He teetered and then he collapsed.

"Molly." The name tumbled from his lips and then his body went deathly still.

"Baby?" Molly crumbled to the floor next to Cruz and touched his face. "Come on. Open your eyes," she begged. "Don't do this to me. It's you and me. Together. Forever. Remember?" She shook her head frantically as she touched his chest. Her hand closed around the stake. "Forever." She pulled the stake free.

Just when Viv thought she meant to turn it on herself, she whirled. She flew at Viv, but Garret caught her.

He anchored one hand around her waist and reached for the stake with his other. He was an older vampire and, therefore, stronger. She soon went slack in his grasp.

"I'm only going to say this once." He tossed her to the ground and held up the stake. "You can end up like your friend there, or you can get the hell out. It's your choice, and you'd better make it fast. Before I change my mind."

"Kiss my ass." Molly lunged at him, in full attack mode.

Viv tackled her, sending her sideways. They both crashed into the door. She grabbed Molly's hair and hung on, fighting to keep her down and away from Garret.

She didn't have to fight long. One minute she was staring up at Molly, holding her at arm's length, and the next, the woman went rigid.

Molly gasped, and blood spurted from her mouth as she pitched forward. Viv rolled out from under her, and that's when she saw the sharp piece of the wooden doorframe that protruded from between her shoulder blades.

Garret stood just inches away, his eyes blazing with a protective light and something else. Something that stalled her heartbeat.

"Are you okay?"

"You saved me," she said accusingly. "Why?"

Because I love you.

That's what his gaze said, but she didn't just want to see it. She needed to hear it.

Before she could open her mouth again, a groan carried from the far corner. She turned just as Matt Keller staggered to his feet. Blood still gushed from his neck, and he looked dangerously pale, but already the wound had started to close.

"Don't tell me. Werewolves have rejuvenating capabilities."

"You know it." He staggered back a few steps and collapsed on the edge of the bed.

"Maybe you should lie down." Viv reached him in the blink of an eye and urged him back down. She checked the wound, and sure enough, the skin had already started to knit back together. "I know how this goes for vampires. A little sleep, and we're fine."

He nodded. "Sleep is good."

"Do you need anything?"

"Just some peace and quiet."

Viv nodded and turned to Garret. "We'd better get them out of here." She motioned to Molly and Cruz. They were still intact, but come sunup, their bodies would start to disintegrate.

Garret nodded, and they spent the next half hour moving the bodies out to his barn. Once they finished, she turned on him.

She'd waited long enough for the truth.

"You never answered my question. Why did you face off with Cruz? You should have been helping him."

"I won't let you die."

"You don't get to make that decision. My father beat you to it."

"No, he didn't." He shook his head. "He took your humanity, but he didn't take your soul, Viv. You're still a good person. You weren't trying to hurt Cruz and Molly. You helped them. You did what they asked of you."

"You never asked."

"I would have. If I had known what you were, I would have. For the chance to be with you again, to touch you, to kiss you, to talk to you, I would have begged."

"What are you saying?"

"That I love you. I've always loved you."

"Because I was a vampire."

"I loved you then—I love you now—in spite of the fact that you're a vampire. And I won't let you sacrifice yourself. You didn't set out to hurt anyone. You did what you thought was right."

"But—"

"There is no but." Certainty gleamed in his eyes, along with a brilliant light that filled her with a burst of warmth. Because he did love her, and he meant every word he said.

"You gave them all a chance to right their wrongs," he went on. "A chance to live. To love. If they didn't want that, if the hunger led them down the wrong path, that's their problem. You don't owe anyone."

But Garret did.

Jake. Dillon. While he hadn't initially attacked them

on purpose, they were his friends. They'd been his friends even though he'd doomed them. They'd stood by him, waiting patiently, searching for the Ancient One.

For Viv.

He wouldn't give her up.

At the same time, he couldn't let his friends down. He'd been content as a vampire until he'd gotten to know Jake. Jake had forced him to remember the man he'd once been, to miss his humanity, because Jake missed his.

Garret saw the truth when he looked at Jake and Nikki. They wanted so much to be together. To be normal. And they were depending on Garret to make it happen.

But Garret couldn't sacrifice the woman he loved—he wouldn't. Tonight had proved as much. They were bonded now. She was his, now and always, and he would defend her until the last dying beat of his heart.

No, he wouldn't sacrifice Viv so that his friends could walk in the sunlight.

He wouldn't have to.

He'd been the one to take Jake's humanity from him, and he could give it back.

"No." Viv shook her head. "You're not going to—"

He pressed a fingertip to her lips. "No more talk. I need to be inside of you tonight."

Their last night.

Because Garret was through living with the guilt and the regret. He owed Jake, and it was time to ante up.

He scooped Viv into his arms and headed for the main house.

21

He CARRIED HER into the house and down the steps into the basement.

His room. She knew it as she stared at the large area with its open rafters and king-size bed.

He dropped her to her feet, flipped on a light switch and then turned back to her. His gaze burned with an intensity that made her body tremble.

She knew what he was going to do.

Not because she read it in his thoughts. Despite the fact that they were bonded, she still couldn't see inside his head because he'd put up a mental wall to shut her out.

No, she felt the truth in the urgent way he touched her, kissed her, as if he wanted to brand this moment into his memory.

She forced her mouth from his. "You can't—" she started, but then he kissed her again, silencing her words.

She slid her arms around him and held him tight, refusing to let go. Not now as he made love to her, and not afterward.

Not ever.

She drew a ragged breath when he tore his mouth from hers to leave a fiery trail down the length of her neck to the hollow between her breasts. Then he released her, his hands going to the buttons of her blouse, his movements urgent as if they had not a moment to spare.

He pushed the edges open and unhooked her bra, baring her aching breasts. Dipping his head, he closed his mouth over one swollen nipple and greedily sucked the sensitive flesh.

She matched his urgency with her own as her hands found the waistband of his jeans. She heard the groan that rumbled from his throat as she trailed her fingers over the bulge of the material. Impatiently she tugged at the zipper and dipped her hands inside.

Hot and hard, his shaft pulsed, swelling even more when she brushed her fingers along its silky length.

He lifted his head and captured her with his heated gaze, stoking the fire already raging inside her. She kissed the pulse at the base of his neck, her hands moving up and down his arousal. She rained kisses over his chest, laving his nipples with her tongue.

His arms wrapped tight around her as he pulled her even closer. "I need to feel your heat around me, your sweet fangs in my neck," he said, his lips a soft vibration on hers.

Then he kissed her again, plunging his tongue inside to explore and savor. He grazed the very tip of one fang, and she felt the stroke between her legs.

When he moved his mouth to leave a burning path

down her neck, she tilted back her head, pleasure rushing to her brain and building the anticipation. His tongue traced the slope of her breast, down around its fullness, and a cry tore from her lips the moment he found her nipple again.

Viv buried her hands in his hair, holding him close, arching her breast into the moistness of his mouth. His fangs were sharp, prickling her soft skin but not biting her. No, he wanted what she'd held back from him the last time.

He sucked, and she felt the waves of heat build inside her, rising higher like molten lava in a volcano, until she felt ready to erupt.

She wouldn't. Not yet. Not until they were really and truly one.

In one swift motion, he unzipped her jeans and pushed them down, making quick work of his own. Then he locked her in his powerful arms and lifted her.

She clung to him, wrapping her legs around him as he slid her down onto his rigid length, the delicious friction sending jolts of electricity shooting through her body, singeing every nerve until she burned as hot as the man inside her.

She didn't know when he moved them. She only felt the bed against her back, the pulsing heat between her legs. Lifting her hips, she grasped his muscled buttocks and pulled him closer, deeper, her desire for him overriding all else.

She rose to meet each fierce thrust, taking all that he could give and wanting more.

So much more.

They came together in a frenzied, primitive act. Hunger made them burn, desperation a potent aphrodisiac that heightened their senses and stirred their appetite.

She reached for him, pulling him down as she felt the first waves of pleasure begin. The beast rose inside of her, and she didn't fight it this time. Need rushed through her, and her entire body went tight. A hiss worked its way up her throat, and she drew back her lips.

His pulse pounded against her tongue, begging her to sink her fangs deep, but she couldn't bring herself to take his blood. She'd taken far too much from him already.

"You didn't take." His voice was gruff against the shell of her ear. "You gave. You wanted me to live and so you gave me back the life that those bandits took from me. You don't owe me anything, baby. I owe you." His fingers splayed at the base of her head, and he pulled her closer, pressing her fangs against his neck until they sank deep.

His sweet essence filled her mouth, and a burst of electricity sizzled across her nerve endings.

"Drink," he urged, and she couldn't stop herself.

She drew him in, relishing the missile of heat that spread through her body and firebombed between her legs.

She sucked harder, faster, feasting at his neck the way her body feasted on his rock-hard erection.

Arching her body, she pulled him in even deeper. He growled and bucked and spilled himself deep inside.

She held on to him as he gave himself to her. His blood. His body. His soul.

The realization hit her, and she forced her mouth away. She stared up at him and saw the emotion blazing in his eyes.

Even more, she felt it in the way he covered her mouth with his own and kissed her. Slowly. Tenderly.

He loved her.

And she loved him.

And for the next few moments, the world seemed to fall away as she clung to him and he held her tight.

"I'm not letting you go," she murmured against his neck, her voice thick with conviction.

She'd been powerless to save her mother all those years ago, but she wasn't powerless now. And she wasn't going to turn her back and walk away from him again.

She would beg. She would plead. And he would listen. He wouldn't leave her.

He wouldn't.

That's what she told herself. But as the minutes slipped by and dawn approached, she couldn't shake the sinking feeling that in his head, in his heart, he was already gone.

HE WAS SOUND ASLEEP.

Viv stood next to the bed and stared down at Garret's muscular body sprawled across the white sheets. He lay on his stomach, his arm still stretched out beside him, covering the indentation her body had made.

He hadn't budged when she'd slipped from the bed, despite the fact that it was still dark outside and he should be at the peak of his strength right now, particularly since they'd just had sex.

But as much energy as she'd given, she'd taken in return by drinking from him, and so he was wiped out. He needed at least an hour or two of sleep to regain his strength.

Then he would climb from the bed and do the unthinkable.

If she didn't do something first.

She touched the smooth sinewy skin of one shoulder and pressed a soft kiss against his temple.

And then Viv pulled on her clothes, grabbed her purse and went to save Garret Sawyer from himself.

IT WAS ALMOST FIVE in the morning, and everything in town had long since closed up shop for the night. The streets were dark and shadowed as Viv drove the short distance to Skull Creek Choppers. The small neon sign blazed in the window. Her senses went into overload, buzzing and humming from being so close to the two vampires inside.

She pulled into the back parking lot, killed her engine and climbed from the front seat. The door was locked, and she knocked. Doubt crawled up and down her spine as she waited for someone to answer. She almost called it quits.

Almost.

But she loved Garret too much to let him sacrifice

so much for her. She knew he was trying to save her, and she wasn't going to let him. Not again.

She was through taking from Garret. It was time for her to give back.

The door opened, and she found herself staring at a tall, handsome vampire. He had long dark hair, blue eyes and a puzzled expression.

"Jake McCann?" she asked, and he nodded.

"My name is Viviana Darland. I have something you want, and I need to give it back." And then she walked into Skull Creek Choppers, spilled her guts about the past and the future and what was going to happen if Jake didn't pop a stake into her right here and now.

And then she waited for him to take the decision out of Garret's hands and put them all out of their misery.

22

GARRET PARKED HIS pick-up near the gate of the eastern pasture and climbed out. A quick leap, and he stood on the other side of the fence where he kept the bucking horses. They were spread out. One stood in the far corner chewing on a hay bale. A few others had galloped over the ridge when they'd heard his pick-up. Only Delilah stood nearby, munching on the remains of one of the hay bales he'd dropped off earlier that week.

"Easy, girl. I'm not here to bother you." Garret held up his hands. "Not this time."

She danced backwards a few steps and eyed him, her eyes wide, fearful, as if she didn't trust him.

She didn't, and she never would, and it didn't matter anymore. Because Viviana Darland loved him.

The truth sang through his head and relaxed his tight muscles. She'd loved him as a man, and she loved him as a vampire and that emotion filled the emptiness that had haunted him for so long.

He realized now that all of the desperate attempts to reclaim his humanity hadn't been because he'd missed what he'd once been…but because he'd hated what he'd become. Restless. Lonely. Empty. He hadn't wanted to be a man again half as much as he'd wanted to feel whole.

The way he'd felt during those few weeks when he'd been with Viv.

But then she'd walked away.

That's what had destroyed him. Not losing his humanity, but losing her. He hadn't spent the past century regretting what he'd become. Other than not being able to tell his folks goodbye, he'd actually been content being a vampire. Sure, he wasn't too keen on the yearly turning, but he'd learned how to control it, with the exception of Jake and Dillon. And while he regretted biting them, he couldn't regret the bond they'd forged.

They were his friends.

His family.

No, he'd come to appreciate the perks of being a vampire. He liked being strong. Reading minds. Being great in bed.

Until he'd watched Jake fall in love with Nikki. Then he'd remembered what it was like to be in love himself—really and truly in love—and he'd missed it.

He'd missed Viv.

She'd come back to him now and given him the most precious gift of all—her love—and he owed her.

His love.

His protection.

He'd already eliminated the vampires threatening her existence. All except for one.

Jake had fought too hard, too long to simply give up the search for his humanity now, not with Nikki still human. Sure, they could go after Viv's father, but he could be halfway around the world for all they knew. They had no clues. And even if they did manage to track him down, Viv would never let them destroy him.

She would sacrifice herself first to save all of them, if for no other reason than to prove that she wasn't like the man who'd made her childhood a living hell.

Vampire or not, she would never willingly hurt anyone.

He knew that now. He knew her.

Her head.

Her heart.

He also knew that he would do anything in his power to keep her safe.

He'd eliminated the two vampires who'd threatened her existence, and now it was time to take care of the last and final threat.

He walked several more feet until he reached a far tree near the edge of the pasture. It was the same tree he'd camped out at that night so long ago when he'd been attacked and left to die.

Viv had saved him, and now it was his turn to repay the favor. He would give Jake and Dillon their humanity back, and the hunt for the Ancient One would end right now.

Sitting down, he leaned back against the tree, his legs stretched out in front of him.

And then he fixed his gaze on the eastern horizon and waited for the sun to rise.

"GARRET." THE NAME whispered on the wind, and Garret thought for a split-second that it was his imagination. Until he felt a nudge against his leg.

He opened his eyes to see Jake standing in front of him. Orange tinged the horizon behind him, and a faint stream of smoke whispered around the vampire. It was almost time now. He could feel it in the lull of his muscles and the weariness that pulled at his eyelids. They drifted shut again, and he felt the nudge of a boot against his leg.

"You stupid sonofabitch." It was Jake's voice again, pulling him from the exhaustion and the dream he was having.

He and Viv were together. She loved him and he loved her and all was right with the world.

"Come on. Get up." Jake's voice grew stronger, reminding Garret that it was just his wishful thinking.

Nothing was right and there would be no happily ever after. Not for him.

But that was okay. She would be safe. Alive.

"Leave me alone," he told Jake when the vampire nudged him again.

"And let you fry for some woman? What the hell is wrong with you?"

He opened his eyes then and stared up at his friend. "She's the Ancient One." He shook his head. "This is the only way."

"Do you love her?" Jake demanded.

"What does that have to do with anything?"

"Do you?"

"I've always loved her."

"Then forget this self-sacrifice crap, get the hell up and do something about it."

"But you and Dillon—"

"—aren't going to last two days without your sorry ass to boss us around." Jake hunkered down in front of Garret. "We need you, man."

"You need your humanity."

"I always thought so." Jake shook his head. "I thought if I could just go back and erase the past hundred or so years, then I would feel different. I would feel hopeful, optimistic, free. I've spent so long being a slave to the hunger, and I just wanted to be free. But then I found Nikki."

"And you wanted it even more."

"Only because I thought it was what she wanted. But she loves me, even if I never become human again. She loves me just the way I am. And she'll keep loving me, for a lifetime or an eternity. Meg feels the same about Dillon." His gaze caught and held Garret's. "And Viv feels the same about you. She loves you, man. Don't blow this." He pushed to his feet. "Get your ass up, and let me take you home."

But Garret couldn't because he knew what Jake was thinking. They would just go after Viv's sire.

"I know about her father," Jake said, as if reading Garret's thoughts. "She told me."

"You talked to her?"

"She came to me and offered herself. She wanted to take the decision away from you. So she told me who she was, and then asked me to kill her." Before Garret could move, Jake held up a hand. "Calm down. I didn't touch her."

"Why not?"

"For the same reason that you're sitting here right now, ready to fry. We're friends, Garret. Now and always. If you love her, that's good enough for me."

"And me." Dillon stepped up behind Jake.

"Ditto for me." It was Nikki's turn. She slid an arm around Jake's waist.

"And me," added Meg as she came up beside Dillon.

"But it's not good enough for me." Viv's sweet voice slid into his ears, and he watched as she stepped from behind the group and walked over to him.

He pushed to his feet then, despite the fatigue that bound his muscles. Suddenly, he didn't feel half as drained as he had a few minutes ago. Not with Viv here. Now.

She fed his strength in a way that went way beyond blood and sex. She fed his soul. With her smiles and her laughter.

"I want more than your love," she told him as she stopped just inches away, determination etching her beautiful features. "I want to fall asleep in your arms and wake up to you every evening. I want you. Every moment of every day. Every day from now until forever. You." She touched him, her fingertips brushing his jaw as she reached out. Her eyes glimmered with emotion and his chest tightened. "Please don't do this."

Garret sighed. It looked as if he had no choice, even if he'd wanted it. And he didn't. "Then we all agree it stops here." He glanced around the small group. "No more searching for the Ancient One. It's over right here and now."

"Right here," Jake added.

"Right now," came Dillon's solemn agreement.

"Besides, I hear that fangs are the new thing this year," Nikki added.

"It's what all of Skull Creek's finest are wearing," said Meg.

Garret grinned and turned back to Viv. His expression faded as he stared at the woman he loved. The vampire he'd always loved.

"Let's get the hell out of here," he murmured. And then he pulled her into his arms and held on tight.

Epilogue

His head hurt like a sonofabitch.

Sheriff Matt Keller forced his eyes open to the blinding morning sunlight that pushed past the drapes. He rolled over onto his back and winced against the pain that beat at his temples.

He felt as if he'd drank the night away and passed out in an alley somewhere. His entire body felt stiff, his muscles tight. A groan worked its way up his throat as he pushed into a sitting position.

He blinked and focused on his surroundings.

And then he blinked again because nothing was the way he remembered when he'd first crawled between the sheets last night.

The door hung from one hinge, and every piece of furniture except the bed had been smashed to bits. There was a sizeable dent in one wall and a litter of sheetrock on the floor. It looked as if Godzilla had faced off with King Kong, and neither had won.

What the hell…?

He closed his eyes and tried to remember. He'd checked the parking lot for Viv Darland's car one more time, then he'd crawled into bed and flipped on the TV to pass the time and wait for her to come in. He'd wanted to talk to her. To get her to confess.

He'd done just that, but only after she'd come knocking on his door. He remembered her accusations, her revelation. The attack.

Holy shit.

He'd been bitten by a vampire.

As if he didn't have enough friggin' problems of his own.

He touched a hand to his neck, but the wound had already healed thanks to his werewolf DNA. The only lingering reminders of last night were the very real images in his head and the Metallica solo that pounded in his head.

Oh, and the little old woman standing in the doorway. Towels overflowed her arms and a disapproving expression etched her face.

She eyed the surrounding mess and arched one eyebrow. "I hope you know this means you ain't getting your deposit back."

He shrugged. "I sort of figured."

She took another look before her gaze zeroed in on him again and dropped to his lap. "You always sleep in your birthday suit?"

He glanced down and sure enough, he was bucknaked. "I like to be comfortable."

"Me, too. Say, you're not a bad-looking fella. If you're interested in a date, I might be able to help you out."

"Thanks, but I'll pass."

"Let me know if you change your mind. There's lots of pretty girls around here."

His body seemed to come alive just at the thought. His gut tightened and his groin stirred. He snatched up a nearby pillow just before the old woman got an eyeful.

"I've got a really busy job. Maybe next time."

"Suit yourself." She shrugged and waddled past his doorway, her orthopedic shoes slapping the pavement outside.

He moved the pillow and stared down at his lap. At the monster that had once been his penis. He'd never been short on equipment. He was a werewolf, after all, which meant he had the whole survival of the fittest thing going on—primitive alpha male, leader of the pack, the whole nine yards.

But this…

This gave new meaning to the word "enormous" and made him wonder what other not-so-little changes lay in store for him now that he'd been bitten by a vampire.

Only time would tell.

* * * * *

FLASHPOINT

BY
JILL SHALVIS

USA TODAY bestselling author **Jill Shalvis** is happily writing her next book from her neck of the Sierras. You can find her romances wherever books are sold, or visit her on the web at www.jillshalvis.com/blog.

To the readers of my daily blog.
Having you there with me on my *I Love Lucy*
adventures makes my day, every day.
This firefighter's for you.

Prologue

"NOW'S YOUR SHOT with me, Zach. I say we get naked."

Exhausted, filthy, Zach Thomas still managed to lift his head and stare at Cristina. "What?"

Just as filthy, she arched a come-hither brow streaked with soot, which made it difficult to take her seriously. So did the mustache of grime. "You and me," she said. "Naked. What do you think?"

He couldn't help it; he laughed. He thought that she was crazy. They both wore their fire gear and were dragging their asses after several hours of intense fire-fighting. All around them, the stench of smoke and dev-astation still swirled in thick gray clouds, penetrating their outfits, their skin. Nothing about it felt sexy.

"Hey, nobody laughs at my offer of sex and lives," she told him. "Not even you, Officer Hottie."

When he grimaced at the nickname, she laughed. "You doing me tonight or not?"

Sex as a relaxant worked—generally speaking, sex as anything worked—but Zach was so close to comatose he couldn't have summoned the energy to pull her close, much less do anything about it once he got her that way. "I can't."

"Now we both know that's a lie."

Firefighting left some people exhilarated and pumped

with adrenaline. Cristina was one of them. Normally he was, too, but they'd just lost a civilian—an innocent young kid—and he couldn't get that out of his head. "I can't," he repeated.

Cristina sighed. She was in her midtwenties, blond, and so pretty she could have passed for an actress playing a firefighter, but she was the real deal, as good as any guy on the squad. She was also tough-skinned, cynical and possessed a tongue that could lash a person dead without trying.

He should know; he'd been on the wrong end of it plenty of times. So he braced himself, but she just sighed again. As sardonic and caustic as she could be, they really were friends. Twice they'd been friends with benefits, but it had been a while. She let it go, rolling her eyes at him, but moving off, leaving him alone.

He stood there a moment more, surrounded by chaos, his gear weighing seventy-five pounds but feeling like three hundred as the radio on his hip squawked. Allan Stone, their new chief, was ordering everyone off the scene except the mop-up crew, who would stay through what was left of the night to make sure there were no flare-ups. Tommy Ramirez, the fire inspector, was already on scene, his job just beginning.

Zach's crew was slowly making their way to their respective rigs. He needed to move, as well, but his gut was screaming on this one—someone had set this blaze intentionally. Unfortunately, it wasn't the first time he'd suspected arson when no one else had. Even more unfortunately, the last two times he'd thought so, he'd been reprimanded by Tommy for having an "authority" issue.

He didn't.

Okay, maybe he had a *slight* authority issue, sometimes, but not tonight.

He could ask Aidan what he thought but Zach knew what his firefighting partn and best friend would say. *Grab a beer, a woman and a bed, in any order.* And if Zach called Cristina back, he could knock out two of the three. Yeah, that was what he should do.

So why he headed toward the burned-out shell of a house instead, he had no idea, except that he trusted himself enough to know something was off here.

Something big.

And he couldn't just walk away from it.

He never could.

1

BROOKE WAS A VIRGIN. Not in the classic sense of the word—that status had changed on her seventeenth Halloween night when she'd dressed as an evil, slutty witch and given in to a very naughty knight in shining armor—but that was another story.

She was a *California* virgin, but as she drove up the coast for the first time and into the small town of Santa Rey, she lost that cherry, as well.

Santa Rey was a classic West Coast beach town, mixing the best elements of Mexico and Mediterranean architecture, all within steps of the beach shimmering brilliantly on her left. There were outdoor cafés, shops and art galleries, skateboarders and old ladies vying for the sidewalks with surfers and snotty tourists, and if she hadn't been so nervous, she might have taken the time to enjoy it all more.

She took a last glance at her quickly scrawled directions, following them to Firehouse 34. Parking, she peered through her windshield at the place, nerves wriggling like pole dancers in her belly.

A new job as a temp EMT—emergency medical technician.

One would think that after all the moves and all the

fresh starts she'd made in her lifetime that *new* would be old hat to her by now, but truthfully she'd never quite gotten the hang of it.

The Pacific Ocean pounded the surf behind her as she got out of her car. The hot, salty June air brushed across her face as her nerves continued to dance. What was it her mother had said every time she'd uprooted them to follow yet another get-rich-quick scheme or new boyfriend or some other ridiculous notion?

It will be okay. You'll see.

And though her mother had been wrong about so many things, somehow it really had always been okay. Today would be no different. The azure sky held a single white puffy cloud hanging high over a dreamy sea dotted with whitecaps and a handful of sailboats. Three-foot waves hit the sand, splashing the pelicans fishing for their morning meal. Nice…if she had to make yet another new start, this didn't seem like such a bad way to go.

Hitching her bag up on her shoulder, Brooke started toward the station, a two-story brick-red structure with white trim and a yard filled with grass and wildflowers swaying in the breeze.

In the huge opened garage sat three fire trucks and an ambulance. One wall was lined with equipment such as hoses and ladders.

Surfboards leaned against the outside of the building. Oak trees dotted the edge of the property, and between the two largest, near the path to the front door, a man swung on a large hammock.

A man with broad shoulders, long legs and the unmistakable build of an athlete. His boots lay on the grass beneath him, as well as a discarded button-down shirt, leaving him in blue uniform pants slid just low enough on his hips to reveal a strip of black BVDs. His white T-shirt invited the general public to bite him. He had his hands clasped behind his head, and a large straw hat covered his face. His stillness suggested he was deeply asleep.

She slowed to a tiptoe, trying not to stare but failing. She was petite, and therefore constantly had to prove to people how strong she could be, but she'd bet he'd never had to prove anything; even from his prone position, he radiated strength and confidence. Of course that long, tough body didn't hurt, with all that aesthetically pleasing sinew defined even as he snoozed.

She envied the nap. She couldn't remember the last time she'd taken one. Or the last time she'd taken a moment to just lie on a hammock and soak up the sun.

Or even just to breathe, for that matter.

A lot of that came from being raised by a wild child of a mother, with little to no stability or security. And though Brooke had been on her own since high school, things hadn't changed much. She'd followed suit, living how she knew, moving around, bouncing from junior college to undergrad to working as an EMT, all in different cities. Hell, different states. Some habits died hard.

But she'd never landed in California before. She'd come to deal with her grandmother's estate, which included a great big old house and no cash to take care of the mortgage. Wasn't that just like an O'Brien.

It left Brooke with no choice but to sell the place off before it dragged her down in debt. Except she had to pack up some sixty-plus years of living first. And hell, maybe while the house was on the market, she could learn more about the grandma she'd never known.

In the meantime, she needed money for the immediates—like, say, eating—and the temp EMT position was for six weeks.

Perfect.

At least on the outside looking in, which was pretty much how she lived her life. Someday she'd like to change that. Someday she'd like to find her niche.

Find where she really belonged…

But for now, or at least the next six weeks, she belonged here. As she moved past the dozing firefighter, the sea breeze stirred her hair and tickled her nose. Then another gust of wind hit, knocking her back a step, and still the occupant of the hammock didn't move, breathing slow and deep, his chest rising and falling in rhythm. She kept tiptoeing past him, then pretty much undid all her careful stealth by sneezing. And not a dainty-girl sneeze, either.

The long body stirred, and so did something deep within her, which was so odd as to be almost unrecognizable.

Lust?

Huh. It'd been a while since she'd felt such instant heat for a guy, especially one whose face she hadn't even seen yet.

His hand reached up to tip off his hat, revealing short, sun-streaked brown hair. When he turned his head in her direction, she caught a quick flash of a face that definitely matched the body, and more of that stirring occurred. He'd been blessed by the gene-pool angels, and freezing on the spot, Brooke watched as two light green eyes focused, then offered a lazy smile. "Bless you," he said.

He had a voice to go with the rest of him—low, deep and melodic. Uh-oh. Lots more stirring and a rise of instantaneous heat, because, good Lord, if she'd thought him virile with his eyes closed, she needed a respirator to look at him now. "Sorry to wake you."

"No worries. I'm used to it. Besides, you're a much prettier sight than anything I was dreaming about."

They were just words but they brought a little zing to her good spots. Good spots she'd nearly let rust. *Whew.* Suddenly, she was actually beginning to sweat. If someone had asked her before this moment if she believed in lust at first sight, she'd have laughed. No, she needed more than hot sexiness in a guy, always had.

But she wasn't laughing now.

Wanting to hear him talk some more, she asked, "What were you dreaming about?"

"We responded to a fire last night and lost a kid."

Some of that overwhelming lust relegated itself to the background of her brain, replaced by something far more real to her than mere physical attraction. *Empathy.* She'd lost people, too, and it never stopped hurting. "I'm so sorry."

"Yeah. Me, too." Shifting his muscular, athletic body in the hammock so that he lay on his side facing her, he propped his head on his hand. "So let me guess. You're the latest EMT."

"Yes. Brooke O'Brien."

"Zach Thomas."

"Hi, Zach Thomas."

His eyes warmed to a simmer, and a matching heat came from deep in her belly. Holy smokes, could he see the steam escaping from her pores? It was so strange, her immediate reaction to him. Strange and unsettling. "What do you mean latest?"

"They've sent us six EMTs so far." He smiled without much mirth. "No, seven. Yeah, you're the seventh."

Okay, that didn't sound promising. "What's wrong with the job?"

"Besides crazy twelve-hour shifts for the glory of low pay and little or no recognition?" He let out a low laugh, and she found that the butterflies in her belly were dancing to a new tune now. Not nerves, but something far earthier.

"No one mentioned that I'm the seventh temp, or that they'd had any problem filling the position."

"Did I scare you off?"

"Did you want to?"

He lifted a shoulder, not breaking eye contact. "If you scare easily, then it'd be nice to know now."

A challenge, and more of that shocking, undeniable sexual zing.

Did he feel it? "I don't scare at all."

At that, something new came into his gaze. Approval, which she didn't need, to go along with that undeniable awareness of her as a woman.

She didn't need that, either, but damn, it was good to know she wasn't alone in this. Whatever this was. Since she wasn't ready to put a finger on it, she forced herself to stop looking at him. "I don't actually officially start until tomorrow, but the chief suggested that I come by, check the place out." And, she supposed, meet the crew, who, it sounded like, were tired of meeting people who didn't stick.

But she'd stick. At least for the six weeks she'd been hired for, because if she was anything, it was reliable.

"Would you like the tour?"

Yes, please, of your body. "No, don't get up," she said quickly when he started to do just that. "Really. I'll manage."

"Door's unlocked," he said, watching her, gaze steady.

"Great. I'll just…" *Try to stop staring at you.* Jeez, it'd been too long since she'd had sex. *Waaaay* too long. "Nice meeting you."

"How about I say the same if you're at work tomorrow?"

"I'll be here." She might be nearly drunk with lust but she knew that much. She would be there.

"Hope so." His light eyes held hers for another beat, and more uncomfortable little zings of heat ping-ponged through her.

Whew. Any more of this and she was going to need another application of deodorant this morning. "I will," she insisted. "I always follow through." She just didn't always grow roots. Okay, she never grew roots. Turning away, she let out a long breath and, hopefully, some of the sexual tension with it, and headed toward the door, which stood ajar. "Hello?"

Utter silence, broken only by a gurgling sound. The front room looked like a grown-up version of a frat house, not quite as neat and organized as the garage, but clean. There were two long comfy-looking sofas and several cushy chairs in beach colors that were well lived in. Shelves lined one wall, piled and stacked with a wide assortment of books, magazines and DVDs. On the floor sat a huge basket filled with flip-flops and bottles of suntan lotion. Another wall was lined with hooks, from which hung individual firefighter gear bags.

She could see the kitchen off to the right and a hallway to the left, but still no sign of life, which was odd—they couldn't all be off on calls, not with the rigs still out front. *"Hello?"*

Still nothing.

With a shrug, she headed toward the gurgling sound, which took her into the kitchen, and a coffeemaker, making away. "Who'd want coffee on a hot day?" she asked herself.

"A crew who's been up all night."

Turning around, she faced sexy firefighter Zach Thomas, and as potent as he'd been lying down, his hotness factor shot up exponentially now that he was standing, even with bed-head—or hammock-head—which was good news for him…and bad news for her.

Letting out a huge yawn, he covered his mouth, then grimaced. "Sorry."

He looked good even when yawning. She was so screwed. "Don't be."

He set down his boots and shirt and stretched. His T-shirt rose, giving her a quick peek at a set of lickable abs. He ran a hand over his hair, which only encouraged the short strands to riot in an effortlessly sexy way that might have been amusing if she hadn't been in danger of drooling.

She'd never been one to lose it for a guy in uniform, so she had no idea why now was any different, but *oh my*.

"We had seven calls last night," he explained. "Fires, an explosion in the sugar factory, a toxic-waste spill at the gas station on Fifth. You name it, we were at it, all night. None of us got more than an hour." Again he ran his hand over his already-standing-on-end hair. "We're wiped. Everyone's sleeping."

Beneath all that gorgeousness, true exhaustion lined his face, and suddenly Brooke saw him as a flesh-and-blood man. "I'm sorry I woke you. Especially after such a rough night."

He lifted another shoulder, not anywhere close to how irritated and frustrated she'd be if she'd had only an hour of sleep. "That's the way this job works. You wanted to meet the crew?"

"I'll come back."

"You want coffee first?"

She opened her mouth to say no thanks, but then she saw it in his gaze. His guard coming up. Here he was, overworked, the place obviously short-staffed, and in his eyes, she was just one in a long line of people that had flaked. That would flake. "You know, coffee would be great."

He turned to the cupboards while she took in the kitchen. The table was huge, with at least twelve chairs scattered around it. On the counter ran a line of mugs the length of the tile. "How many of you are stationed here?"

"We're on three rotating shifts, with only six firefighters and two EMTs each, which makes us…twenty-four? Down from thirty, thanks to some nasty cutbacks."

A medium-size station, then, but huge compared to the private ambulance company she'd last worked for, where there'd been only four on at all times.

She'd have to be far more social here than she was used to. The firefighters worked twenty-four-hour shifts to the EMTs' twelve, but it was still a lot of time together. She told herself that was a bonus, but really it just drove home that, once again, she was the new kid in class.

Zach eased over to the coffeepot. "Black, or jacked up?"

"Jacked up, please."

He reached for the sugar. Without her permission, her

eyes took themselves on a little tour, starting with those wide shoulders, that long, rangy torso, and a set of buns that—

He turned and, oh perfect, caught her staring.

At his butt.

Arching a brow, he leaned back against the counter while she did her best imitation of a ceiling tile. When she couldn't stand the silence and finally took a peek at him, he was handing her the mug of coffee, his eyes amused.

"Thanks," she managed.

"You're not from around here." He poured another mug for himself.

All her life she hadn't been "from around here," so that was nothing new. Getting caught staring at a guy's ass? That was new. New and very uncomfortable. "Is that a requirement?"

"Ah, and a little defensive," he said easily. "You look new to Santa Rey, that's all."

"And you know that because…?"

"Because of your skin." Reaching out, he stroked a finger over her cheek, and instantly she felt as if all her happy spots sparked to life. She sucked in a breath.

So did he.

After a pause, he pulled his finger back. "Huh."

Yeah, huh.

"You're pale," he said. "That's what I meant. You're obviously not from a beach town."

Okay, so they weren't going to discuss it. "I'm just careful, is all."

Zach nodded slowly. "I didn't mean to ruffle you."

Even though he was clearly ruffled, too. He slid his feet into his boots, leaving them unlaced as he set down his coffee and shrugged into his uniform shirt.

Maybe he hadn't meant to ruffle her, but that's exactly what he'd done, was still doing just by breathing. "I'm a big fan of sunscreen."

With a nod, he came close again, his gaze touching over her features. "It was a compliment. You have gorgeous skin, all creamy smooth." Again, he stroked a finger over her cheek, and like before, she felt the touch in a whole bunch of places that had no business feeling anything.

He was ruffling her again. Big-time ruffling going on, from her brain cells to all her erogenous zones, of which she had far more than she remembered.

"Back East?" he guessed.

"Massachusetts." Brooke was trying not to react to the fact that he was in her personal bubble, or that she was enjoying the invasion. "You, uh…" She wagged her finger toward his shirt, still partially opened over the invitation to bite him, which she suddenly wanted to do. "Didn't finish buttoning."

"You distracted me."

Yeah. A mutual problem, apparently. This close, he seemed even taller and broader, and now his surfer good looks were only exaggerated by the firefighter uniform. "Are the surfboards outside yours?"

"Why?" He flashed a smile that must have slayed female hearts across the land. It certainly slayed hers. "Because I look like a surfer?"

"Yes."

"Do you surf?"

"I've never tried," she admitted. "I'm not sure it'd be a good idea."

"Why?"

"I'm…" She paused, not exactly relishing telling this gorgeous specimen of a man her faults.

"A little uptight?" he guessed, then looked her over. "Maybe even a little bit of a perfectionist?"

"Are you suggesting I'm anal? Because I'm not."

He just kept looking at her, a little amused, and she caved like a cheap suitcase. "Okay, I am. What gave me away?"

"The hair."

Which she had in a neat braid. "Keeps it out of my way."

"Smart. And the ironed cargoes?"

She slid her hands into her pockets. "So I hate wrinkles."

A smile tugged at the corners of his mouth. "Yeah, wrinkles are a bitch."

Damn it. He was gorgeous *and* perceptive. "Fine. I'm a lot anal."

He let out another slow and easy grin.

And something within her began a slow and easy burn.

Oh, this wasn't good. It was the opposite of good. "Maybe I should just come back—"

But before she could finish that thought, a loud bell clanged, and in the blink of an eye the surfer firefighter went from laid-back and easygoing to tense and alert.

"Units two and three, respond to 3640 Rebecca Avenue," said a disembodied voice from the loudspeaker.

"That's me." Zach set down his mug as movement came from down the hall.

People began filing into the front room in various stages of readiness, most of them guys—really hot guys, Brooke couldn't help but notice—half of them pulling on clothes, some shoving on shoes, others giving orders to others. All looked exhausted, and somewhat out of sorts. Having been up all night, they couldn't be thrilled at having to move out now, but she still expected someone to ask about her, or even acknowledge her, but no one did.

"Mary's temp is here," Zach said into the general chaos. "Brooke O'Brien, everyone."

People gave a quick wave, one or two even quicker smiles, and kept moving. Zach squeezed her shoulder as he headed to the door, once again a simple touch from him giving her a jolt. "See you around, New Hire Number Seven." And just like that, he was gone.

They were all gone.

Yeah. Definitely still the new kid.

2

BROOKE SPENT that night walking through the three-story Victorian her grandmother had so unexpectedly left her, marveling that it was in her name now. She'd never met Lucille O'Brien, who'd been estranged from her only child, Brooke's mother, Karen, so it'd been a shock to everyone when Brooke had been contacted by an attorney and given the details of Lucille's will.

As she'd been warned by the attorney, every room was indeed filled to the brim with…stuff. For Brooke, for whom everything she owned could fit into her car, this accumulation of stuff boggled the mind. All of it would have to go in order to sell the house, but she didn't know where to start. Her mother had been no help, wanting nothing to do with any of it, not even willing to come West to look.

But Brooke was glad she'd come. If nothing else, being in Santa Rey, experiencing that inexplicably over-the-top attraction to Zach, staying here in the only place her family had any history at all, gave her a sense that she might actually have a shot at things she'd never dared dream about before.

She finally decided to go top to bottom and headed to the attic. There she went to the first pile she came to and found a stack of photo boxes that unexpectedly snagged her by the throat. The way she'd grown up hadn't allowed for much sentimentality. None of her few belongings included keepsakes like photos. She'd told herself over the years that it didn't matter. She *liked* to be sentiment light.

But flipping through boxes and boxes of pictures, she realized that was only because she hadn't known any different. Karen and Lucy hadn't spoken in years, since back when Brooke had been a baby, so she hadn't known her grandmother, or how the woman felt about her. But some of the pictures were from the early 1900s and continued through her grandmother's entire life, enthralling Brooke in a way she hadn't expected.

She had a past, and flipping through it made her feel good, and also sad for all she didn't know. She and her mother weren't close. In fact, Karen lived in Ohio at the moment, with an artist and wasn't in touch often, but now Brooke wished she could just pick up a phone and share this experience.

That she had anyone to pick up a phone and call…

She fell asleep just like that, surrounded by her past, only to wake with a jerk, the sun slanting in the small window high above her. She had two pictures stuck to one cheek, drool on the other. She'd been dreaming about the big house, filled with memories of her own making.

Was that what she secretly wished for? For this house to represent her roots?

Was that what she needed to feed her own happiness?

She glanced at her watch and then panicked. Tossing off the dream and the photos, she raced through her morning routine, barely getting a shower before rushing out the door, desperate not to be late on her first day at work.

The hammock by the firehouse was empty, and she ignored the little twinge of disappointment at not getting to gawk at Zach again. Not that she was going to gawk. Nope, she was going to be one hundred percent professional. And with that, she stepped inside.

"Well, look at you. You really came back."

Danger, danger…sexy firefighter alert. Slowly she turned and looked at him, thinking, *Please don't be as hot as I remember, please don't be as hot as I remember—*

Shit.

He was as hot as she remembered. He didn't look tired this morning. Instead, the corners of his mouth were turned up, and his eyes—cheerful and wide-awake—slid over her, making her very aware of the fact that while she might have a little crush going, it was most definitely, absolutely, a two-way thing.

Which didn't help at all.

"Guys," he called out over his shoulder. "She's here."

"Number Seven showed?" This from a tall, dark and extremely drool-worthy firefighter in the doorway to the kitchen.

"Meet Aidan," Zach said to Brooke. "He dated New Hire Number Two and she never came back, so he has orders to stay clear."

"Hey, I didn't plan on the shellfish giving her food poisoning," Aidan said in his own defense. "But just in case…" He flashed a smile at Brooke, a killer smile that rivaled Zach's. "We'd better not go out for shellfish."

Several more men crowded into the hallway to take a look. Yeah, they really did make them good-looking here. Must be the fresh sea air. "Hi," she said, waving. "Brooke O'Brien."

The bell rang, and everyone groaned, their greeting getting lost as they headed for their gear.

"Aidan and I roll together," Zach said, stepping into his boots. "With Cristina and Blake." He gestured to two additional firefighters, the first a tough-looking beautiful blond woman who smiled, the other, male, tall and lanky, not smiling.

Zach shook his head. "Or, as we call Blake, Eeyore."

Okay. Brooke wasn't smiling, either, so she put one on now, but it was too late; they'd turned away.

"You're with Dustin," Zach called back.

Dustin, who looked like Harry Potter The Grown-Up Years, complete with glasses, raised his hand. "We're the two EMTs on this shift. Nice to meet you. Hope you orientate fast."

She hoped so, too.

Dustin gestured to the door, nodding to the two firefighters not moving. "This is Sam and Eddie. Their rig wasn't called, so they get to stay here and watch *Oprah* and eat bonbons."

They took the ribbing with a collective flip of their middle fingers, then vanished back down the hall.

"Actually, they're scheduled to go to the middle school on Ninth this morning and give a fire safety and prevention speech to the kids," Dustin told her with a grin. "They'll eat their bonbons later. Let's hit it, New Hire Seven. It's a Code Calico."

"Code Calico?"

But he was already moving to the door that led directly to the garage and the rigs.

Cristina brushed past Brooke and set her mug in the sink. "Good luck."

"Am I going to need it?"

"With Dustin, our resident McDweeb? Oh, yeah, you're going to need it."

"What's a Code Calico?"

Cristina merely laughed, which did nothing to ease Brooke's nerves.

Blake poked his head back in the door. He'd pulled on his outer fire gear, which looked slightly too big on his very lean form. "Hey, New Hire. Hit it means hit it."

So she did what was expected of her—she hit it. Dustin drove, while she took the shotgun position. "So really, what's a Code Calico?"

Dustin navigated the streets with a familiar sort of ease that told her he knew what he was doing, not even glancing at the GPS system. "Want to take it?"

"Take it?"

"Be point on the call." He glanced at her. "The one in charge."

She sensed it was a test. She aced tests, always had. That was the analness in her, she supposed. "Sure."

He pushed up his glasses and nodded, but she'd have sworn his lips twitched.

Huh. Definitely missing something.

When they pulled onto a wide, affluent, oak-lined street, she hopped out and opened the back doors of the rig.

"Gurney's not necessary on this one," Dustin told her.

Behind the ambulance came the fire truck. Zach and the others appeared, smiling.

Why were they all smiling?

Before she could dwell on that, from between the two trucks came an old woman, yelling and waving her cane. "Hurry! Hurry before Cecile falls!"

The panic in her voice was real, and Brooke's heart raced just as Dustin nudged her forward, whispering in her ear, "All yours."

This was the job, and suddenly in her element, her nerves took a backseat. Here, she could help; here, she could run the show. "It's okay, ma'am. We're here now."

"Well, then, get to it! Get my Cecile!"

"Where is she? In the house?"

"No!" She looked very shaky and not a little off her rocker, so Brooke tried to steer her to the curb to sit down, but she wasn't having it.

"I'm not sitting anywhere! Not until you get Cecile!"

"Okay, just tell me where she is and I'll—"

"Oh, good Lord!" The woman blinked through her thick-rimmed glasses, taking a quick look at the others, who stood back, watching. "She's another new hire, isn't she?"

"Yes," Brooke said. "But—"

"What number are you?"

Brooke sighed. "Seven."

"Well, get a move on, New Hire Number Seven! Save my Cecile!"

"I'm trying, ma'am. What's your name?"

"Phyllis, but Cecile—"

"Right. Needs my help. Where is she?"

"That's what I'm trying to tell you!" The woman jerked her cane upward, to a huge tree in front of them. Waaaay up in that tree, on a branch stretched out over their heads, perched a cat.

A big, fat cat, plaintively wailing away.

Brooke turned and eyeballed Dustin, who seemed to be fascinated by his own feet, and that's when she got it. She was going through some ridiculously juvenile rite of passage. "I'm beginning to see how they got to number seven." Good thing she was used to being the newbie, because she hadn't been kidding Zach yesterday. Little scared her, and certainly not a damn cat in a damn tree.

"Hurry up!" Phyllis demanded. "Before she falls!"

"I'll get her." Zach had separated from the others and walked toward the tree.

Oh, no.

Hell, no.

They'd wanted to see her do this, they were absolutely going to see her do this.

"Brooke—"

"No." She kept her eyes on Phyllis. "Cecile is a cat," she clarified, because there was no sense in making a total and complete fool of herself if it wasn't absolutely necessary.

"Yes," Phyllis verified.

Okay, it was going to be absolutely necessary. Damn, she hated that.

By now, Barbie Firefighter Cristina was out-and-out grinning. Cutie Firefighter Aidan was smiling. Harry Potter look-alike Dustin was, too. Not Eeyore, though. Nope, Blake was far more serious than the others, she could already tell, though she'd have sworn there was some amusement shining in his gaze.

Zach was either wiser, or maybe he simply had more control, but his lips weren't curved as he watched her. Quiet. Aware. Speculative.

Sexy as hell, damn him. Fine. Seemed she had a lot to prove to everyone. Well, she was good at that, too, and she stepped toward the tree.

"Brooke—"

She put a finger in his face, signaling Don't You Dare, and something flashed in his eyes.

Respect? Yeah, but something else, too, something much more base, which would have most definitely set off one of their trademark chain reactions of sparks along her central nervous system, if she hadn't been about to climb a damn tree. "I can do this," she said.

His eyes approved, and even though she didn't want it to, that approval washed through her.

So did that sizzling heat they had going on.

Oh, he was good. With that charisma oozing from his every pore, he could no doubt charm the panties off just about any woman.

But though it had been a while since anyone had charmed Brooke's panties off, she wasn't just any woman.

Reminding herself of that, she stepped toward the tree.

3

ZACH WATCHED how Brooke handled herself and something inside him reacted. He didn't know her, not yet, not really, other than that they had some serious almost chemical-like attraction going, but she was crew, and as such, she was family.

Except he felt decidedly un-family-like toward her. Nope, nothing in him looking at her felt brotherly.

Not one little bit.

The gang was being hard on her, there was no doubt of that, but he'd seen many new hires hazed over the years—six in the past few weeks—and it had never bothered him.

Until now. This bothered him. *She* bothered him, in a surprising way. A man-to-woman way, though that wasn't the surprise. It was that he felt it here, at work.

People came in and out of his life on a daily basis. It was the nature of the beast, that beast being fire. Every day he dealt with the destruction it caused, and what it did to people's existence. Hell, he'd even experienced it in the most personal way one could, when he'd lost his own parents to a tragic fire. He coped by knowing he made a difference, that he helped keep that beast back when he could.

What also helped were the constants in his life, and since the loss of his mom and dad at age ten, those constants were his crew. Aidan, his partner and brother of his heart. Eddie and Sam, fellow surfers. Dustin, resident clown, a guy who gave one hundred percent of himself, always, which usually landed him in Heartbreak City. Blake, whom he'd gone to high school with and who'd lost his firefighting partner Lynn in a tragic fire last year, a guy who'd give a perfect stranger the heavy yellow jacket off his back. Even Cristina, a woman in a man's world, who was willing to kick anyone's ass to show she belonged in it. All of them held a piece of Zach's heart.

For better, for worse, through thick and thin, they were each other's one true, solid foundation. They meant everything to him.

But the emergency community they lived in was a lot like the cozy little town of Santa Rey itself—small and quirky, no secrets need apply. Everyone knew that the constant gossip and ribbing between the crew members acted as stress relief from a job that had an element of danger every time they went out. Zach had always considered it harmless. But looking at it from Brooke's perspective, that ribbing must feel like mockery.

She dropped her bag to the ground and walked to the tree.

She was going to climb it for the cat. And hell if that didn't do something for him. He didn't interfere—she was Dustin's partner, not his—but he wanted to. The chief would have a coronary, of course, but the chief wasn't there throwing the rule book around as he liked to do. Zach wasn't much for rules or restrictions, himself, or for drawing lines in the sand—which hadn't helped his career any. Nor did he make a habit of stretching his emotional wings and adding personal ties to his life. How many women had told him over the years that he wouldn't know a real relationship if it bit him on the ass?

Too many to count.

And yet he felt an emotional tie now, watching Brooke simply do her job. It shouldn't have been sexy, but it was. *She* was sexy, even in the regulation EMT uniform of dark blue trousers and a white button-down shirt, with a Santa Rey EMT vest over the top, the outfit made complete by the required steel-toed boots.

She made him hot. He thought maybe it was the perfectly folded-back sleeves and careful hair twist that got him. Her hair was gorgeous, a shiny strawberry blond, her coloring as fair as her hair dictated. He knew after any time in the sun—and in Santa Rey, sun was the only weather they got—she'd probably freckle across that nose she liked to tip up to nosebleed heights. She was petite, small-boned, even fragile-looking, and yet he'd bet his last dollar she was strong as hell, strong enough for that tree.

She looked up at the lowest branch, utter concentration on her face. A face that showed her emotions, probably whether she wanted it to or not. It was those wide, expressive baby-blue eyes, he knew. They completely slayed him.

She put her hands on the trunk of the tree and gave it a shake, testing it. Nodding to herself, still eyeing the cat as if she'd rather be facing a victim who was bleeding out than the howling feline on the branch twenty feet above her, she drew a deep breath.

Unbelievable. She was slightly anal, slightly obsessive and more than slightly adorable.

And she had guts. He liked that. He liked her. She was

taking his mind off his frustration over the Hill Street fire and Tommy's investigation. But while his career was shaky at the moment, hers was not, and she was going to climb that damn tree if no one stopped her. "Dustin."

Cristina shushed him. Blake, the one of them who couldn't stand to see anything suffer, even before losing Lynn last year, shot her an annoyed look. Zach leaned toward Dustin. "Stop her."

"On it." The EMT stepped forward and put his hand on Brooke's shoulder, saying something that Zach couldn't quite catch, though he had no problem reading her expression.

Relief that she didn't really have to climb the tree.

Embarrassment that she'd let them all fool her.

And a flash of a temper that made him smile. Good. She might be reserved, but she wasn't a doormat.

Aidan grabbed the ladder. Zach helped him. As he passed a brooding Brooke, their eyes met before he climbed the ladder to reach Cecile.

Yeah, quiet and reserved, maybe, but also a little pissed. So was Cecile, but she was one female he could soothe, at least, and when he brought the cat to Phyllis, he had to smile.

Brooke had the older woman sitting on the curb and was attempting to check her vitals, which Phyllis didn't appear to appreciate.

"Ma'am," Brooke said, "you have an elevated blood pressure."

"Well, of course I do. I'm eighty-eight."

Brooke lifted her stethoscope, but Phyllis pushed it away. "I don't need—Cecile! Give me my baby, Zachie!"

Blowing a loose strand of hair from her face, Brooke gave Zach a look. *"Zachie?"*

"Small town." With a half-embarrassed shrug, he handed the cat to Phyllis.

"I used to change his diapers," Phyllis told her, and patted Zach's cheek with fingers gnarled by arthritis. "You're a good boy. Your mother would be so proud of you."

He'd found it best not to respond to these types of statements from Phyllis, because if he did, she'd keep him talking about his family forever, and he didn't like to talk about them. He thought about them every day, and that was enough. "I thought we decided you were going to keep Cecile inside."

"No, *you* decided, but she hates being cooped up." She nuzzled the cat. "So how's all your ladies, Zachie? Still falling at your feet?"

Brooke arched a brow but Zach just smiled. "You're my number-one lady, Phyllis, you know that." Her color wasn't great, plus her breathing was off, which worried him. She'd probably forgotten to pick up her meds again. He crouched at her side and took her hand. "You're taking your pills, right?"

She bent her head to Cecile's, her blue hair bouncing in the breeze. "Oh, well. You know."

With a sigh, he reached for Brooke's blood pressure cuff. "May I?"

Their fingers brushed as she put it in his hand, and again he felt that electric current zing him, but as hot as that little zap was, he didn't take his gaze off Phyllis. "You know the drill," he said, gently wrapping the cuff around her arm as above him he heard Brooke say to Dustin, "So did I pass the test?"

"Yep. Nice job, New Hire Seven."

"You've got to keep the cat inside," Zach said to

Phyllis, handing back the blood pressure cuff to Brooke, making sure to touch her, testing their connection. Yep, still there. "Cecile's not safe out here, Phyllis."

"She's safe now."

"Yes." With effort, he shifted his mind off Brooke and focused on Phyllis. "We have a new chief."

"Yes, of course. Allan Stone. Santa Rey born and raised, back from Chicago to do good in his hometown. I read all about him in the paper."

Everything was in the Santa Rey paper. Not that Zach needed to read it. Not when he and the chief were becoming intimately familiar with each other; every time Zach put his nose into Tommy's business regarding the arsons, he got some personal one-on-one time in the chief's office. "After all he saw in Chicago, he's not going to think this qualifies as an emergency."

"But it was an emergency."

"I'm sorry, Phyllis."

"Yes." The older woman sighed. "I know. I'm old, not senile. I get it." She lovingly stroked the cat, who sprawled in her lap, purring loudly enough to wake the dead. "It's just that Cecile loves the great outdoors. And you always come—"

Seemed his heart was going to get tugged on plenty today. "That's my point. We can't always come. If we're here when there's an emergency, then someone else might go without our help. I know you don't want that to happen."

"No, of course not." She hugged the cat hard. "You're right. I'm sorry."

"No apologies necessary." He scratched the cat behind her ornery ears and rose to leave.

Brooke blocked his path. She still held her stethoscope and blood pressure cuff, looking sweetly professional while she tried to maintain her composure, but her annoyance at being played was clear.

"I'd like to talk to you," she said primly.

He enjoyed that, too, the way she sounded so prissy while looking so damn hot. So put together, so on top of everything, which perversely made him want to rumple her up. Preferably the naked, hot and sweaty kind of rumpled. "Talk? Or bite my head off?"

"I don't bite."

"Shame." Passing her, he headed back to his rig to help Aidan put away the ladder. But she wasn't done with him yet, and followed.

"I nearly climbed that tree, Zach. Without the benefit of the ladder, I might add."

Aidan shot Zach a look that said Good Luck, Buddy and moved out of their way. Zach turned to face a fuming Brooke. "No one was going to let you climb that tree."

"Really? Because I think that the crew thinks I was sent here to amuse them."

"You have to understand, you're the seventh EMT—"

"To walk out, yeah yeah, got it. But I'm not going to walk out. I'm not."

"I believe you."

"You do?"

He smiled at her surprise. "I do. And I was never going to let you climb that tree, Brooke. Never."

She stared at him for a long, silent beat. "Is your word supposed to mean something?"

He was a lot of things, but a liar was not one of them. Not that she could possibly know that about him yet. "Hopefully it will come to mean something."

She continued to look at him for another long moment, then turned and walked away with a quiet sense of dignity that made him feel like an ass even though, technically, he'd done nothing wrong.

OVER THE NEXT FEW DAYS the calls came nonstop, accompanying a heat wave that had everyone at the firehouse on edge, Zach included. If they'd had the staff that they used to, things would have been okay, but they didn't. So they ran their asses off in oppressive temperatures with no downtime, while the higher-ups got to sit in air-conditioned offices.

By the end of the week, they were all exhausted.

"Crazy," Cristina muttered on the third straight day of record-high temperatures *and* calls. "It's like with the heat wave came a stupid wave."

They were all in the kitchen, gulping down icy drinks and standing in front of the opened freezer, vying for space and ice cubes. Cristina rubbed an ice cube across her chest, then gave poor Dustin the evil eye for staring at her damp breasts.

Zach didn't blame Dustin for looking; the view was mighty nice. He did worry about the dreamy look in the EMT's eyes. Dustin tended to put his heart on the line for every single woman he met, which left him open to plenty of heartbreak. If Cristina caught that puppy-dog look, she'd chew him up and spit him out. Instead, she elbowed everyone back and took the front-and-center spot for herself.

"You forgot to take your pill this morning," Blake told her, not looking at her chest like everyone else but nudging her out of the way so he could get in closer.

"I'm not on the pill," Cristina said.

"Not that pill. Your nice pill."

Dustin snorted and Cristina glared at him, zapping the smile off his face.

Zach cleared some space for Brooke to get in closer, and she sent him a smile that zapped him as sure as Cristina had zapped Dustin, but in another area entirely.

He wished she was rubbing an ice cube on her chest. He maneuvered himself right next to her. Their arms bumped, their legs brushed and every nerve ending went on high alert.

The bell rang, and with a collective groan, they all scattered. It was exhausting, and *he* was seasoned, as was the crew. He could only imagine how Brooke felt. If he'd had time to breathe, he'd have asked her.

As it was, they couldn't do much more than glance at each other, because between the multitude of calls, they still had the maintaining and keeping up of the station and vehicles, not to mention their required physical training.

But he did glance at her.

Plenty.

And she glanced back. She appeared to hold up under pressure extremely well; even when everyone else looked hot, sweaty and irritated, she never did. Look sweaty and irritated, that is.

Hot? That she most definitely looked.

It'd been a long time since he'd flirted so slowly with a woman like this, over days, mostly without words. A very long time, and he'd forgotten how arousing it could be. He figured if they had to pass each other one more time without taking it to the next step—and he had plenty of ideas on what that next step should be, all involving

touching and stripping and nakedness, lots of nakedness—they'd both go up in flames.

One late afternoon a week and a half into Brooke's em-
ployment, he headed toward her to see about that whole
thing, but of course, the bell rang.

It was a kitchen fire, with a man down. Zach and Aidan
were first on scene, with Dustin and Brooke pulling in
right behind them in front of a small house that sat on a
high bluff overlooking the ocean. By the time they got
inside, the fire had been extinguished by the supposedly
downed man himself, who was breathing like a lunatic
and looked to be in the throes of a panic attack. Zach and
Aidan checked to make sure the doused fire couldn't
flare up and then began mop-up while Dustin tried to get
the guy to sit, but he wasn't having it.

"No." Chest heaving, covered in soot, he pointed at
Brooke. "I want her. The chick paramedic."

Everyone looked at Brooke. For some reason, she
looked at Zach. He wanted to think it was because they'd
been looking at each other silently for days, building an
odd sense of anticipation for…something, but probably it
was simply that he'd been the first person she'd met here.

"I'm an EMT," she told the victim. "Not a paramedic."

"I don't care." The guy was gasping for air, clutching
at his chest. "It's you or nothing."

HER OR NOTHING. Brooke could honestly say that she'd
never heard that sentence before, at least directed at her.
She looked at the crew around her, all of whom were
looking at her, perfectly willing and accepting of her
taking over.

And in that moment, she knew. They might tease her

and call her New Hire, but the truth was, they treated her as a part of their team, a capable, smart part of their team, and she appreciated that. "What's your name?"

"Carl."

"Okay, Carl. Let's sit."

"I'm better standing. Listen, I was just cooking eggs, but then the pan caught fire."

"It's okay," Brooke assured him. "The fire's out now. Let's worry about you."

"I have a problem."

Yes, he did. He was pale, clammy and sweating profusely. "Let's work on that problem."

"It's, uh, a big one. It won't go away." Still breathing heavy, the guy looked down at his fly. "If you know what I mean."

Everyone stopped working on the kitchen mop-up and looked at the guy's zipper, and Brooke did the same.

He was erect.

She glanced at the guys. Dustin pushed up his glasses. Aidan busied himself with the cleanup. Zach rubbed his jaw and met Brooke's gaze, his own saying that he'd seen it all, but not this.

Carl shoved his fingers through his hair, still trying to catch his breath. "See, I was supposed to have this hot date last night, but Mr. Winky wasn't working. So I took a vitamin V."

"Vitamin V?" Brooke pulled out a chair and firmly but gently pressed him into it. "What's vitamin V?"

"Viagra."

Brooke processed that information while Carl stared down at his lap with a mixture of pride and bafflement. "It worked, too. A little too well."

"Okay." Brooke opened her bag and began to check his vitals, carefully not looking at the guy's zipper again.

"So…can you fix this? I've never had a twelve-hour case of blue balls before. Could it…kill me?"

"No one's dying today." Behind her, Dustin was checking in with the hospital, as was protocol. From the victim she took the basics: name, age, weight, etc. Dustin set down his radio and turned to her. "We have a few questions."

"Not you," Carl said, shaking his head. *"Her."*

"Right." Dustin wrote something down and pushed the piece of paper toward Brooke. It was the questions the E.R. doctor wanted answered. She paused, tucking a non-existent stray piece of hair behind her ear while she tried to figure out how to do this and keep Carl's dignity, not to mention her own. "Carl? How many Viagras did you take?"

"Oh. Um." He looked away, catching Aidan's and Zach's eye. "Just the one."

Brooke gave him a long look. She was not a pushover, not even close. "One?"

"Okay, two."

"Are you sure?"

Mr. Vitamin V caved. "Four. Okay? I took four. I really wanted to do this." Still breathing unsteadily, he put his hand on his heart. "Am I going to have a heart attack? Because I feel like I'm having a heart attack."

Brooke was waiting on Dustin, who was talking to the E.R. about the four pills. "Just hang tight for a second."

"Hanging tight. Or at least my boys are." He smiled feebly at his joke. "Do I have to go to the hospital?"

"Finding that out now." She did her best not to squirm, extremely aware of all the eyes on her, especially Zach's, as Dustin gave her another piece of paper, which she read. *Oh, boy.* "Carl, when did you last have sex?"

Carl blinked. "When did I last have sex? Are you kidding me? That's why I took the pills in the first place!"

Again Brooke accidentally met Zach's gaze. He was cool, calm, and not showing a thing, but she felt her own face heat. If she had to answer this question, she'd have to admit that she couldn't even remember. "We need to know when you last ejaculated."

"Oh." Carl let out a long breath. "Jesus. Yesterday. In the shower."

Nodding, she made the note.

"Twice."

Brooke dropped her pen.

"That's normal, right?" He looked at Aidan, Dustin and then Zach for affirmation. "Back me up here, guys. It's just what we do, right?"

Aidan got really busy, fast.

Dustin scribbled on his notepad.

Zach just raised a brow.

"Damn it!" Carl slapped his hands on the table. "Don't you guys leave me out here hanging alone! Tell her."

Dustin sighed, then after a hesitation, nodded.

Aidan, too.

Brooke looked at Zach, who met her gaze evenly, not looking away, neither embarrassed nor self-conscious as he nodded, as well.

Carl was waiting for her next question, but she couldn't stop staring at Zach, couldn't stop picturing him—

Oh, perfect. And here came the blush.

Dustin nudged her and she jumped, jerking her gaze off Zach.

"Really, it's what guys do," Carl was still saying.

It was what guys did.

Drive her crazy.

They made the decision to transport, and while loading the patient in the small kitchen, Brooke bumped into Zach. She looked into his face, feeling hers heat, watching him smile as if he knew what she was thinking.

It's what guys do...

She moved past him but their arms touched, and damn if she didn't feel her stomach quiver. Because their arms touched. How ridiculous was that? If he ever touched her in a sexual way, she'd probably come before he even got her clothes off.

"You okay?" he murmured. "You're looking at me funny."

"Me?" Her voice was as high as Mickey Mouse. "No. Not at all." *I was looking at you like I wanted to gobble you up for my next meal, that's all.*

He cocked his head and studied her a moment. "Sure?"

"Sure." Liar, liar...

4

"HEY, NEW HIRE SEVEN," Cristina said several days later, the next time she saw Brooke. "Any more Viagra calls?"

Brooke looked over as Firefighter Barbie entered the fire station living room grinning from ear to ear. "Brooke. My name is Brooke."

"So. You ever have a patient with a perma-boner before?"

"No. That was a new one," Brooke admitted.

"At least you didn't have to climb a tree to get to him, huh?"

"At least he was human."

Cristina laughed and walked past Blake, who was on the computer, and affectionately rumpled his hair. "You get the message that your sister called?"

"Yep, thanks."

"Kenzie sounds good. I saw her on *Entertainment Tonight* last night, she was being interviewed about being nominated for a daytime Emmy for her soap."

"I taped it."

"We still all having dinner tonight, right?"

"Yep."

Brooke knew that they did that a lot, got together. All of them. They'd asked her to join them weeks ago, on her first night, but she had been anxious to get started packing up her grandma's house. Now that she'd been doing that for two weeks, she'd love to be included, but didn't know how to ask.

A lifelong problem—not knowing how to belong. But for the first time in her life, she wanted to. She didn't know if it was her grandmother's house with all that family history, or the way she yearned and burned for Zach at night, or just wanting more for herself from life, but she wanted to be a part of this team. A part of their family. At least for the month she had left. Then, when she did go, she'd have these memories. She'd have her own history to look back on and remember.

Cristina leaned over Blake's shoulder. "Got anything good today, Eeyore?"

Blake pulled open a drawer and held out a candy bar. "Careful," he warned. "I rigged it. The person who eats that is going to turn sweet."

"Not a chance."

With a sigh, Blake went back to the computer.

Brooke headed into the garage to restock their rig as end-of-shift protocol dictated. And then, blessedly, she was off the clock. Stepping outside, she was immediately hit by a sucker punch to the low belly area—not by the hot, salty summer air, but by good old-fashioned lust.

Zach stood on the bumper of the truck, hose in hand, leaning over his rig, squirting down the windows. Stripped to the waist, his skin glistened with a light sweat. She broke into a sweat, too, just from looking at him.

His back was sleek, smooth and sinewy, and improving the already fantastic view was the fact that his pants had slid low enough to once again reveal a strip of BVDs, blue today. His every muscle bunched and unbunched as he moved, hypnotizing her, fusing her to the spot. She didn't mean to keep staring, she really didn't, but was unable to help herself as she eyed his sun-streaked hair, his rock-solid and ready-for-action body, all corded bulk honed to a fine edge, topped with so much testosterone she could hardly breathe. He looked like the perennial surfer boy all grown up—and it hit her.

This might be more than a crush.

"If you come help, you can get a better view."

Oh, for God's sake. She jerked her gaze off him and pretended to search her purse for her keys while silently berating herself. "I'm sorry, I—"

"Are you kidding? A pretty woman looks at me, and she's sorry?"

"I wasn't looking—"

Tossing aside his hose, he lithely hopped down from the rig and came closer, letting out that damn slow, sexy smile of his. "Anal, uptight *and* a liar?"

"Okay, so I was looking." She crossed her arms and tried not to look at his chest but it was right in front of her, drawing her eyes. "But I didn't *want* to be looking."

With a soft laugh, he turned the tables, letting his gaze slowly run over her, from her hair to her toes and then back up again, stopping at a few spots that happily leaped to hopeful attention.

"Stop it." God, was that her voice, all cartoony-light and breathless? "What are you doing?"

"Looking," he murmured, mocking her. "And I wanted to."

"Okay, you know what? You need a damn shirt. And I'm going now."

Leaning back against the rig, he smiled, and damn

if it didn't short-circuit her wires. "Have anything special planned for your days off?" he asked. "Visiting friends, family?"

No. Fantasizing about you...

Unacceptable answer. She'd be working on the house. The house that she was beginning to wish was hers in more than name, because being there reminded her of exactly how rootlessly she'd lived her life, and how much she'd like to change that. Going through decades of family history had brought it home for her. It was exhausting, almost gut-wrenching, but also exhilarating.

And honestly? Flirting with Zach was the same.

But no matter what the house represented to her, no matter what someone like Zach could represent to her, she still didn't know how to get there.

How to belong. "I don't have either friends or family here."

"Everyone back East?"

She hated this part. Telling people about herself, getting unwanted sympathy. "My mother's in Ohio. I'm an only child. And I haven't made any friends here yet."

He didn't dwell or give her any sympathy. "I thought we were friends."

She gave him a look.

"Aren't we?"

"I don't know."

"Let's do something, then, and you can decide."

"I can't. I'm closing up my grandmother's house before it sells, and I've only got a month left in town."

"You think you'll be able to leave Santa Rey without falling in love with it? Or the people?"

She looked into his eyes, wishing for a witty response.

But the truth was, she fell a little bit more for her grandma's house every single night she slept there. "I don't know."

"Do you know how you feel about surfing?"

"I'm pretty uncoordinated."

"I'm a good teacher."

Uh-huh. She bet he was.

"Come on, say yes. I'm betting you don't take enough downtime."

"I take lots."

He arched a brow, and she let out a breath. "Okay, so I don't."

"Is that because you like to be so busy your head spins, or because you don't know how to relax?"

"Is there an option number three?"

"You work a stressful job."

"So?"

"So…" He smiled. "Maybe you should let that hair down and just be wild and free once in a while."

"Wild and free. Is that what you do?"

"When I can."

She hadn't expected him to admit it, and she ran out of words, especially because he was still standing there with no shirt on.

"Not your thing, I take it," he said. "Letting loose."

"I've never thought about it." Okay, she'd thought about it. "I'm not sure how to…let loose," she admitted, going to tuck her hair behind her ears. But he shifted closer and caught her fingers in his.

That electric current hummed between them. He looked at their joined hands and then into her eyes. "Maybe it's time to think about it," he said silkily and stroked a finger over the tip of her ear, causing a long set of shivers to race down her spine. Then, with a look that singed her skin, he walked off.

She managed, barely, not to let her knees give and sit right there on the ground. He wanted her to relax? Ha! So not likely, and not just because he wound her up in ways she hadn't anticipated. Relaxing, getting wild and free, those were all alien concepts for her. No matter what her secret desires were, she had responsibilities, always had. She didn't have time for letting loose.

But, as he'd suggested, she thought about it. Thought about it as she drove home—yes, she'd begun to think of her grandmother's house as home—and she thought about it as she finished the attic. She thought about it, dreamed about it, fantasized about it…

Ironically enough, in the pictures that chronicled her grandma's life, she saw plenty of evidence that her grandma had known how to relax, and be wild and free.

How was it her grandmother had never insisted on getting to see her only grandchild?

It made her sad. It made her feel alone. She had missed out on something, something she needed badly.

Affection.

A sense of belonging.

Love.

Damn, enough with the self-pity. Having finished the attic, she moved down a floor to box up her grand-mother's bedroom. There she made an even bigger find than pictures—her grandmother's diaries. Brooke stared down at one dated ten years back, the year she'd graduated from high school.

I tried calling my daughter today but she's changed her number. Probably long gone again on another of her moves. Of course she didn't think to let me know the new number, or where she's going.

She's still mad at me.

I really thought I was doing the right thing, telling her what I thought of her bohemian life-style and the shocking way she drags that child across the world for her own pleasure. I thought she needed to hear my opinion.

For years I thought that.

Now I know different. I know it's her life to live as she wants, and if I'd only arrived at this wisdom sooner, I wouldn't be alone now, with no one to belong to and no one to belong to me.

Brooke remembered that year. Her mother had gone after some guy to Alaska, and she'd entered junior college in Florida, feeling extremely…alone. Hugging the diary to her chest, she stared blindly out the window, wondering how different her life might have been if stubbornness hadn't been the number one trait in her grandmother's personality…

Or her mother's.

Or hers…

IF ANYONE had asked, Zach would have said he spent his days off surfing with Eddie and Sam, and replacing the brakes and transmission on his truck.

What he wouldn't have mentioned was how much time he spent thinking about Brooke. They most definitely had some sort of an attraction going on, one he wanted to explore. He wished she'd taken him up on spending some of their days off together. His weekend might have turned out differently if she had.

But with too much time to think, he'd gone over and over the Hill Street fire, the one he was so sure had been arson.

Tommy wouldn't give him any info. He and Tommy went way back to when Tommy had sat on the hiring board that had plucked Zach out of the academy, but the inspector wasn't playing favorites. Sharp as hell and a first-rate investigator, he was as overworked as the rest of them and frustrated at Zach's pressing the issue. All week his response had remained the same: "I'm working on it."

Still, Zach found himself driving to the site, where he'd gotten an unhappy shock. Back on the night of the fire he'd only had three minutes before the chief had ordered everyone out, just long enough for him to catch sight of *two* points of origin. One in the kitchen beneath the sink, the other in the kid's bedroom inside a wire-mesh trash can.

But now the kid's bedroom had been cleaned, and there was no sight of the wire-mesh trash can or flash point marring the wall.

And no sign of an ongoing fire investigation.

What *didn't* shock Zach was finding Tommy waiting for him at the start of his next shift.

Tommy was a five-foot-three Latin man with a God complex compounded by short-man syndrome. Added to this, ever since his doctor had made him give up caffeine, he'd been wearing a permanent surly frown; now was no exception as he stalked up to Zach as he got out of his truck. "We need to talk."

Zach shut his door without locking it. No one ever locked their doors in Santa Rey. "Still off caffeine, huh?"

"The Hill Street fire."

Zach sighed. "What about it?"

"I just left the scene."

"Okay." Zach nodded and grabbed his gear bag out of the back of his truck. "So maybe you can tell me what happened to the second point of origin, the one I saw in the kid's bedroom the night of the fire."

Tommy's jaw bunched. "The fire is out. Your job is done."

Zach turned to look at him, and it was Tommy's turn to sigh. "We found the point of origin in the kitchen. Beneath the sink. There were rags near the cleaning chemicals, which ignited. The fire alarm was faulty and didn't go off. It wasn't called in by anyone in the house, but by an anonymous tip reporting smoke."

"There was a metal trash can in the kid's room—"

"Zach, stop." Tommy's voice was quiet but his eyes were intense. "The chief's signing off on the report today. Accidental ignition."

"He can't sign off. It's arson."

"I'm not having this conversation." Tommy turned and started to walk away. "Not with you."

"Are you kidding me?"

Tommy looked back, regret creeping into his expression. "Look, you're not the most credible of witnesses right now, okay? There were those two other fires earlier in the season that you cried arson—"

"*Cried arson?* What am I, the boy who cried wolf?"

"Just leave the case to those who are trained, Zach. I've got a helluva workload right now and I don't need you—"

"I don't care about your workload. We're *all* over-worked. What I care about is making sure that whoever killed that kid pays his due."

"*My* job, Zach. My job."

"But you don't believe it was arson."

Tommy gave him one hard, long stare. "I never said that."

"What the hell does that mean?"

"Look, I get that after what happened to your parents, that you'd see arson in every fire, but—"

No. Oh, hell, no. "We dealt with that in my interview, remember? That fire was years ago and has nothing to do with this."

"Are you saying that what happened to them when you were a kid has nothing to do with you being a fire-fighter?"

"I'm saying that I know what I saw on that Hill Street fire."

"No, you don't." Tommy scrubbed a weary hand over his face. "Listen, you should have several strikes on your permanent record by now, but I've always stepped in for you. I trusted you, and now I'm asking you to trust me."

"To do what?"

"To not go over my head with this. The chief is getting pissed off, Zach. And when he's pissed, he reacts. You know that by now. So do this, for me." He paused. "*Please.*" And with that, he walked away.

Zach watched him leave in frustrated disbelief before turning to go inside, coming face-to-face with Brooke.

"Hey," she said softly.

"Hey." Before he could ask how much she'd over-heard, she put her hand on his arm and literally gave him a physical jolt. Gave her one, too, by the way she pulled her hand back. Jesus, when they finally touched each other sexually—and they would—he was convinced they'd spontaneously combust.

"You okay?"

Better now, he thought. "Yeah." He took her hand in his, and felt the jolt all the way to his toes. "Quite a zap."

"Yeah."

Something about her made him forget his troubles. Well, not forget, but be able to ignore them, anyway. Her eyes were soft and also somehow sweet. After nearly three weeks, Number Seven had finally let her guard down, and damn, but it looked good on her. He wondered if she wanted to put that concern to good use, because he had several ideas—

"Are you sure you're okay?"

Soft, sweet, sexy, and too perceptive. "I'm fine."

"Because it's understandable if you're not. I'm here if you wanted to—"

Oh yeah. He wanted to. He wanted to in his bed, in hers, with her panting out his name as she came all over him.

"—talk."

He blinked the sexy vision away. "No. Not talk."

She blushed but didn't go there. "I'm sorry about your parents."

So she'd heard everything. "It was a long time ago."

"And it doesn't change what you saw at that Hill Street fire."

He stared at her, a little stunned. "No, it doesn't." He felt his heart engage, hard. "You're different, Brooke O'Brien."

"I've heard that before."

"Different good. Different great."

She didn't believe him, that was all over her face. "If you'd gone surfing with me," he said, "I could have shown you, proven it to you."

"Maybe another time."

Now that, he could get behind. "I'll count on it."

With an unsure but endearing nod, she walked away.

5

IF BROOKE HAD TALKED with Zach for even another minute, she'd probably have thrown herself at him. She wouldn't have been able to help herself. He'd been standing there, looking fiercely unhappy, and her ears had been ringing with all she'd heard Tommy say to him—about his parents, about that kid dying, about how Zach needed to stay out of it. God, she'd wanted to grab him and hug him and kiss away that look on his face.

Even now she wanted to, hours later, sitting by herself in the house.

Good thing she was off duty for two days. Two days in which to get herself together and find some semblance of control. Because there were other ways to offer comfort than sex, for God's sake. She could buy a Hallmark card, for instance. Or make cookies.

But neither appealed. No, she wanted to offer a different kind of comfort all together.

A physical comfort.

A grip. She needed one. So she buried herself in packing. By the time her weekend was over, she'd gotten to the halfway point, setting aside a shocking amount of boxes to keep.

Keep.

Odd, how she wished she could keep even more, but she'd talked herself out of that, going only for the photos and diaries, still surprised at the sentimental impulse. What was she going to do with it all and no house to keep it in? Oh sure, her name was on the deed of this one, but that was temporary.

Like everything in her life.

The answers didn't come, not then, and not when she drove to work for her next scheduled shift. As she got out of her car, her eyes automatically strayed to the hammock, empty of one übersexy firefighter. Not there.

And not washing his rig, half-naked. His rig was parked, though, so she knew he was here, somewhere. Pulse quickening for no good reason other than she was thinking about him, she stepped inside her new home away from home and found a big poster had gone up in the front room, announcing the chief's upcoming big birthday beach bash.

A party.

She wasn't great at those. Turning to head into the kitchen, she ran smack into a warm, solid chest.

Zach's T-shirt didn't say Bite Me today. It didn't say anything. No, this one was plain black, half-tucked into loosely fitted Levi's that looked like beloved old friends, faded in all the stress points. He had his firefighter duffel bag over his shoulder and was clearly just getting here for his shift, same as her.

"Hey." It was the low, rough voice that had thrilled her in waaaay too many of her dreams lately. "You showed."

At the old refrain said after all these weeks only to make her smile, she found herself doing just that even as her body came to quick, searing life. She had it bad for him, and it was as hot and uncontrollable as a flash fire. "I told you, I finish everything I start."

He smiled a bad-boy smile, and touched her, a hand to hers, that was all—and the whole of her melted. "Everything?" he murmured.

Oh, boy. She recognized the heat in his gaze, and felt a matching heat in her belly.

And her nipples.

And between her legs.

A kiss. She wanted just one kiss. Was that so bad?

"Because I think we've started something very interesting here. Something we should finish. What do you think?"

"I…uh…"

"I'm all ears," he murmured and shifted just a little closer. So close that she had to tip her head up to see into his eyes, giving her an up-front and personal view of the scar that slashed his right eyebrow in half.

Her gaze dropped from that scarred brow to his mouth. *Way* too dangerous. Also too sexy-looking for his own good, for *hers*—his smile too easy on the eyes, his *everything* too easy on the eyes.

"Brooke?"

"Don't I hear a fire bell?" she managed.

He chuckled softly. "No, but nice try." He shifted to let her move past him, but somehow they ended up bumping against each other, softness to hardness. For a brief breath she closed her eyes and allowed herself to absorb it—his scent, his proximity, the feel of him brushing up against her.

She'd had no idea how much she'd craved this nearness, a physical touch; that it was *him,* the object of her secret nighttime fantasies, only intensified the sensation.

He put his hands on her arms, sensuously slid them up and down, and she forgot they were in the firehouse, forgot that they should really make at least an attempt to be discreet. Hell, she forgot to breathe. "Zach." She tore her gaze from his and looked at his mouth.

A mouth that let out a low, rough sound of hunger, and then, blessedly, *finally*, was on hers, and then she was kissing him with *her* mouth, with her entire body, and most likely her heart and soul, because, good Lord, the man could kiss. He gave her everything—his hands, his body, his tongue—and when they broke apart for air, he stared down at her in astonishment. "Damn."

"What?"

"Just damn." Eyes a little dazed, he took a step back, looking off his axis enough to send a surge of lust and power skittering through her, but she managed to control herself. Controlled and composed. Yeah, that was her, one hundred percent put together.

With hard nipples.

And a telling dampness between her thighs.

"You ever feel anything like that before?" he asked.

"Truthfully? It's been so long, I can't remember."

His soft but not necessarily amused laugh ruffled the hair at her temple and ran down her spine. "Love your honesty."

She didn't. And she didn't love the idea that anyone could have seen that wild kiss they'd just shared. What was the matter with her? She turned away, but he caught her, a hand curving around her shoulder. "Don't go."

She needed to. *So* needed to. "Listen, maybe we could forget about this, at least until I figure out what it is."

His hand slid down her arm, settling on her waist,

where his thumb lazily stroked one of her ribs. The motion liquefied her bones and altered her breath. "Forget it? I don't think that's possible. Did you feel that?"

"I felt…something." Which she was fighting. She wasn't sure why, when she'd wanted that kiss more than her next breath—but that hadn't been just any kiss. No. And being with him wouldn't be just sex, either, and she knew herself enough to know that she wasn't quite equipped to walk away. Not from that.

And she *was* walking away. In a matter of weeks. Her job would be over, her grandmother's home on the market… "It's natural that we'd feel…" She watched him arch a curious brow. "This. Natural. I'm a woman, you're a man." A really, *really* hot man, but still. "Natural," she repeated again, and tried to mean it. "We've been working hard, and not relaxing, and…"

His head dipped to hers, his eyes a lethal combo of heat and good humor. "So you'd feel this with everyone, then? Say, Dustin? Or Blake?"

"Okay, no. But—"

Triumph surged in his eyes to go with that heart-stopping heat. "Maybe we should do something about it."

Yes, cried her body. Oh please, yes.

A bell sounded, thank God, and before she could form a response, the call went out for all the firefighters, no EMTs required.

Aidan popped his head in for Zach, who nodded, then looked down into her face. "We can finish this when I get back."

"No need," she said quickly.

"Oh, there's a need."

And then he was gone.

BROOKE SPENT most of the day out on transport calls with Dustin, and though she gave her all to what she was doing, her mind wandered. Not to the house she needed to sell, or how it was going to make her feel to leave a place she was slowly, reluctantly, started to think of as hers, but to a man and his kiss, and to the fact that he was making her yearn and burn when she never yearned and burned.

"Where are you today, New Hire? Disneyland?" Dustin shot her an exasperated look after having to ask her the same question three times in a row.

"I'm sorry. I'm preoccupied."

He pushed up his glasses. "It's because you guys haven't knocked it out yet. That's very preoccupying."

She stared at him. *"What?"*

"Come on. Are you going to tell me that you don't want to be with Zach?"

"Yes," she said quickly. "I'm going to tell you that. I don't want to be with…"

He waited patiently, but the lie wouldn't come off her damn tongue. Frustrated, she turned to look out the window, watching the town go by. Farmers' market. An art gallery. An outdoor café. "It's personal."

"Hey, don't worry. Your secret's safe with me. Hell, I've got the same problem."

"You want to have sex with Zach?"

He pushed up his glasses again, grinned, and pulled into the station. "Not quite." He hopped out and walked away whistling, getting inside before she could ask him *who* he had the same problem with.

Zach and Aidan's rig was in the garage, and her heart skipped a beat. The kiss, the kiss, the kiss…it was all she could think about. That, and getting another. And then she stepped into the kitchen and found Zach just standing there, looking ten kinds of wow.

He was in his gear, a little dusty, a little sooty and a whole lot sexy. He was still practically shimmering with adrenaline from the fire he'd just fought, looking far too edgy to be the laid-back, easygoing surfer guy she knew him to be.

And far too much for her to handle, no matter how much her body sent up a plea to let it do just that. He was too experienced for her, too…everything.

She'd spent too much time in her life trying to get somewhere, trying to find herself, to let a man like this in. Unfortunately, right now, at this very second, she wasn't thinking about finding herself. She was thinking about seeing him naked. "Hey. You okay?"

"Yeah."

But that was a lie, and that haze of lust he always created faded a little as she stepped closer. "Did anyone get hurt?" Or God forbid, like in the Hill Street fire that she knew haunted him, die.

"No."

But the memory of something bad was etched in the drawn, exhausted lines of his face. He took his losses hard, very hard, and that fact only deepened how she felt about him.

"I'm just tired," he said. "And needed a moment alone."

"Oh. I'm sorry." And she went to leave, because she understood that, but then he added, "I don't want to be alone from you."

She turned to look at him, but he'd moved closer and

she bumped right into him. Her chest to his, his thighs to hers, and she actually let out a shuddering sigh that might have been a moan.

"What was that?"

Oh, just her brain cells blowing fuses left and right. "Nothing."

Snagging her hand, he held her close, peering into her face. "You let out a…sound."

"Yes. It's called breathing."

His hand slid to her waist and gently squeezed. "It sounded like more."

How about a sexually charged, needy whimper? Did it sound like that? "No."

His gaze searched hers for a moment. "Maybe we should talk about the kiss."

Kisses. Plural. "Probably we shouldn't. It might lead to…"

More.

He was waiting for her to speak.

"I think I heard the fire alarm."

"Huh," he said, sounding curious.

"What?"

"You're not as honest as I thought."

"Yes, I am."

"Really?" His hand slid to the small of her back and stroked lightly. "Then what are you thinking right now?"

That he'd look mighty fine naked. "That I'm hungry."

Not a lie. She *was* hungry. For his yummy body.

"Brooke…"

"Yeah. Listen." She let out a breath. "I'm trying to resist you here, okay? I'm failing miserably, but I'm trying."

"Why?"

Wasn't that the question of the year. "Because this is unlike me, this thing we have going on. I don't flirt, and I certainly don't do…whatever it is *you're* thinking right now."

"Never?"

"No, not—not in a long time."

"That's just not right, Brooke."

Just the image of what they were talking about gave her an odd shiver and changed her breathing, and she realized he wasn't breathing all that steadily, either. "Not helping, Zach."

He laughed—at himself, at her, she had no idea really, but she found herself staring up at him, torn between marveling at the ease with which he showed his emotions and laughing back because the sound of his genuine amusement was contagious. "Happy to amuse you."

"I'm sorry." Still smiling, he sighed. "Ah, hell, that felt good. Laughing."

"Laughing at me felt good."

"Oh, no." Gently, he tugged on her ponytail. "Definitely laughing with you, I promise. And I should be resisting, too. But I can't seem to do that."

His words caused more of those interesting shivers down her spine, and to other places, as well, secret places that wanted reactivating. Standing there in the hallway, way too close to this sexy man, a smile wanting to split her face, laughter spilling in her gut, she realized something.

Whether she'd meant to or not, she'd made roots here, temporary ones, but roots she would treasure and remember always. And now she wanted to strip naked and let him do things to her, lots of things, things that would create more lasting memories that she could take with her. "So how often, when you give that look to a woman, when you talk to her in that low, sexy voice, when you touch her, do her clothes just fall off?"

When he opened his mouth, she shook her head. "No, you know what? I'm sorry. Don't answer that. Because I was on board for that. The clothes-falling-off thing. But…"

"But…?"

"But I'm not mixing business and pleasure, no matter how sexy you are. I can't, much as I want to. I just can't, not for anything less than a meaningful, lasting relationship, a real connection."

Her own words shocked her but she found she meant them. To the bone. Being in her grandmother's house had obviously sent that yearning within her rising to the surface, and she couldn't help it. "I mean it. I'm sorry if I let you think otherwise, but I really do."

Looking torn between bafflement and disappointment, he nodded. "Okay."

"I'm sorry if I led you on. If it helps, I led myself on, too. I hope we're still friends." All that was left to do was walk away gracefully, when in her heart of hearts she didn't want to walk away at all. She started with one step, a baby step, and then another. "I also hope that the rest of your shift goes well," she managed.

"Thank you. That's…friendly of you."

Was he was mocking her? "Well," she said primly, backing to the door. "Just because we're not going to…"

"Mix business and pleasure," he supplied helpfully.

"Yes." Because obviously he was not looking for a deep or meaningful relationship, or he'd have said so. "It doesn't mean that we can't get along."

"I think," he said slowly, in a tone she couldn't quite place, "that we're not going to have a problem in that department."

No. No, they weren't.

She nodded, and managed to turn and leave, but in the hallway, alone, she leaned back against a wall and let out a long breath. There. That hadn't been hard or awkward.

Ah, hell. It'd been plenty of both.

But she'd done the right thing. Now she wouldn't fall for him and mourn him after she left. Yep, definitely the right thing.

Damn it. Why couldn't she have gotten all self-protective after she'd gotten to see him naked? Brooke turned around to look at the closed kitchen door, nearly going back in, but she restrained herself.

The right thing.

6

SEVERAL SHIFTS LATER, Brooke was sitting outside the fire station on a rare break, laptop open, flipping through a national job database to see where she might go after the house sold and this job ended in a few weeks.

The warm sun beat down on her, the waves across the street providing the perfect white noise. It should have been incredibly peaceful. Instead, she was thinking about Zach. About the kissing. About her opening her mouth and saying that she wasn't going to mix pleasure and business.

She'd meant it, but she *really* regretted saying it.

Cristina came outside. She wore her blue uniform trousers, a pair of kick-ass boots and a tiny white tank top, which emphasized a figure that a Playboy model would envy. Chomping into a red apple, she glanced at Brooke. "Are you actually relaxing, New Hire?"

"Brooke. My name's Brooke." This was now a three-week-old refrain between the two of them.

Hard to believe she'd been in California for so long already, but it was a fact. And as she always did, Cristina shrugged. "Hey, I called Number Four Skid Mark, so consider yourself lucky."

She would. Cristina might be sarcastic and caustic but

she was brutally honest, emphasis on brutally, and loyal to a fault. In short, if you were on her good side, you had a friend to the death. Brooke knew the two of them weren't there, not even close, but at least she didn't have a nickname she couldn't live with.

"There's no point in remembering your name when you all eventually quit," Cristina continued.

"I'm not leaving until my six weeks are up. I'm just past halfway."

Leaning back against a tree, Cristina studied Brooke with interest. "People who aren't from around here rarely stick."

"Gee, really? Even with your sweet and welcoming attitude?"

Cristina smiled. "It's too bad you're not sticking. You could grow on me."

"I *am* sticking. Until the job is over."

"Speaking of sticking, I hear you were sticking to Officer Hottie's lips. That true?"

Oh, boy. "Officer Hottie?"

"Yeah. So were you?"

"That's…" She settled for the same line she'd given Dustin. "Personal."

"How personal?"

Wasn't that the question. She and Zach had only kissed, but it seemed like more, and there'd been lots of close encounters since… All she knew was that the wild sexual tension seemed unrelenting.

And overwhelming.

She really wanted to face that tension, and release it.

Let loose.

Assuming Zach still wanted to.

"I know my faults," Cristina said into her silence. "I'm sarcastic, mean and I don't like many people. But Zach? I like him. A whole lot. He's going through a tough time, and he's vulnerable."

The thought of big, rough-and-tumble Zach being vulnerable might have been funny only a week ago but Brooke knew Cristina was right. "The arson thing?"

"The chief's riding Tommy's ass, and Tommy's riding Zach's. Zach could just shut up and walk away from it all, but it's not in his blood to walk away, not when he knows he's right. I care about him, we all care about him, and he needs to stay focused."

"How do I threaten that?"

"You're messing with his head. *I'm* the only one who does that."

As warnings went, it wasn't exactly subtle. "I didn't realize you two were dating."

"Oh, I wouldn't call it dating," Cristina said with a smile.

Okaaaaay. "What would you call it?"

Cristina just looked smug, then, standing up, grabbed hold of a tree branch above her. "Any new interesting calls lately?"

"Hard to top Viagra Man, but I'm sure there's something just around the corner. What are you doing?"

"Pull-ups." She did five in a row, and still managed to talk normally. "Cats and hard-ons. Interesting job, you have to admit."

"True."

"So where are you going when this is over?"

"Don't worry. It'll be far, far away." Brooke just wished she knew where. She always knew—but this time nothing was coming to her.

Looking pleased, Cristina executed ten more pull-ups, then dropped to the ground to do push-ups.

Brooke went back to her laptop. Cristina didn't seem to mind being ignored, and Brooke tried for some peace and quiet. When another set of footsteps came up the walk, she didn't even bother to look up. She was busy, very busy, thank you very much, and needed no more distractions.

"Didn't anyone ever tell you that all work and no play will make you a very dull girl?"

Everything within her went still at the sound of Zach's low, husky voice. He wore his uniform, looking just hot enough that she felt little flickers of flame burst to life inside her. "Maybe I like dull."

"Nobody likes dull."

"I don't know." This from Cristina, now doing sit-ups on the grass like a machine. "I can believe she likes dull."

With an irritated sigh, Brooke closed her laptop yet again and stood. She'd find another place to study. Some place where the not-so-subtle barbs couldn't pierce her skin. Some place where there were no gorgeous, sexy firefighters making her yearn for things she shouldn't, like a connection, a real connection. And letting loose... She made it to the door before a big, warm hand hooked her elbow and pulled her around.

For a guy who only moved when he needed to, she was surprised at how fast he'd caught her. "I'm busy," she said with unmistakable irritation. She used that tone when she needed someone to back off, and it'd never failed her.

But it failed her now. Utterly.

"Yes, I can see that you're very busy."

Cristina, apparently finished torturing her body, walked past them with a smirk.

But Zach just studied Brooke's face. "You're always busy. You like it that way."

So damn true. But they weren't going there. "Where were you?"

"A meeting with the chief."

He was no longer amused, and she read between the lines. "How did it go?"

"Terrific."

"Really?"

"Sure. All I have to do is learn to respect authority, and everything will be just terrific. So were you and Cristina bonding?"

Nice subject change, she thought, but she saw misery in his eyes, and she didn't want to poke at it. "Yeah. We're like this." She held up two entwined fingers.

He smiled.

"Officer Hottie?" she asked. "Really?"

He had the good grace to wince. "If it helps, I don't answer to it." It was just the two of them in the yard now, with no company except the light breeze and waves. Perfect time to tell him she wanted to mix business and pleasure, just once. He stood close enough that she could see flecks of dark jade swimming in that sea of pale green. He hadn't shaved this morning, and maybe not yesterday morning, either, and she could feel the heat radiating off his body and seeping into hers. She could smell him, too, some delicious, intoxicating scent of pure male that had her nostrils twitching.

Bad nostrils. *Tell him...*

"Cristina doesn't mean to be rude," Zach said.

It made her laugh. "Yes, she does."

"Okay, yeah. She does."

"You're all a very tight unit. I get that loud and clear."

"We are. It's what makes us so good. But there's room for more. There's room for you. You could fit in, if you wanted to."

Her greatest fantasy… "*If* I wanted to?"

"Yeah, well, you have a tendency to stand on the outside looking in."

"No, I don't."

He just looked at her, all patient and quietly amused, and she sighed. "Okay, I do."

"But you don't want to be on the outside looking in."

How was it that he knew her? "We both know I don't really fit in."

"You could."

"Uh-huh. Cristina's waiting with open arms."

His expression was serious now. "She's had it rough and is a little distrustful, that's all. It has nothing to do with you."

She had a feeling it wasn't only Cristina who'd had it rough. "You're sleeping with her."

Brooke hadn't meant for that to escape from her lips. She wanted to pretend it hadn't, but Zach's brows had shot up so far on his forehead they vanished into his hair.

"Not that it matters," she said quickly, trying like hell to backtrack. "Because it doesn't."

"It doesn't?"

She shook her head. "It doesn't. It really doesn't. It really, really, *really* doesn't—"

He set a finger on her lips and she shut up.

"Cristina and I are friends," he said quietly. "We have been for a very long time."

She wrapped her fingers around his wrist and pulled it away. "And more than friends? Have you been more than friends for a very long time, as well?"

"Twice. A very long time ago."

She didn't want to acknowledge the relief that flooded through her at that. "You might want to remind her of that part the next time she's going around marking her territory."

"She has no territory to mark. Or I never would have kissed you like I did." He ran a finger over her jaw.

A simple touch.

But there was nothing simple about the way her body reacted, starting with the breath backing up in her throat and her nipples tightening as they hoped for some attention, too. So much for not mixing business and pleasure, because there was pleasure when she was with him. Lots of it. "Oh boy."

His gaze met hers. "Oh boy bad, or oh boy good?"

"We're friends."

"Yes."

"Th-that touch felt like...more."

"Did it?" He smiled innocently. "Then *you're* the one mixing the business with the pleasure, aren't you?"

She stared at him, but he only smiled, touched her again, then walked off, leaving her to talk to herself. "Am not," she whispered.

But she was.

She *so* was.

THE NEXT DAY, Brooke and Dustin hit the ground running and never slowed. They delivered a baby at a grocery store, transported a set of conjoined twins, stood by at a bank robbery and helped locate two fingers belonging to a construction worker, who'd lost them in a pile of sawdust thanks to the blade of his handsaw. It was early evening before they finally made their way back to the station, where a delicious smell had Brooke's nose twitching.

"Ohmigod," Dustin moaned. "Smell that?"

"Tell me it's for us."

"If there's a God."

Following the scent into the kitchen, they found the crew grabbing plates and helping themselves to a huge pan of lasagna. Zach was already seated at the table, his uniform trousers and a gray T-shirt spread taut over that hard body.

Brooke's gaze locked on his. They hadn't spoken since yesterday, where she'd done that whole mixing-business-with-pleasure thing, confusing their issues.

Her issues.

The memory of their kiss—that deep, hot long kiss— was *still* burned in her mind. In spite of herself, she wanted another one, and she had a feeling it was all over her face.

"Ah, man," Aidan moaned loudly from the table, mouth full—which didn't stop him from loading more in. "This lasagna is better than sex."

Cristina snorted. "Then you're doing it wrong." She took a bite, then also moaned. "But, oh yeah, baby, this is a close second. Nicely done, Officer Hottie."

Zach rolled his eyes. "Thanks. I think."

Brooke stared at him as she sat. "You cooked?"

"Well, we tried letting Cristina cook," Aidan said. "Remember, Eeyore?" He nudged Blake with his elbow. "For your birthday?"

"Disaster," Blake confirmed with a dour nod.

Aidan nodded, winking at Brooke as he successfully ruffled Cristina's feathers. "Cristina here burns water with spectacular flare."

"Hey, I've got other talents," Cristina said.

Aidan grinned. "Sure you do."

Cristina waved her fork in his face. "Don't make me kick your ass."

"You cooked," Brooke repeated, looking at Zach.

"Why are you so surprised?"

"Because—" Because it was a hidden talent, and now she was wondering at his other hidden talents. "I'm just impressed, that's all."

"Well, welcome to the twenty-first century," Cristina muttered, still glaring at Aidan. "Where men cook. And in case you haven't heard, us women can vote now, too."

Everyone laughed, and Brooke rolled her eyes, but when she looked around, she realized they weren't laughing *at* her at all. She was included in the joke.

Zach was gazing at her, his mouth curved, looking relaxed and easygoing and, damn it, gorgeous, and something came to her in that moment.

She belonged.

Aidan and Cristina were still bickering, Blake and Dustin were thumb wrestling for the last serving of lasagna, Sam and Eddie were shoveling in their food and laughing over something…they were all as dysfunctional as they could be, and they were a family.

And she was a part of it.

Sam took the last of the lasagna and everyone protested. "Hey, there's two kinds of people in here—the fast and the hungry. I'm the fast, that's all."

Zach smiled at Brooke with a genuine affection that stole her breath.

And replaced it with heat.

Oh boy, a lot of heat.

"Hey," Sam said. "Don't forget, I need everyone to sign up for party duty. The chief's b-day bash isn't going to throw itself."

"Yeah, and why are we doing this again?" Blake asked, classic Eeyore.

"To have an excuse to have a party," Eddie explained.

"To kiss up, you mean," Blake said, sounding disgusted with all of them. "Don't forget the kissing-up part."

"Well, maybe if Zach spent some time kissing up—" Sam accompanied this with kiss-kiss noises "—he wouldn't be called to the principal's office to get spanked every other day."

Zach sighed.

Cristina reached across the table and squeezed his hand. "I'd rather be spanked than hold my tongue."

"Me, too," Aidan said, in between mouthfuls of food. "Me, too."

"Yes, but…" Blake sent Zach a frustrated look. "It wouldn't hurt to lay low, let the chief get distracted by someone else's ass once in a while."

Zach shook his head.

No can do on the lying low thing, apparently.

"I can tell on Sam," Eddie suggested. "For leaving porn in the bathroom. Maybe that would take some of the heat off Zach."

"Hey, what did porn ever do to you?" Sam protested.

They all laughed, and Zach smiled, but Brooke could see that it didn't reach his eyes.

Later, she sought him out in the kitchen. He opened the refrigerator for a bottle of water, then leaned back against the counter, taking a long drink. He was behaving himself. Not mixing business and pleasure.

He was also quiet. Hurting.

Telling herself she was crazy, she walked toward him and took the water from his hand.

He just looked at her.

"That friend thing…" she started.

"Yeah?" He gripped the edges of the counter by his sides, and she wondered if that was to ensure he didn't touch her. She wished he could have put those hands on her, but she'd seen to it that he wouldn't try.

For her own good.

Damn, she was tired of for her own good. "If we're friends," she said softly, "then I should be able to do this."

"What?"

She set her hands on his chest, then let them glide up around his neck, bringing her body flush to his as she hugged him.

For one beat he held himself rigid, then with a low, rough breath, let his hands drop from the counter and come around her, hard.

She didn't look into his face, knowing if she did, she'd kiss him again, and this was just a hug, comfort.

Friendship.

So she pressed her face into his throat and held on.

"Brooke," he murmured, and the hand he had fisted in her shirt low on her back opened, pressing her even closer as he buried his face in her hair and just breathed her in. "Brooke—"

The kitchen door opened, and Eddie looked at them, brows raised. "If I cook tomorrow," he asked, "can I have the same thank-you?"

MUCH LATER THAT NIGHT, back at her grandmother's house, Brooke thought about the evening. About the hug and her reaction to it. Partially, because her body was still revved from what should have been an innocent touch, but there was more to it.

According to Sam, she could be the fast, or the hungry. But when it came to her life, she'd always been the fast, never slowing down, never relaxing, always doing, going, running. And for what? To always end up alone, wondering what she was missing? She'd come here out of duty, but she'd also wanted to find herself. Maybe…maybe she couldn't do that at the speed of light, maybe she had to slow down. Maybe *that's* what was missing.

She needed to give herself time to catch her breath, time to relax.

Needed to do that whole let-loose thing.

Moving through the kitchen with a mug of tea, she looked out the window at the dark night and thought about it, thought about Zach. As she did, a now-familiar tingle began low in her belly and spread. And suddenly, she had a feeling she knew exactly how she should be letting loose. And it included mixing business and pleasure.

A *lot* of mixing.

7

ZACH RAN in the mornings. It woke him up, kept him in shape and gave him time to think. Typically, he thought about work or, more recently, Brooke. He really liked thinking about Brooke.

But this morning, after having a dream about the arson fire, it wasn't Brooke on his mind, and he changed his routine, running past Hill Street. When he reached the fire site, he thought maybe he was still dreaming.

The place had been demolished, razed.

He stared at it in disbelief. On a hunch, he ran back to his house, got into his truck and drove to the site of a different fire, the one from a few months previous, a fire he'd also "cried" arson to Tommy about and had gotten his wrist slapped for.

That property was also demolished.

And the one before that? Yeah. Demolished. Standing at the edge of the third lot, where nothing remained but dirt, he pulled out his cell phone, but didn't hit any numbers as his last meeting with the chief ran through his head. He'd been asked, and not very nicely, to do his own job and no one else's.

Somehow he doubted stalking the fire sites would be considered doing his own job.

Shit.

Tommy Ramirez had told him to be on his best behavior, but that was proving damn hard to do. Driving home, he called Aidan, but had to leave a message. While waiting for a return call, he tried to distract himself with a Lakers game but his mind kept wandering to the arson.

He couldn't let it go. Driven to do something, Zach pulled out his laptop. He'd already typed up all his thoughts and notes on the fires. Now he needed to talk it out with someone, and oddly enough, the person that kept coming to mind wasn't Aidan, but someone with sweet baby blues and a smile that pretty much destroyed him.

Brooke. He was driven by her, too, because, damn, she was something. She was something, and…and she wanted a relationship.

Driven as he was, he didn't do relationships. Relationships always came to an end, and he hated endings. He didn't need a shrink to attribute that to losing his parents so young, to growing apart from the brother he had nothing in common with except grief and, in a way, losing him, too.

No, he didn't like endings, and therefore, avoided beginnings.

Still, Brooke drew him. She was a little buttoned-up, a little rigid, and—and hell. She had a smile that could melt him from across town, and a way of looking at him that suggested she could see right through to all his flaws, and she didn't mind those flaws.

Jesus. He went back to his laptop, burying himself. He had property deeds, architectural plans, records of sales, and looked it all over for the hundredth time to see if there were any obvious connections.

When his doorbell rang, he figured it was Aidan. When he opened the door, it turned out to be a beautiful redhead.

Nope, not Aidan, but his neighbor Jenny with a pizza in one hand, a six-pack dangling from her other, and a fuck-me smile firmly in place.

"Hi, neighbor." She lifted the pizza. "Interested?"

She was a high school librarian, but nothing about her was a stereotypical keeper of books. She hosted a weekly poker party, enjoyed car racing, and brewed her own beer. They were friends, and so far, *just* friends, but she'd made it clear that she was ready for that to change. Now here she was, flirting. Normally he'd flirt right back, but he didn't. Stress, he decided. Stress and frustration. "I'm sorry, Jenny. It's not a good time—"

"Don't even try to tell me you're not hungry. I'll have to take your temperature." She pushed her way in, carrying the food, swinging the beer. "Everyone has to eat."

True. And she'd obviously decided the way to his heart was by way of his stomach, maybe with a side trip past other certain body parts. Up until a few weeks ago, he might have been happy to take that side trip, but he no longer wanted to. Not with another woman on his mind.

Jenny turned to face him, and her smile slowly faded. "What's the matter?"

"I'm not sure." Yes. Yes, he was. He wanted a blue-eyed, sweet, sexy EMT with a smile that slayed him.

And only her.

"Zach?" Jenny waved a hand in front of his face. "You look like you were just hit by a train."

Uh-huh. The Brooke train. At some point, probably during the wild kiss, he'd decided no one else would do. *Holy shit.*

Jenny set down the food and popped the top off two of the beers, handing him one. "Here. You look like you could use this now."

"Thanks." He took a long pull.

"So who is she?"

"I didn't even know there was a she until two seconds ago. How did you know?"

"It's all over your face."

He scrubbed a hand over his face, images of Brooke coming to him. That very first day when she'd woken him, or when she'd so fiercely approached Code Calico, and then Viagra Man...or the way she'd looked at him with her heart and soul in her eyes when she'd said she wanted a relationship.

"Damn," Jenny said softly, still staring at him. "She's...special, isn't she?"

"I—yeah." He managed to meet her gaze. "I'm sorry."

"Not as sorry as I am." With another sigh, she stepped toward him, and in a show of how stunned he was, managed to nudge him down to the couch with a single finger. Then she plopped next to him and clinked her bottle to his in a commiserating toast. "You're good and screwed, you know that, right?"

He leaned back and shook his head. "You have no idea."

ON THE DRIVE to work, Brooke took in the high morning surf on her left, and the joggers, walkers and bikers on her right. She'd lost track of how many times she'd moved in her life, but all of those places had been big cities. She had to admit small-town living appealed. Little to no traffic, good parking spots...

But she was almost four weeks down, and only two to

go. Past halfway. Soon enough she'd be gone, far away
from here, starting over yet again. She'd found jobs available in both Seattle and L.A., and had filled out applica-
tions, telling herself there was just something about the
West Coast.

But actually, there was just something about Santa
Rey, and it had little to do with the great weather and everything to do with the fact that in spite of herself, she
was making ties here.

Blake was on his laptop when she entered the firehouse, and at the sight of her, he jumped guiltily, quickly
slapping the computer shut.

"Don't worry," she quipped. "Your porn is safe with
me."

Instead of laughing, he grabbed his laptop and left the
room.

Cristina was on one of the couches reading a *Cosmo*.
She flipped a page. "Hey, New Hire. Maybe you should
read this when I'm done. There's an article here on how
not to scare off men."

Brooke shot her an exasperated look. "One of these
days you're going to call me Brooke."

"I doubt it. Oh, and don't forget to read this article.
'How Not To Be Annoying At The Work Place.'"

Giving up, Brooke went into the kitchen. Her eyes automatically strayed to the counter—the scene of her two
indiscretions: one a heart-stopping kiss, the other the best
hug she'd ever had. Letting out a breath, she poured
herself some iced tea and was adding sugar when the door
opened behind her.

"Hey."

At just the one word, uttered in that easygoing, low,

husky voice, she dropped her spoon. "Damn it." She crouched down, and so did Zach, handing her the spoon, smiling at her. He was in uniform, filling it out with that mouthwatering body, but there was something…quiet about him today. Something quiet and, frankly, also outrageously sexy.

He helped her up. "You've been getting sun." He touched the tip of her nose. "And a few freckles." He stroked his finger over her cheek, her jaw.

Her body was so pathetically charged her toes curled at his touch. That's what happened when she spent her spare time dreaming about seeing him naked.

"You're looking at me funny again. Do I have something in my teeth?"

"No."

"Do I smell bad?"

That tugged a laugh out of her. He smelled delicious, and she suspected he knew it. "No."

"Then what?"

"I dreamed about you," she admitted.

"Ah. Were we mixing business and pleasure?"

She opened her mouth to say yes, oh most definitely yes, but then shut it again. No need to give him more power.

He just laughed softly. "We were, weren't we?"

She felt the blush creep up her cheeks.

"Yeah." Another low laugh and a naughty grin. "We were."

"Zach—"

"Was it good?"

She bit her lower lip but it must have been all over her face because his eyes went all sexy and sleepy. "Off the charts, huh?"

She closed her eyes. Oh yeah, off the charts.

Tell him you want to do the mixing in person. She was still trying to find the words when he said with a smile, "So, exactly how off the charts were we?"

"Zach!" yelled Dustin from the other room. "Phone!"

Zach sighed. "I'll be back. Don't move."

When he was gone, she let out a breath and fanned her face, saying the words she'd meant to say in front of him. "I was wrong. I *want* to mix business and pleasure. Just once." She smacked her own forehead. "How hard is *that* to say?"

Behind her, someone cleared his throat.

Oh, God. Wincing, she turned around. Blake had come in the back door in his silent way and stood there. "Sorry."

She just closed her eyes.

"No, it's okay. I didn't hear anything."

"Nothing?"

"Nothing," he said.

"Really?"

"Nothing except you want to jump his bones."

"I didn't say that!"

"Then I didn't hear it." He strode to the refrigerator, where he scrounged around and pulled out a soda, raising a brow when he realized she was still staring at him. "What? I won't tell anyone."

"Everyone tells everyone everything around here."

He acknowledged that with a shrug of his shoulders.

"Okay, you know what? I'm going to need a secret of yours."

He choked on his soda. "What?"

"That way I can guarantee that neither of us will talk."

Blake looked at her, then turned away. "I don't think that's a good idea."

"Are you kidding? It's a great idea."

His narrow shoulders were tense now. "But my secret is really someone else's."

"What do you mean?"

"Nothing. Never mind." Abruptly, he set his soda on the counter and walked out.

"Blake?"

But he was gone, carrying her very revealing secret. And then the fire bell went off and she put it out of her mind.

LATER THAT DAY, Brooke and Dustin were in the kitchen devouring a box of cookies between them while standing in front of the opened refrigerator trying to cool off.

"We're having a poker game Friday night at Cristina's," Dustin said. "You should join us."

"Did you ask Cristina?"

"Don't worry about her. She'll be happy to see you."

"Happy? Really? Cristina?"

"Okay," he said with a fond smile. "So she can be aloof, but it's just a facade. She's really just a toasted marshmallow."

"What did you call me?" Cristina came into the kitchen. She was in the bottom half of her fire gear, with a snug T-shirt on top. Her hair was pulled back and she looked hot, grumpy and irritated as she grabbed a handful of cookies.

"A *toasted* marshmallow." Dustin grinned at her, leaning back against the counter. "Crispy on the outside, soft and gushy on the inside."

Cristina hopped up on the counter next to him and set her head back against the upper cabinets, arms and legs spread in the aggressive sprawl of an alpha female who knew her place in the world. "Dustin?"

"Yeah?"

"The next time you call me a marshmallow, I'm going to pound you into the ground." She uttered this threat with her eyes closed, without moving a single muscle. "Next time."

Dustin winked at Brooke. "Definitely crispy on the outside."

"I can be a marshmallow sometimes, too," Brooke said.

A sound escaped Cristina, who still didn't move or open her eyes. "You don't know crispy. Dustin? Get me a water?"

"Ah, but I didn't hear the magic word."

"Get me a water. *Please.*"

"See?" Dustin grinned as he reached for a glass. "Soft and mushy."

"I'll have you know there's not a single inch of soft and mushy on me anywhere," Cristina muttered without her usual heat, making Brooke take a closer look at her. The female firefighter looked pale and just a little clammy, alerting her to the fact that maybe Cristina wasn't just being her usual pissy self, but might actually be in pain. "Hey, are you okay?"

"Migraine." Dustin filled the glass, which he gently nudged into Cristina's hands. Then he lay a cold, wet compress over her forehead.

"Thanks." Cristina let out a sigh. "Christ, this sucks. I'm going to the chief's party tonight. No matter what, I'm going."

"You should go home and sleep this off," Dustin said.

"I know. But first…" She sat up and groaned. "I've got to clean out my unit from that last call. Blake's doing something for the chief, so—"

Dustin set his hand to the middle of her chest and held her down. "If you're going to get rid of that headache, you need to sit real still and you know it."

The bell rang, and Cristina moaned, covering her ears as dispatch called for her and Blake's unit.

Dustin headed for the door. "I'll tell them you can't. They can get a different unit."

"Dustin—"

"Save it." He left the room.

Brooke looked at Cristina, so carefully still, pale and clearly miserable. "Can I get you anything?"

"Got a spare head?"

"Why don't you go home and go to bed?"

"I can't go anywhere until the rig is cleaned. We've got an inspection today."

"I know. We're all in the same boat."

"Oh, really? Are you on probation for falling asleep and not hearing a call?"

"Uh, no."

"Do you have a recent traffic violation?"

"Well, no, but—"

"Then get the hell out of my boat." Cristina sighed and straightened, looking positively green now. "Okay, I'm getting up. Watch your shoes."

"Stay." Brooke didn't quite dare put her hands on Cristina as Dustin had done, but she held them up. "I'll clean out your rig for you."

Cristina pulled the cold pack from her head and stared at Brooke. "Why? What do you want?"

Brooke let out a little laugh. "I'm offering to do something nice for you, even though you're not all that nice to me, and you're questioning it?"

"I'm less than 'not all that nice' to you, I'm downright bitchy. So the question stands, New Hire. Why would you do my job for me?"

Brooke shrugged. "Why not?"

Cristina just stared at her, the pain evident in her eyes but not hiding her cynicism. "The question isn't why not, but *why?*"

"Maybe I like to help people."

"We all do. Hence our jobs."

"Maybe I just do it nicer than you."

A ghost of a smile crossed Cristina's lips at that, then she very carefully covered her eyes with the compress again and leaned back. "Everyone does everything nicer than me."

"True," Dustin agreed, coming back into the room. "You're officially off duty, Cris."

Cristina peeked out from the cold pack to shoot him a look.

"You're sick. Take the break."

Cristina sighed. "Go away. Both of you just go away and let me die in peace."

Dustin lifted her off the counter.

"Hey!"

"If you won't put yourself to bed, I'll do it for you."

"Oh, sure, wait until I'm debilitated before you finally make a move on me."

He stared down at her, clearly shocked, his glasses slipping down his nose. "You want me to make a move on you?"

She didn't answer.

"Cristina?"

"There's a very real possibility I'm going to throw up on you. So if you could stop talking, that would help."

"And if you could stop trying to tell me what to do when you're as green as a leaf, that would help."

She laughed very very softly. "Assertive, too. Who knew? Hey, New Hire?"

Already heading for the door to go clean Cristina's rig, Brooke glanced over. "Yeah?"

"Thanks."

"A PARTY," Brooke muttered to herself. She'd showered and was now standing in the center of the bedroom she'd made hers, the first bedroom in her life that she loved without reason.

She had no idea if that was because her grandmother had put silly white-lace curtains over the window, which ruffled prettily in the wind, or if it was the dark cherry antique furniture. Or maybe it was because she'd come here looking for an exterior change of pace and had found an interior change of pace instead.

Because deep inside, she'd settled here. Her heart had engaged, for this town, this house.

For a man…

She stared into the closet. She had only one thing appropriate for a party on the beach, and that was a pretty little halter sundress she'd bought on a whim and had never worn.

With a sigh, she pulled it on, then didn't look at herself in the mirror. She did not want to change her mind. In that vein, she slipped into a pair of flip-flops and headed directly toward her car before she could come up with a million and one reasons not to go, starting with needing to work on the house and ending with because she was nervous.

Being nervous was not an option.

Not only was she going to go to this party, she was going to go and relax.

Let loose.

She needed to remember the concept. She needed to live the concept. She was going to smile and laugh. She was going to let go. And maybe even manage to do so with one wildly sexy Zach Thomas.

If he was still interested.

Please let him still be interested.

She drove to the beach, parked and got out of her car, the salty air brushing at her hair, the waves pounding the surf sounding all soft and romantic. Then she glanced over at the man getting out of the truck right next to her and her heart knocked hard into her ribs.

Zach wore board shorts and a T-shirt, his body looking at ease and beach ready. His eyes, though…not so relaxed. Nope. As she watched them lock on her, they were filled with the same hunger and frustration she felt, and she knew.

He was most definitely still interested.

8

IT HAD BEEN a shitty day all around, Zach thought as he got out of his truck. He'd had another unpleasant phone call with Tommy, who refused to tell him what was happening with the arsons. Then he'd covered for Cristina on three calls and as a result, hadn't been ready for their monthly inspection, and the chief had chewed him out.

Zach had almost not come tonight.

But now, looking into Brooke's eyes, he was suddenly glad he had. Very glad. Just taking her in, he felt a visceral reaction clear to his toes. For the first time since he'd met her, she wasn't dressed for the practicality of their work. No uniform trousers and matching shirt, no steel-toed work boots, no carefully controlled hairdo that said. *Back off. The rest of me is wound as tight as my hair.*

Not that *that* look didn't have some hotness to it.

But tonight she was in a pale blue sundress of some lightweight material that hugged toned limbs and a body that reminded him she was in shape.

Great shape.

She'd left her hair down, the strawberry blond strands falling in soft waves just past her shoulders, lit softly by the moonlight. A few long bangs were swept to one side, curving along her cheek and jaw, emphasizing her face.

A beautiful face.

Looking at him.

Smiling at him, with just a hint of nerves.

And he stood there, a little stunned, because when she smiled for real it lit up her face and her eyes, revealing humor and a sharp intelligence, and…and a sexual awareness that sparked his.

Hell, his had been sparked from the moment he'd first set eyes on her, but once he'd realized she wasn't going to play, he'd tried like hell to redirect.

She wasn't going to play. Playing wasn't her thing. He needed to remember that. He really did. Turning, he headed down the beach. Not to the party, not yet. He needed a moment—

"Zach?"

Alone. He'd needed a moment alone, away from her, to clear his head, where he couldn't see her looking at him, so sweet and sexy, smiling that smile—

A little breathless, she ran around to the front of him, one hand stopping her loose hair from sliding into her face, the other spread on her dress as if to keep it from blowing up in the wind.

Torn between hoping for a gale-force wind or running away, he stood there instead, rooted to the spot. "You look…"

"Silly, right?" She smoothed down the fabric but the breeze continued to tease the flimsy material, lifting it, revealing her lovely thighs for one all-too-brief, tantalizing glimpse. "I know. I should have stuck with something more practical—"

"Amazing," he managed. Even the sound of her voice lifted his spirits. Somehow she made him feel better by just being. "I was going to say you look amazing."

"Oh." She flashed another kill-him-slowly smile. "It's just a dress."

"I like it. I like the lip gloss, too." It smelled like peaches, and he wondered, if he leaned in right now, would she let him have another taste of her?

Just one.

Who was he kidding? One taste wouldn't cover it. Neither would two. Nope, nothing less than an entire night of tasting would be good enough.

Tipping back his head, he stared up at the star-littered sky, taking a moment to draw in the salty air, to listen to the waves.

But that moment didn't give him the peace he needed. Not when she was still looking at him, her gaze wordlessly telling him that she wanted him, too. "You should head on over to the party." He gestured with a hitch of his chin to the bonfires already going about a hundred yards down the beach, and the growing crowd.

In spite of what Zach thought of him, the new chief was extremely popular.

"Can we walk first?" Brooke gestured in the opposite direction. "Just us?"

Walking alone with her on a moonlit night along the beach? A fantastically bad idea.

"Please?"

No. Absolutely not.

She held out her hand. "Sure," his mouth said without permission from his brain, and taking her hand, he led her down the path to the water. There they kicked off their flip-flops and walked with the surf gently hitting the shore on their right, the cliffs on their left and the moonlight touching their faces.

Pretty damn romantic, which didn't help.

A wave splashed over their bare feet and legs, and the bottom of Brooke's dress got wet, clinging like plastic wrap.

Perfect. Just what he needed. Brooke all wet.

Letting out a low laugh, she gathered the material in her hands, pulling it up above her knees as she backed farther up on the sand.

He thought she'd turn and head toward the party, but she didn't. She kept going.

And like a puppy on a leash, he followed.

"It's beautiful, isn't it?" she asked.

He took in her profile, the small smile on her glossed lips, the few freckles across her upturned nose, her hair flying around her face. "Yes," he agreed. "Beautiful."

Her gaze flew to his. "I was talking about the scenery."

"I know."

"But you weren't looking at it."

"No."

"I…" She let out what sounded like a helpless sigh. "You were saying that I'm beautiful?"

"Yes."

"See, that's the thing."

"There's a thing?"

"Well, you make me feel a thing." She looked away. "A few things, actually."

Uh-huh. And that made two of them.

The breeze continued to toy with the wet hem of her dress and his mind at the same time. He took in the empty beach, the myriad alcoves and cliffs lining the shore, forming lots of private little spots where they could escape to without being seen.

Where he could slowly glide that dress up her legs and—

"*Ouch.*" She hopped on one foot, then bent to pick something up. "A shell."

He traced his finger over it in the palm of her hand. "I used to have jars and jars of these when I was little."

"You grew up here?"

"Yep. Santa Rey born and bred. My parents were surfers. I think my first words were surf's up."

She laughed, but then the sound faded. "You miss them. Your parents."

Lifting his eyes from the shell, his gaze collided with hers. "It was a long time ago, but yeah. I miss them."

"I lost my dad before I was even born, and I still miss him."

"What happened?"

"He died in a car wreck. My mom…she didn't really recover. She never settled in one place again, or with one man."

"That must have been rough on you."

"Not as rough as losing both parents." She squeezed his hand.

Yeah, it'd been rough. He and his parents had lived in an old apartment building on the beach. It'd been run-down, but it had fed their surf habit. He'd remembered every second of the night their building had caught fire. Every second of hearing his mother scream in horror at being stuck in the kitchen, surrounded by flames. Every second of watching his father battle those flames to try to get to her. The fire department had been volunteer at the time. They'd done the best they could, but their best hadn't been enough to save his parents. Their rescue effort had been a recovery effort pretty much from the start.

"Your older brother raised you?"

"He did."

"Does he live here, too?"

"No, Caleb's a high-powered attorney in L.A. Driven and ambitious…we're very different." He smiled. "He's still after me to do something with my life."

"Firefighting isn't doing something?"

He shrugged. "Well, it's not going to get me fame and fortune, or into a cushy old-age home."

"You don't care about any of that."

"No."

She nodded, looked down at her fingers, then back into his eyes. "We're very different, too. You and I."

"I know."

"Are you okay with that?"

Zach felt a smile tug at his mouth. "I happen to like the differences between a man and a woman."

She let out a soft laugh. "I meant that you're laid-back and easygoing, and I'm…not."

"I don't judge my friends."

"Yeah, about that." Her gaze dropped to his mouth. "I have a question."

He hoped like hell it was something like, *Can I kiss you again?*

She hesitated, then shook her head. "I need to walk some more."

"Okay." But he was saying this to her back because she'd already started walking, not along the water this time, but up the sand toward the bluffs, where they could move over rocks the size of houses. She did just that, climbing one, reminding him that she was a capable, strong woman who spent her days lifting heavy gurneys.

He followed behind her, enjoying the way her dress bared her back, her arms, how it kept catching between her legs.

With a huff of frustration, she finally hiked the dress to midthigh so she could move easier, a sight he greatly enjoyed from his lower vantage point.

Her panties matched her dress.

Then she vanished from view. "Brooke?"

"Up here."

He found her on a ledge the size of his pickup truck, sitting with her arms wrapped around her knees, her face turned out to the ocean, the waves tipped in silver from the moonlight. "Isn't it amazing?" she whispered.

Yeah. Yeah, it was, but she was even more so. He sat next to her so that their shoulders touched, and for a long moment neither of them spoke.

"The waves are mesmerizing." She sighed. "I could watch them all night."

"You should see them beneath a full moon."

"I've rarely taken the time to just sit and watch waves. Actually, that's not true. I've *never* taken the time to just sit and watch waves." She let out a long breath and looked at him.

"You had a question," he reminded her.

A ghost of a smile crossed her lips. "I was thinking maybe I'm too rigid. For instance, I shut down this thing between us without giving it full consideration. I said I wanted a relationship, but the truth is, I'm leaving in a matter of weeks. I couldn't really have a relationship, anyway. Plus, you were right about me not relaxing enough. Letting loose. I need to try some of that." She paused and looked at him for a reaction.

"Okay," he said carefully. "So…"

"It's just that I'm not exactly sure how to start." She flashed an insecure smile. "I've always been in school, or working. It's not really left a lot of time for anything else. I mean, I've had feelings for guys before, of course, but…but not in a while. A long while, actually." She paused again. "Do you understand?"

He was trying.

With a sigh, she took his hand. "I'm attempting to come on to you." She brought his hand up to her chest, over the warm, creamy skin bared by her halter dress to her heart.

He looked down at his long, tanned fingers spread over her, feeling the curve of her breast beneath his palm, and the way her heart beat wildly, and then stared into her eyes.

"Just once," she said very softly, "I want to be wild and crazy without worrying about anything. No meaning, no strings, no falling for anyone, just…let loose."

"I want to be very clear," he said, just as softly. "You're looking to—"

"Have sex."

"Have sex." She wanted to have sex. Just once. Had she been dropped here by the fantasy gods? How the hell had a shit-spectacular day turned so perfect?

"Zach? Am I doing this wrong?"

He let out a low laugh—it was for real. "You're not doing anything wrong, believe me. But…" He looked around them, at the rock. "Now?"

"Yes, please."

Again, he laughed. *Laughed.* "Here?"

"*Here.*"

His entire body reacted to the thought, so apparently he was on board with the here and now.

"Just the once," she clarified.

"To be wild and crazy."

She smiled. "That's right. And no falling. No messy emotions. Promise me."

"No falling. No messy emotions." He was so ready, his board shorts had gotten restricting, but he hesitated. "Brooke. What if that doesn't work?"

"Well, of course it'll work. We'll take our clothes off and lie on them, and then—"

He interrupted with a smile. "Trust me, I know how to do *that* part. I meant, what if once isn't enough? What if we still go up in flames when we look at each other at work? What if afterward, someone gets hurt?"

"Won't happen," she said so firmly that he was momentarily stymied by the fact that she was so sure she wouldn't want him again. "You just promised me no falling," she said. "I promise it right back. I'll be leaving town before I can start worrying about any sort of meaningful relationship."

True, all true, but...

"Besides, I'm not exactly the type to ignite any sort of wild passion, so—"

"Whoa." He was still reeling from her certainty that she would get him out of her system so easily. "*What?*"

She lifted a shoulder. "I'm awfully buttoned-up, Zach. Ask anyone."

"I'm asking you."

"It's years ingrained. Far too long a story to tell you now, but—"

"Give me the CliffsNotes version, then." This he had to hear. Not the type to ignite wild passion? Was she serious?

"I just put the prospect of sex on the table," she said. "And you want to talk? See? Proof right there that I don't ignite passion."

"Oh, don't worry. We're going to have sex on the table. Or on the rock." He smiled when just the words brought a blush to her cheeks. "But first I want to hear the long Brooke story."

"Really?"

She sounded so surprised that it squeezed his heart. Had no one ever bothered to try to get beneath her skin? "Really."

"Well…you already know I came here from back East."

"Boston. And before that, Florida."

"You remembered."

"I'm a good listener."

"And a good cook. And a surfer. And—"

"This is about you," he reminded her.

"But see, that's my point, Zach. I'm not good at a bunch of things like you are. I've never had the time to be. Before college, I lived in South Carolina. Before that, New York. Before that, Virginia. Before that…so many other places I can't even remember them all."

"Because your mom liked to move around a lot after your father died."

"Yeah."

So Brooke had been dragged around like a rag doll, with no say in her life until she'd been on her own. No wonder she liked her careful control. "Sounds tough."

"It doesn't matter—this isn't a poor-me story. My point is, I got my uptight analness from my childhood, or lack thereof, but I could be worse, and yes, I realize you're thinking that'd be quite a feat, but it's true. In any case, I've led a sort of wanderlust life."

"When all you really wanted was stability. Comfort."

Again, she revealed surprise that he got her. "Yes. And then my grandmother died and shocked everyone by leaving me her great big old house, chock-full of sixty-plus years of stuff, even though she didn't know me. I shouldn't have cared, but I did. I couldn't just let strangers box it up and get rid of it."

"Of course not."

She looked around, at the rock, the ocean, gesturing wide. "So here I am."

"So here you are. In a house. A home, actually. That's probably new to you."

"Very." She lifted a shoulder. "At least for another few weeks, until the job's over, and the house sells. It's going on the market this weekend." She met his gaze, and in hers the truth was laid bare. No matter what happened, despite the danger of caring too much, or falling a little too hard, she didn't want to miss out on this.

Neither did he. The wind kicked, stirring the warm evening. Her bare arm bumped his, a strand of her hair slid along his jaw as he slowly pulled her closer.

She tipped her head up to his, eyes luminous as her hand came up to his chest. She waited until their mouths nearly touched before she held him off. "I'm going to let loose tonight, Zach." Her fingers dug in, just a little. "Consider yourself warned."

His pulse leaped. So did other parts of his anatomy. "I think I can handle it."

"Sure?"

"Very," he murmured, stroking a hand down her hair, her back, cupping her sweet ass and scooting her a little closer, closing his eyes when her mouth brushed over his jaw, then met his.

Oh, yeah. He ran his hands down her body, half braced for her to come to her senses and stop him.

Any moment now…

Instead, she kissed him just the way he liked to be kissed, long and deep and wet, and raw, helpless pleasure flooded him.

And instead of her coming to her senses, he lost his.

9

AT ZACH'S RESPONSE to her kiss—a thrillingly low, rough sound from deep in his throat—Brooke melted and kissed him again, and then again…

"Brooke."

Lifting her head, she looked into his eyes.

His breathing had gone uneven, and against her body she could feel his, solid and warm and…hard.

Very hard.

She put her hand to his chest and felt the solid thudding of his heart. "Don't change your mind."

"*No.*" Eyes hot, a low laugh escaped Zach. "No. But we could go to my place, or—"

"No." She wanted another kiss. She loved the way he tasted, the way he smelled, so innately male she could hardly stand it. How long since she'd felt this way? Too long, that's all she knew. "Right here. It'll help me relax, Zach. I really need to relax."

Laughing silkily, he slid his hands to her waist, squeezed, then let them glide up her ribs, stopping just before her breasts. Her aching breasts. "Anything to help," he murmured, leaning in to kiss her again.

That worked. So worked. He wanted her. She could feel it in the tension in his broad shoulders, in the taut muscles of his back. Knowing it gave her a heady rush of power, and she demanded more, pressing closer.

His hands slid down her back, pulling her onto his lap, making her momentarily lose concentration as she tried to remember—did she have on pretty panties?—but then she couldn't think at all because his hands were skimming beneath her dress and were on those panties, and he let out another of those sexy rough sounds…

Oh yeah, letting loose worked. She should have tried it a long time ago. Already it was beating back the inexplicable loneliness she hadn't been able to put a name to. With Zach, she never felt alone; it was part of his appeal. He fascinated her. He had from the start. He was such a presence, so virile, so physical—especially right this minute.

"Brooke?"

He wore his intense firefighter face, or maybe that was just his intensity, period, but mixed in with it was need and desire, stark, glorious desire—for her. "Yes?"

His eyes were on hers as his hands continued to mess with her mind. "What are you wearing beneath this dress?"

"Not much."

The sound he made gave her another heady rush, and she gripped the hem of his T-shirt. Helping her, he tugged it over his head, then pulled her back in. The full physical contact made her hum, and then his fingers played with the tie at the back of her neck, the only thing holding up her dress, and the breath evaporated in her lungs.

"Your skin is so soft." He was touching as much of it as he could, running his hands up and down her sides, her arms, her back, under her dress, pressing his face to her throat. "And you smell so damn good…"

He smelled good, too. So good she leaned in and put her mouth to his shoulder, opening it on him because she needed a taste, just a little teeny tiny taste—

He sucked in a breath when she bit him.

"Sorry," she managed behind a horrified laugh when he lifted his head. "I'm sorry. I couldn't help it, I just had to—"

The words backed up in her throat as the front of her dress slipped to her waist. He immediately filled his hands with her breasts. "Sorry," he murmured, repeating her words. "I couldn't help it, I just had to."

She would have laughed again but his thumbs slowly rasped over her nipples, and any laughter vanished. Unbelievable. She was closer to an orgasm than she'd been during the last time she'd actually had sex. "Zach…"

"Relaxing yet?" His voice was low, silky.

"T-trying."

"Good. You keep trying." Bending her back over his arm, he dragged hot, wet, openmouthed kisses down her throat and across a breast, and sucked her into his mouth.

At the feel of his tongue stroking her nipple, she gasped, and then again when he settled her so that his erection pressed against the core of her.

He felt hard, very hard. And big. She looked into his glittering eyes, gulping as his hands slid down her thighs, then up the backs of them to play with the edging of her panties.

Oh, God. This was happening. They were doing this. She untied his board shorts.

He hooked his thumbs in the sides of her panties.

She tugged his shorts down, freeing the essentials.

He repeated the favor with her panties and slipped his hardness between her legs, using the rough pad of one finger to stroke her.

She quivered. "Zach—"

He did it again, adding a second finger, and she tightened her legs on his hand so he couldn't stop, because if he did she was going to die.

"I won't stop," he promised, reading her mind, playing in the slippery heat he'd generated, a heat she'd forgotten existed.

"Condom," she managed.

He went utterly still, then pressed his forehead to hers. "Christ. I don't—Brooke. I didn't think about—"

"I have one."

His gaze, so steamy hot it singed everything it touched, met hers.

"In my purse. It's been there for a while..." She fumbled for the zippered compartment. "I wish I had two—"

His laugh was soft and sexy as he took it from her fingers. "This'll work for now."

Biting her lower lip, she nodded, touching his chest, his flat abs, and then lower still, where his shorts were opened.

He stopped breathing.

So did she.

Bold in a way she hardly recognized, she wrapped her fingers around him. Loving the way that made him let out a rough oath, she slowly stroked. Swearing again, he slid the skirt of her dress up to her waist, baring her to the night and his searing gaze.

"Um..."

"Relaxed yet?"

"Not quite, no." Her dress was now bunched across her

belly, leaving her hanging out in the wind. Literally. Relaxed? Try wound up tighter than a coil.

"Lie back, Brooke."

Doing so would pretty much spread her out like a feast. "Yeah, but—"

He merely laid her back himself. Towering over her, he slid a leg between hers and glided his hands down her arms to join his fingers with hers. "How about now? Relaxed now?" he murmured, pulling their entwined hands up, over her head.

Was he kidding? She was so far from relaxed she couldn't even remember the meaning of the word. He was holding her down in the dark, only the moonlight slashing across his face, making him look like a complete stranger. But instead of the logical response of panic, she arched up against him, wanting more.

He gave it to her. Lowering his mouth to within a fraction of hers, he nipped at her lower lip, then danced his tongue to hers, long and sure and deep, and she gave back everything she got.

She was a different woman with him, someone who let herself live and love. And she wanted to be loved, more than she'd imagined. Closing her eyes, she rocked into him, moving impatiently against him, her fingers digging into the muscles of his back. "Zach, please."

"I plan to. I plan to please you until you—"

"Relax?"

"Come." He slid down her body, kissing her stomach, her ribs. "And then again." Making himself at home between her thighs, he smiled wickedly. "And again."

Oh, God. If he kept at it, she was going to go off in approximately two minutes—

He gave a slow, sure stroke of his tongue and she revised her estimation to two *seconds*. His hands skimmed up her legs to her inner thighs, holding her right where he wanted her, and then he added a finger to the mix and she couldn't have stopped from exploding to save her life. It hit her like a freight train, and he made her ride it out to the very end, slowly bringing her down...

After a moment, or maybe a year, she came back to her senses and realized she lay there on the rock, staring up at the stars, her hands fisted in Zach's hair, holding him to her in a way that would have horrified her if she'd been capable of rational thought, which she wasn't. Not quite yet.

He pressed his lips to one inner thigh, then the other, then crawled up her body, his mouth trailing hot and wet kisses along her skin as he went. She ran her hands up and over his back, his shoulders, and he let out a quiet sound of pleasure.

Taking her face in his hands, his mouth came back on hers as he pushed inside her, filling her so that she thought she might burst, holding her there on the very edge with fierce thrusts that sent pleasure spiraling through her, so far beyond anything she could have imagined. They never stopped kissing, not until the end when she fell apart for him again, and when he did the same for her, his head thrown back, her name on his lips.

When it was over, he rolled to his back so that they lay there on the rock side by side, breathing like lunatics, staring up at the stars, listening to the ocean crashing onto the sand just below them.

"That was..." She let out a half laugh. Words failed.

"Yeah." His voice was husky, rough. "That was."

Turning her head, she looked at him and felt her heart

catch at the sight of him, all long, defined grace, lit only by the silvery moon, which was a good color for him. Hell, any color would be good for him with that mouth-watering body.

Shifting to his side, he smiled as he reached for her and pulled her against him.

A cuddle.

Damn it, he really knew the moves, didn't he. Hard to keep her distance with him, that was for sure. But she was letting loose, so what the hell. Brooke scooted in as tight as she could get, loving the steady thud of his heart beneath her ear, loving the warm strength of his body all around hers, loving the feel of his hands skimming over her. "Maybe we should get up before we forget we only had the one condom."

His answer was a soft laugh, and he pressed his mouth to her ear. "There are plenty of ways around that."

She stared into his naughty, bad-boy smile, a smile that assured her that whatever *ways* he had in mind, she was going to like them. Her body was already halfway to another orgasm at just the thought. "The party."

"Yeah." He let out a breath. "Right."

"I mean, we should go, right? Blake said you need the kiss-up points with the chief." She sat up, looking for her panties, which were behind them, lying on top of his shorts. It was silly, given what they'd just done, but it looked so intimate. Too intimate. Snatching them both, she tossed him his shorts, and watched him pull them on that body she could happily look at unclothed for hours.

Days.

Weeks.

Oh, God. So much for keeping her head.

She spent the next few awkward seconds trying to right her dress, and not having much luck until he turned her away from him and tied her halter himself. "Brooke?"

Just the sound of his voice did her in. Closing her eyes, she swallowed hard. "Yeah?"

Zach stroked a finger down the back of her neck, evoking a shiver and a yearning that weakened her knees again. "I loved watching you let loose."

"Twice."

He grinned as he pulled on his shirt. "I still think we should try for a perfect hat trick."

"Party," she said weakly, tempted to do just that. "We're going to the party."

THEY WALKED down the beach toward the party together, Brooke's mind working overtime. The hot, sexy guy walking alongside her had seen her naked.

Touched her naked.

Kissed her naked—

"Well, well. What do we have here?"

Brooke jerked her thoughts to the present and looked at Cristina, who stood in front of them on the sand in a tiny bikini top and a pair of board shorts riding low on her trim hips. "You two look quite... *flushed* this evening."

Just behind her, the chief's birthday bash appeared to be in full swing. There was a big bonfire and several barbecues going. Music blared out of a set of speakers, and people were sitting on the sand, standing around the fire or dancing. Aidan was swaying like peanut butter on jelly with a pretty brunette. Dustin and Sam were happily flipping burgers. Blake was adding logs to the fire.

There were a bunch of other people, as well, from different shifts and different firehouses. In the center, enjoying the attention, stood Chief Allan Stone himself. A tall man in his fifties, he had the air of an army general and commanded respect—even fear—on the job. But tonight he was smiling and looking more comfortable than Brooke had ever seen him.

But mostly all she could see was the cynical twist to Cristina's lips as the female firefighter took the time to scrutinize Brooke from head to toe.

Brooke could only imagine what she looked like, and shifting uncomfortably, glanced down at herself. Yep, her dress was a wrinkled mess, not a surprise given that ten minutes ago it'd been rucked up to her waist.

Zach reached out and pulled something from her hair. A piece of dried seaweed. Perfect.

"I'd call the cute police," Cristina said dryly, "but they wouldn't know who to arrest first." And with that, she turned and walked back to the fire.

"She knows," Brooke whispered.

Well, she wouldn't go back and change it even if she could. She'd be remembering tonight for many, many nights to come, and would undoubtedly get all hot and bothered all over again at the remembering, and maybe even ache over what might have been, but she wouldn't take it back.

"Ready?" he asked.

She nodded, and they joined the crowd. Zach was immediately pulled away and put on barbecue duty, leaving her standing on the outskirts, a little bit anxious. Which was ridiculous. She'd just been bare-ass naked on a rock, she sure as hell could handle this.

Dustin came up to her and offered a plate of food.

He waited until she'd taken a big bite of the burger. "Hungry, huh?"

She slid him a glance. "Yes."

He nodded and said nothing else. Just stared a little glumly at the dance floor where Cristina was dirty dancing with someone Brooke had never seen before. "Why don't you ask her to dance?" she asked.

"Because she'd think it was funny."

"Funny that you have a crush on her?"

"I don't have a crush on her." He sighed. "Okay, I do. *Shit.*"

Sam and Eddie brought Brooke a drink. "To replenish the fluids," Sam explained. Both men looked at her expectantly.

"What?"

"You tell us," Eddie said.

Instead, she took another large bite of her burger.

"Don't you have anything you want to share?" Sam looked hopeful. "With your two best friends?"

"We're best friends?"

They both nodded eagerly. "So if something was on your chest," Sam said. "And you just needed to, you know, get it off—"

"In detail," Eddie added. "We're all ears."

Her burger congealed in her gut. "You know?"

"Oh, we know all."

She looked at Dustin, who grimaced, then nodded. She handed him back the plate, and Eddie the drink, and then walked off. She stopped at the water's edge.

"Stop sulking, will you?"

Brooke turned and faced Cristina. "I'm not sulking."

"Pouting, then. Look, this is a fire station. We're all

walking God complexes who put our lives on the line every day, and yet socially? Immature as high school kids. Come on—" she snorted when Brooke scoffed "—we love to talk. You've given us something new to talk about. Deal with it."

Brooke sighed. "How long will it last?"

"Until it's over."

"It is over."

"Please."

"It is. It was a one-time-only thing."

"Okay, now I *know* you're crazy."

"Why?"

"Why would you sleep with that man only once? That's just a waste of all that hotness."

"I'm leaving in a few weeks. We agreed it was just a letting-loose thing."

Cristina stared at her, then laughed. "And let me guess. You're already regretting that stupid decision."

Brooke looked away, into the bonfire. "No." *Yes.*

Cristina just shook her head. "Well, lucky for me, your shortsightedness is another woman's gain." And she walked away in her sexy little top and shorts, heading directly toward Zach, stopping to hug Blake.

Zach stood at one of the barbecues, holding a long spatula, flipping burgers and laughing at something Aidan was saying to him. Just looking at him, something happened inside Brooke. A clutch. A quiver.

What would it be like if she wasn't leaving? she wondered.

But she always left.

Always.

Besides, she'd said no strings. She'd insisted. She'd

come here tonight, just wanting to let go, to live and, oh boy, had she. She just hadn't realized that in doing those things, something else would happen.

In spite of her promise, she'd begun to fall for Zach.

She watched as Cristina took the plate out of his hands and handed it to Aidan before drawing Zach over to where people were dancing, proceeding to grind up against him in tune to the music.

"Here."

Brooke stared down at the proffered beer, then into Blake's face.

"You looked like you could use it," the tall, thin firefighter said gently.

"I…"

"Drink. Then we'll dance. If it makes you feel better, you can rub all over me like she is with Zach. I'm a good friend like that."

"I'm not jealous or anything."

"Okay."

"I'm not."

He just nodded.

And she drank the beer, then took him up on his offer to dance.

10

AFTER DANCING with Cristina, Zach moved to the coolers to get a drink. He pulled out a soda, then stood there with the waves at his back, looking for Brooke.

She'd been dancing with Blake, but now was with Sam, who was making the most of his time with her. Twice the firefighter's hands slipped to her ass, and twice Brooke lifted them to her waist.

Sam grinned in a can't-blame-a-guy-for-trying way, and Zach considered going over there and tossing him into the ocean, but he didn't.

An hour ago, Brooke had been in *his* arms, panting his name as she came all over him. She'd let loose now. Washed him right out of her system and that was fine. Hell, that was great. He'd just move on, too, and—

"You holding up?" Tommy asked, stopping next to Zach, sipping a beer.

"Why wouldn't I be?"

"Haven't heard from you in a few hours. Couldn't figure out if I should be worried, or if it was because you were finally trusting me to do my job."

Zach let out a long breath. "And how is that going? Your job?"

Tommy just took a drink.

"Shit. Don't tell me it's not going."

"I'm not saying that. I'm not saying anything."

"Well, then, say something."

"You're just going to have to trust me a little bit longer."

Unfortunately, he really had no choice. Tommy walked away, and Zach watched Brooke dance some more. Her cheeks were flushed, her hair a little wild. She'd definitely loosened up tonight, and he couldn't tear his gaze off her. Forcing himself to, he moved to stand by Blake, who was back at the bonfire.

The other firefighter tossed a log into the flames, watched it catch. "You could just ask her to dance."

"Who?"

Blake shook his head in disgust, then tossed another log into the fire before swiping a forearm over his sweaty brow. He didn't look so good, and Zach frowned. "You okay?"

"Yeah."

"Why don't you take a break, let me relieve you for a few?"

"I've got it."

Blake had been quiet and down all year since Lynn had died. Of all of them, Zach thought maybe he at least knew a little of what he was feeling. "Blake—"

"I said I'm good."

Great. They were both good.

And they were both liars.

For Zach, the next few days whirled by, a blurry, crazy merge of calls. He didn't sleep well, and finally gave up even trying, ending up at the firehouse kitchen table with his laptop, going through all his gathered arson information to distract himself from daydreaming about the feel of Brooke's curves, the taste of her skin…

And then the object of his fantasies walked into the room.

She was early for her shift, looking a little sleepy and a whole lot sexy as she headed directly toward the coffeepot on the counter.

They hadn't had a chance to speak alone since she'd worn that pretty dress with her hair down, her body soft and giving and sweet.

So goddamn sweet.

Her mouth was still soft and sweet now, but she was back in the uniform, complete with her hair all carefully pulled back.

Buttoned-up.

It didn't matter. He remembered what she looked like with her hair down, not to mention without her clothes, and he wanted to undo her all over again.

He wanted that. *He,* the one who'd not wanted a relationship.

Jesus. He really needed more sleep.

Brooke doctored herself some coffee, then looked at him. "What are you doing?"

Since the answer to that was, "something I shouldn't be," he shut the laptop.

"You and Blake. I caught him looking at porn, too."

"Excuse me, but I was *not* looking at porn."

Over her mug, she raised a brow. "What was it Viagra Man said? Guys will be guys?"

"For God's sake." He opened the laptop back up. "Come here and look for yourself."

"Oh no, thank you." She was laughing now, and lifted her free hand. "What you do in your own spare time—"

Reaching out, he grabbed her hand and tugged her over, letting go just before she fell right into his lap, where he really wanted her.

She sat in the chair next to him and looked at him for a long beat; he looked back.

"Hi," she whispered.

He smiled. "Hi."

Turning her head, she stared at the screen, at the list of property deeds and the records of ownership he'd been studying, and her smile faded.

"The fires," she said quietly. "The arsons."

"Yeah. Doing some research." Which was getting him nowhere. Nothing matched. None of the current owners, none of the past owners, none of the three properties were related to each other in any way. After all these weeks, he was at an impasse, and was afraid Tommy was, too.

"You're trying to link them together."

He wasn't supposed to be doing any such thing. He certainly shouldn't be discussing it.

"What about the way the fires were started?" she asked.

They'd all been started in a wire-mesh trash can, with a second point of origin as bait for the investigator to find and be misdirected, but he was afraid he was the only one who knew that. "Similar," he admitted.

"Suspects?"

He stared at her. She wasn't lecturing him on how stupid it was to risk his job digging into this. She wasn't telling him all the reasons why these fires hadn't been arson. She was sitting here, believing him, believing *in* him. "Most arson is committed by the owners. But the owners of these properties aren't connected in any way that I can see."

"New structures? Or old?"

"Newer."

"What about contractors, then?"

"All different."

"Okay, then. Back to location." Standing up, Brooke paced the length of the kitchen and back again. Leaning in over his shoulder, she typed on the keys of the laptop. "If we compare their footprints…"

He couldn't stop staring at her, bowled over by her analytical mind, her quick thinking. "I already did."

"And?"

And her scent was extremely distracting. As was the way her breast gently pressed into his arm. "They were all different square footage," he told her. "Different building types. Different everything."

"Show me."

He brought up the map he'd created. Her arm was resting on his shoulder. Her skin looked so damned silky, and he knew from experience that she tasted amazing.

Everywhere.

"There's got to be a connection." She was studying the screen, her brow furrowed, her mouth grim. "Somewhere."

She believed in him. The knowledge was staggering. "Brooke."

"Somebody is connected in some way. An employee, a relative, someone…" She was thinking, chewing on her lower lip, eyes still glued to the screen, and he couldn't take his off her.

"Maybe—"

"Brooke."

Her gaze cut to his questioningly.

And he lost his breath. Instead of talking, he tugged on her hand, so that she was forced to lean in closer until she lost her balance.

He caught her.

And then he kissed her.

With a soft murmur, she wrapped her arms around his neck and kissed him back. Oh yeah, *this* was what he'd needed for days—hell, maybe his entire life—and he kissed her until they had to break apart to breathe.

They were still staring at each other when the kitchen door opened and Aidan walked in. "Hey."

Brooke leaped back to her chair like a Mexican jumping bean.

"Anyone got food?" Aidan asked.

"Uh…" Brooke put her hands to her cheeks. "I have cookies on the top shelf."

"Score." Aidan helped himself while Brooke rose to her feet.

"Gotta clock in," she said and, with a last glance at Zach, left the room.

Zach thunked his head to the table.

"What?" Aidan took two fistfuls of cookies and plopped himself down next to Zach, peering at the laptop. "Trying to link them." He nodded. "Hey, maybe if you—"

"Aidan."

"Huh?"

He had to laugh. "I was sort of in the middle of something with Brooke."

Aidan blinked. "Oh. You mean…" He pointed a finger at himself. "You wanted me to leave you two alone?"

"Man, you are quick."

"I thought you two already knocked it out."

Zach winced, and Aidan sat back. "Wow."

"What?"

"Nothing."

"Oh, it's something."

"Okay. You're falling for her."

The door burst open again and Brooke stood there looking more than a little ruffled.

Aidan got to his feet. "Apparently I'm supposed to leave you two alone."

Zach rolled his eyes.

Brooke just kept staring at him until Aidan was gone. "Did you know everybody is talking about us? Why is everyone talking about us? It feels like we're twelve and in middle school."

"Since there's sex involved, let's call it high school. Ignore it. It'll blow over."

She glared at him. He couldn't help it; he laughed. "It will."

"You're not bothered at all?" she asked.

"I'm just saying it's what they do. Seriously, it'll all fade away if you just—"

"Yeah, yeah. Let it go. But maybe I'm not like you, all cool and calm and so laid-back that I have to be checked for a pulse."

Before he could say anything to that, she sighed and rubbed her eyes. "I'm sorry. That wasn't fair. I guess I'm still having bad new-kid flashbacks."

He moved toward her and lowered her hands from her face. "We're adults, and we made a decision. A decision that turned out to be the best night of my entire summer. Don't regret it, Brooke. Please don't."

As she looked at him, her eyes softened. Her body softened, too, and she nodded. "It *was* nice, wasn't it?"

"Nice?" He shook his head. "Nice is a walk in the park. Nice is a sweet goodbye kiss. Nice is a lot of things, Brooke, but it doesn't come even close to covering what we did on that rock."

"Okay, so maybe nice isn't quite the right word. How about good? Do you like that word better?"

He looked into her eyes. Beyond the irritation was a light that said she was playing with him now, but he'd show her good. Backing her to the refrigerator, Zach covered her mouth with his, swallowing her little gasp of surprise, a gasp that quickly turned into the hottest murmur of undeniable need and hunger he'd ever heard when his tongue swept alongside hers.

And though he'd meant only to show her up, he ended up showing himself something. That she fit against him as if she'd been made for the spot. That her scent filling his head, and the feel of her hands fisting in his shirt fueled his hunger as she sighed into his mouth, until it became so damn arousing he couldn't bear it. Pulling back, he stroked a hand down her body and felt her knees buckle.

His own weren't so steady, either, but a fierce sense of satisfaction went through him. Still holding her between the refrigerator and his own hard, aching body, he looked down into her face. "Tell me again that that was merely *good*. I dare you."

"Okay." She licked her lips, an action that didn't help calm him down any. "Does shockingly incredible work for you, Officer Hottie?"

He rolled his eyes but could admit that yeah, shockingly incredible worked far better. "So what now?"

"The million-dollar question, Zach? From you? Really?"

He found himself staring at her. Holy shit, had he actually asked, "What now?"

"Yeah," she said into the charged silence. "That's what I thought. There's *nothing* now. Both of us know it. We just have to remember it."

LATER THAT DAY, after having been out for hours on a series of nonemergency transport calls, Dustin and Brooke were directed to a familiar address for another Code Calico.

"How about you take it this time," Brooke said to Dustin.

He looked amused. "You catch on quick."

"I try."

"You're trying a lot of things lately. Or people. What?" he said innocently when she sent him a long look. "Just wondering about the status."

"I'm not asking you the status of *your* love life."

"Ha!" He grinned victoriously. "So you admit there *is* a love life."

They arrived on scene, mercifully saving Brooke from having to answer, since she didn't know the answer. The truth was, she no longer knew anything at all about what she and Zach were doing. Stepping out onto the sidewalk, she craned her neck, searching the three large trees out in front of Phyllis's place for the cat.

No Cecile in sight.

"Dustin," she said, watching as Aidan and Zach pulled up, moving with steady purpose toward the house, not the yard. "What's going on?"

Dustin put the radio mic back in its place, his expression suddenly serious. "It's not Cecile after all. Grab your bag."

For a split second, she stared at his back as he headed to the front door, then grabbed her bag and ran after him.

Inside the house, the shades were drawn, but she could still see well enough. As her grandmother's place had been, the house was filled to the brim with furniture from another era, upon which knickknacks covered every inch. But there wasn't a speck of dust anywhere, even the wood floors had been shined.

"In here!"

She and Dustin followed Zach's voice down a hallway, its walls hidden by photographs from at least five decades, to a bedroom filled completely with lace. In the center, on the floor, lay Phyllis. Far too still at her feet sat Cecile, gaze glued to her mistress, tail twitching.

Zach was kneeling at Phyllis's side, holding her hand, saying something to her.

Phyllis, eyes closed, responded with a nod. "Yes, Zachie, I can hear you. Tell Cecile I'm okay. She's worried."

"Phyllis, about your meds." Zach spoke calmly, evenly, any personal concern well tucked away, but Brooke could see it in his eyes. "Did you forget to take them?"

"No, I took my damn pills. You hound me enough about it, I don't forget."

"Okay, good." Zach squeezed her hand. "That's good."

Dustin moved in and crouched at her other side, and began taking vitals. Brooke recorded everything, all the while watching Zach be so sweet and gentle and kind.

Why she was surprised, she had no idea. She'd seen him in action before, with many victims by now, and he was always sweet and gentle and kind.

He'd been nothing but those things with her, as well.

And once, on a rock beneath a star littered sky, he'd been much, much more…

When it was determined that Phyllis had to be transported to the hospital, Zach helped get her on a gurney, where the older woman began to panic. "I can't leave. What about Cecile?" Reaching out, she gripped Zach's shirt with an iron fist. "I don't want to go!"

"Phyllis." Zach took both her hands in his. "Your doctor wants you to meet him at the hospital. He wants to stabilize your condition—"

"Condition shmondition. I don't have time for him. I'm fine. Completely fine, I'm telling you."

But she wasn't. Her color was off, her breathing coming too shallow and too fast, and, given the grimace on her face, she knew it, too. "Damn it," she said, sagging back. "Damn it. I'm not going." But she said this much weaker than before. "I'm not. You can't make me."

"Phyllis." Zach stroked back her gray hair as he leaned on the gurney to look into her eyes. "You do this for me and I'll take care of Cecile. Okay?"

"You'll take care of her?"

"I promise."

Phyllis covered her mouth with a shaking hand and nodded. "Your mother would be so proud of you. I hope you know that."

He squeezed her hand. "Just get better." He gestured to Dustin and Aidan, and they carried her out of the bedroom, navigating down the tight, cramped hallway.

Zach looked around Phyllis's room with an unreadable expression. Then, with a sigh, he grabbed the unhappy cat and tucked her into the crook of his arm. Turning to leave, he found Brooke watching him.

As it had since the beginning, their odd connection caused a spark to pinball off her insides, from one erotic zone to another, and all the ones in between—but this wasn't about their crazy physical attraction. Standing there, looking at him, she suddenly knew. It didn't matter that she'd told herself she wouldn't get her heart involved.

It already was.

"You okay?" she whispered.

"Yeah. It's just that she—" Shutting his mouth, he shook his head. Brooke moved closer and put her hand on his arm.

Something went between them at the touch. Not the usual heat but something much, much more.

Yeah, her heart was involved. Big-time.

PHYLLIS RESISTED getting into the ambulance. She wanted to stay home, she wanted her cat, she wanted everyone to get the hell away from her. She even tried a diversion technique.

"There was a man in my yard," she claimed suddenly as they loaded her inside the rig. "Did you see him? He was holding something."

"Phyllis," Dustin said gently. "You're going to the hospital. If not for me and Brooke, then for yourself."

"I recognize his face, I just can't quite place him…"

"It's going to be okay." Brooke sat with her and held her hand. "You're going to be okay. We're just going to the hospital so your doctor can check on you—"

Phyllis shook her head, her eyes cloudy as she struggled to get up. "You people are idiots."

Brooke sighed. "You promised Zach you'd do this, remember?"

The old lady closed her eyes. "Zachie."

"Yes. He gave you his word that he'd take care of Cecile. And you gave him yours that you'd go get checked out."

Phyllis's mouth tightened, but she stopped fighting at least. Zach's name had calmed her down.

Brooke had a feeling Zach had that control over every woman in his life, whether he realized it or not.

"There really was a man in my yard with a blowtorch, or something like one," Phyllis grumbled, sounding more like her old self.

In the back of the unit as she was, Brooke couldn't see out. She met Dustin's eyes in the rearview mirror and he shook his head. He didn't see a man.

Brooke squeezed Phyllis's hand.

The older woman held on with surprising strength as she looked into Brooke's eyes, her own filled with grief and fear. "I really want to stay home."

"You'll go back soon."

"Promise?"

She was so scared. Brooke's throat tightened, burned. If there was one thing she never quite got used to, it was the helplessness she felt over the things she couldn't make better. "Yes," she whispered. "I promise."

AFTER DROPPING Phyllis off in the ambulance bay of the E.R., Brooke and Dustin were called to another transport. The minute they were free again, Brooke tracked down a nurse to find out what she could about Phyllis's condition.

The nurse pulled her chart. "She's in renal and heart failure."

Brooke's brain refused to process that. "What?"

"Yes, the doctor was just with her."

"Oh my God."

"It's been happening for quite a while. Apparently the patient has actually known for months. She'll be staying a while this time."

"But—I promised her she'd be back home soon."

The nurse frowned at her over the chart. "It's not your job to make promises of any kind."

"I…" Brooke knew that, so she had no idea why she'd done so. "I didn't know about her condition."

"Of course not, because you're not her doctor." The nurse looked down her nose at Brooke, reigning supreme. "Do yourself and your future patients a favor and don't make rash promises. Don't make any promises." Spinning on her heels, she walked away.

Brooke staggered to a chair and let her weak legs sink until she was sitting. Renal and heart failure…

"Rough day?"

She looked up at Zach, in full firefighter gear and looking a little worse for wear himself. "Yeah. Rough day." Damn it, she could barely speak past the huge lump in her throat. "But not as rough as Phyllis's."

"So you know."

When she nodded miserably, he sighed and crouched in front of her. He was in her space but in a very lovely way, his big body sort of curled around her protectively, his eyes easy and calm and full of something she hadn't known was missing in her life.

Simple and true affection.

"I've got Cecile at the firehouse," he said. "Happily scratching the furniture and terrorizing the crew."

He'd made a promise and had followed through. For some reason, that got to her. "Zach. I screwed up."

"We all do."

"I promised Phyllis she could go home soon. But—" Her voice cracked and she stopped talking. Had to stop talking because she couldn't stand the thought of breaking a promise. Her past was a virtual wasteland of promises broken by her mother, and she'd made it a rule to never, ever do the same thing.

Zach let out a long breath, then reached for her hand.

"Now's probably not a good time to be nice to me," she managed. Damn it, she hated this. Hated that she'd failed, much less failed a woman she cared about. "When I'm near a breakdown and someone's nice, I tend to lose it."

"You should know I'm not so good with tears."

She pulled her hand free and closed her eyes. "Well, then, you're not going to like what's coming next." Eyes still shut, she felt him shift his weight. When he didn't speak, she figured that he'd left her by herself, which was definitely for the best. With a sigh, she opened her eyes, prepared to be alone.

As she always had been.

But to Brooke's shock, he'd never left her side.

11

ZACH WATCHED Brooke's expression register surprise on top of the pain already there. She'd really believed that he'd walked away. Tears or no tears, he wouldn't have left a perfect stranger, but she'd actually expected him to abandon her. He knew that wasn't a reflection on him, but on her own experiences. People didn't stick in her life.

Odd how he wanted to. "Phyllis wouldn't want you to lose it over her."

"I told her everything would be okay. I *promised* her. But everything isn't going to be okay."

He knew that, too. Heart heavy, calling himself every kind of fool, he sank into the chair next to her and leaned his tired head back to the wall and studied the ceiling.

It didn't matter that he wasn't looking at her. He could still see her; she'd been imprinted on his brain. A body made for his. A mouth that fueled his fantasies. Eyes that destroyed him with every glance. "Promises are a bad idea all the way around."

Especially the one he'd made to her. Not to fall for her. Man, that one was going to haunt him.

"I know."

Brooke still sounded way too close to tears for his comfort. Turning his head, he found her watching him, eyes still thankfully dry. "Don't be too hard on yourself. We all break promises."

"Some of us do it more spectacularly than others."

"I don't know about that."

She stared at him for a long moment. "Zach…I've not handled any of this well."

"This."

"The new job. Making friends at the new job." She lowered her voice. "You."

"What about me?"

"Sleeping with you and thinking I could just walk away. It was supposed to be letting loose, but you should know I'm having some trouble with that whole walking-away portion of the plan. I have no idea how people do the one-night thing, I really don't."

"There was no sleeping involved."

"What?"

"Our night. We didn't sleep. It's an important clarification, because sleeping implies intimacy."

"What we did felt pretty damn intimate," she said.

"Temporarily intimate. There's a difference. Now, if we'd been getting naked every night since…that would be true intimacy." He looked at her, wanting a reaction, but hell if he knew what kind of reaction he wanted, or why he was even going there.

"You agreed readily enough," she reminded him. "And it's what you do, anyway. Light stuff only."

She was watching him carefully, and sitting there in the hospital chair, surrounded by strangers, the scent of anti-septic and people's suffering all around them, she was clearly waiting for him to deny it. And given how he kept baiting her about it, it made sense that she was confused.

But what he wanted didn't really matter. Not when she was out of here in less than two weeks. But apparently his mouth didn't get the message from his brain because it opened and said, "Whatever this is, clearly we're going to drive each other nuts for the next two weeks, so we might as well take it as far as we can."

She blinked. "You mean…"

"Yeah."

At his hip, his pager beeped. Hell. Rising to his feet, he looked down into her still surprised face. "Think about it."

"I…will."

ZACH'S CALL was to an all-too-familiar address for a house fire.

Phyllis's.

When they pulled down her street, his stomach hit his toes. The house was lit up like a Fourth of July fireworks display. The flames were hot, fast and, as it turned out, unbeatable. Even with Sam and Eddie's engine already there, and two others from neighboring firehouses, in less than twenty minutes they'd lost the entire structure.

Afterward, with the crew all cleaning up, Zach slipped inside the burned-out shell. He moved through the clingy, choking smoke, down the blackened hallway where Phyllis's pictures were nothing but a memory. Inside her bedroom, he took in the soot, water and ashes.

And a wire-mesh trash can, tipped on its side.

On the wall above it, black markings flared out, indicating a flash burn. Probably aided by an accelerant.

Just like the Hill Street fire.

And the two before that.

Jaw tight, Zach stared at the evidence, pulling his cell

phone out of his pocket to take a picture, which he e-mailed to both Tommy and himself. This time, whatever happened, he was going to have his own damn evidence, because no way had Phyllis had a wire-mesh trash can in here, not in the lacy, frilly, girly room.

His cell phone rang, and when he saw Brooke's name on the I.D., he experienced a little jolt. *I've thought about it,* he imagined her saying. *Do me, Zach…*

"I just heard about the fire," she said instead, sounding tight and grim. "Zach, when we were taking Phyllis out of the house, she tried to tell us that someone was standing on the edge of her property, watching us. A man with a blowtorch."

His fantasy abruptly vanished. *"What?"*

"She was fighting us, trying to stall, saying whatever she could to get us to let her go back into the house. We didn't listen to her. And now…"

"And now you just might have helped catch a serial arsonist," he said firmly. "If you were here, I'd kiss you again."

She let out a breath. "But what if—"

"Don't kill yourself with the what-ifs," he said. "I've been there. They don't help."

"OLD HEATING element," Tommy told him the next morning when he found Zach waiting at his office. "Shoddy, unreliable, and as we saw firsthand, dangerous. Thank God Phyllis was still in the hospital and not at home."

Zach just shook his head. "This was no more accidental than the Hill Street fire. The trash can—"

"Zach—"

"Look, Phyllis said she saw a guy standing on the edge of her property with a blowtorch."

Tommy sighed and retrieved two Red Bulls from a small refrigerator on his credenza. "I can't discuss the investigation."

Zach declined the caffeine-rich drink. "Thought you were off caffeine."

"Sue me." Tommy drank deep and sighed again. "Just don't tell my wife."

"Tommy—"

"Look, I talked to Phyllis myself this morning. She's incoherent and in and out of consciousness. She doesn't remember a damn thing about yesterday. Not a guy with a blowtorch, or if she had a wire-mesh trash can or not."

"That's the drugs talking."

"That's all we have. The fire was put out, Zach. It was a job well done on our part. No injuries, no fatalities."

And that was the bottom line. Zach got that. He just didn't happen to agree. "It was also arson."

"Goddamn it."

"I suppose your next line is for me to leave this one alone, too."

"Yes," Tommy said very quietly. "It is."

"You got the picture I sent."

"I got the picture."

"You'd better be on this, Tommy."

"You need to go now, Zach."

Yeah. Yeah, he did, before he did something he might deeply regret. Like lose his job.

When he finally got to the fire station and went to the kitchen for something to put in his empty, gnawing gut,

Brooke was there. He'd hoped to see her last night at his place. In his bed. But clearly she'd thought a little too much. He tried to move past her, but she grabbed his arm.

"Brooke, don't." He felt raw. Exposed. If he let her touch him right now, it might make him all the more vulnerable. Pulling free, he backed up a step and came up against the damn refrigerator.

She merely stepped in against him, trapping him there. He could have shoved past her, but he didn't. Her warm, curvy body pressed to his, her eyes wide and open, reflecting her sorrow, her sympathy.

"The house is completely gone?" she asked.

"Yes."

"Was she right about the guy she saw? Was it arson?"

"I believe so."

"Tommy—"

"Told me again to stay out of this."

"Oh, damn. Zach, I'm sorry." She slid her hands up his chest to cup his jaw. "I'm so sorry."

But not sorry enough to have come to him last night. Knowing that, he might have been able to resist what she did next, except he didn't. She pressed her mouth to his cheek, and then to the corner of his mouth, and then, because he'd apparently lost his mind, he turned his head and hungrily met her lips with his.

Reason went out the window. Everything went out the window as he did his best to inhale her whole. She had her arms wound around his neck, her hands fisted in his hair. He had a hand up the front of her shirt cupping her breast over her bra, the other down the back of her pants, when he vaguely heard someone clear his throat behind them.

Shit.

Lifting his head, he locked eyes with Blake over Brooke's head.

"Bad time?" Blake asked drolly.

Brooke squeaked and hid her head against Zach's chest.

"Very bad," Zach said.

Blake gestured to the refrigerator at Zach's back. "But I'm hungry."

With a choked sound, Brooke stepped away from Zach. Without a word, she walked out of the kitchen.

Blake just arched a brow, gesturing to the fridge.

"Jesus." Zach pushed away from the refrigerator and let Blake at it.

THE NEXT NIGHT, off duty and at home, Zach sat at his own kitchen table with all the evidence he had on the arson fires so far spread out on a board laid in front of him. He was trying to connect the dots instead of thinking about Brooke when the doorbell rang.

It was pizza delivery by Aidan. His partner handed off the extra-large, loaded pie and pushed past him to get inside.

"Well, gee," Zach said dryly. "Come on in."

"We've got to talk." Aidan moved into the kitchen and helped himself to a beer in the refrigerator. He twisted off the top, drank deeply, then gave Zach a long look.

"It's not good," Zach guessed.

"It's you. And what you're doing."

"Look, we're both adults. If we decide to go at this until she leaves, it's our business."

Aidan looked confused. "Huh?"

"You're not talking about Brooke?"

"No." Aidan cocked his head. "Although, I did hear some interesting rumors today, which I ignored. Erroneously so, apparently."

"It's no big deal."

"Okay."

"It's just casual."

"Okay."

"But Jesus, the way everyone's going on about it, I might as well marry her."

Aidan's eyes nearly bugged out of his head. "Whoa. The M word? Out of *your* mouth?"

"It's just a word."

Aidan was still eyeing him like a bug on a slide. "Why are you harping on this?"

"Because you are."

"I said okay about twenty minutes ago, dude. It's all you."

Zach opened the pizza box, pulled out the biggest piece and stuffed a bite in his mouth. "Jenny brought me pizza a while back. Hers was better."

"That's because hers came with a hot bod. You boinking her, too?"

"No."

"Then can I boink her?"

Zach sighed. "Why are you here again?"

"To yell at you. But not for the women. I only wish I had half your woman problems."

"Hey, you've had your problems."

"Name one."

"Okay, how about you doing Blake's soap-star-diva sister and not telling him about it."

Aidan winced. "Hey, she wasn't a soap-star diva at the

time. And besides, I was really young and really stupid back then."

"Uh-huh."

"You're unusually testy. You're either PMSing, or those new rumors are definitely true."

"Which are what exactly?"

"That you and Brooke nearly did it up against the refrigerator. Which, by the way, if it's true? *Nice.*"

"Do you ever think of anything besides sex?"

"Alas, rarely." Aidan grabbed his own huge piece of pizza.

"Fine. But I don't want to talk about Brooke."

Aidan shot him an amused look. That rankled. "Okay."

"I don't."

"Fine. Let's talk about a little thing called arson. You told Tommy you thought Phyllis's house fire was deliberately set."

"Yes."

"Are you crazy?"

"It *was* arson."

"Okay, but Tommy is the best investigator this town has ever had and you know it, which means he's on it."

Zach opened his mouth to speak, but Aidan stopped him. "And you also know he has the biggest mouth this town has ever seen. Everyone is talking about you."

"So what?"

"So what? You love this fucking job, that's what. You work your ass off. You're one of the best in the whole damn city, and there's a lieutenant position coming up that you're going to take yourself right out of the running for because you won't leave this alone."

"I can't leave it alone."

Aidan sighed. "You're that damn sure?"

Zach pointed to the material he'd been working on.

Twisting one of the kitchen chairs around, Aidan straddled it, steepling his hands over the back and setting his chin on them as he studied the board on the table. After a long moment, he let out a breath. "Mysterious points of origin. Metal trash cans. And now, maybe a blowtorch." He shook his head. "So what now?"

Zach sat heavily and for the first time put words to the terrible thoughts in his head. "I'm not sure. But look at this." He tossed down the photos he'd taken of the razed properties.

Aidan shifted through the pictures. "Who ordered the demolitions?"

"I'm working on that."

Aidan finished his beer, silent.

"I know. I'm crazy." Zach shoved his fingers through his hair. "I feel crazy."

"No." Aidan shook his head. "Someone is systematically destroying evidence. Tommy either knows this, or…"

They stared at each other at the unspoken implication that Tommy could be behind any of it.

"You're not crazy," Aidan said. "And you need to get to Phyllis before someone convinces her to destroy any more evidence we can use."

"We?"

"Partners," Aidan said. "For better or worse."

LONG AFTER Aidan had left, Zach stood on his back deck, staring out at the night, his mind whirling.

Arson.

Brooke.

Restlessness…

He was surrounded by the life he'd chosen, a life both exhilarating and challenging. He loved it. And yet there was no denying he'd shut himself off from the very thing that people would say mattered most.

Love.

Had he really done that because of losing his family so long ago? Or had it just been an excuse, a handy reason not to let himself get hurt? If so, that had backfired, because he'd gotten hurt, anyway. Whether he was ever with Brooke again almost didn't matter—his emotions were involved.

She hadn't come to him tonight, either. That left him two choices: be alone, or go to her.

Easy enough choice. He went inside and grabbed his keys, and then whipped open the door—to find Brooke standing there, hand raised to knock.

12

BROOKE STOOD on Zach's front steps, having gotten his address courtesy of Dustin. One minute she'd been at her grandmother's, absorbing the sensation of feeling at home inside a house for the first time in…well, ever, and the next, she hadn't been able to stop her mind from wandering to Zach. She had no reason for being here. None.

Okay, that was a lie. She knew. And her body's reaction to the sight of him, all big, bad and slightly attitude-ridden, cemented it.

She was here to, what had he said? Take it as far as they could.

He wore a T-shirt and jeans, no shoes, no socks. Simple clothes.

Not such a simple man. "Hi," she said.

"Hi." He let out a breath and hooked his hand around her elbow, pulling her up the last step and closer to him. In the dim light he was all lean lines and angles and hard muscle as he jangled his keys in his other hand. "I was just coming to see you."

Her heart skipped a beat or two. "You were?"

"Yeah. I got tired of waiting for you to finish thinking." He moved aside so she could come in, but she hesitated.

"Give me a second," she murmured.

"Okay. For what?"

"For my brain to catch up with the rest of me." She smiled nervously. "It's my body that brought me here, you see. For some of that letting loose we're so good at."

He smiled, and her body began to tingle.

"Maybe you should let your body lead on this one," he suggested in a very naughty, silky tone.

"You think?"

"Oh, yeah."

"Just sort of let my brain take a rest?"

"Exactly." Gently crowding her in the doorway, he put his hands on her hips and his mouth to her ear. "So, are you going to come inside?"

"That was going to be my question to you."

His soft laugh stirred the hair at her temple and all her good spots. Then he slid his arms around her and gave her a hug, and along with the lust came such a rush of affection that her heart hurt. She buried her face in his throat and held on tight. "Okay," she said. "Maybe I'll come in for a little while."

"Great idea. We could—"

"Let loose?"

"Anything you want," he murmured, pulling back to look into her eyes. "I wanted to see you tonight."

Her breath caught. "You're seeing me."

"Yeah. I am. I see you, Brooke. The real you."

"With lines like that, you're awfully hard to resist."

"I'm trying to be." Pushing the door shut, Zach kissed her and, turning them both, backed her to the door. This freed up his hands, which he used to cup her face, a touch that turned her on more than any other. "I needed this connection tonight."

"With me?"

"Only with you." He kissed her again, his mouth making its way over her jaw to her throat.

"Zach?"

"Mmm-hmm."

"Zach."

"Right here." His hands slipped beneath her shirt and her eyes crossed with lust.

"I don't have a condom this time. I forgot to put a new one in my purse."

He shoved his hand in his pocket and pulled out...

"Three." Her knees wobbled as she let out a shaky laugh. "Think we can use them all in one night?"

"I have more in my nightstand."

"Oh," she breathed, staring at him.

At her expression, he let out a shaky laugh. "God, Brooke. I don't know what the hell it is about you, but you always make me..."

"What?" She needed to know. "I make you what?"

"Well, it's a bit of a problem." He pressed against her, and she could feel that he did have a problem. A big one.

"Oh my. I see."

"Do you?" His voice was a rough whisper against her ear. "Any ideas?"

"Uh, well, I do have a few. You know, all in the name of assisting a friend in need."

Against her skin, he grinned. "Is that what you're going to do, give me some assistance?"

"I'm a giver, Zach."

He was still laughing when he kissed her this time, and so was she, but his tongue sliding against hers had all that good humor fading away. Pulling up his shirt, Brooke put her hands on his chest, his hard, warm chest, while he lifted her, sandwiching her between his body and the door, rocking into her, and at the sensation, she thunked her head back against the wood, a needy moan escaping her lips as his mouth latched on her neck.

"Love that sound."

So she repeated it, and with a groan, he peeled off her shirt. Beneath she wore only a camisole. He slid the straps off her shoulders, then tugged it to her belly, exposing her breasts. "Look at you," he whispered in awe, leaning in, running his tongue over a nipple then sucking it into his mouth.

She found her fingers in his hair, and tightened her grip, arching up into his mouth. "Now, Zach. Please, now."

Now must have worked for him. He went directly to the button on her shorts while she yanked at his jeans. Somehow, he managed to tear open one of the condoms, and then with their clothes still half on and half off, he slid into her.

Time slowed.

Or stopped.

Or something.

It just felt so right, having him inside her, filling her. It was the only thing that made sense in her unsettled life, the only thing…and she didn't want it to end.

"Brooke." That was all, just her name, as if he felt everything she did. Then he was kissing her, moving within her. Her vision burst into a kaleidoscope of colors, and her blood rushed through her head, roared in her ears. She barely heard herself cry out as she came, or the answering low, strained groan from him as he followed her over.

Lifting his head, he slapped a hand on the door to keep them from hitting the floor. His eyes were dark and sexily sleepy as he looked into her face.

"How was that for some letting go?" she asked, still breathless.

His eyes were still scorching. "If I were to say it wasn't quite enough...?"

"I'd have no choice but to make use of those two other condoms you're carrying."

"Because you're a giver."

"That's right."

They made it to his shower, where Zach smiled down at her in a way that said he was rough and ready, all tough sinew wrapped around enough testosterone to leave her weak in the knees.

His hands were all over her, up and down her back, smoothing her wet hair from her face, skimming her breasts, her hips, her bottom, her thighs, between them...making her groan softly in his mouth, because yeah, his fingers knew her, knew exactly what to do to make her gasp. "Zach—"

"God, you're wet."

She managed a laugh, though it backed up in her throat when he slid a finger into her. "That's because I'm in the shower."

He played that finger inside her, in and then out. "This isn't from the shower."

Before she could respond, he dropped to his knees, pressed her back against the tiled wall and slid his hands up her thighs. "This is from me. You're wet from me." Using his fingers to part her, exposing exactly what he wanted, he leaned in and kissed her, then groaned in pleasure at her taste.

"Me," he repeated thickly, with unmistakable satisfaction.

He was right. Even now, after knowing him in a way she knew few men, he could merely look at her and turn her on.

And his touch...

He wasn't done with her, not even close. "Oh, God," she gasped as he, with gentle, heart-stopping precision, used his tongue, his teeth, his fingers, driving her right to the very edge and holding her there until she gripped his wet hair in her hands, silently begging him to finish her off.

Which he did, and she came again. Exploded, actually. Maybe imploded. She couldn't tell because she departed from her own mind for a few minutes, and when she'd have slipped to the tile in a boneless, orgasmic heap, he caught her. Caught her and surged to his feet, once again pressing her back to the wall, bending his dark, wet head to rasp his tongue over a nipple.

"Wrap your legs around me," he commanded, his voice a low, husky whisper as he lifted his head and impaled her with that dark, direct gaze. "There—God, yeah. There..."

Her breath caught again when he rocked his hips to hers, entering her. He pushed again, going deeper this time, and her entire body welcomed him.

"Don't," he growled when she arched into him. "Don't move, not yet—"

But she couldn't help it, and he swore again as he moved, a slow thrust of those hips, gliding against her sensitized flesh, wrenching a horrifyingly needy whimper out of her as her head thunked back against the wall.

He had his arms low around her hips. One slid up her

back, his fingers slipping into her hair, cushioning her head, protecting it from the tile. "God, you feel amazing." He let out a slow, rough sound of sheer pleasure. "You're so beautiful, so goddamned beautiful..." He thrust into her, wrenching low moans from both of their throats, which comingled in the fogged-up shower as he moved within her...

She'd already come, but she was there again, right there, primed and ready to go, his rhythm knocking her right off her axis. "Zach—"

"I know." Again he bent his head, this time to watch the sight of himself sliding in and out of her body, the pull and tug of their glistening flesh, hers so soft and pliant and wet, his wet, too, but hard, hard everywhere—his chest, his abs, his thighs, between them—

That was it, that was all she took in before her mind went white with blinding pleasure. Vaguely, she felt him follow her over, but she was gone, simply gone.

WHEN SHE COULD breathe once more, Brooke looked into Zach's eyes, which were still dazed enough to stir her up again. She'd wanted to let loose and, oh boy, had she. She'd wanted a change—well, being naked with a man was a huge change. She'd wanted to belong, and she'd found that, too.

She tightened her grip on him so he couldn't move, couldn't break free, not yet, and he pressed his hips to hers as if he didn't want to let go, either.

But then she realized how ridiculous that was. She didn't cling, ever, and she was sure he didn't, so she forced herself to relax her hold, to free him.

But he remained right where he was, muscles still

quaking, eyes still a bit glazed over, just holding her, and something happened to her in that moment, something ripped deep in the region of her chest.

Oh, no. No, no, no…

She was not going to fall in love.

At least not any further than she already had…

Only she wasn't stupid, or slow-witted. She knew the truth. Knew it was far too late. Needing to lighten the mood, she lifted her head and smiled. "Two condoms down…"

He let out a half laugh, half groan.

"Hey, if you're too tired for that third one, I understand."

Eyes glittering at that challenge, Zach bit her lower lip. He then proceeded to teach her a whole new kind of appreciation for her handheld showerhead—and she risked her knees to return the gesture.

By the time they hit his bed and tore open the third condom, she'd "let loose" multiple times and she was one quivering, sensitized nerve ending who could do nothing *but* feel.

And she felt plenty.

So damn plenty.

"Jesus," Zach breathed shakily in her ear some time later. "That third time was…"

"Yeah."

Turning his head, he softly kissed her throat, then her lips, coming up on an elbow to look into her face. "If we don't have the words for it, I say we keep going."

There were many, *many* reasons why she should get up and go home, but there was only one reason why she turned into his arms.

13

ZACH WOKE UP with a hard-on and a smile, both of which vanished when he realized he was alone.

Great. Terrific. Brooke wasn't clingy, and he'd always liked that in a woman. Unable to pinpoint the basis for his sudden irritability, he took a shower, and just looking at the showerhead, remembering its use last night, had him smiling again.

He dressed and stopped to visit Phyllis at the hospital on the way to work. She wasn't awake but he left her flowers and a Polaroid of Cecile sprawled on the fire-house couch, looking like the Queen of Sheba.

The picture reminded Zach that Tommy hadn't called him regarding the photo he'd sent, and something niggled at him, just in the back of his brain, a connection that he couldn't quite put together. It bugged the hell out of him.

At the station, he headed directly for the kitchen and caffeine. He found Cristina raiding someone's lunch and Cecile meowing at her feet for handouts.

Cristina looked at Zach, then did a double take.

"What?" he asked, looking himself over to see if he'd put his pants on backward.

"Hey," Dustin said, coming into the room, gesturing to the sandwich in Cristina's hand. "That's mine."

Cristina took a bite, still staring at Zach. "You know what."

"Not a clue," Zach told her.

"*My* sandwich," Dustin said again.

With a shrug, Zach headed for the coffee, but Cristina muttered something beneath her breath and, frustrated, he turned back to her. "Spit it out then."

She put her hands on her hips. "You're flaunting your just-gotten-laid airs."

"Hello," Dustin said to the room. "Am I invisible? That's my sandwich."

Cristina sighed and handed it over.

Brooke came in but stopped short when she saw them all. A smile slipped out of her at the sight of Zach, one that had *we had great shower sex last night* all over it, and it was adorable.

Cristina saw it and rolled her eyes as Brooke headed to the coffeepot. "Jesus. You two did it *again?* You know it's a dry summer when even the New Hire is getting more than me."

At that, Brooke spilled coffee over the edge of her mug and onto her fingers. *"Ouch."*

"Karma," Cristina told her.

"Hey, Cranky Pants." Dustin tossed Cristina back the sandwich. "Maybe I should go bring you some Wheaties instead."

"I'd rather get lucky."

"You could get lucky," Dustin responded. "Anytime."

"No, I can't." She opened the Baggie and took another bite, still frowning. "My vibrator broke."

Dustin's jaw fell open.

Zach handed him a mug of coffee and gently tapped his chin until his mouth closed. "Easy there, big D."

"Seriously, look at this face," Cristina demanded of Dustin, waving the sandwich around. "Does it say I've gotten any good action lately? Does it say freshly laid? Does it say orgasm central? No, it does not."

Zach glanced at Brooke, who was desperately trying not to look at any of them. He didn't want to brag, but he was pretty damn sure she'd visited orgasm central just last night, compliments of *him*.

Dustin cleared his throat. "You could try a man," he said to Cristina. "You know, instead of a vibrator."

"A *live* penis? Gee, why didn't I think of that?" Cristina poured a pound of sugar into her coffee, stirring so hard some of it splashed out.

Zach leaned in. "A little less anger, you might scare away the penises. Or is it peni?"

She pointed at him. "You, of the Recently Had Sex Club, shut up. You don't get to give me advice."

Brooke went even more red.

"How about me?" Dustin asked. "Can I give you advice?"

"*Hell,* no."

"Why not?"

"I don't take advice from a man who throws his heart into every relationship, only to get it crushed."

"If you don't put yourself out there, then why bother?"

Cristina stared at him as if she'd never seen him before. "You're hopeless. A hopeless romantic."

"You say that like it's a bad thing."

"It's…it's…" But for the first time in, well, history, Cristina seemed to run out of words.

THEIR FIRST CALL of the day came in for a large fire in a warehouse across from the wharf, and all units responded.

By the time Zach and Aidan pulled up, black smoke stretched hundreds of feet into the blue sky like a vicious storm cloud, and the chief was setting up the ICS— Incident Command System. The street was a chaotic mess, making it difficult to get close, but the police were working on directing the civilians out and the fire units in.

Word had come through that there were several people trapped in the warehouse, and Zach eyed the inferno critically. "Not good."

"Going to be tricky," Aidan agreed as they pulled out their equipment.

The chief sent a group of them to the south side of the building, where the missing people had last been seen. Sam, Eddie, Cristina and Blake manned the hoses, while Aidan and Zach prepared to enter the building.

"Now," Blake yelled from the rig, gesturing them in as the gang beat back the flames.

Aidan and Zach went in together, immediately choking on the thick, unrelenting smoke in spite of their protective masks. Visibility was ten feet at first. But only a few yards in, that was cut in half.

"You see red?" Aidan yelled.

"No, but I hear popping like Rice Krispies, so it's coming." In fact, it was earsplitting.

They had no idea where their victims were so Aidan gestured for Zach to go left, and he'd go right. About twenty feet down the dark, smoky hall, Zach heard a woman screaming. "Got one," he said via radio to Aidan, pounding on the doors as he went, stopping at the one from behind which came the screaming.

The wood was hot to the touch.

A door opened behind Zach, and as he turned, a man stumbled right into his surprised arms.

"Claire," the man gasped, and fought to get past Zach. "I hear her, I have to get to Claire!"

The guy was half-unconscious, and the size of a linebacker, an overweight linebacker. Zach gripped him tight, completely supporting his weight. Clearly the guy couldn't go after anyone in his condition. Hell, he couldn't even walk on his own. "You're not going anywhere—"

"I've got to get to Claire! Claire, it's me, Bob! I'm coming!"

"I'll get her."

"No, I—" That's all Bob got out before his eyes rolled up in the back of his head and he slumped to the floor, a dead weight.

Zach hunkered down to sling him over his shoulder, but Bob suddenly came to life, and with what seemed like superhuman strength, grabbed his ankle and tugged.

Zach hit the floor hard.

"Claire!" Bellowing, Bob crawled over him toward the office door.

Zach rolled and managed to hold him down. "You can't go in there. You don't have a mask. I'm taking you out—"

Good old Bob slugged Zach in the gut.

Zach absorbed the blow, using precious oxygen as he got the guy in a choke hold just as the ceiling began crashing down in flaming chunks, one narrowly missing the man's head, and only because Zach yanked him out of the way. "You're wasting time! Wait here—"

"No!" Bob charged for the door, but on the way there, a huge piece of burning tile fell, hitting him hard enough to slam him to the ground, where he finally was still.

Great. Now Zach had to get Bob out and to medical help before he could go for Claire, whose screams were already fading.

Calm but furious, Zach hoisted the man up in the classic fireman's hold and made his way back down the hallway. Luckily, Aidan met him halfway. "Take him," Zach directed. "I'm going back for the woman."

"We've got orders to get out now. The roof's unstable."

No shit. "I can get to her quick." Hands free, Zach turned back. The smoke was even thicker now, pouring in through the walls, making it seem like night. He couldn't see his hand in front of his face.

But worse, Claire was no longer screaming.

Then Eddie and Sam showed up, their lights barely cutting through the darkness. "Zach! Out of here!"

"I know—hold on!" He opened the office door. Behind him he heard Eddie and Sam yelling into their radios for lines of water to come through the office windows and the roof. They were going to get their asses kicked for breaking protocol, but Zach had never been so happy to see them in his life. "Claire!" he yelled as flames roared out the door, right at them, attracted by the new source of oxygen.

From outside, the hoses beat the flames back enough for them to move in; they found Claire crumpled on the floor beneath a desk. Zach dropped down and pulled her toward him. With Eddie flanking one side and Sam the other, he carried her into the hallway, where they were shoved back by flames coming from both directions now.

"Go back the way you came!" came the chief's voice via radio. "Out the way you came!"

They wouldn't make it. They needed a faster way—the office windows. But they couldn't get to them without hoses.

"Do it," Blake shouted into their radio. "I'm on the roof, I'll cover you."

Shocked, they all looked up, and through the burning ceiling, they could see an arc of water coming through.

Blake.

"Hurry!" he yelled down to them. "Move it!"

Eddie went out the window first, straddling the ledge, reaching back for Claire. Sam went next. Waiting until the ladder cleared, Zach took one last look over his shoulder at the flames rushing them, but Blake still had his back.

"Go," Blake shouted as the ceiling started to cave.

"Jesus, Blake!" Zach's heart stopped. *"Get back!"*

"I will when you're out—"

But a thundering shudder silenced them both. Zach made to leap for the ladder, but the ceiling crashed down. As he yelled Blake's name, everything went black.

"TWO FIREFIGHTERS are down," Dustin said grimly, setting down the radio.

Brooke's heart stopped. "Oh my God. *Who?*"

Dustin didn't meet her eyes.

She grabbed his sleeve. *"Who?"*

"Blake and Zach." He grimaced, but tried to sound reassuring. "Don't worry, they'll get them out."

"Ohmigod, they're trapped?"

The male victim Aidan had carried out was sitting on the curb holding an ice pack to his head, and at this news, he moaned. "It's my fault. I freaked out. And now Claire's trapped in there, too."

"She's out," Dustin told him. "She's in the ambulance, where you should be."

"Oh, thank God." The man surged to his feet, grabbing Brooke's hand, his eyes wet. "I'm sorry. I'm so sorry—"

She shook her head. "You need to sit down—"

"No, I'm fine. I'm just so damn sorry—"

Dustin brought him to Claire, while Brooke stared up at the building, which was a virtual inferno.

Zach was in there.

She took a step toward it but Dustin was back, blocking her path. *"What are you doing?"*

"I need to get closer."

"You're not a firefighter. And we're hospital-bound, Brooke. Two vics, remember? It's our job."

Damn it, he was right. The job. The job always came first. It was what she'd signed on for, and she'd never before minded it taking over her life. Not once.

Unfortunately, she'd given herself a taste of *real* life here in Santa Rey, and she liked it. Hell, loved it.

But now the person who'd given her that taste of life was in danger of losing his.

BROOKE AND DUSTIN were still unloading their patients at the E.R. when word came from the fire scene that they had the flames eighty percent contained, and the injured firefighters had been evacuated safely.

Alive.

And on the way to the hospital.

Brooke took her first deep breath since she'd heard the words *firefighters* and *down* in the same sentence. She and Dustin tried to wait but an emergency call came in for them—a woman with chest pains needed assistance.

While Dustin drove, Brooke called Aidan.

"Blake's in surgery," Aidan said, sounding tense and stressed. "Badly broken leg."

Ohmigod. "Zach?"

"A concussion, broken wrist and a few second-degree burns. I know that sounds bad, but he's going to be okay, Brooke."

Relief hit her like a tidal wave, but she couldn't lose it because they'd arrived at their call, where she and Dustin found a three-hundred-and-fifty-pound woman stuck in her bed, needing assistance to the bathroom.

"You said you had chest pains," Dustin said.

"Right. I do. But I think it's heartburn."

"Are the pains gone now?" Brooke asked.

"Yes. Completely."

"Ma'am, we still need to bring you in to be checked—"

"Okay, so I never had chest pains. I called because you people won't come out unless it's serious."

They were speechless.

"Would you hand me my TV remote?" she asked them. "Oh, and that box of doughnuts?"

Brooke stared at her. She'd missed being at Zach's side for this, for a woman who couldn't reach her damn remote so she'd called 911? She handed over the remote but not the doughnuts. "Ma'am, the 911 system is for *real* emergencies—"

"It was a real emergency."

Dustin still couldn't speak.

"Hey, I'm sorry, but *Grey's Anatomy* is repeating and I missed it the first time around."

"*Medical* emergencies," Brooke said tightly.

The woman finally had the grace to look a little abashed. "I know, but who else am I going to call?"

"You could do it yourself." No longer speechless, Dustin was clearly furious. "Consider it your daily exercise."

They left there in silence, and it was several long moments before either could speak.

"That didn't just happen," Dustin finally said.

But unfortunately it had, and they had another call, and then another, and it was several hours before Brooke could get another status check on Zach. By that time he'd been released from the hospital and was at his house, supposedly resting.

She wanted to get over there, needed to get a good look at him herself and make sure he was okay, but the chief put their rig on overtime; neither she nor Dustin was going anywhere.

It killed her.

She'd always given her heart and soul to her job, and that had always fulfilled her. But she could see that was no longer the case. Zach's accident had driven home to her that work was *not* enough.

Here in Santa Rey, she'd found more.

14

WHEN THE DOORBELL rang late that night, Zach was in bed, nicely doped up, flying high on whatever the doctor had given him. Aidan had already brought him dinner and had stayed for a movie, but was gone now. Jenny had brought another movie and a few of her pole-dancing pals by, but they'd left, too.

And now someone else was ringing… He sat up very carefully, and then stayed there, head spinning. He'd never been injured on the job before and wasn't quite sure how it had happened. He remembered nearly getting outside the burning building, but that was all until he'd woken up to a headache from hell and Aidan pulling his sorry ass out of the fire just before it ate them both alive.

He knew the dangers of his job. Hell, he knew the dangers of life, but that reality hadn't hit him since his parents had died.

It hit him now. He could have died.

Morbid thought, but he was a realist. If he'd died, life would go on. People would mourn, sure, but no one's basic existence would change with his passing, and that meant facing something uncomfortable—he hadn't made much of a dent.

After his parents' death, he'd just gone along, minding

his business, working hard, playing even harder, and that had always been enough for him, because why go for more when life was so damn short? He'd always looked at his colleagues, the ones who'd tied themselves down with marriages and kids, and had been thankful it wasn't him.

But now he couldn't help but wonder if he'd missed out on something that he'd never fathomed.

The doorbell rang again.

"Coming!" he called out, then instantly regretted it because that hurt. Note to self: *don't yell.* Getting out of bed wasn't too much of a problem, but remaining upright proved to be. It turned out his head didn't feel quite attached, and he brought up his uncasted wrist to hold it in place as he made his way to the door like someone on a three-day drunk. He managed to unlock it, then sagged back against the wall, weary to his bones of the jackhammer going off inside his skull. Everything hurt—his wrist, the burns on his left shoulder, arm and chest...

The door creaked open. "Zach?"

Ah, he knew that voice. He knew what it sounded like when she was in the throes of an orgasm, panting, sobbing for breath. He knew what it sounded like when she was slowly drifting back to him, and his name rolled off her tongue as if maybe, just maybe, he were the best she'd ever had.

At the sight of him, she let out a little gasp. "Zach, you shouldn't be up."

"You rang."

"Oh, God. I'm sorry." And then her hands were on his waist, gently pulling him away from the wall so she could slip her shoulder beneath his good one and wrap an arm around him, supporting his weight. "Okay?" she asked.

He slung his arm around her and smiled into her face. "Okay." She was wearing a tank top and capris, looking as if she was learning to fit into the beach world after all. Her hair had been pulled back as usual, neat and tidy as could be, so he tugged on her ponytail, just enough to have some strands slipping free. "There," he said. "A little messy. I like you that way best."

"Bed," she said firmly.

"I thought you'd never ask."

She gave him a look. "What do they have you on?"

"Good stuff."

"Sounds like it." One arm was firmly around him, the other hand low on his abs. He wouldn't have thought it possible, but she was actually completely supporting him, even though he was a foot taller and probably had seventy pounds on her.

As he'd always known, the little city girl was a helluva lot tougher than she looked.

At the top of the stairs, she kept moving to his bedroom. He was just dizzy and shaken enough to let her put him to bed, although he did attempt to pull her down with him. "You need liquids," she said. "Water? Tea?"

"A kiss."

"Both," she decided, and vanished.

Uptight, stubborn as a mule, know-it-all, anal woman.

When she came back and set a tray on his nightstand, he struggled to open his eyes, surprised to find even that took effort. "I'm cold," he said. "Possibly hypothermic."

"I'll get you a blanket."

"You're supposed to offer to strip down and press

your heated body to mine. It's in all the movies. The girl always strips."

"Zach." With her hands on her hips, and her hair suitably messed up thanks to his doing, Brooke looked so pretty and sexy he couldn't think straight.

And she had no idea. No idea at all that she messed with his head just by being. "You really should be out by now," he said, bemused.

"I'm not leaving you alone."

"I meant out of my head." He closed his eyes. "I can't get you out of my damn head."

What if *she'd* gotten hurt today? What if *she'd* died? At the thought, his throat closed up. Just refused to suck air into his lungs, because apparently he'd screwed up and let himself care. If something ever happened to her...

He'd never put words to his biggest fear before, but he was doing so now. And he didn't like it. Not at all.

"Zach." Softly, gently, she cupped his face. "You're in my head, too. *Way* too much."

He hadn't planned to go there—had, in fact, never planned to go there again. His parents dying had nearly been the end of him. "It's the drugs for me." He closed his eyes. "What's your excuse?"

She was quiet a moment. "Maybe you've proven irresistible."

He tried to laugh, but that hurt, so he sobered up quickly. "If it'd been you..."

"But it wasn't. I'm fine." She stretched out next to him on his bed and gently pressed her body to his aching one, easing his pain with no effort at all.

With a sigh, he pulled her closer, holding her tight, tucking her head beneath his chin, wondering how it was that suddenly, with her here in his arms, everything felt all right.

"Are you really okay?" she whispered. Pulling back, she looked up into his face. Her eyes were bright, and warm, and so open Zach could see into her soul.

Was he okay? He didn't feel it. Things had gotten a little crazy in that fire—maybe it was just residual adrenaline making him need her so. "If I said I'm not okay, what would you do?"

Her fingers drifted over his chest in a touch he knew she meant to be soothing, but was actually having an entirely different effect. "I'd do everything in my power to make you comfortable."

"Then, no." He went to shake his head, but the pain stopped him cold. "Definitely not okay."

"Tell me what hurts."

He looked deep into her eyes and saw so much. So much that he had to close his own.

Coward. Yeah, despite the tough-guy image his job gave him, he was a coward. At least he knew it, knew his limitations, knew that loving her, loving anyone, was something he couldn't do. "What hurts?" He stayed very still. "Everything hurts like hell."

Leaning over him, she very carefully kissed his jaw beneath a bruise. "Does that help?"

"Yeah," he decided. "Yeah, definitely."

"How about here…" She kissed him again, closer to his ear this time, making his breath catch.

"Uh-huh."

"Maybe I should kiss all your hurts."

"Okay."

"Tell me where," she murmured.

"Here." He pointed to his throat.

Nodding somberly but with a hint of humor in her beautiful eyes, she obediently kissed his throat, slowly, hotly, with a touch of tongue that shot all the blood in his head to his groin in zero point four.

"Where else?" she asked against his skin, her hand slipping down his side, then back up again, lifting his T-shirt as she went. "Here?" She kissed him over the bandage on his left shoulder and part of his chest, and then the other side, where there were no bandages, just skin, and he felt his heart leap. "Zach?"

"Yeah, there—" He broke off on a shaky breath when she licked his nipple and then began a trail of hot, wet, openmouthed kisses down his torso, southbound.

"Maybe here, too?" She was at his abs now, her fingers toying with the string tie of his sweats. She stopped to glance up at him with an expression that said there was nowhere on earth she'd rather be than right here licking him.

He could come from just looking at her. "Everywhere," he said hoarsely, and felt her yank on the tie and slip her hand inside, beneath the material, wrapping those magic fingers around him. "God, Brooke."

"Shh." She worked his sweats down. "I'm healing you here." Her lips hovered over him and he held his breath, which came out in a rush when she kissed him.

And then drew him gently into her mouth. He lost himself for a while after that, but managed to tug her up before he exploded. "Skin to skin," he whispered, and with an eager smile, she pulled off her clothes, and then with such slow care that he was aching by the end of it, she removed the rest of his, as well, before raiding his nightstand for a condom. Shaking with need, he pulled her down over the tip of him and kissed her as she spread her legs, straddling his, and brought him home.

Sensations swamped him, but then she began to move so that he slid in and out of her, in and out, and he lost his breath again. Time drifted away, his entire world shrinking down to the feel of her surrounding him, milking him, and he had to fight the inclination of his own body to let go and fly.

"Are you hurting?" she murmured, her mouth on his jaw, her hands—just her hands had him letting out a groan of agonized pleasure. "Zach?" She stilled. "Am I hurting you?"

"*Killing* me." He swept his one good hand down her back to grip her sweet, sweet ass, loving the way she panted his name softly in his ear. Slipping his fingers in her silky wet heat, he stroked and teased, doing his damnedest to bring her up to speed to where he was, which was standing on the edge, teetering, so desperate for the plunge he shook with it.

"Zach—"

Unable to help it, he thrust up into her. She was letting out soft whimpers with every breath, assuring him she was as turned on as he.

"Zach, I'm going to—"

"Do it. Come," he murmured against her mouth. "I want to feel you."

And she did. She came completely undone for him, on him, her unbound hair in his face, her fingers tightening painfully in his hair. She was breathless, crying out, and he was gasping as her tightening thighs and the slow grind of her hips set off his own climax. He followed her over, swamped with a tidal wave of unnamed emotion as he poured himself into her.

A WHISPER, then a low male laugh broke through Brooke's subconscious, and then it all came back to her. Going to Zach's house, him answering the door, her taking in all that rumpled, surfer-boy glory.

Taking him to bed, taking him *on* the bed, seeing the look in his eyes that told her he was way more invested in her than he wanted to believe or admit…

She opened her eyes. Yep, still in bed with Zach. Actually, she was wrapped around him like a pretzel, thankfully with the covers up to their chin, because at the foot of the bed stood Aidan, Sam, Cristina and Dustin.

"Definitely, he's doing better than Blake," Dustin said. "Blake didn't have a woman with him in his hospital bed."

They were holding fast-food bags, and, as Sam so cheerfully held up to reveal, porn. "To cheer you up."

"But apparently Brooke had other ideas on how to cheer him up," Cristina said.

Dustin shushed her.

"Well, she did." Cristina gave him a little shove. "And as I told *you* before you turned me down, sex is really good for cheering people up."

Everyone looked at Dustin, who shifted uncomfortably. "Maybe I don't like casual cheer-up sex," he said in self-defense.

"Everyone likes casual cheer-up sex," Cristina scoffed. "*Normal* people like casual cheer-up sex."

"Maybe I like it to mean something." Dustin looked into her eyes. "Maybe I want to know it's going to happen again."

She jabbed him in the pec with a finger. "I told you, I don't make plans."

Dustin lifted a shoulder, wordlessly admitting they were at an impasse.

Cristina glared at him, then at the others. "And what are you all looking at?"

In unison, eyes swiveled away from the train wreck waiting to happen, to the other train wreck that had already happened.

Brooke, in Zach's arms.

In his bed.

Surrounded by goggling eyes.

"Get out," Zach said to them all. "And Aidan, I want my key back."

"You gave it to me for emergencies."

"Is there an emergency?"

"Well, I thought junk food and porn constituted one, but I can see I was mistaken."

"Brooke's hair is down," Sam noted. "That's new."

"Out." Zach pointed at the bedroom door with his injured arm. *"Now."*

When they'd filed out, Brooke covered her face. "This is bad. I fell asleep—"

"It's okay."

"They thought it was funny!"

"It is funny," he said. "A little."

Slipping out of the bed, she hurriedly reached for her clothes. Hearing the guys in the kitchen, digging into the food, she felt naked.

Very, very naked. "I've got to go."

"At least stay and eat."

She couldn't stay. Not right now. Not when she'd just

realized that in her heart, she was like Dustin, and not cut out for this lightweight sex thing. In spite of herself and her promise on that night on that rock, her damn heart had opened to Zach.

How stupid was that? She'd fallen all the way, leaving herself vulnerable to pain. And there would be pain. She was okay with that, but she needed a moment, a few moments, before she could smile and mean it.

"Hey. *Hey,*" he said when she turned away, snagging her hand, pulling her back. "Brooke? What is it?" The bruise on his jaw had darkened, the white bandage wrapped around his left shoulder stark against his tanned skin. He had bed-head again, and tired eyes that said he was hurting like hell.

He didn't need this, the burden of her feelings. "I need to go home for clothes before work," she said, faking a smile. "That's all."

He was quiet while she pulled on her shirt, so quiet that she finally glanced over to find him looking at her. And in his eyes was a wariness because he felt things for her, too, she knew he did, feelings he kept inside because he didn't intend to let them go anywhere—but what was worse was the comprehension she found there.

Oh, God. Despite her best effort, he could see what she was feeling. "Yeah, I really, *really* have to go."

With a wince, he sat up in bed. "Brooke—"

"No." She shook her head. "Please don't say anything."

"I'm sorry."

Oh, God. "Don't be silly. You have nothing to be sorry for."

"Yes, I do. I'm sorry that I can't give you what you want."

Casually as she could, she slipped into her shoes and attempted to wrangle her hair. "And what is it you think I want?"

Reaching out, he grabbed her hand again, stilling her frenetic movements, waiting until she looked at him. "Love," he said quietly.

She managed a light laugh. She realized she might be pathetically needy when it came to that particular emotion, but love hadn't exactly been prominent in her life. She'd come here to Santa Rey a little bit in limbo, but the one thing she'd known was she'd wanted that to change. But she'd made Zach a promise *not* to get attached, *not* to have messy emotions.

She'd failed on both counts.

"Brooke." He stroked a strand of hair from her face, all the while holding her gaze with his so that she couldn't look away to save her life. In these eyes were affection, heat…and a brutal honesty. "I don't want to hurt you. I never wanted to hurt you, but—"

"It's not your fault—"

"I wanted a physical relationship with you, you know that. And now I'm holding back, you know that, too. It's just that if you're going to add love into the mix—" He grinned ruefully. "Well, you can't. I don't seem to have the parts required to do love. So you can't fall, not for me."

Her throat tight, she nodded. "I know."

Only she also knew it was too damn late.

15

ZACH SLEPT on and off for two days. Or rather he tossed and turned for two days. He spent his third night at home surrounded by the guys, grateful not to still be in the hospital like Blake, who'd suffered a more serious head trauma, his leg broken in four places, and two cracked ribs, and was by all accounts cranky as all hell.

Zach was glad for the company. Sort of. But mostly he kept thinking about the fact that Brooke hadn't come back, and that this was her last week in town, and that he was an idiot.

"Why are you moping around like you lost your puppy?" Sam asked.

"I'm not."

The guys all exchanged a careful-with-the-deluded-patient look, and he sighed.

Yeah. He was moping.

Because he'd sent away the best thing that had ever happened to him.

"You've got pizza, beer and us," Eddie joked. "What else could you need?"

"Brooke." This from Aidan, his mouth full of pizza and a knowing look in his eyes. "He wants Brooke."

"No." Sam shook his head. "Our Zach's not much of a repeater."

Zach opened his mouth, but in lieu of absolutely nothing to say in his defense, shut it again.

"If I had Brooke looking at me the way she looks at you, I'd become a repeater," Dustin said as he reached for more pizza.

Yeah, but Zach was a moron. Brooke wouldn't be looking at him like that again. He'd made sure of that.

"You're only saying so because you got laid by the woman of your dreams," Sam pointed out. "Cristina."

"Cristina?" Zach blinked. This was news. "Since when?"

"Since last night," Sam informed him. "Dustin fixed her car and then she slept with him."

Not one to kiss and tell, Dustin tried to hold back his stupid grin and failed.

"Cristina's not going to settle down," Aidan warned Dustin. "She's not the type."

"She might, for the right guy," Dustin said, pushing up his glasses. "It could happen."

"You're asking to be crushed," Aidan told him. "Like a grape. *Again.*"

"Actually," Zach said quietly, "you never know."

"Then why aren't you seeing Brooke?" Aidan asked. "With only one week in town left, that makes her the perfect woman in my eyes."

"So why don't *you* date her?" Eddie jeered.

"Maybe I will."

Suddenly the pizza Zach had consumed sat like a lead weight in his gut. He tried to picture Brooke moving on and dating any one of these guys. His friends.

Then he had to admit it wasn't the pizza weighing his gut down. "No."

Aidan raised a brow. "What?"

"Nothing." Zach tossed his pizza aside. "She can date whoever she wants."

"Really?" Aidan said dryly. "So you wouldn't care if I ask her out?"

Zach opened his mouth, shut it, scrubbed a hand over his eyes and sighed. "We've been friends for a long time."

"Years."

"Yeah. And I've always said you should go out with whoever floats your boat, but…"

"But?"

"But if you go out with Brooke, I'll have to hurt you."

Dustin laughed and clamped him on the shoulder in commiseration.

Aidan just arched a brow that said, *You're in deep.*

Didn't he know it.

LATER THAT DAY, the bad news came from Zach's doctor—he wasn't cleared to go back to work until his cast came off, which was a minimum of three weeks away.

Three more weeks without work just might kill him, not that the doctor seemed to care, and not that the chief seemed to, either, when he called to check on Zach.

"Enjoy the time off. We'll be waiting for you."

"I want to come in," Zach said. "I could handle light duty—"

"No. We want you back, Zach, but sound."

Sound. What the hell did that mean?

But as the mind-numbing boredom set in, Zach had to admit he didn't feel so *sound.* He sat on his couch with the remote, but nothing on daytime TV interested him.

Nothing on his bookshelf interested him. Hell, even the porn didn't interest him. He couldn't go surfing because of the cast and bandages. He couldn't work.

All he could do, unfortunately, was think. *Way* too much thinking going on. About Brooke, about... Brooke.

It was another whole day before he remembered.

The arson fires. He'd actually come close to figuring something out...something really important. He called Aidan. "Where was I with the arson stuff?"

"Close to screwing up your career."

"Come on. We've fought hundreds of fires, and out of all of those, I'm only talking about four—"

"Five."

"—So how in the hell is that screwing up my career—"

"Five fires."

"What?"

Aidan sighed. "Let's get real crazy, okay? I think that the warehouse fire was arson."

"Why?"

"Gut feeling. Too many things went wrong. And guess what Tommy told me when I mentioned it?"

"I'll go out on a limb here and say, 'Mind your own fucking business?'"

"Bingo."

"Did you look around afterward?" Zach asked. "Get sight of the point of origin?"

"No, I was sitting by your side in the hospital after saving your sorry ass."

"Damn it."

"You're welcome."

After they hung up, Zach went out onto his deck and

stared off into the night. Maybe it was exhaustion, maybe it was pain, maybe it was simply that he didn't want to face the fact that his chest hurt, and so did his heart.

Or that he missed Brooke.

Over the years, he'd slept with enough women to lose count, and that had never bothered him any, but now he wondered what it would be like to stay with the *same* woman instead of moving on each time? To have some familiarity? A real relationship with depth instead of just heat?

He bet there was comfort in that, which he'd never had any use for before. But now, honestly, he could use a little TLC.

Zach hadn't taken his pain meds in two days, so showering was a bitch, but he got through it, dressed and walked out to his truck. He stopped short at the sight of Brooke getting out of her car.

She was carrying a bag from the local sandwich shop and wore an expression that said she wasn't too sure of her welcome, an expression that changed to disbelief when she saw the keys in his hand. "What are you doing?"

"I was going to ask you the same thing."

"I'm bringing you something more substantial than pizza or McDonald's." Her eyes met his. "Now you."

"I was coming to see you."

She let out a breath. "Okay, you have no idea how I both love and hate that. You shouldn't be driving. How are you feeling?"

Like I missed the hell out of you. "Great."

She arched a brow.

"Good."

"Zach."

"Okay, like shit. I feel like complete shit."

With a sigh, she stepped close, and did something he hadn't expected, given how things had gone the last time he'd seen her.

She hugged him.

For a moment, just a heartbeat, really, he stood still, shocked, because normally when he pushed someone away, they willingly went. After all, he was a master pusher when it came right down to it. And he'd all but thrown her feelings for him back in her face.

But Brooke, petite, sweet-but-steely-willed Brooke, hadn't just held her ground with him, she was pushing back.

If that didn't grab him by the throat.

Unable to resist, he slid his arms around her, pulling her in tight. Bending his head, he buried his face in her hair, breathing her in.

Keep it light, keep it casual…

But then she was pressing her mouth to his cheek and he was turning his head to meet her mouth, and as he deepened the kiss he knew the truth.

He didn't want to push her away anymore. He really didn't. So he hoped like hell someone threw him a line, because he was going down.

"You need to get back inside," she murmured. "You're pale."

Pale, and apparently stupid, because he kissed her again.

Deep.

Wet.

He was in the middle of working on the long part, but she pulled back. "Careful, I'll hurt you—"

Shaking his head, he kissed her again, then dropped

his forehead to hers. "No." Drawing a deep breath, he straightened and pulled free. "I'll hurt you."

"Oh." She stared up at him, then took a step back and nodded. "Right."

They were still just staring at each other when Aidan pulled up, followed by all the guys.

Incredible timing, as always.

"Okay," Brooke said. "I'm going to go."

"No, don't."

"No, really. It's okay. I just wanted—" She thrust the bag of food in his hands. "Here."

"Wait—"

"Listen, I know I wear my heart on my sleeve and feel too much, but I'm not slow. I really did hear you the other day, what you were trying to say. You don't want me to get invested, and I get it. I'm leaving and all that, and this was never about that kind of thing. I just want you to know that I understand, and there's no hard feelings."

Damn, she killed him. "Brooke—"

"Don't." She shook her head. "Don't go there. Not now."

"Fine. Later, then. Just please stay until I get rid of these guys?"

She glanced at them all getting out of their cars. "Okay, but Zach? That kiss…"

He couldn't help looking at her lips again. He could still taste her. "Yeah?"

"That didn't feel like a hey-how-are-you kiss. Or even a one-night-stand kiss." She moved in and whispered for his ears only. "It felt like a helluva lot more."

Yeah. It had.

"So you might want to think about that next time you tell yourself I'm the only one going to get hurt here."

EVERYONE ENTERED Zach's house, carrying food and news of their day. Brooke joined them because Zach had asked, but mostly because she wanted to. She wanted to be with them.

With Zach.

He sat sprawled on the couch, and if it hadn't been for the cast, the bandages and the slight paleness of his face, she'd never have guessed that he'd nearly died.

Her heart tightened at that, but she'd always licked her wounds in private, so stressing about what could have happened, as she had been doing since the fire, would have to wait.

Sam tossed her a soda.

Dustin handed her a plate.

Aidan kicked a chair her way.

She sat in the chair, holding the soda and plate, staring at the group talking and laughing amongst themselves, a huge lump forming in her throat.

She really was part of them. She belonged. And hadn't that been what she'd been looking for at the beginning of the summer? A place to belong?

Zach sipped his soda, his eyes hooded as he watched her over his drink.

She watched him back.

Around them, the laughter and noise went up a notch, but Zach didn't join in. Probably because he was hurting far more than he'd let on. She could see it in the grim set of his mouth and the lines of exhaustion on his face. He eyed the pizza on the coffee table in front of him but didn't take a piece.

He loved pizza.

"You okay?" Aidan leaned in to ask her quietly.

"Not me I'm worried about."

They both eyed Zach. "Let's try this." Aidan tossed two slices of pieces on a plate, then handed it to Zach. "Hey. The annual picnic is in one week."

"So?"

"So we need an anchor for the tug-of-war against Firehouse 32."

"I repeat. So?"

"So no pansy-asses need apply. Eat up."

"Not hungry."

"Really? You like being home all day, watching *Oprah,* eating bonbons?"

Zach opened his mouth, probably to tell Aidan where to go, but the doorbell rang again, and in came Cristina, carrying a tray of cupcakes.

Everyone looked at Dustin. Everyone except Cristina, that is, alerting Brooke to the fact that something was going on. Happy not to be at the center of the gossip mill for once, she watched with fascination as the blonde shuffled around without her usual cockiness.

"The grocery store had a small fire in their bakery." She set the tray down and grabbed a cupcake in each hand before looking at the gang, carefully avoiding Dustin's eyes. "So, what's up?"

"Nothing," everyone but Dustin said.

Cristina sighed and faced the silent and clearly brooding Dustin. "Okay, fine. I'm sorry." She offered him a cupcake. "Very sorry."

Dustin stared down at the double chocolate fudge cupcake, eyes shadowed, mouth unaccustomedly tight. He didn't take it. "What's this?"

"It's called dessert. It's what people do when they're sorry. They bring people treats."

"Why are you sorry?"

"You know why."

"Say I don't."

Cristina sighed. "I'm sorry I got mad when you wouldn't have sex with me again."

Dustin raised a brow in tune to the juvenile catcalls from the guys.

"I *am* sorry, all right?" Cristina ignored everyone else. "Jesus! Would you just eat a damn cupcake?"

"I don't think so."

"Oh my God." Cristina sighed again, looking at the others, all of whom got real busy with their cupcakes. "Look, I really needed to get laid, okay? It'd been too long and you might have noticed that I was a little on edge."

"Was?"

She rolled her eyes.

"Maybe you're on edge for other reasons," Dustin said. "Ever think of that?"

"No." She waggled the cupcake in front of his nose. "Are you going to take this or not?"

Dustin took it, then licked the frosting while studying Cristina thoughtfully.

The room was unusually quiet now. Brooke was especially so, mostly because she really felt for Dustin. He'd put himself out there and was now hurting.

She knew the feeling.

"I'm sorry, too," Dustin said, mouth full of frosting.

Cristina went still. "For?"

"For not having more meaningless sex with you."

Sam let out a choked laugh and, without taking her eyes off Dustin, Cristina pointed at him.

Sam shut up.

"Does that mean you want to?" Cristina asked Dustin. "Have more meaningless sex?"

"No."

Cristina looked deeply disappointed, but tried to hide it. "Okay."

"*I'll* have meaningless sex with you," Eddie said. When Cristina rounded on him, Aidan helpfully stuffed a cupcake into Eddie's mouth to keep him quiet.

"Or you could try it my way," Dustin suggested to Cristina.

Cristina turned back to Dustin and blinked.

Dustin didn't.

Zach sighed, and with some struggle, stood up, gesturing the others to follow him, clearly not wanting to stay and witness the bloodshed.

This time, Cristina pointed at Zach. "Don't move. Did you put him up to this?"

"Give me some credit," Dustin answered for him. "I've had it bad for you since day one. There's no way you haven't noticed."

"Whoa." Cristina staggered back a step and collided with a wall. "What? What the hell did you just say?"

"I gave you an offer for sex," Dustin said calmly. "As I believe you were lamenting about your continued lack of."

"After that," she whispered.

"I said give me some credit. Of course Zach didn't put me up to this."

"No, after that." She swallowed hard. "*What the hell did you say after that?*"

"The part where I said I've wanted you since day one?"

"Yeah. Hang on." And she sat, right there on the floor. "That."

With a sigh, Dustin got up and crouched in front of her. "It's not a death sentence, Cristina."

"Ohmigod."

He sighed again. "I was hoping for a more articulate response than that."

"Articulate?" She looked bowled over, but he just waited, and she swallowed hard. "Okay, articulate. How about…" She shook her head as if at a loss. "Thank you?"

He arched a brow. "Thank you?"

"Look, I'm trying to be polite here, but I really need to throw up. Are you crazy? You've got a thing for me? You don't even know all my faults."

"I think I know a lot of them," he said dryly.

"Ohmigod."

"You're starting to repeat yourself. Let's go for a walk."

"A walk."

"Yes. On the beach."

"Are you trying to romance me?"

"Uh-huh. Is it working?"

"I don't know. Maybe. No more talk about…wanting me. Promise?"

"Take my hand, Cristina."

She stared at his proffered hand, and then took it. "You should know I'm not putting out on the first date."

"Maybe on our second, then."

That shook a laugh out of her and, shocking Brooke and probably everyone else, Cristina allowed Dustin to pull her out the door.

Brooke watched them go, something deep inside her aching. Then she realized Zach was looking right at her. What she'd give to know that he was aching, too, but whatever he was thinking, he kept it to himself.

A LITTLE WHILE LATER, Zach managed to escape to the kitchen, where he leaned on the sink and stared out the window. He could still hear his friends talking and laughing in the other room. He was grateful for them, but he wished they'd all go away and leave him alone with Brooke.

The door opened and he turned hopefully, but it was Tommy.

"How are you feeling?" the inspector asked.

"I'd be better if you'd convince the chief to let me go back to work."

"No can do."

"Tommy—"

He held up a hand. "I agree with you about those fires," he said quietly. "Okay? You're right. They're arson, all of them. I've always believed you." He let that sink in. "But believing you wasn't the problem. My investigation was—is—undercover."

Zach stared at him. "Because...you suspected me."

Tommy's expression was apologetic but firm. "Past tense."

Zach let out a breath. "Jesus, Tommy."

"I know you want to come back to work, but I'm advising you to wait."

"You don't think—"

"What I think is that you're in danger."

"What the hell does that mean?"

"You've been a damn thorn for me, Zach, and we're

on the same side. Imagine how the bad guy feels about you."

"I don't understand."

"You're getting close. Close enough for the arsonist to try to hurt you. He burned Phyllis's house because you care about her. Then at the warehouse fire, you were hit."

"By a burning piece of ceiling."

"By a chunk of debris, yes, but I've been at the site. I think it was thrown at you."

Zach staggered to a chair and sat.

"I've combed every inch of that site," Tommy said. "You went back in where you weren't supposed to, and I believe you almost caught the arsonist red-handed."

"But the only people inside at that point, besides the victims, were firefighters."

Tommy just looked at him, and that's when he finally got it. They weren't looking for some nameless criminal.

It was someone they all knew.

16

AFTER EVERYONE had gone, Brooke grabbed a trash bag
and started to clean up.

"Leave it," Zach told her, weary to the bone. "I can do
it."

She put her hands on her hips. "You're going to do it?"

"Yes."

"Even though you've barely moved all night?"

He lifted a shoulder, which pulled at his burns and had
pain shooting through him. He didn't make a sound, he
very carefully didn't make a sound, but she was at his side
in a heartbeat.

"Damn stubborn man," she murmured, helping him
up.

Suddenly, all he could think about was how her hands
felt on him. "What are you doing?"

"Putting you to bed."

Just the words had his body leaping to attention. Even
in pain and pissed off at the world, he could still get it up
for her. "Sorry, but I'm bound to disappoint you tonight."

"Shut up, Zach."

Upstairs in his room, she got him onto the bed. He
looked up into her face. Her beautiful face. She was
worried sick, and, he realized with some shame, that he

was not the only one hurting. "I talked to Tommy tonight. He said he believed me."

"What?" Brooke went still. "Oh, Zach," she breathed. "I'm so glad! Does he know who the arsonist is?"

This was the hard part. "He suspects an inside job."

"Inside…" Her mind worked fast, and she gasped. "No."

"The warehouse fire wasn't an accident." He went to reach for her and gritted his teeth at the pain.

"I'm going to get your meds and water. Don't move."

When she was gone, he tried to pull off his shoes, but the cast on his arm felt heavy. Plus, moving hurt. Not feeling up to taking off his own damn shirt, much less his pants, he lay back on the bed, out of breath and frustrated.

"Why don't you get undressed?" she asked, coming back into the room with a glass of water and a pill.

He closed his eyes. "Yeah. Good idea."

"Need help?"

"No. I can do this. Seriously."

"Seriously? Get real, Zach." He felt her hands pulling off his shoes, heard them hit the floor one at a time. "Because, seriously? You are full of shit." Carefully, with a surprisingly gentle touch considering the sarcasm in her voice, she helped him out of his shirt. "So what else did Tommy say?"

"That I've pissed off the arsonist."

She went still. "You're in danger?"

"I'm safe here."

Her eyes searched his as her hands slid over his bare chest.

Instead of the pain he'd felt for days, all he felt was the touch of her warm hands. She was better than Vicodin. Then she trailed those hands down and reached for the buttons on his Levi's. "You still need my help, right?"

Oh, yeah. He nodded, and pop went the first button. And then the second, and suddenly Zach was breathing as if he'd been running.

She wasn't breathing too steadily, either.

"Okay, maybe I'd better do this." His hands were shaking as he pulled open the rest of the buttons, but shoving the denim down his legs required grating his teeth and lifting his hips. By the time he got them down a mere inch, he was beginning to sweat.

"Here." She got on the bed for leverage, straddling his lower legs, and pulled his jeans down to his thighs, revealing the fact that he'd gone commando that morning.

Which left the part of him that was the happiest to see her bouncing free.

Her eyes widened.

"I told you I should do this."

"I'm sorry." She was still staring.

"Not helping."

At that, Brooke actually snickered, but he could hear the breathlessness in the sound.

And the wanting.

"Yeah," he managed. "Still not helping."

"Right." She scrambled off his legs.

Good. Great. She was going away. But then she pulled his jeans the rest of the way off, tossing them to the floor. Leaving him buck naked.

"You…need a blanket."

Which was beneath him. He rolled toward her just as she leaned in to try to pull it out from under him, and they bumped into each other.

"Sorry," she gasped, but in countering her own movement, she bumped into him again.

They went utterly still.

He had his hands on her arms. She had hers braced on his chest, and she was still staring at the part of him boring a hold in her belly.

"Zach?" she whispered.

"Yeah?"

"You seem to need some..." Her gaze met his. "Letting loose."

He laughed, which hurt like a son of a bitch.

"Yeah?"

"Oh, yeah. It's just what I need." *You...* And with that, he tugged her overtop of him.

AT THE FULL BODY CONTACT with Zach, what happened within Brooke was what happened every time—a shockingly intense, insatiable hunger arose. "Zach—"

"I know. Condom."

She leaned over and grabbed one from his nightstand, while he tugged at her zipper, but his fingers were shaking. "Why are you wearing so many clothes?"

"I have no idea—" Before she got the words out, Zach had her capris down and pushed open her legs. Pretty damn talented for a man with one arm. Then he lifted her up and thrust into her.

Their twin groans of pleasure mingled in the air.

Her hands were braced on either side of his face, her head bent low to his. Staring into his eyes, she was startled at how easily she lost herself in him.

Every.

Single.

Time.

Brooke had no idea how she could want him this way,

as if she would die if she didn't have him. The hunger filled her so that she could think of nothing else, and she rocked her hips, a movement that wrested a grunt from him. His good hand gripped her, holding her still. "Don't move." His voice was like sandpaper. "God, don't move, or this'll be over—"

She moved. She couldn't help it; she had to. She rocked her hips again, absorbing the low, rough sound torn from deep in his throat. Leaning over him, she went to bury her face in the crook of his neck but he caught her, cupped her jaw and held it so that she could do nothing but look right into his eyes as he met her thrust for thrust, until she began to tremble, then burst. He was right with her, pulsing inside her even as she shattered around him.

"Yeah." He breathed a shaky sigh as she sagged over top of him, a boneless puddle of raw nerve endings. "Just what the doctor ordered." She felt his mouth press to the side of her throat and closed her eyes, letting the drowsiness take her—which was infinitely preferable to facing the fact that she had no idea how she was going to walk away from this man.

BROOKE AWOKE to the sun pouring in through the window and splashing all over her face with startling cheer.

But she always shut her shades, so...

She jerked upright. Yep, she wasn't in her bed, she was in Zach's. Legs entwined, arms entwined, no covers in sight because their body heat had been enough. Once again she'd slept the entire night wrapped around him as if...

As if she belonged here.

Zach stirred, opened an eye. He had two days' growth on his jaw, and some serious bed-head, and he looked so hot she wanted to gobble him up.

Again.

"Overslept," she said, and tried to free herself. "Going to be late—" She broke off when he merely tightened his grip on her. "What?"

"Just wondering if it worked. If I'm suitably relaxed or if maybe we should kept working on it."

She stared into his gorgeous, sleepy face and remembered his warning not to fall in love with him. "You're fine." She scrambled up, glanced at the clock again on the off chance it had miraculously changed in her favor. "Where the hell are my panties?"

Zach came up on an elbow and surveyed the room. "There."

On his lamp. Perfect. Her bra was draped over a bedpost like a trophy. Snatching it up, she glared at him, just lying there looking like sin on a stick. "I'm late," she said more to herself. Very late. Late for the rest of her life, which was right around the corner. In fact, she was meeting the real estate agent today to discuss an offer she'd received on the house yesterday. With a sigh, she headed toward the door.

"Brooke?"

She turned back. "Yes?"

"Be careful out there."

"I always am."

"I know. But…"

But now one of them was a possible arsonist and had hurt Zach. Anyone could get hurt. She got that. "I can take care of myself."

"But—"

"And after next week, I'll be on my own." Because that brought a lump to her throat, she had to swallow hard to continue. "I realize that last night was mostly my doing, but you should know, I got an offer on the house. Three more shifts, and I'm gone."

He closed his eyes, but not before she saw a flash of emotion much deeper than affection. "I know."

"Goodbye, Zach."

Now he opened those eyes again, and let her see his sadness. "Is that it? Goodbye, the end?"

"What else is there?"

When he opened his mouth and then shut it, she shook her head. "Exactly. Goodbye, Zach."

WELL, WHAT HAD she expected, a marriage proposal? She'd only met him five and a half weeks ago, and he wasn't exactly known for being a commitment king. Brooke drove to work, not acknowledging the burning in her eyes, doing her damnedest not to think about the fact that he'd let her walk away.

He'd let her say goodbye.

She pulled into the parking lot. With Zach and Blake both still out, plus several others hit by a flu bug, she was on the B shift for the first time, with a whole new gang, and she found herself working with an EMT named Isobel. Adding to her stress, Brooke was the scheduled driver for the day, which began the moment she got out of her car and the bell rang.

"Watch your speed," was Isobel's most common refrain, uttered every two seconds on every one of their many, *many* calls. Isobel had a cap of dark hair and darker eyes, both her expression and demeanor screaming, *I know I'm a woman in a man's world, but hear me roar.* "Watch that turn—"

"I'm watching."

"Watch—"

"I'll keep watching," Brooke said evenly, each and every time, though by the afternoon, she didn't feel so even. She missed Dustin. "Believe it or not, I've actually driven once or twice before."

"You can never be too careful is all." Isobel eyed the speedometer. "Watch—"

"Okay." Brooke took a deep breath. "Still watching."

"Sorry." Isobel flashed a small, conciliatory smile. "I know I'm a pain. I'm just overly cautious."

Nothing wrong with that. If only Brooke had watched over her own broken heart as cautiously…

Isobel was blessedly quiet until they turned on Third Street, heading toward their call, an outdoor beach café with a kitchen fire, where one of the cooks had passed out from the smoke and hit his head. A hundred yards ahead, the light turned red.

Isobel pointed. "Watch—" Then she caught herself, and cleared her throat. "Nothing."

Brooke pulled up behind two fire trucks. They had the fire contained, but the flames were still impressive, leaping fifty feet into the sky. She and Isobel got out of their rig and immediately one of the firefighters came up to them. "The vic vanished on us. We're still looking for him."

Isobel went back to the radio to report the information. As Brooke took in the fire, she was shocked to see Blake there, standing just off to the side. He was supposed to still be recuperating in the hospital. She'd visited him the day before, and he'd been in no shape to be up. Worried, she moved to his side. "Blake?"

A low, raw sound escaped him and she took a closer look. He wasn't in his gear. He couldn't have been, not with the cast on his leg. His jeans were cut over the cast, and he wore a sweatshirt that looked odd, given it was at least eighty-five degrees outside. He leaned his weight on a crutch, but what caused Brooke concern was how pale he looked, and the fact that he was sweating profusely. "Blake?"

He didn't respond. Eyes locked on the flames, face tight, he seemed miles away.

When she set her hand on his arm, he nearly leaped out of his skin. "Hey, just me." She sent him a smile he didn't return. "You all right?"

"Yes."

"You don't look it. You're in pain."

"Nah. I've got enough pain meds in me to change my name to Anna Nicole Smith."

With a low laugh, she turned back to the rig and saw Isobel had located their vic. He was shaking his head, pushing her hands away before walking off. He didn't seem to want treatment. "Looks like we don't have a transport after all. Can we give you a ride?"

When Blake didn't answer, she looked at him—he was limping away with shocking speed. Running after him, Brooke caught up just as he got as close as he could to the flames without igniting. "Blake, what are you doing?"

At the sound of her voice, he jerked. "Brooke?" He blinked, as if surprised to see her, as if he didn't remember seeing her only two seconds ago.

"Okay, you know what? You're not okay." She put her hand on his arm. "Let's go sit down."

"What are you doing here?"

"I'm working. On you. Why are you out of the hospital?"

"I don't know." He closed his eyes. "I'm sorry. I just...I'm sorry. For everything."

"Come on. Let's get you back." Away from the fire and the pain she suspected he was suffering. "We're in the way here."

He looked around and blanched. "God, I'm sorry."

"For what, Blake?"

"I can't..." He shoved his fingers through his hair and turned away from her, but not before she saw a suspicious sheen to his eyes. "I'm so damned sorry. I should have handled this better. I should have stopped it sooner."

"Blake? Stopped what sooner?"

Staring at the flames, he appeared transfixed. "I don't want to lose another partner. Or a friend."

"What do you mean? Blake, done *what* sooner?"

"Lots of things, actually." He walked off, but again she stopped him.

"I don't think being alone is what you need, Blake."

"Please." He jerked free, his face tortured. "Just leave me alone. There's nothing you can do to stop it from happening."

"What do you mean?" But she was afraid she knew, or at least was starting to know. "Blake—"

"It's not what you think."

But she was suddenly sure it was *exactly* what she thought. The arsonist was someone from within their own ranks. Possibly, terrifyingly, the someone standing right here in front of her. "Okay, let's go over to the ambulance, and—"

"Isobel needs you."

Brooke turned back to the rig and saw Isobel waving at her frantically.

"We have a call!" she was yelling.

Brooke turned back to Blake. "I have to go but I want you to come with me—"

But she was talking to herself. *"Blake?"*

He'd vanished.

17

BROOKE RAN BACK to the rig. Hopping into the driver's seat, she pulled out her cell phone.

"No talking on the phone while you're driving," Isobel said.

"I'm not driving yet." She punched in Zach's cell phone number.

"We have a call. Eighth and Beach."

"I know, but this is an emergency, too." She got Zach's voice mail. Damn it. "Zach," she said, very aware of Isobel listening to every word. "I need to talk to you. ASAP." She shut the phone and tried to order her racing thoughts. "We need to get someone else to take this call. Blake—"

"There is no one else. We need to go, now."

"Fine." She handed her cell over to Isobel. "Call the station, have someone come to get Blake. Then call Tommy Ramirez. Tell him—" What? What the hell could she say? All she had were suspicions. "Tell him I need to talk to him. That it's urgent. Ask him to meet us at the hospital after we pick up our vic."

But Tommy didn't meet her. So after Brooke and Isobel had turned their patient over to the E.R., she tried the chief, and shock of all shocks, got him.

"This better be important, O'Brien," he said in his sharply authoritative voice. "I'm in a meeting."

"It's about Blake."

The chief was silent for a single, long beat. "What about him?"

Brooke moved away from Isobel so that she could speak frankly. "He was at the scene of the Third Street fire today, and he didn't look right. And…" Oh, God, how to say this? "And I think he was trying to confess to arson."

"You *think?* What the hell does that mean? And what arson?"

"He wasn't coherent. He—" She frowned at the static in her ear. "Sir? Hello, Chief?" She'd lost him. *"Shit."*

"You're not supposed to swear while in uniform," Isobel said.

Brooke contained the urge to wrap her fingers around Isobel's neck and drove them back to the station.

The chief was there, waiting for her. "Blake isn't at the hospital or at the fire."

"What's going on?" Cristina stood in the doorway, looking unnerved. "What's the matter with Blake? Eddie went to go get him but he couldn't find him."

"He's missing," the chief said. "And he's not answering his cell."

"He was at the Third Street fire," Brooke told Cristina. "He was walking with a crutch, definitely disoriented— *oh my God.*"

The chief turned on her. "What?"

"What if he went *into* the fire?"

"Why would he do that?" Panic raised Cristina's voice. "He wasn't suited up, he wasn't working—"

"But he wasn't himself," Brooke said slowly, reviewing their conversation. "He was rambling, not making much sense, and just staring at the flames."

"Rambling about what?" Cristina cried.

"He kept saying sorry about the fires, like he was trying to confess."

Cristina gasped and covered her mouth. "He didn't—he wouldn't—"

"He didn't look good, and then we got a call. He'd vanished."

The chief headed for his truck with long strides while Cristina dragged Brooke inside, where she sank to the couch in the living room.

"That building is gone," Brooke said. "Completely gone. I should have stopped him. I should have—"

"You couldn't have stopped him," Sam said, coming in behind them. "And he's not that stupid."

Cristina let out a low sound of grief.

"Look, he hasn't been the same since Lynn died," Sam told her. "We've all tried to talk to him about it, but you know how he is. He's Eeyore. He's stubborn. But not stupid," he repeated. "No way did he go into that fire."

"He was hurting," Cristina whispered. "He lost his partner."

"And *he's* dealing with it." Dustin said this very gently, coming in from the kitchen. "You can't do it for him."

Covering her face, she sank to the couch next to Brooke. "This. *This* is why I like to alienate people. Goddamn it, you made me forget to alienate him and now I care!"

"Cristina." When she didn't answer, Dustin crouched at her side. *"Cristina."*

"Caring sucks," she whispered through her fingers.

He pulled them from her face. "Not always."

She just stared at him.

"Not always," he repeated softly. "What I feel for you doesn't suck. And what I'm hoping you feel for me doesn't suck."

"Damn it." She closed her eyes. "It doesn't. It only scares the living hell out of me. You should brace yourself now." She opened her eyes. "Because I'm maybe falling in love, too. And it's all your fault."

Dustin looked staggered as he drew a shaky breath.

"Don't you have anything to say?"

"Thank you?"

She stared at him, then with a shocked laugh at having her own words tossed back at her, she lunged up and hugged him tight.

Desperate to take her mind off Blake, Brooke tried to be happy for her partner. Putting himself out there had paid off for Dustin, in a big way. It was right then that she realized she hadn't put herself out there for Zach at all. Instead, she'd done the opposite, hiding behind her six-week time limit. She'd even said goodbye already.

"You okay?"

She opened her eyes to Aidan. Was she okay? She was leaving a job she loved in less than a week. Her grandmother's house was all but sold in spite of the fact that beneath all the clutter, she'd discovered a gorgeous, well-tended home that seemed to say *Don't sell me* every time she walked in the door.

The truth was, this decision to move yet again wasn't being dictated by family or school or anything but her own fear.

Funny, really.

And damned ironic.

All her life she'd been racing from one spot to another, and now she was free to do as she chose, go anywhere she wanted, and…and all she wanted was to stay.

With Zach.

"Brooke?"

She looked at Aidan. "It's nothing. I'm fine."

"Even if that was true, if you're fine, how's Zach?"

"When I left there, he was in a little pain but—"

"Not what I meant."

"Yeah." She sighed. "He was…good."

"He's the master at good. Look, I love the guy, but—"

"I'm sure you two will be very happy together."

"You're funny." He shook his head. "Look, neither Zach nor I have ever really needed a woman in our life."

"I know. I get it."

"No, see that's the thing. Zach looks at you differently. He has from the beginning. If you leave, it'll be like losing his parents all over again. Or his brother."

"He lost his brother?"

"Caleb moved to L.A. the day Zach turned eighteen, pretty much deserting him. Can't blame the guy. He hadn't signed on to be a parent, but still, it was rough on Zach. He's not good with opening up. He's afraid."

She tried to picture the big, laid-back, easygoing Zach Thomas afraid of anything. After all, the man faced danger every single day on the job without so much as a flinch.

But that wasn't the same.

In a way, work was much easier because it was pure testosterone and adrenaline. Putting himself on the line probably made Zach feel better about his losses, almost as if he were offering himself up to fate, as well. And as a bonus, he never had to open up emotionally, except with these guys, the brothers of his heart.

She got that; she'd done the same with her chosen career.

But Cristina and Dustin had managed to find something real, and Brooke wanted that. It was time, *past* time, to get it for herself, because if she'd learned anything today, it was that life was too damn short not to go for it. She stood up.

"What are you going to do?"

"It's…complicated."

"The best things are." Aidan hugged her. "I hope it's good complicated."

"I hope so, too."

"I TRIED CALLING you, Zachie."

Zach sat at the side of Phyllis's hospital bed. "I'm sorry. I can't find my cell phone. I think I lost it in the warehouse fire."

"Don't worry." Her voice sounded shaky. "You asked me not to demolish the house if someone asks, and I won't. I was just telling Blake the same thing."

"Blake came here to see you?"

"Yes. He wanted to talk about my house fire."

"Why?"

Phyllis had a razor-sharp memory, but she'd been too doped up on meds for anyone to take advantage of that. Until now, apparently. "Because he was there. Yes," she said at his surprise. "It finally came to me. It was Blake I saw standing on the perimeter of my property, holding a blowtorch."

The air deflated from Zach's lungs. Blake at the scene

just before the fire, with an ignition device… "Phyllis, are you sure?"

"Well, when I brought it up, he said no, my memory was all twisted from the trauma, but…" She shook her head. "But I don't believe it. I remember."

Blake was the missing link? Blake connected all the fires?

Blake was the arsonist?

It made no sense, and yet…and yet in a crazy way it made *perfect* sense—Blake's ongoing obsession with fire, any fire, and his need to be near it, even the bonfire from the chief's birthday party. "Phyllis, listen to me. I need you to trust me, okay? I have to go but I'll be back."

"Will you bring Cecile?"

"I'll bring you more pictures of her, I promise."

When he got to the parking lot and into his truck, he remembered—no cell phone. Running back inside the hospital, he went straight to a pay phone and called Tommy.

Tommy listened to every word and then said, "Go home. You hear me? Get home and keep your ass right there or I'll get it fired."

"You can't do that."

"Trust me, I'll find a way."

Frustration beat at Zach as he drove home, feeling useless and helpless—two emotions he couldn't resent more. God, Blake… *Could it be true?*

And yet the evidence was there, at least circumstantially. The blowtorch at Phyllis's was huge. And he'd been quiet and withdrawn and secretive for months, pushing all of them from his life.

Zach had to go see him, had to look into Blake's eyes and judge for himself.

But Blake wasn't home, so Zach went back to his place and paced a groove into his living room floor, which did nothing for his adrenaline level.

At the knock on his door, he opened it to the one person he'd have given everything to see.

Brooke, still wearing her uniform, eyes shadowed, mouth grim, looking like the best thing he'd seen all damn day.

"Damn, are you a sight for sore eyes," he said.

"I'm not supposed to be here," she said. "I forgot to clock out at work."

"Good. Because I'm not here, either. I'm on my way to find Blake's ass and probably get mine fired."

"You know where he is?"

"No."

They both stood there and stared at each other, unsure what to say next.

"I'm really not here," she finally said again, "telling you that I take back my goodbye."

"Then I'm not really doing this." Hauling her to him, he covered her mouth with his.

She sighed in pleasure and sagged against him, fisting her hands in his shirt to keep him close.

As if that was necessary.

"Zach," she murmured. "We need to talk."

"Yeah."

But then she nipped at his lower lip, making him groan. He stroked his tongue to hers, his hands running down her body, filling them with her glorious curves. "We'll talk," he promised her. "In a minute. Maybe ten." He needed to lose himself in her before he faced the unthinkable—that one of their own was an arsonist.

Not going there, not yet. He kicked the door shut, tugging her upstairs to his bedroom.

She stared at his bed. "First I really need to tell you what I came for—"

"You haven't come yet." He nudged her onto the bed and followed her down. "But you're going to."

18

ZACH'S WORDS sent a shiver of desire skittering down Brooke's spine. In his eyes was a fierce intensity—for her, which she loved, but also the same grief she'd seen in Cristina's.

He knew about Blake.

He kissed her, hard. She knew he was hurting and destroyed over Blake's betrayal, that he was trying to lose himself in her. She understood. She wanted to get lost in him, too.

He pulled off her shirt, and she did the same for his, sliding her hands up his heated skin, feeling the hard planes beneath quiver for more. "Are we letting loose again?"

"No." His mouth slid over her neck, her shoulder, making its way toward a breast. "This time it's more, damn it." He curled his tongue around her nipple.

Sinking her fingers into his hair, she arched up into his mouth. "More?"

"Everything's all fucked up." His voice was low, raw, as he slid a hand into her panties.

His physical pain matched the mental anguish in his eyes, and both broke her heart. "I know."

"Except this, with you." He tugged her panties down to her thighs to give him better access. "I don't usually do this."

"Pull a woman's pants down?"

"No, smart-ass. Get into a relationship."

When his gaze caught hers, she couldn't look away. "Is that what we're doing?"

"I thought you were safe. You're leaving, for Christ's sake. You're outta here. Can't get much safer than that."

Moved by his pain and frustration, she pressed her forehead to his. "Zach."

"I mean, I wasn't going to fall for a woman with one foot already out the door. It was never going to happen."

She closed her eyes.

"But goddamn it, it did."

Before she could open her mouth, he covered it with his. Reality had no place then, no place at all. Until she smelled smoke. "Zach—"

"I know. We're both idiots."

"No." She coughed. *"Smoke."*

"Uh-huh. I think I'm on fire."

"No, I mean *real* smoke." Just as she said this, his smoke alarm went off.

"What the—" Eyes hot, body hard, his face was a mask of frustration as he lifted his head and sniffed the air. "Shit, it *is* smoke." He pulled free and leaped off the bed, staring at the wisps curling beneath the bedroom door.

"Zach!"

"I see it." He tossed her his phone from the nightstand. "Call it in!" He ran into the bathroom, coming out with towels, which he shoved under the door to block the smoke while she called 911.

Coughing, choking, Brooke dashed to the window and then gasped. Zach peered over her shoulder and swore.

Down on the grass far below stood Blake. He was

propped up on one crutch, face gray, holding a blowtorch as he looked right at them.

Zach threw Brooke her clothes and shoved his feet into his jeans. Then he reached under his bed and pulled out a portable rope ladder. "My house is on fire. My damn house is on fire. I'm going to kill him."

But Brooke was still staring at Blake, who had tears running down his face as he limped toward the door, vanishing inside.

"He's in—" Brooke gasped, still coughing. "Zach, Blake's inside." The smoke tightened in her lungs so that she couldn't talk.

Zach covered her mouth with a towel. "Breathe into that." He tossed the ladder out the window. Straddling the ledge, he reached for her. "Come on. You're going down and out. Quickly." He pulled her out the window and onto the rope. "Don't stop until your feet touch the ground. Got that?"

Right. Don't stop. Except she wanted to stop. She wanted to stop time and go back to a few minutes ago, when he'd been about to bury himself deep inside her, telling her he'd fallen. "I'm not leaving you."

"Go!" His voice was already hoarse, his eyes flashing fear and anger. "I'm getting Blake, then I'll be right behind you—"

"Zach—"

"Brooke, listen to me." He gave her a little shake. "You have to be out of here for me to do this."

"But—"

"No, I mean it. I can't lose you. I can't." He set his forehead to hers. "I can't do this with you still in here, in danger."

He meant he couldn't lose another person who meant so much to him. Brooke's heart swelled until it felt too big for her body.

"Please go," he said, hugging her hard. "Because if something happens to you—"

"It won't, it won't. I'm going." She squeezed him tight, breathing through the towel and still coughing. "But you should know something. I love you, Zach."

He looked staggered. "Brooke."

"I do. I love you." It'd probably sound better if she could talk more clearly, but she could tell he understood. "And I swear to God if you die in here, I'll come find you and kill you again."

He choked out a laugh. Off in the distance they could finally hear sirens. *"Go."*

"Going." And down the ladder she went, leaving him to face Blake alone.

BROOKE SAT ON the curb, staring up at the flames. Dustin kept trying to put the oxygen mask over her face, while dabbing at a nasty cut on her arm that she'd managed to get from the rain gutter on her way down the ladder. She kept slapping the mask away, not taking her eyes off the house.

Where was he? Sam, Eddie and Aidan had all gone in after Zach and Blake. Why weren't they—

Finally the door burst open and Sam and Aidan appeared, with Zach between them, Eddie just behind.

No Blake.

Shoving the blanket off her shoulders, Brooke went running toward them.

"Brooke," Zach was saying to Isobel. "Where the hell's Brooke?"

"Here," she managed.

At the sound of her voice he whipped around. He still wore only his Levi's. Dirt and ash were smeared over his chest and torso, blackening the bandages from the last fire he'd been in. He was bleeding from several cuts, as well, and couldn't stop coughing. His eyes were wild, though they calmed at the sight of her as he hauled her into his arms.

"Blake?" she whispered.

Eyes revealing his misery, he shook his head. "We found the blowtorch, and his hard hat. Nothing else."

Heart heavy, she hugged him tight, but she didn't get to hold on to him for long. The scene was chaotic as all hell. Tommy appeared, and the chief, not to mention every rig out of their firehouse, plus too many police units to count.

Zach was pulled aside. "For questioning," Aidan told her.

"He didn't do anything wrong—"

"They know that," he quickly assured her. "But with Blake gone—"

"Gone?"

"They didn't find a body, but—" His voice broke, and he cleared his throat. "But they expect to. There's going to be an internal investigation. Zach wants me to take you to the hospital for stitches—"

"I've got her, you stay with Zach." Dustin flanked her on one side, and Cristina was on the other, looking devastated over the news about her partner.

They took her to the hospital, where she received eight stitches and a tetanus shot. Exhausted and woozy, she let Dustin take her home, where she had a message waiting from her Realtor about the offer on the house.

Was she taking it?

Good question. She'd gotten her asking price. Didn't that just put a nice neat bow on her life. The end of yet another era...

Dustin called in for an update. The fire was out; Blake was presumed dead. Cristina showed up with Thai takeout and a brown bag. The three of them sat around Brooke's table, grimy and filthy, stuffing their faces.

"I still can't believe it was Blake," Cristina said very quietly. "That he—" She broke off, her voice choked. "He was a pyromaniac. In some ways we all are, or we wouldn't do this, but he was mentally ill. Tommy said that looking back, you could see he started unraveling when the chief came from Chicago, right about the time that Lynn died." She closed her eyes. "He needed help."

Dustin squeezed her hand. They ate in silence, an emotional but companionable sort of silence until Cristina looked at the stack of boxes filled with the stuff Brooke hadn't been able to make herself get rid of—the photos, the diaries—all things that had helped Brooke find the missing parts of herself. "Looks like you've been busy, Brooke."

She raised a brow. "Did you just call me Brooke?"

"That is your name, right?"

"I thought it was New Hire to you."

Cristina shrugged. "You stuck."

Her throat tightened. "Yes, but the job's nearly over."

"You could apply for a permanent position."

She'd never done anything permanent. But this, with the people she now thought of as her friends, felt very permanent. And wasn't that part of what she'd been searching for? "I'm ready for the booze now."

Cristina lifted a brow.

"The brown bag you brought. It's alcohol, right?"

Cristina pulled out a bottle of bubble bath and Dustin laughed.

"What?" Cristina demanded.

"You're so damn cute."

"Oh, shut up." Cristina squirmed, looking uncomfortable. "I'm new at this girl-pal stuff, okay? I thought she might want to just soak, and God, I know, it's stupid."

"No." Brooke hugged her. "It's perfect."

They stayed for ice cream, and two more calls for info, of which they got very little except that Zach was still at the fire site.

After Dustin and Cristina left, Brooke drew herself a bubble bath and lay back, soaking.

Thinking…

A knock at her front door stopped that and her heart. It wasn't Zach, it couldn't be Zach. He was no doubt still with the chief and Tommy. It was probably the real estate agent, whom she'd not yet called back. Wasn't ready to call back, not when she felt as if she'd found all her answers right here in this house—answers about her life, and how she wanted to live it. Which was pretty much the opposite of her grandmother and mother.

Brooke didn't want her memories stuck in boxes in some attic. She wanted to share them with real people. She wanted to create new ones every day.

The knock came again. Wrapping herself in a towel, she went to the door. "Who's there?"

"Me."

Oh, God. She whipped open the door.

Zach stood there in his jeans and someone's firefighter jacket, opened so that she could see he was still as grimy as she'd been only a few moments ago. It didn't matter.

One minute she was holding on to the door and the next moment she was holding on to him.

"Brooke," he murmured, his hand fisting in the towel at her back.

She pulled away to look into his face. "Are you all right?"

"Yeah."

"Your house?"

"Not so much."

"Oh, Zach."

"Aidan's putting me up at his place, but I needed to see you."

"I needed to see you, too. Are you sure you're okay?"

"I am now."

"I feel sick about Blake."

"Yeah." Zach blew out a breath. "They found a stack of wire-mesh trash cans in his garage. The chief is saying he was always a pyromaniac, that this job was just a cover to be near fires, that his illness got too much for him so he started setting fires to put them out. Then I started stirring it all up, which made it worse, and he went crazy." He shook his head. "He was one of us, Brooke. How the hell did this happen to one of us?" He turned in a slow circle. "And there's something else bugging the hell out of me. How did Blake manage to order the properties demolished? He didn't have that kind of pull. It doesn't make sense to me."

She just shook her head and hugged him again, closing her eyes to breathe him in. "You're safe. That's all that matters right now. The rest of the questions will get their answers later."

His eyes cut to the stack of boxes. "You've been busy. Did you take the offer on the house?"

"Not yet."

"Where will you go?"

"I—I'm not quite sure."

"You probably have lots of choices," he said quietly, still looking at the boxes.

"I don't know. I like this coast, a lot."

He turned back to her. "Yeah?"

"Yeah." She swallowed past a lump of emotion the size of a basketball. "There's lots of coastal cities hiring EMTs right now."

"Including Santa Rey."

"I know." Brooke ran her hand over his sooty chest. "I have a tub filled with hot, bubbling water. Interested?"

"As long as you're in it."

"That could be arranged."

They ended up draining the tub so he could shower the grime off him first, then filling it back up. Then they climbed in together, her back to his chest, his legs alongside of hers, his arms surrounding her, cast carefully out of the water. For a long moment he just pressed his jaw to hers. "Rationally, I knew you weren't going to die today," he murmured. "But I've found I'm not always rational when it comes to you."

"Ditto." She was grateful that he couldn't see her face, or the tears that suddenly filled her eyes. *Rational* had gone out the window weeks ago, somewhere around that night on a rock overlooking the ocean.

"Brooke?"

She shook her head and forced herself to laugh. "What does rational have to do with us anyway? We just clicked, that's all."

He ran a finger up her wet arm, leaving a trail of

bubbles and goose bumps. "We could keep clicking. If you weren't leaving."

Craning her neck, she looked into his face.

There was no humor in his gaze, not a single drop. "I realized something that first day with you," he said quietly.

"What, that I was going to be a pain in your ass to dump?"

"That my lifestyle, the one I've reveled in for so long, had finally caught up with me and bit me on the ass. Because for the first time since losing my parents, something was going to matter. You were going to matter, Brooke."

She stared at him. "Is that why you wanted to keep this light?"

"That, and because it was what I thought you wanted."

"You told me I shouldn't fall in love with you. Remember?"

"Yeah, that's because I'm insanely stubborn. I've always thought I was so damn brave. I mean I put myself on the line every single day on the job." He laughed, and it was not in amusement. "But not my heart. Never my heart. And that doesn't make me brave at all. It makes me a coward."

His gaze held hers. "Until I met you. I met you and something happened. The walls crumbled. I put my damn heart on the line for the first time in years, with absolutely no backup, no safety net. And it worked. It felt right," he said sounding staggered. "Hell, it felt amazing." Zach shook his head. "I want to be with you, Brooke."

"For tonight."

"For tonight," he agreed. "And tomorrow night, too."

She looked into his eyes, feeling a little kernel of hope and love, so much love she couldn't draw a breath.

"And the night after that. I want all your nights. I love you, Brooke. But there's something even more shocking."

She managed to breathe. "Are you sure? Because that's…that's pretty shocking."

He finally smiled and, oh baby, was it worth the wait. "Turns out I wasn't out there without a backup at all."

"No?" she whispered.

"No." He cupped her face, stroked his thumbs over her jaw. "You're my backup. You're my safety net. You're all that I need."

"So…"

"So stay. Stay here in Santa Rey with me. Or go. But take me with you."

Now Brooke was the one staggered. "You'd leave here?"

"My home is wherever you are."

Twisting all the way around, she propped herself up on his wet chest. "I don't want to go anywhere."

"You don't?"

"Nope. I know you planned to stay at Aidan's house, but I have this big place all to myself, and I don't really want to leave it, or my job. I think New Hire has a certain ring to it, don't you?"

Laughing softly, Zach pulled her close. "How does New Hire *Thomas* sound?"

Her breath caught. She could hardly speak. "Like everything I ever wanted."

*Runaway bride Payton Harwell thinks she's hit rock
bottom when she ends up in jail – in Australia!
But then sexy rebel Brody Quinn bails her out and lets
her into his home, his bed, his life. Only Payton's
past isn't as far away as she thinks it is...*

Turn the page for a sneak preview of

The Mighty Quinns: Brody
by Kate Hoffmann

*available from Mills & Boon® Blaze®
in January 2010*

The Mighty Quinns: Brody
by
Kate Hoffmann

Queensland, Australia—June, 2009

HIS BODY ACHED, from the throbbing in his head to the deep, dull pain in his knee. The various twinges in between—his back, his right elbow, the fingers of his left hand—felt worse than usual. Brody Quinn wondered if he'd always wake up with a reminder of the motorcycle accident that had ruined his future or, if someday, all the pain would magically be gone.

Hell, he'd just turned twenty-six and he felt like an old man. Reaching up, he rubbed his forehead, certain of only one thing—he'd spent the previous night sitting on his arse at the Spotted Dog getting himself drunk.

The sound of an Elvis Presley tune drifted through the air and Brody knew exactly where he'd slept it off— the Bilbarra jail. The town's police chief, Angus Embley, was a huge fan of Presley, willing to debate the King's singular place in the world of music with any bloke who dared to argue the point. Right now, Elvis was only exacerbating Brody's headache.

"Angus!" he shouted. "Can you turn down the music?"

Since he'd returned home to his family's cattle station in Queensland, he'd grown rather fond of the accommodations at the local jail. Though he usually ended up behind bars for some silly reason, it saved him the long drive home or sleeping it off in his SUV. "Angus!"

"He's not here. He went out to get some breakfast."

Brody rolled over to look into the adjoining cell, startled to hear a female voice. As he rubbed his bleary eyes, he focused on a slender woman standing just a few feet away, dressed in a pretty, flowered blouse and blue jeans. Her delicate fingers were wrapped around the bars that separated them, her dark eyes intently fixed on his.

"Christ," he muttered, flopping back onto the bed. Now he'd really hit bottom, Brody mused, throwing his arm over his eyes. Getting royally pissed was one thing, but hallucinating a female prisoner was another. He was still drunk.

He closed his eyes, but the image of her swirled in his brain. Odd that he'd conjured up this particular apparition. She didn't really fit his standard of beauty. He usually preferred blue-eyed blondes with large breasts and shapely backsides and long, long legs.

This woman was slim, with deep mahogany hair that fell in a riot of curls around her face and shoulders. By his calculations, she might come up to his chin at best. And her features were…odd. Her lips were almost too lush and her cheekbones too high. And her skin was so pale and perfect that he had to wonder if she ever spent a day in the sun.

"You don't have to be embarrassed. A lot of people talk in their sleep."

Brody sat up. She had an American accent. His fantasy women never had American accents. "What?"

She stared at him from across the cell. "It was mostly just mumbling. And some snoring. And you did mention someone named Nessa."

"Vanessa," he murmured, scanning her features again. She wasn't wearing a bit of makeup, yet she looked as if she'd just stepped out of the pages of one of those fashion magazines Vanessa always had on hand. She had that fresh-scrubbed, innocent, girl-next-door look about her. Natural. Clean. He wondered if she smelled as good as she looked.

Since returning home, there hadn't been a single woman who'd piqued his interest—until now. Though she could be anywhere between sixteen and thirty, Brody reckoned if she was younger than eighteen, she wouldn't be sitting in a jail cell. It was probably safe to lust after her.

"You definitely said Nessa," she insisted. "I remember. I thought it was an odd name."

"It's short for Vanessa. She's a model and that's what they call her." Nessa was so famous, she didn't need a last name, kind of like Madonna or Sting.

"She's your girlfriend?"

"Yes." He drew a sharp breath, then cleared his throat. "No. Ex-girlfriend."

"Sorry," she said with an apologetic shrug. "I didn't mean to stir up bad memories."

"No bad memories," Brody replied, noting the hint of defensiveness in his voice. What the hell did he care what this woman thought of him—or the girls he'd dated? He swung his legs off the edge of the bed, then raked his hands through his hair. "I know why *I'm* here. What are *you* doing in a cell?"

"Just a small misunderstanding," she said, forcing a smile.

"Angus doesn't lock people up for small misunderstandings," Brody countered, pushing to his feet. "Especially not women." He crossed to stand in front of her, wrapping his fingers around the bars just above hers. "What did you do?"

"Dine and dash," she said.

"What?"

Her eyes dropped and a pretty blush stained her cheeks. "I—I skipped out on my bill at the diner down the street. And a few other meals in a few other towns. I guess my life of crime finally caught up with me. The owner called the cops and I'm in here until I find a way to work it off."

He pressed his forehead into the bars, hoping the cool iron would soothe the ache in his head. "Why don't you just pay for what you ate?"

"I would have, but I didn't have any cash. I left an IOU. And I said I'd come back and pay as soon as I found work. I guess that wasn't good enough."

Brody let his hands slide down until he was touching her, if only to prove that she was real and that he wasn't dreaming. "What happened to all your money?" he asked, fixing his attention on her face as he ran his fingers over hers. It seemed natural to touch her, even though she was a complete stranger. Oddly, she didn't seem to mind.

Her breath caught and then she sighed. "It's all gone. Desperate times call for desperate measures. I'm not a dishonest person. I was just really, really hungry."

She had the most beautiful mouth he'd ever seen, her

lips soft and full…perfect for— He fought the urge to pull her closer and take a quick taste, just to see if she'd be…different. "What's your name?"

"Payton," she murmured.

"Payton," he repeated, leaning back to take in details of her body. "Is that your last name or your first?"

"Payton Harwell," she said.

"And you're American?"

"I am."

"And you're in jail," he said, stating the obvious.

She laughed softly and nodded as she glanced around. "It appears I am. At least for a while. Angus told me as soon as he finds a way for me to work off my debt, he'll let me out. I told him I could wash dishes at the diner, but the owner doesn't want me back there. I guess jobs are in short supply around here."

Brody's gaze drifted back to her face—he was oddly fascinated by her features. Had he seen her at a party or in a nightclub in Fremantle, he probably wouldn't have given her a second glance. But given time to appreciate her attributes, he couldn't seem to find a single flaw worth mentioning.

"Quinn!"

Brody glanced over his shoulder and watched as Angus strolled in, his freshly pressed uniform already rumpled after just a few hours of work. "Are you sober yet?"

"You didn't have to lock me up," Brody said, letting go of the bars.

"Brody Quinn, you started a brawl, you broke a mirror and you threw a bleedin' drink in my face, after insulting my taste in music. You didn't give me a choice." Angus braced his hands on his hips. "There'll be a fine. I figure a couple hundred should do it. And you're gonna have to pay for Buddy's mirror." Angus scratched his chin. "And I want a promise you're gonna behave yourself from now on and respect the law. Your brother's here, so pay the fine and you can go."

"Teague is here?" Brody asked.

"No, Callum is waiting. He's not so chuffed he had to make a trip into town."

"I could have driven myself home," Brody said.

"Your buddy Billy tried to take your keys last night. That's what started the fight. He flushed the keys, so Callum brought your spare." Angus reached down and unlocked the cell. "Next time you kick up a stink, I'm holding you for a week. That's a promise."

Brody turned back and looked at Payton. "You can let her out. I'll pay her fine, too."

"First you have to settle up with Miss Shelly over at the coffeeshop and then you have to find this young lady a job. Then, I'll let you pay her fine. Until you do all that, she's gonna be a guest for a bit longer."

"It's all right," Payton said in a cheerful voice. "I'm okay here. I've got a nice place to sleep and regular meals."

Brody frowned as he shook his head. It just didn't feel right leaving her locked up, even if she did want to stay. "Suit yourself," he said, rubbing at the ache in his head.

Payton gave him a little wave, but it didn't ease his qualms. Who was she? And what had brought her to Bilbarra? There were a lot of questions running through his mind without any reasonable answers.

MILLS & BOON

Blaze

On sale 18th December 2009

(2-IN-1 ANTHOLOGY)
THE MIGHTY QUINNS: BRODY & FLASHBACK
by Kate Hoffmann & Jill Shalvis

The Mighty Quinns: Brody

Runaway bride Payton thinks she's hit rock bottom. But then sexy rebel Brody Quinn lets her into his home *and his bed*! Still, her past isn't as far away as she thinks…

Flashback

Fireman Aidan has always known how to keep his cool. Until an old flame, soap star Mackenzie, returns. Now Aidan has no hope of controlling his desires!

A FEW GOOD MEN
by Tori Carrington

Four sizzling-hot soldiers, four complete short stories! Fighting together in Iraq Eric, Matt, Eddie and Brian have become a family. But now they're home, each of these brave bachelors is ready to find a woman of his own.

SECRET SEDUCTION
by Lori Wilde

Tanner is an undercover bodyguard protecting surgeon Vanessa at the exclusive Confidential Rejuvenations clinic. Keeping her close won't be a problem – it's the sizzling sexual chemistry between them that Tanner has to worry about!

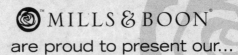

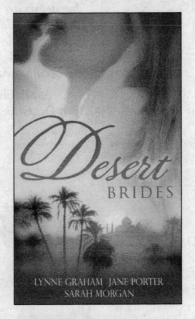

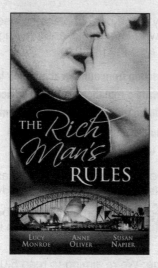

millsandboon.co.uk Community

Join Us!

The Community is the perfect place to meet and chat to kindred spirits who love books and reading as much as you do, but it's also the place to:

- Get the inside scoop from authors about their latest books
- Learn how to write a romance book with advice from our edit
- Help us to continue publishing the best in women's fiction
- Share your thoughts on the books we publish
- Befriend other users

Forums: Interact with each other as well as authors, ed tors and a whole host of other users worldwide.

Blogs: Every registered community member has their own blog to tell the world what they're up to and what's on their mind.

Book Challenge: We're aiming to read 5,000 books and have joined forces with The Reading Agency in our inaugural Book Challenge.

Profile Page: Showcase yourself and keep a record of your recent community activity.

Social Networking: We've added buttons at the end of every post to share via digg, Facebook, Google, Yahoo, technorati and de.licio.us.

www.millsandboon.co.uk

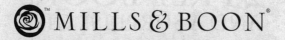

2 FREE BOOKS
AND A SURPRISE GIFT

We would like to take this opportunity to thank you for reading this Mills & Boon® book by offering you the chance to take TWO more specially selected titles from the Blaze® series absolutely FREE! We're also making this offer to introduce you to the benefits of the Mills & Boon® Book Club™—

- **FREE home delivery**
- **FREE gifts and competitions**
- **FREE monthly Newsletter**
- **Exclusive Mills & Boon Book Club offers**
- **Books available before they're in the shops**

Accepting these FREE books and gift places you under no obligation to buy, you may cancel at any time, even after receiving your free books. Simply complete your details below and return the entire page to the address below. You don't even need a stamp!

YES Please send me 2 free Blaze books and a surprise gift. I understand that unless you hear from me, I will receive 3 superb new books every month, including a 2-in-1 book priced at £4.99 and two single books priced at £3.19 each, postage and packing free. I am under no obligation to purchase any books and may cancel my subscription at any time. The free books and gift will be mine to keep in any case.

Ms/Mrs/Miss/Mr _____ Initials _____

_____

Surname _____

Address _____

_____

_____ Postcode _____

Send this whole page to: Mills & Boon Book Club, Free Book Offer, FREEPOST NAT 10298, Richmond, TW9 1BR